PENTACLE

M.R. HAUCK

Beaten Track
www.beatentrackpublishing.com

Pentacle

Published 2022 by Beaten Track Publishing
Copyright © 2022 M.R. Hauck

All rights reserved.

No part of this publication may be reproduced, stored in a retrieval system, or transmitted, in any form or by any means, without the prior permission of the publisher, nor be otherwise circulated without the publisher's prior consent in any form of binding or cover other than that in which it is published and without a similar condition including this condition being imposed on the subsequent publisher.

The moral right of the author has been asserted.

Paperback ISBN: 978 1 78645 562 8
eBook ISBN: 978 1 78645 563 5

Beaten Track Publishing,
Burscough, Lancashire.
www.beatentrackpublishing.com

For you
Who left abruptly
JCJ 1990-2022

CONTENTS

CONTENTS

I.
GIFT

You caused me to weep
You caused me to moan
You caused me to lose my home
Little girl, little girl
Where'd you sleep last night?
Not even your mother knows
In the pines, in the pines
Where the sun never shines
We'll shiver when the cold wind blows

– Lead Belly, "In the Pines"

ONE

THOSE PANTS DO nothing for your ass.
Are you sure you want to wear such a low-cut top?
Yellow is not your color.

I could hear his voice inside my head that day, as I could every day since the day we met, all snide judgement and thinly veiled put-downs. I reminded myself that today would be the day that voice stopped its incessant string of noise; today he would finally, at long last, be held accountable in a way he'd never been in his entire privileged life. I stood in front of my mother's dressing room mirror, adjusting my top, making sure it was neatly tucked into my dress slacks, leaned closer to rub lightly at a small smudge of mascara beneath my left eye. I'd been forcing back tears all morning. Whether they were from gratefulness and joy, or pure terror, I couldn't tell, because I felt all that and more, all at once.

You look fine, I told myself, replaying in my head what the self-help book on tape had told me, *perfectly fine. You are confident. You are at ease. You are safe. And today is the day you walk through those doors his bitch, and back out of them a free woman.*

The ride to the courthouse was tense, my father silent behind the wheel, my mother fussing over her jewelry, unable to be quiet to save her life.

"Honestly, Maurice, I don't understand why we *all* need to be there," she said as if I wasn't sitting in the back seat, my hands twisting around themselves and my stomach clenching with every bump. "The verdict is just for Claire. It hasn't got anything to do with us. It's like they're punishing us for being her parents by

3

forcing us to lose valuable daytime hours sitting in a courtroom, sweating in our good church clothes."

My father shrugged. "Judge requested."

And that was all. My mother tutted, going back to her inane diatribe about her tangled jewelry—*Why did she wear so much of it, then?* I wanted to ask—and dropped the subject. I gazed out the window at the overcast day, the heavily pregnant clouds threatening rain. A fat drop splatted against my window to confirm my suspicions.

The courthouse was full of people milling around in what my mother called their "church clothes." There were a few people in jeans and T-shirts, lounging around on the uncomfortable chairs as though this were their living room instead of a house of judgement, but most of them were dressed like me: business casual, bright colors, extra neat.

I swallowed hard, all nerves. The trial was basically over, today was merely a way for the jury to deliver their verdict, and I was 99.9% sure it would end in my favor. The difficult part— my testimony, in which I was compelled to describe in gruesome detail everything my ex-husband had done to me physically, mentally, and emotionally—had been over for days. It took two of those days for the defense to grill me until I cried on the stand and the judge called a recess. He patted my shaky hand as I stood, and smiled sympathetically. One juror, an elderly redhead with a cloud of thin, frizzy hair, had had her hand pressed to her heart, her eyes tearful. My lawyer told me today was going to be a formality only, and then this whole messy business would be in the past, and I could go home a rich woman who no longer needed to be under the heel of anyone ever again.

My lawyer, who was a sweet, tall man in his early forties named Arlo Mattingly, arrived fifteen minutes before we were set to go in, smiling. He hugged me when he got to my little knot of family, shook hands with both my parents, and squeezed my shoulder. "How you holding up, Ms. Shaw?"

He used my maiden name in his Mississippi drawl, which relaxed me immensely. No longer being Mrs. Dane Wilson was comfort enough, even now, when I was at my most nervous. "Doing alright. You know…as well as I can be."

"I hope I didn't keep you waiting long."

"Oh, no, we only got here about—"

"It's been *thirty-five* minutes, actually. Claire made us leave *early*," my mother chimed in, her mouth pursed in disapproval. "I said we'd be fine if we left a little later, but she absolutely insisted we wait around in this stuffy place full of *criminals* instead of at home in our air-conditioned townhouse. I swear. It's as if *she's* eager to know if she's going to get a life sentence, when she's the one who got—"

"Marilyn," my father said quietly, touching his wife's hand. "Don't be unkind. Claire's just nervous, is all."

My mother folded her arms, pulling away from his hand. "She could have been nervous at home."

Arlo smiled at her, his big, fake lawyer smile my mother loved. "Claire was probably right to have you leave so early. Construction on Tulane has made parking a nightmare. It's what held me up, and y'all live further away from the courthouse than I do. And I can assure you, ma'am, all of the criminals are backstage in orange jumpsuits, not out here."

He tipped a wink at me and I felt my shoulders unclench. He really was good, was Arlo, and he made every effort to ensure I felt safe and protected, even from my parents. I think he knew that Dane Wilson wasn't my first abuser, just the one who left the most visible wounds.

"All parties for the case of Shaw v. Wilson! Shaw v. Wilson, please come forward!" Bellowed the officer near the chambers.

I jumped, and Arlo put a hand on my elbow to steady me. "Ready, Ms. Shaw?"

"Ready as I'll ever be." We walked forward as a group, me feeling like my head wasn't attached to my body, like I was floating inexorably towards that bailiff and his booming voice, my pulse everywhere at once, pounding with the rhythm of my feet on the ugly, stained carpet.

Inside the courthouse itself, it was quiet. My ex-husband was already there (how?), smirking at me as I entered flanked by my lawyer and my mother, my father bringing up the rear, the three of them looking for all the world like my honor guard, my safekeepers. He sat there, smiling that indulgent smile that I always found so passive aggressive, with his little round glasses perched on his nose and his thick, curly blond hair (artfully long) parted to the side, looking, in his navy blue pinstripe suit, like the professional he wished he was. He gave me a once over and I could hear his voice

Does nothing for your ass

Are you sure you want to wear

Yellow is not your color

in my head, so loud, so clear, but Arlo was steering me into the hard wooden swivel chairs that hurt my ass, and my parents were gone to sit way in the back of the empty spectator section, and my pulse was singing a high-pitched whine in my ears. I was thirsty beyond reason and looked to Arlo for help. He saw my plight immediately, and brought out from his interior jacket pocket a tiny plastic bottle of miraculously cold water. He cracked the top for me—my hands were shaking and sweating, and I could never have done it alone—and handed it to me. I tried to sip, but I gulped once, twice, three times, a bit of the water escaping the side of my mouth and rolling down my chin to land in a splat on my blouse. I heard Dane snicker from the other side of the room, but I didn't—couldn't—look.

"All rise for his Honorable Judge Richard Clement!" the bailiff boomed, his voice too loud in that overwarm, empty room.

We all stood as the judge made his way to his high seat, a raven on the bust of Pallas, here to tell me if this feeling of sinking into my own private hell would be forever or nevermore. He flapped his robe and settled down, beaky nose and wild silver hair completing the birdlike look. He glanced at Dane, then at me, nodded, and struck his gavel.

The bailiff shouted, "Be seated!"

We sat. The jury, whom unto now hadn't even pinged on my radar, so thrown was I by Dane's presence, were the first to be addressed by Judge Clement. His voice was deep and gravelly, the voice of a long-time smoker, but carried in a way that commanded attention without ever rising above a conversational level. "Ladies and gentlemen, are you ready to hand down your verdict in this case, so these good people can go home in a timely manner?"

Good people, as though Dane was included in that after all I'd recounted on that witness stand. I shuddered, cold now despite the closeness of the room.

The jury nodded. Judge Clement folded his hands pensively in front of himself. "Would the foreman of the jury please rise?"

The jury foreman, a balding, portly man with a walrus moustache and thick glasses who looked uncomfortable in his tweed suit with too many buttons done up, stood up, paper in hand. He cleared his throat loudly, adjusted his footing, and said in a high voice incongruous to his frame, "Your Honor, we the jury have reached a verdict in the case of Shaw v. Wilson."

"And how do you find?"

Sweat trickled from my hairline, staining the collar of my yellow (*not your color*) blouse. My hands twisted against each other like they were fighting, and Arlo, bless him, reached over to take one of them, threading his fingers through mine and giving me a squeeze.

"We find the defendant, Dane Wilson, on four charges of domestic battery—"

You stupid cunt, I'll give you something to cry about. Shut up. SHUT UP!

"—not guilty. And on five charges of torture, both physical and emotional—"

You're a fucking joke, you know that? And you'll never get out of this, honeybaby; I won't let you. Hold still, damn you. I don't want to burn myself. Just you, Claire. Hold still or it'll be worse.

"—not guilty. And, finally, on the..." the juror stopped, his eyes darting to me sitting, sweating bullets behind the mahogany table, and cleared his throat again. "On two counts of marital rape—"

Don't pretend you don't want this. I'm your husband. This is your duty. This is my right. Open, Claire, open now or I'll get that thing you don't like to open them for me.

"—not guilty." He sat abruptly, making his chair squeak, his eyes watery and his body limp as though delivering the verdict was a difficulty level akin to running a marathon. Perhaps it was.

I couldn't move. Couldn't speak. Couldn't even cry. There were a few seconds of silence in the courtroom that were so loud and drawn out as to be a wind tunnel to eternity. Arlo was frozen, rigid, his mouth hung open in a gawp of surprise. Dane's lawyer was up and hugging him, the two men banging each other on the back like their favorite football team had just won the playoffs.

Judge Clement sighed, pinched the bridge of his nose. When he looked up again, his face was a mask of disgust. "The court will uphold your verdict, but I must say, as a man and a husband, I feel absolutely no pleasure in saying these words: Mr. Wilson, you are free to go." His small, piercing blue eyes turned to me. "Ms. Shaw,

I will remain, until the day I die, disgusted and supremely baffled by what has happened here today, and for this I am truly sorry."

He banged his gavel. It was over.

I nodded to him and his sad, sympathetic eyes, tears finally welling up and spilling over onto my cheeks. I still could get no words out, but the need to scream until my throat bled was rising like vomit in my chest. I felt if I started screaming, I'd never stop, but then Arlo was tugging at my elbow, whispering in my ear, "Come on, Claire, let's get you out of here."

From somewhere in the back, I heard my mother whisper, "…waste of time."

I let Arlo lead me away. What else could I do? As we got to the low gate that separated the spectators from the judged, I made the mistake of glancing towards Dane. He was already staring at me, that wolfish grin of *winning* plastered all over his stupid face, that same look he had after every time he made me bleed.

"Better luck next time, sweet cheeks," he said in that familiar way that made my skin crawl, and winked.

And oh, I could feel that scream of pain and rage coming, that scream I was never allowed to utter because he liked me quiet, he liked me submissive, he liked me too scared to make any noise at all. And now, he'd won. I would be forever silenced about the five years I spent in purgatory with him, the minor devil that held the pitchfork with which he stabbed at all my vital places while he laughed and cavorted and people gave him a pass and questioned why I stayed and what I had done and why didn't I fight back?

But how does one person fight a demon on their own?

I swallowed that scream as I swallowed his bullshit for five fucking years, allowed Arlo to hand me over to my parents (but only after hugging me long and hard with tears in his eyes, apologizing over and over), and rode home through driving rain in the back seat of the grave-silent car neither feeling the bumps nor seeing any of the scenery. I was far, far down in my own head, reliving Dane Wilson's Greatest Hits.

I drifted up the stairs to my childhood room in a fog, locked the door behind me, and fell face-first onto my too-small bed. It wouldn't do to have my mother burst in just now, when my tears were flowing freely and my heart was a raw, open wound. I cried as quietly as I could while the thunder rolled outside, the sobs turning my face beet red from the pressure of being silent, my grief so large that I had a pounding headache in minutes. Luckily, my room had an en suite bathroom (as well as posters of rock stars from my teenage years), so when I dragged myself to pee and get some Tylenol for my head, I didn't have to look at anyone else in the household, with mascara and snot running down my face, when I went to do it. As if I *could* look anyone in the eye after all that.

A couple of hours later, a sharp pounding on my door startled me from a light, anxious dose, and my mother shouted (as though the door were made of cement instead of cheap plywood from Home Depot), "Claire? Are you coming down to dinner? Everyone is, yet again, waiting on you."

Everyone meaning her and my father. I'd told them time and time again not to wait on me, that I was an adult and sometimes my job kept me later than their 6 p.m. dinner time, but my mother insisted dinner was for family, and that they would wait, though she never seemed happy to do it. I never understood why she offered if she hated the idea of waiting so much. But I couldn't go downstairs, not today, to eat with my father who avoided my eyes and my mother's constant string of minor judgments. Or worse—her *advice*. I clutched my purple shag pillow closer to my face and said nothing. There was nothing to say.

After a minute, I heard my mother tut in frustration and stomp off back downstairs.

I. Gift

I went back to work less than a week later. I had to. I just couldn't stay in the house anymore, hiding from my parents up in a bedroom full of the past. It wasn't my choice to move there, but the house I'd lived in when I was married was in Dane's name, and while my job paid well enough, I hadn't had enough time to save anything to get a place of my own. He'd never allowed me to. He'd controlled the finances, and once my bank account was my own again, I found he'd emptied it, savings and all, before the change could be made. The idea of staying with friends that would ask too many questions made my skin crawl, so back to my parents I went. Even with my mother's snide remarks and my father's withdrawn affections, at least here I wasn't required to verbally relive everything to please some horror-porn quota that made me worthy of a room.

Work wasn't much better. The people I worked with knew very little beyond my divorce, and perhaps thought the lawsuit was over my alimony being too small. In fact, it was nonexistent, but they didn't know that. There were no whispers about the battered woman in the cubicle facing the window, but there were no queries about my well-being either. That was fine with me. I'd rather they think I was a gold digger than treat me like an exhibition at a freak show. *Step right up and see her, folks, the Beastly Beaten Beauty! For the low, low price of ab-so-LUTE-ly nothing! Don't worry, folks, she never fights back!*

Anything but that.

I did my work, kept my head down, answered all the backlogged emails, and responded to the banal good-mornings from my coworkers. By lunchtime I was caught up, listened to the chatter of people leaving in pairs and groups to go out and get a bite while I pulled my lunch sack from under my desk. I bit into the turkey sandwich I'd made before my mother was up, looking out the window that faced the park. From the third-floor window, I could easily see over the sea of treetops—bikers, joggers, and a few couples getting in a little exercise on their lunch break. I chewed thoughtfully, watching them. What would happen if I just up and disappeared today? Never returned to this office? I came to the conclusion that because nobody here really knew me or cared to know me, I'd never be missed if I left. I could ditch this job if I wanted to, become one of the people having a midday stroll in the sun, alone, on my own terms.

There was kind of a magical feeling in that notion, the knowledge that my life *could* change from here, didn't *have* to continue as it always had. This job, this office, stank of my life with Dane. In the drawer to the left of my computer was the box of emergency Band-Aids, in case he left a burn where some coworker innocently coming over to plop more work on my desk could see. In the foothold was the heating pad I kept to sit on when the stripes across my ass from his belt were still fresh enough to sting. On the windowsill was the potted peace lily I hated that he'd given me as an afterthought on our third anniversary (and *only* a day late because he'd forgotten again), another thing for which he felt I hadn't expressed enough gratitude.

And you really should be more grateful for the things people do for you, Claire.

That red rage rose in my throat again, that feeling of a scream unreleased. I watched a couple holding hands pass slowly under the shade of a live oak, their bodies pressed together in oneness, in joy, totally in sync with one another. I had never had that even once, and I allowed myself to feel anger at all the things Dane had done, all the parts of myself I allowed him to take, all the good memories that could have been, that had been ripped viciously from me by a selfish man who only knew how to brutalize the people he loved.

"No more," I said out loud in the silent, empty office, my voice all gravel and unshed tears. "Not one day more."

And then, in my furious, red mind, a plan began to hatch.

TWO

"I JUST DON'T UNDERSTAND, I really don't," my mother fumed for what felt like the hundredth time. "This is so sudden and so, *so* out of character for you. I didn't raise you to run away from your problems like this."

"I'm not running away," I responded, stuffing a pair of sweatpants into my duffel bag. "I'm just…taking a vacation."

"A vacation? You quit your *job*, Claire."

"I know," I sighed, straightening up to pop my aching back. "But it wasn't a good fit for me, anyway. I'll have another one by the time I get home, don't worry."

"And where do you think that'll come from?" Her spindly arms were folded tightly together, her face pinched and apprehensive. She had never liked *not knowing*, and I wasn't giving her satisfactory answers. "If you expect us to support you more than we already are, we won't do it. We've given you leeway until now because of your…situation…but it's been nearly a year with no forward progress. Are you running away because of the verdict? Because Dane won instead of you?"

I gathered up all of my bathroom supplies, counted them out as I tucked them into the side pockets of the duffel. "No. And also yes. I can't keep living like this, Mom, with people looking at me like I have a disease. I can't keep going to the same places I used to go when I was with him, run in the same circles. It all hurts, brings up old memories. I need to do this to reset, so I can have a fresh start. I need to figure out who I am without him, what that person wants out of life, and…learn how to put this all behind

13

me. I need to find a way back to myself again. Isn't that what you keep saying I need to do?" I shot her a look as I zipped up my bag. "'Pull yourself up by your bootstraps, Claire, and move on.' So that's what I'm doing."

She glared at me, miffed her own words were being used as a counterattack. "I didn't mean move to *Shreveport*, of all places."

"I'm not moving, Ma, I'm taking a sabbatical. And the cabin isn't in Shreveport; it's in Homer, about forty minutes from the city."

"Some city," she grumbled. "With what money, exactly, are you taking this—what did you call it—*sabbatical*, of yours?"

"If you must know, ever since Dane stole my money and I got full control of my account again, I've been saving up. My plan was to move out of here by the end of the year, and I discovered that even with renting a cabin for a month *and* quitting my job, I have enough tucked away to still do that and pay all my bills, besides."

I fished around in the jackets draped over my desk chair, searching for my favorite: a beautifully worn leather bomber, the first thing I'd ever bought with my own money when I moved away from home at twenty-two. I put it on, liking very much how the lining felt sliding over me, how protected I felt encased in the animal hide. "Plus, Candace said she needed an accountant at the bookstore, and since we're friends, she'll not only hire me right away, but pay me nearly double what I was making at the firm."

"Sure," my mother scoffed. "As if you're worth *that* much to a little independent bookstore."

"They're a chain now," I said, hoisting my bag onto my shoulder. "And it's already done. I accepted the position, with one month leeway to do this thing for myself. She said she totally understood. So that's all your problems with me solved now, right?"

She was taken aback by my speech. And if I'm honest, so was I. Marilyn Shaw was rarely spoken to as though she didn't have absolute authority, so the idea that the daughter she'd taken pity on had gone behind her back and had the audacity to take steps that yanked the power out from underneath her stopped her in her tracks. She stared daggers at me for a moment, then smacked her lips. "Claire, I am not your enemy."

"I never said you were."

"You treat me like I am," she said, the waterworks beginning to well. I braced myself for the pity party display I knew was coming. "I don't understand why you hate me so much. Was I not a good mother?"

I said nothing, just stood waiting with my bags in my hands as she blocked my only exit. I hated when she did this, just to make me feel guilty, hated the knowledge that it was working.

She continued, "I was never on a mission to be cruel to you, Claire. You did enough cruelty to yourself, staying with that man for as long as you did, if he did those things to you—"

I bristled. "He *did* do those things to me."

"*If he did,* I wish you had just walked away from him as easily as you're walking away from your father and me. I never wanted to hurt you, just make you understand that bad things happen to everyone. Schools get shot up, people get cancer, wars break out, bombs are dropped. Mothers have heartless, ungrateful daughters." She sniffled. "Bad things happen to everyone."

"Yes they do," I said quietly, willing myself not to give her what she wanted, swallowing the tears that threatened to come pouring out. I held my head up, meeting her gaze, unwavering in my purpose. "But this happened to me. Now can you please move out of my way? I'd like to say goodbye to Dad."

She stepped to the side.

THREE

"*I* N ONE...HUNDRED...FEET, TAKE *a left onto...Cranesbill... Lane.*"

"OK, OK, I'm going," I muttered, squinting in the early evening gloom at the street signs, hoping Cranesbill Lane wasn't one of the many signs missing due, I presumed, to local teens with nothing better to do.

Luckily it wasn't, and I turned my chugging Saturn hatchback—a machine nearly as old as I was—right, waited for my next instruction from the GPS mounted on my crumbling dash. It was the first cold snap of winter, and I banged the dash with my palm so hard that the plastic casing shuddered, willing the heater that had been broken since the previous March to rise up from its grave. It didn't, so I rode without it on a drive that was longer than I anticipated, vibrating as much from the chill in the air as from the gravelly road under my severely balding tires. The neighborhood here was sparse; very few houses dotted the little lane that was more glorified dirt road than street. I bumped over a deep pothole, silently begging the front tire that creaked with every turn to stay attached just a little while longer. I didn't want to get stranded in this place, even though I was the one who had chosen it to begin with.

You should have known better than to do this, Claire, my mother's voice intoned.

Look at you, big girl, out on your own, Dane laughed, giddy with my impending failure. *Christ, you are worthless.*

"*In...five hundred...feet, your destination will be on the...left.*"

I growled as I shifted down, slowed to a crawl so I could better see where the place was. There were no streetlights here, the only light that of the moon and about a million stars I could never see in the city, but there…there…just ahead, a dim porch light on the front of a small, slanted house.

"You have arrived at your destination."

I pulled up into the gravel driveway, killed the engine, and pulled the parking brake, listening to the engine tick and cool as I collected myself. The ad on Airbnb had said to come here to get the key to my cabin, that the owners would supply me with directions and an escort if I couldn't find it on my own, but this little house looked nothing like the cheerful home of a host that I had expected. This house was incredibly small, with peeling white paint and tiny, dark windows, with just a battered Ford truck in the driveway. It felt stupid, all of a sudden, to be knocking on a stranger's door after driving five and a half hours, and simultaneously felt too late to do anything but exactly that. I started to wonder if I was in the right place, if I was walking into danger, if my mother was right and this was a huge mistake.

"Fuck you," I said to every voice in my head that told me to turn around and go home like a good little girl, my fingers gripping the wheel so hard my knuckles were bloodless. I unsnapped my seat belt and hauled myself out into the night.

A blast of icy wind hit me right in the face, blowing my hair into my mouth. I struggled to get it out of my eyes and close the door with my hip. If it was the first cold day of the season down in the city, then here, further north and in the sticks, it felt practically glacial. I pulled my leather jacket tighter around myself and strode to the front door, rapping on the wood frame of the screen door with my already icy knuckles. I stood there, shivering, rubbing my armored arms with my palms, and wondered if I had indeed gotten the address wrong.

Stupid little girl, Dane sneered.

Finally, blessedly, the doorframe squalled as the screen opened. Weak light backlit a wrinkled, ageless woman with curlers in her hair, a housecoat and slippers on, and a lit Pall Mall stuck in the corner of her mouth. She didn't open the screen, but peered out at me, vaguely suspicious.

"Well, what is it, missy?" she asked sharply. "Don't suppose you're selling Girl Scout Cookies."

"No…uh…ma'am," I said, trying for respectful but earning a squint from the woman inside. "My name is Claire Shaw. I rented the cabin from you and your husband off of Airbnb."

She gave me a once over, taking the cigarette from her mouth to flick ash through a crack in the screen, then craned her skinny neck back and shouted, "*Earl!* The tenant's here!"

"Chrissakes, woman, I'm in the kitchen, quit hollerin'!" The heavy sound of boots on wood brought Earl into view. I immediately thought of the actor who played Hazel on *The Umbrella Academy*. Earl was a mountain of a man, broad, tall, and husky, with a round, pleasant face, owlishly large brown eyes, and an incongruously tiny moustache. He dwarfed his wife, who still stared at me with trepidation. "Well, hi there. You must be Ms. Shaw."

"I am." I smiled at him, shivering. "The blurb for the cabin said to come here for the key."

"That it did," he replied, nodding. "But you showed up a sight later than we thought you would."

I checked my phone. It was 7 p.m. "Sorry. It's a five-hour drive."

Earl whistled. "You must really want to get away."

"Yeah, haha, I do."

"Well, let me get you the keys and we'll head out." He looked past me toward the Saturn. "I guess I don't have to tell you that machine won't make it up to the cabin. No roads up there, and no paths wide or clear enough. You can leave it parked here, but we're gonna have to hoof it. About a mile, mind. You alright with that?"

I looked down at my frayed Converse sneakers. "I think I'll manage. I'll get my things."

The walk to the cabin was not uneventful, as Earl talked a blue streak the whole way. Ten feet in, I tripped in a hole in the ground and Earl caught me deftly with his calloused working-man hands, hoisting me by my biceps and righting me. As heavy as his footsteps had been in his home, they were equally as silent out there in the woods. He used a battery-powered work light to light our way, the LEDs lighting up the trees and throwing crazy shadows around us. I looked back ten minutes into the walk to see nothing but darkness with pinpoints of starlight, and felt immediate apprehension being out here with this hulk of a man, small and insignificant in my city-girl clothes. I looked down at my feet, saw the path to my cabin was nothing but a hunter's machete cut track, and not much clearer than the thinner paths through the underbrush. Not a place I could run easily if I found I needed to. I gulped.

My mother clucked, *Excellent decision making, Claire, following a strange man into the woods.*

"This time a'year," Earl said, his voice muffled by the dense trees around us, "the woods get fairly quiet. No hunters come out here nummore, on account of the game moving territories about ten years back. These days there's very few bears about, but you may see a fox or a coon or two, if you're lucky. Once we had a cougar running wild, et up all the livestock at Jefferson Farm up yonder." He threw a thumb noncommittally to his right. "But that's about it. There's deer about, big fat fuckers, if you pardon my French, miss, but they're more scared a' you'n you are a' them."

"Actually, I would think it was really cool if I saw some deer right outside my window," I said, huffing along behind him. He walked fast for a big guy, and I was at least a foot shorter, carrying a heavy duffel, a cloth shopping bag of electronics, and my purse.

Earl laughed. "Oh, yuh, I imagine you might think it's *cool*. But you wanna watch for the bucks. If they're in rut, they'll use those beautiful racks folk so love mounting on their walls to tear right through *anything* that gets in their way. Mind this hole, now."

I followed him, stepped with some difficulty over the "hole" (which was really a very deep ditch about four feet across) while he shone the light on it for me so I wouldn't trip. At the top were four long, deep divots that made the earth look scooped out, like it had been made with a small backhoe. "What do you think did this? A deer?"

"Hmm. Mebbe so, mebbe not," Earl pondered before he turned and continued walking up the path. "Passing animals do all sorts of weird shit, pardon my French, but there's more'n that to be worried about out here. If you don't mind, I'd like to pass on some old country boy knowledge to you, miss, so's I'm not responsible for you getting yerself in a mess out here. Would do my conscience a world a'good."

I smiled at him, though he couldn't see it. I found that despite my misgivings, I wanted to like Earl very much already, and chided myself for ever thinking he was anything but good-natured. "I'd be happy to take whatever advice you have."

"Yuh," he nodded, not looking at me. "Now I say there's no hunters about, and there's not—no legal ones anyway. There's bound to be a poacher or two with all these fat-ass deer around, pardon my French. If you go for a jaunt during the day, wear high contrast clothing and look human. Wouldn't want some jittery meth head mistaking you for an animal. There's some right purdy views about a half mile into the woods—a waterfall, a little lake, a field that grows so many flowers in spring it's like one a'them Monets—but you're gonna want to stick to the paths. They're out there, but somewhat hard to faller, so tomorrow afternoon, if'n y'like, I'll come out here on my four-wheeler and point y'whur to go."

"I'd like that very much, thank you."

"Welcome. Now this is the most important bit, so listen close, miss." Earl stopped and turned to look at me in the lamp light, his round face pink with exertion and his expression grave. "Do not, under any circumstances, try to go out in these woods alone at night. I don't doubt your intelligence, so I feel I don't have to tell you that the woods are different at night than they are in the daytime. Folks that known this place their whole lives get turnt 'round and lost in minutes. You might hear an animal crashing around outside and want to go investigate. Don't. Stay inside. You may think to yourself 'it's just a short walk to Earl's house,' and in the daytime, you'd be right. But not at night." He looked pensively out at the dark trees. "Not at night."

He was silent for a moment, and though he was a kind man, silence always made me nervous, so I spoke up. "I promise I won't wander the woods at night."

"Good," Earl said absently, his eyes roving around the woods still. Wind shook the branches, made them whisper to each other, dark conspirators surrounding the two small beings in their midst. I moved from foot to foot, uneasy. Then all at once he seemed to rouse himself, shook his head as if to clear it, and resumed his cheerful tone. "Good, good, good. Cabin's just a few minutes further."

And with that he began walking again, his catlike footfalls making no sound in the leaves that crunched under my shoes when I fell into step. And he was honest—the cabin appeared not more than five minutes later, as though by magic. One minute there was nothing but a wall of trees, and the next, as Earl turned us due east, there was a cabin. It was very small, just two rooms, but it sat cozy in its nook of trees like a fairy tale cottage, the door a happy mouth flanked by two smiling eyes that reflected Earl's lamp. He mounted the two steps to the porch, and I followed, dropping my bags gratefully into the rocker that sat there.

"She's somewhat tiny, but she's got all the amenities," Earl said, pulling his wad of keys from his pocket and sifting through them as he spoke. "Y'got a kitchen, coffee pot and coffee for tomorrow morning, as I see y'got no groceries. Bathroom fixtures are all new and installed by yours truly, with its own water heater round the back. There's a TV with cable that's also hooked up to me and the wife's Netflix account if y'want a movie. Bedding is all new with one a'them fancy memory foam mattresses, quilt's handmade by my mama years ago. There's a Piggly Wiggly and a gas station in town, if'n yer bucket a'bolts can make it, and a Walmart Supercenter in Shreveport that's chock full of anything a soul could want. But that's about an hour out from here, not countin' the walk."

He found the keys and pulled them off the ring, dangled them out to me. I reached for them, but he pulled them back. "You remember what I said about the woods at night?"

"I...yes," I replied, that sprig of uneasiness growing again, unsure of this enormous, work-strong man holding the keys to my freedom out of reach. "I won't go out for any night walks, and I won't follow any sounds. I promise."

Earl smiled. It was a smile as broad as he was, gentle and relieved. He handed over the keys and I relaxed.

"Oh, before I go," he said, once more digging in his pocket to produce a tattered scrap of paper with a phone number scrawled on it in blue ink. "This is us at the house. In case you *do* see a cougar or something like that sniffing around, or you need anything, you call. And sorry about Lilyanne." He rubbed a hand on the back of his neck, suddenly shy. "She can be a right cunt to new folks. Pardon my French, miss."

I laughed out loud, taking the paper. "Don't worry about it. Us city folk are plenty scary, I reckon."

He laughed his big man's laugh and held the light so that I could open the door to the cabin and fumble with the light switch, which he reached in and lit for me instead of watching me struggle any longer. Once he was satisfied that I was safely ensconced in my cabin and his due diligence was done, he tromped down the stairs, waved once over his shoulder, and disappeared into the blackness of the woods.

I shut the door on the night and leaned against the frame, my shoulders sagging. Finally, at long last, I was alone.

FOUR

EARL HAD SAID I might hear animals traipsing around in the woods at night, and he was right. That night, while I settled in and put away my things, I could hear the fauna of the woods skittering, stomping, scratching their way past what I thought of as my retreat. I ate a Lean Cuisine—Earl was wrong about that, I had brought *some* groceries with me—sitting on the porch in the rocker, wrapped in Earl's mother's blanket, and listened to an owl hoot somewhere close by. I scanned the tree line but didn't see it, something I knew I'd just have to get used to. Sometimes, in wild places, you just don't get to see the things that follow you, even if they're right on top of you. I fell asleep with the window cracked despite the cold, listening to the sound of the wind in the trees, and was sound asleep in seconds.

The next day I ventured down the path back to Earl's house, stepping carefully over fallen logs, keeping my eye on the track that seemed to want to disappear every hundred yards. I'd made coffee—the good kind, strong, with chicory—but I was hungry, and I would have to go into town to stock up if I was going to stay up here for any length of time. I ate an ancient protein bar I had in my purse while I walked, enjoying the warmth of the morning sun that cut through the cold. I'd fallen asleep in my clothes the previous night, but figured there was no reason to stand on ceremony out here in the sticks.

I came upon that divot in the ground I'd nearly stepped in the previous night. It was bigger by daylight, the edges more clearly defined in the sun. I bent to look closer, munched another bite of my bar. I held my hand up to it, finger splayed to match the divots, closing one eye and squinting. And yes, from this angle, I decided it looked very much as if a giant hand had scooped a fistful of earth, and, as there was no evidence that the resulting pile had been set down anywhere nearby, hurled it off into the distance. Something behind me stepped on a twig, making it snap. I whirled around, heart beating hard

Look at you, so frightened. I love it when you're frightened. You listen so...much...better...when you're just a little scared, Claire...

but saw nothing. Of course. I took a few deep breaths to slow my pulse.

"OK," I said to no one, to the woods, to the giant with the huge hand that pitched a curveball with the Earth itself, "stop being a spooky little bitch and get on it."

I'd be lying if I said I didn't speedwalk the rest of the way down that path, though.

There was nobody outside when I got to Earl's, and the truck was gone, so I assumed he and his wife had lit off to work. Country people wake up early and work long hours, and it seemed they were no exception.

I got behind the wheel of the Saturn and bump-rattle-squeaked into town. When I got there, I discovered a McDonald's that looked like it had been pulled directly out of the eighties, and swung into the drive thru. I wolfed down my sausage, egg, and cheese McGriddle with strawberry jam

Really, Claire, it's like you want *to be one of those sad, fat women whose husbands don't find them attractive anymore*

sitting on the hood of my car in the parking lot before I set out in search of the Piggly Wiggly. I stopped for gas first, topping up my shitmobile just in case I had to make the drive to Shreveport for missing essentials

Always prepared unless it's important to someone else, huh, honey

then found the market less than five minutes later. Homer wasn't a big town, but it was sprawling, with everything far flung from everything else. And would wonders never cease, it turned out I didn't have to go to Shreveport for essentials after all, so that was alright.

The locals gave me something of the hairy eyeball—I was new, I stuck out, with my black clothes and hair streaked pink and orange—but that was to be expected, and that was alright too. It felt good to shop for chicken breasts and eggs in a place where nobody knew me, where no one whispered to each other about my *divorce* as though it were a crime, where no one gave my bruised face a sympathetic stare as they rang up my purchases. Here, in this Piggly Wiggly, was as much freedom as I had at the cabin, and *that* was best of all. Here I was no longer the former Mrs. Dane Wilson, the beaten wife who won the battle and achieved escape velocity but ultimately lost the war against the stones that tied her to the Earth. The clerk at the register, a slight, blonde teenage girl rabidly chewing gum, smiled to me as she told me my total, and I smiled back as I handed over the debit card that was mine, all mine.

It wasn't until I humped the groceries into the hatchback that I realized I'd bought too much to carry in one trip to the cabin. I hoped against hope as I drove southeast that Earl or his wife would be home when I got back, and one of them would be willing to help me. Lilyanne seemed an unlikely source— I could feel her mistrust of me from the moment she'd opened the door last night—but Earl was much more affable and eager to please. Luck was with me that day, and when I crunched into the gravel drive, Earl's truck was sitting there, a sleeping beast of an automobile. Only in the light of day could I see that it was white like my Saturn, but dirty with patches of grey where the paint had peeled off.

Moo, I thought. I spied Earl's wife in their side yard, wearing a huge sunhat tied under her chin, unfurling a hose to water the flowers that dotted the front garden, and got out hallooing to get her attention.

She turned and put a hand up to shield her eyes. "Oh, it's you. Help you?"

"Yeah," I replied, smiling at her despite her frown. Maybe if I was friendly enough she'd warm to me, I reasoned. She didn't smile back. "I went into town and got groceries, and, uh, haha, I guess I got too much."

She gave me another of those appraising once overs. "And?"

"And..." I faltered, unsure of myself in the face of this woman who gave nothing away. "Well...Earl said something about a four-wheeler last night?"

"Did he now." It wasn't a question. But she thumbed over her shoulder the same as her husband had the night before, to indicate the fenced back yard. "He's out back, fixing that fuckin' chainsaw again." Unlike her husband, she didn't say *pardon my French* when she swore. "Suppose he'll be willing to help yer, if'n he ain't too busy, that is."

I thanked her (she only grunted in response) and made my way to the back fence, which was open on this side of the house. I could hear Earl speaking, muttering to himself, and when I stepped in, I saw his bulk hunched over a small chainsaw that was laid on a piece of plywood between two sawhorses. He fiddled with a delicate piece, trying to reach it with the screwdriver in his hand, but his hands were too big, and he kept missing. He swore gently every time.

"Help you?" I said, not wanting to startle him, unconsciously mirroring the way his wife had spoken to me moments before.

He looked up, his eyes unseeing and confused for a moment, before breaking into a sunny grin. He got up, wiping the sweat off his face with a handkerchief, then wiping the grease from his hands with the same. "Miss Shaw, as I live and breathe! Seems you made it into town OK in that contraption of yours?"

I smiled right back. "Sure did."

"Find everything you needed, did you?"

"Yes, sir, I did."

He looked pained. "It would do my ego a dern sight a'good if you'd dispense with the 'sir' from now on."

"As long as you call me Claire instead of Ms. Shaw," I laughed, then came up to where he was working and looked down at the chainsaw. "Is there something you need help with, Earl?"

"Well, I wouldn't, if not for these sausages at the ends of my hands." He held up his fingers as if to prove how big they were. "There's a little screw inside here that I just can't reach n'matter how hard I try. And Lilyanne, she won't get her hands all greasy."

"Maybe I can help."

"Oh, miss, I can't ask you to get all dirty on my account."

"What about a trade? I undo this screw for you with my tiny little fingers, and you get your four-wheeler and drive me and my heavy groceries out to the cabin."

Earl looked surprised for a moment, then slapped his knee and let out that big, hearty laugh that did my soul good every time he employed it. "Shoot. I'd say that's the best deal I've had presented to me in a dog's age. Done."

He held out one of his large, dirty mitts to shake, and I took it, enjoyed his warm, calloused grasp that was both gentle and firm. In the day it was much easier to convince myself that Earl meant no harm, with his good nature and his kind eyes. I decided right then to put any ill-tempered thoughts about Earl to bed forever.

That was trauma talking, and I knew it. If there was one person on this Earth who wasn't out to harm me, it was this man who was renting me his cabin and had been nothing but nice. I wasn't so broken that I was beyond noticing that.

The chainsaw was fixed in no time, and then the two of us gathered my groceries. I'd never ridden a four-wheeler before, and the roar that little engine put out pleased me to no end. Earl had hung some of my bags on the handlebars, some on his wrists, and I had the rest on mine. I sat behind him and clung for dear life as we bounced, jostled, thumped down the path to the cabin. The ride only took five minutes, but it was the most fun I'd had in months. I loved the icy wind in my face, the sound of the engine, the feeling of barely-held-onto safety. This was the type of danger a girl could get used to. Earl helped me bring my groceries inside, then blatted the little horn on the front of the four-wheeler to say goodbye. I watched him go.

What a dear, sweet man, I thought. *He'd make an excellent father.*

The thought about him brought up an image of my own father from when I was little. He spun me around on the tire swing in our backyard that hung from a huge weeping willow, pushing me so high that I screamed in delight and could see over the fence into our neighbor's yard for split seconds of time. It was a stark contrast to how he was now. He barely looked at me, wouldn't even hug me, hardly spoke to me directly. He would defend me still, in his way, but never offer words of comfort or even so much as touch me. Gone were the days of his inside jokes with me, his warm and loving embrace, gone too the days of making me cry with laughter. Those days had been taken from both of us, by the mere knowledge of what had happened to that little girl, how she'd ended up. He pulled away, some of which had to do with my mother, but also perhaps because it hurt him to know.

But that loss hurt me too, and I felt it more acutely than anyone.
I'd lost so much, so much I'd never regain.
 If *he did that, I wish you had just walked away*
 If *he did that*
 IF
I sighed and closed the door to the cabin.

FIVE

ARL SAID THE cabin had all the amenities, but he'd sold it short with his description. Like the TARDIS, the outside belied the inside, which was spacious and clean, with just a hint of rustic flavor. It was indeed all one room except for the bathroom, the kitchen melding into the living room going seamlessly into the bedroom. The floors were polished hardwood, not parquet as I'd expected, a light buttery brown that gleamed in the soft recessed lighting that had a dimmer switch. The couch was new, plush, a blue microsuede affair with throw cushions that opined in cross stitch such phrases as HUNTING FOR LOVE and HOME SWEET HOME. The walls were painted a cool, pastel yellow, which made everything seem more open and inviting. There were a small wood coffee table and end table in the sitting area, as well as a black IKEA nightstand with three drawers next to the queen-sized, extremely comfortable bed that had crisp, soft new sheets in pale blue and four (four!) extra-large down pillows. The duvet was also down, warm and comforting when I wrapped myself in it, and the blanket Earl's mother had knitted added a pop of bright, country colors. There was generic art on the walls—a painting of a buck standing in a field lit by soft summer light, ducks flying over treetops, and in the kitchen, a print of chefs making boiled seafood. But the bathroom was the real star of the show.

It was painted light, cool-toned blue, lit only by a row of five Edison bulbs in a strip above the sink. The sink was white, the bowl scalloped, with silver fixtures that seemed far too elegant for a cabin in the Louisiana woods. There were two beige mats on the floor—one in front of the sink, one by the tub—that were so fluffy and soft I almost felt guilty stepping on them with bare feet. And then there was the little window over the tub, letting in diffuse light through frosted glass. Oh, what a tub. Clean, gleaming white porcelain with claw feet, so deep that I could submerge my entire body in hot water if I so desired, and still have room to spare.

And that night, I did in fact desire. After dinner—grilled chicken breast with lemon and parmesan pasta and *why are you so eager to get fat, Claire*—I ran the water as hot as I could stand it and sank myself down, gasping, into the water. I put on music, listening to the tinny speaker on my phone pour out Lou Reed's "Perfect Day," and relaxed, glad indeed for the perfect day that I got to spend with me. I breathed deeply of the steam, letting it unclog my stuffy nose after trekking around in the cold for so long, my head leaned back on the lip of the tub. It was so quiet tonight, the only sounds my beating heart, my breathing, and the music switching over to Lizzo, who confirmed that all the rumors were true.

For the first time since booking this place, I allowed myself room to think, really think, about what I was doing here. This cabin made an excellent retreat in which to collect myself, but it still felt like what I was doing *was* retreating, from my past and my current situation. It felt like running away. I sang along with Lizzo, musing on how I wasn't anyone's

Honey
Lover
Whore
Bitch

wife anymore. I was hardly anyone's *friend*, and I wasn't much of a daughter either,

Honestly, Claire, you're so dramatic
so what was I? And what did that person want?
I knew what she didn't want.
I'll give you something to cry about
I'll show you what it feels like to
You want this don't you yes you

But as for what she *did* want, I hadn't a clue. I'd spent so much time hiding, making myself small for the comfort of other people, being *silent* when I wanted to scream, that *I* was the ghost living in the haunted house that was my body, covered in hidden scars. I tried to hold back my tears, but then it occurred to me: I no longer had anyone to hold them back *for*.

So I cried. I cried loud and long, fat, rolling tears of grief and anger for all that I had lost to other people who didn't deserve me, and for myself, who deserved more than I gave her. I cried for all the times I hid myself to avoid the wrath of my ex-husband, to avoid the pitying stares of others, to avoid the sharp questions of my mother, to avoid the sad silence of my father. I cried for every time I was angry and didn't let on so as not to be inconvenient to someone else. I cried for everything I'd missed out on: love, happiness, fulfillment, growth. I sat in that hot water and scrubbed myself clean, finally clean, of the filth that had hung around me in a miasma of sorrow for so long, and I cried while I did it. I cried until I was empty, then I sat still in the water and held myself. There was no one else to hold me.

When I felt that I could stand, I hauled myself up out of the rapidly cooling water, dizzy from the heat as much as from the outpouring of emotions that had been bottled up so long. I dried myself carefully, wiping the tears from my face first, spreading them all over my body even as I toweled off the rest of me, anointing myself with my grief. I stepped out and reached for my phone, stopping the music, wanting silence.

And then I heard it.

At first I thought the trees were just shifting in the wind, but then I heard that it had a different rhythm, off somehow to the beat of the nighttime. And there were no other sounds. The owl from last night wasn't hooting, no animals skittered in the underbrush, no leaves rustled, nothing. I stopped where I was, nude and clutching a towel to my chest, hand still outstretched to my phone, and listened. There was nothing for a moment, and then...

Clump. Clumpclump.

THUMP.

The thump hit the side of the cabin and I cried out softly, keeping it in as much as I could. I'd had a fair bit of practice at this, so I barely made a sound even though my heart was revving up and my temples throbbed from holding in the scream. I slowly turned, needing to look, not wanting to, but when I saw the bathroom window, it was only blackness outside the frosted glass. I swallowed hard and wrapped my towel more tightly around me, stepping quietly forward.

My plan was to go to the window and crack it just a tiny bit, so I could see what was out there. I did not get to enact that plan. As I stepped into the still-full tub as quietly as I could, I reached for the latch on the window. When I popped it, it gave a tiny *click*, and that was enough.

Suddenly, the window was full of moonlight as something moved quickly to the right, and then I *did* scream, falling backwards and splashing back down into the tub in an effort to get away. Water splattered over the sides of the tub and soaked the floor. As the clumping sounds retreated from the cabin, I pulled myself up, dripping, slammed the latch back home and practically ran, soaked and naked, to make sure all locks were locked and all the lights were on.

34

My brain was shouting the entire time, *He's here, he's here, he found you, he's coming, not safe, not safe, NOT SAFE!!!* But I managed to get another towel to redry myself and then get clothes on in case the intruder came back, in case it *was* Dane, so that at least I wasn't naked when

You like it when I

and if he burst through the front door. I shook the whole time, my eyes darting to every window in rapid succession, continually dropping things and swearing under my breath. But everything was silent, not so much as a rustle from the woods after that. Only the breeze through the trees, the creaks and groans of a house settling in for the night.

I didn't sleep much, even with every light on in the house, and both the duvet and knitted blanket wrapped around me. I drank coffee at 3 a.m., when I finally gave up and waited impatiently until 9 a.m. to call the number Earl had given me.

"H'lo," he said, obviously still groggy. Even country people sleep in on Saturdays.

"Hi, Earl," I said, my voice too high pitched for my liking. I cleared my throat and tried again, willing my voice to sound more calm than I felt. "Something weird happened over here last night and I was hoping you could help ease my mind."

"I'll surely try," he said, sounding a bit more awake now. "What happened?"

"Uh…well…this is going to sound kind of crazy, but I think someone was trying to look in on me in the tub. I heard these weird shuffling noises, like walking? And then when I tried to look outside, they ran into the woods."

"*What?*" He was all the way awake now. I heard Lillyanne's voice in the background and Earl covered the receiver momentarily, talking back to her in a muffled voice before coming back. "I'm gonna call up Wiley Goodrich, one a'my friends who's a cop.

And maybe Laurie out at Wildlife and Fisheries for good measure, I tell you what. That bathroom window is *high*, even I can't see in it tall as I am, so if it wasn't a guy with a stepladder, it was definitely some kinda animal. Though I'd be hard pressed to think a'one. Y'ok, Claire?"

I was so relieved not to be called *dramatic* and have someone instead ask how I was, that I almost started crying again. "Yeah, I'm OK. I'll feel better once I know what it was."

"Me too. Stay inside till I get there with Wiley and Laurie, you hear?"

"I hear." And I did. I didn't want to be outside by myself right now, even in the daytime. It felt like my haven had been violated. Like nowhere was safe. Usually I had a very keen mistrust of the police and their many questions (*How did you get those bruises, ma'am? Did you fall? Clumsy you!*), but this time was different. I wanted very much for Earl and his friends to get here as fast as they could.

I waited nearly an hour before I heard the distinct rumbling of four-wheelers coming up the path to the cabin. I twitched back the curtains and saw Earl on one, and two people I didn't know on the other. The second four-wheeler was driven by a slight man in his mid-fifties that I presumed was Wiley, who bore the brown uniform of all small-town police officers, a gun on his hip and a walkie on his shoulder. He spoke into it as the person riding behind him swung a leg over and dismounted, brushing leaves off the front of her green trousers and windbreaker before re-tucking her orange shirt, emblazoned with a deer's head and a fish. This was Laurie, I reasoned, as I watched her tuck her long brown ponytail through her cap and reseat it on her head. She was smiling and chatting with Earl, and looked younger than both men, but had an air of kindness that made me feel brave enough to open the door.

"Hey there, Claire!" Earl said, waving. "Come on out and meet two'a the ne'er-do-wells I know."

I stepped carefully down the stairs and came over to Earl, who swept a hand in the direction of the brunette. "This beauty is Laurie Kemper, daughter of the dumb bastard, pardon my French, that I call my brother."

"Daughter-*in-law*," Laurie said, and reached to shake my hand. "Stop making us sound like a bunch of inbred hicks, Early." She shook my hand warmly, her own in padded gloves. "Nice to meet you. Early tells us that you came here all the way from New Orleans? And you're staying a whole month?"

I gave her a nervous smile. "That's right."

Laurie whistled. "Choo. Can't imagine what we have up here in Homer that could ever compare to a city like that."

I resisted the urge to tell her I was more interested in what Homer *didn't* have, but instead said, "I needed a break. New Orleans is so crowded, all loud and busy. Unless you're a drinker, it's not that fun of a town to live in."

"And I suppose you're not a drinker?" A voice like sandpaper spoke up from my left and I turned towards it, to the man still straddling the four-wheeler, with his hands stuffed in his armpits for warmth. His eyes were steely blue, much like Judge Clement's, but instead of holding any kind of compassion, he had that beady-eyed stare cops have that tells you you're guilty until proven innocent.

"I don't. Well, not much anyway," I replied truthfully, but I was already sweating under that stare despite the cold. "Maybe a drink or two when out with my friends, but that's it."

He scrutinized me, his craggy jaw working. "Did you happen to have a drink or two last night, as well?"

Had you been drinking the night you said he

"Wiley Goodrich!" Laurie said tersely, smacking him on the arm so hard he rocked in his seat. "This young lady is *not* here being interrogated." She turned to me, shaking her head. "Fuckin' cops. *Men* cops. Am I right?"

I let out a breath I was previously unaware I was holding and nodded vigorously, making her laugh. It had an infectious, musical quality that got me laughing too, as much at her calling me *young lady* as at her assessment of men and cops. Then Earl caught the giggles. Wiley groaned and rolled his eyes, but that only made us laugh more, and soon he was chuckling too.

"OK, OK, I came on a bit strong," he said, waving his hands as he pulled one long leg over the four-wheeler and stood. "My apologies, ma'am. Now would you like to tell me why myself and the lovely Mrs. Kemper are out here freezing our cheeks off on a Saturday morning?"

"Sure," I said, but then my mouth stalled out. How did I explain what I saw, what it felt like, the notion that my ex-husband might be out there in the woods, waiting to beat and rape me into submission? I couldn't bear the thought of watching their faces change with that knowledge, especially pleasant-faced Earl who might stop speaking to me the way my father had, all because he didn't know what to say. I cleared my throat. "Last night I was in the tub, and I heard what sounded like footsteps outside the window. When I went to look out, whoever or whatever it was ran away. The sound of it was big, heavy, you know? And I called Earl because…because…"

"Because you're a woman alone, who's so used to city sounds that every sound in the woods seems like a threat, and you got scared," Wiley finished, nodding. "Yuh, seems about right. I can tell you, ma'am, that the likelihood of there being a *person* who came spying on you is slim, but I'll investigate anyway. More likely it was an animal of some kind."

"That's where I come in," Laurie piped up. "And Wiley's probably right. Whatever came by for a visit probably wasn't human. There have been reports from other people in the area of something big doing damage to fences, equipment, and the like. Mike Dooley had two sheep carried off just the other night, in fact. So we suspect a bear or a cougar is to blame. Dangerous, sure, but only if you go outside to try and get a peek. Can you show us the bathroom window, please, Claire?"

I opened my mouth to protest, to tell her that no bear or cougar could *cover the light of the window* if Earl was too short to do so, but thought better of it. Maybe I wanted to be wrong about what I'd seen, maybe being told that it was nothing to be afraid of would be just the kind of comfort I needed. Like Laurie had said, an animal, even a deadly one, couldn't harm me unless I went outside to confront it. "It's over here."

We walked in a group to the back of the cabin, me in front, Wiley and Laurie behind me, Earl bringing up the rear. I remembered walking through the courtroom in a similar way a couple weeks back, to be handed a very different kind of verdict in regards to my future. Here, the stakes weren't as high. Here, no matter the outcome, I was going to win.

Better luck next time, sweet cheeks

When I rounded the corner and saw what was there, I pulled up so short that Wiley collided with my back with a grunt.

"Choooooo," Laurie said over my shoulder, awe in her voice. "Something *big* paid you a visit. Been digging too, so that's probably what you heard. I'm gonna have to log this one in."

Directly under the bathroom window, the earth was hollowed out, as though a giant hand had scooped it up, four long, spindly gouges at the top of the hole.

SIX

I T WAS HARD over the next few days to get anything done, so plagued was I by the thought of what had left that hole behind. Laurie had assured me that "Wilds n' Fishies" was on the case, and that my story would light a fire under the chief's ass to find whatever had been roaming around in the woods causing trouble. Officer Goodrich had told me he'd keep a wary eye on things too, just in case, and had given me a business card with his personal mobile number on it before he left. Earl had hung back for a few minutes after they'd gone to ensure I felt safe out there alone. I said I did, but I lied, and spent four days jumping at every sound from outside. Nights weren't much better. What sleep I did get was plagued by dreams of Dane, all the things he'd done to me over those five long years, and I woke up sweating and aching like I'd been hit all over again more often than I woke up rested.

On day five after my night visitor, I sat on the porch, sipping my coffee with shaky hands, listening to birds chatter to one another in the trees. It was one of those rare cloudless Louisiana days, and no longer as cold as it had been, but a light breeze blew.

Such a perfect day, I thought, *I'm glad I spent it with you.*

And then realization hit. I had rented this cabin for myself to get *away*, away from everything that had happened, away from everything I had been, and what was I doing? Falling into old habits. Jumping at shadows. Allowing some outside force to control my life and what I did with it. That bright red rage welled up in my throat again, as sizzling hot and bitter as bile.

"Fuck this," I said out loud, and went inside to get dressed.

An hour later, after a hearty breakfast of bacon, over medium eggs, and toast to dip in the yolks, I stepped outside in my Converse, sweatpants, and an old The Damned T-shirt I'd bought at their House of Blues concert before I even met Dane. I looked at my GPS, which gave me an idea of where the waterfall was, pinned the location of the cabin, and headed out. Earl said you could get lost easily, but technology and daylight were well on my side this day as I found the path he'd said would lead me right to it.

It was slow going. I had to climb over fallen trees and go around underbrush too thick to slog through. The cold would keep the snakes inside their holes, but I made sure to make a lot of noise so as not to startle a raccoon or fox that might be waddling about nearby.

I sang to myself as I slogged along, a snippet of a song I'd heard long ago, *"Little girl, little girl, don't lie to me—tell me where did you sleep last night?"*

Laurie had told me that the thing outside my cabin might be a bear, and Google told me bears were more often than not deterred by loud noise, so I sang as I went. I soon got bored with the song swirling in my head and turned on Spotify. I kept the phone handy, watching the map lest I get too far away from the path, and found that the waterfall wasn't as far away as I'd thought.

I'd brought my tote along, filled it with three bottles of water, two sandwiches, a protein bar, and an apple. I didn't plan to eat it all, but I suppose subconsciously I was preparing to be lost in the woods for a while.

Prepare for the worst, hope for the best, was one of my mother's favorite witticisms, and as much as I hated to admit it, in this instance it was pretty good advice.

I heard the waterfall before I saw it, a gentle trickling at first and then a rushing sound akin to traffic on the freeway, but more organic. I clambered over the trunk of a long-dead oak tree and there it was, cascading beautifully down over rocks and mossy banks, feeding the river below it with the river above. It wasn't a very wide or deep river (in fact it was more like an overblown creek), but the water was cold and refreshing when I dunked my hands in, clean, clear, and lovely. I found a particularly flat boulder whose top was somewhat bafflingly free of moss, and sat cross legged on it, pulling out a bottle of water and a sandwich. I was halfway through it in a flash, ravenous after my athletic trek.

When I was done, I put the wrapper in my tote, stripped off my shoes and socks, and dangled my feet into the water. I lay back, allowing the crisp coldness of the river to flow around my wiggling toes, my arms pillowing my head as I gazed up onto the canopy above me. Birds flitted to and fro in the boughs, hunting, fucking, feeding their young, making homes with one another. I felt a deep loneliness watching them, longed for a life that had never been, and probably would never be, mine. That I might pair off with someone again in the future was the furthest thought from my mind.

I would rather be alone for the rest of my life, I thought, *than ever again allow that kind of madness in. There's too much risk with people. Too many unknowns.*

The unknown. Wasn't that always what I had been afraid of, what had kept me rooted in the house with my parents, and then kept me standing by the side of someone so hateful as Dane? Didn't I always pick the devil I knew? The path of least resistance?

I growled in frustration, pressing my palms to my eyes. That had always been my pattern, and it was such a hard pattern to break. I couldn't allow myself to think of a future version of myself that wasn't alone, because I had no idea what to expect from myself now that I was. I'd divorced my husband, quit my job, and walked out on my mother crying for me to stay. These were all good things, certainly, but they left me firmly in the path of the unknown, and much to my chagrin, I found I was afraid.

I hugged myself, squeezing my leather jacket closer to me, the tears coming back to spill grief in cleansing tracks down my sweaty face. "I'm just gonna have to be enough for me."

The snap of a twig brought me back, and I flipped over on my stomach, my legs coming up too, pulling me into a crouch. I had no idea I could move that fast, but I had, and now I was poised, tense, searching for whatever had made the sound.

There was more rustling to my right and I whirled around, shouting, "Whoever's out there, I will *fuck you up.*"

What I meant I had no idea, seeing as I wasn't exactly the musclebound type, nor did I possess even so much as a butter knife to use as a weapon. The crunch of leaves coming closer made me draw in a sharp breath, and I clutched the handle of my tote bag, ready to ditch my shoes and run barefoot through the forest like a hunted hare if a human being stepped out of those trees. The sound of heavy footfalls got louder, and I thought this was it, the thing from outside the cabin must be here, it was ready to claim its meal and my bones would bleach on this rock until time wound itself down and then…

…then, from between two gnarled and ancient cypress trees, stepped the largest and most beautiful deer I've ever seen. He was huge, at least two hundred pounds even now in the winter when most deer are thin, with antlers so expansive he had to turn his head to step between the trees. His fur was a dark sable, deep black in places on his back, his throat and stomach a pale, delicate speckled grey. His eyes, watery black pools, caught mine and held them, his ears tipping forward as he chewed thoughtfully on foliage.

43

A giddy chuckle of relief escaped me. "Oh, buddy, you just scared the shit out of me, you know that? Jesus, Buck."

I sat heavily back down on the boulder, wrapped my arms around my knees, and watched him. He was utterly majestic as he bent his long neck down to take another nibble of clover, and when he came back up, still regarding me, his rack looked like two huge, gnarled, black hands pointed to the sky in supplication. I had this warm feeling spreading through me despite the wind picking up, with those wild eyes on mine, a sense of peace. Here was a creature for whom the unknown was home. He lived with uncertainty, not knowing if there was a hunter nearby ready to kill him for his antlers, unsure where his next meal was coming from, with no family to speak of, and yet he lived. He trusted that his home would provide for him, trusted that I wasn't his enemy.

"I want to be more like you, Buck," I said to him, and it was true. I wanted to trust in my own senses to protect me. I wanted to trust in my own judgement. I wanted the freedom to choose where and with whom I spent my time. I wanted to be as wild and gentle as the buck that stood, chewing, twenty feet away.

But equally, I knew that all of that would take time, take effort. There was an uneasy peace in the knowledge that the enemy of my growth was, now, only myself.

The deer snorted loudly. He pawed the ground, making divots in the soft earth, then bobbed his head up and down as if to confirm my thoughts. His ear twitched back, listened to some secret sound in the woods only he was privy to, then turned his bulk back to the forest and disappeared into the leaves as suddenly as he had appeared.

I put my shoes on, gathered my things, and began the trek back to the cabin, lost in thought, singing to myself.

"In the pines, in the pines, where the sun never shines— we'll shiver the whole night through."

SEVEN

I MADE MYSELF DINNER, feeling lighter than I had in days. I ate with gusto, polishing off an eight-ounce steak, a pile of mashed potatoes with mushroom gravy, and a forest of roasted broccoli. After eating, I took a shower to wash the dirt and sweat from the day's exertions off of myself, not even thinking about the beast that had come to the window nights ago. It felt like the person who'd been afraid was a different entity altogether—remote, far in the past. Once dressed, I retired to the porch to read and smoke a couple of cigarettes from the "emergency" pack I kept in my purse.

Men don't like it when girls smoke. Sends the message that you're easy.

Christ, Claire, you taste like an ashtray. If you want to burn, I'll show you a burn.

There was no one around to punish me for my pleasure, and I sat on the porch, rocking, buzzing with nicotine, full, content. I'd brought myself two books to read—the new Stephen King and a worn and spine-broken copy of *The Princess Bride*—and discovered that I'd soon need to go to town to get a few more. Having the quiet surround me, having the *time* and *space* to read what I liked

Why do you read such trash? Ugh, these aren't books for young women.

was a precious thing indeed. My brain soon caught up to give me back my reading speed from high school, when I'd average five books a month. I made a mental note to ask Earl if there was

45

a Books-A-Million in Homer. Even if there wasn't, the thought of a jaunt to Shreveport wasn't as daunting as it had been a week ago. I took a last long drag and got up to stub my cigarette in the grass.

Clump. Clumpclump. Clump.

I froze. The sound had come from directly ahead. I sat, hardly daring to shiver, in the rocking chair and peered out into the woods. The wind whipped my hair into my eyes. I made no movement to push it away. My eyes began to water, my vision blurred. I could only see the first row of trees; the rest were steeped in pitch blackness. The moon was all but gone now, its weak light no help at all as I tried with my paltry human vision to squint into the copse of trees and make sense of the sounds I was hearing.

Clumpclump. Clump c-clump. Shhhhhhhnikt...

The last sound was like someone dragging a knife over a wood block, a scraping sound I associated with pushing chopped vegetables into a bowl, but long and drawn out. My skin prickled, my limbs tingled with suspense.

"Buck?" I said, my voice shaky. "That you, buddy?"

There was silence for a beat, then, from much too close and to my left, a heavy *CLUMP,* and the sound of wood splintering.

I turned and ran into the cabin, locking the door behind me, my heart pounding so hard I thought it might leap from my throat and land with a wet *smack* on the floor. Laurie had told me if I heard anything, to go immediately inside, because if it was out *there*, and I was in *here,* whatever animal that had killed those sheep and caused that hole under my window couldn't do me any harm. But it didn't feel like that was true. Not at all. I wondered vaguely if bears or cougars were fond of karate chopping the fuck out of logs at night.

Clump. Clump. Clump. CLUMP. CLUMP.

Right beyond the porch.

"Oh *fuck!*" I squeaked, falling to my knees behind the door as those sounds stopped and were replaced by a listening, watchful silence. I glanced over to my bed, where I'd left my phone, which contained the lifelines that were the phone numbers of the people who could help me. It was too far to reach from where I sat. I would have to get up and risk the thing outside seeing movement in order to get it. And with the lights on and the windows so close, it certainly would. "Shit, shit, *shit!*"

More sounds from outside startled me, but I couldn't scream. *Shhh, shhhhhhh, shhhhhhhh, CRACK...SKRRREEEEERNK...*

The sound came from *above* this time and vibrated the cabin floor where I sat, that wood scraping sound and then a metallic scream as though something were rubbing itself on the gutters and the gutters were losing.

But the gutters are twelve feet in the air, thanks to the steps. Definitely not Buck. Definitely not a bear, either. I pressed myself harder against the door, grimacing as more scraping sounds emanated from outside.

Clump...CRACK

The sound of splintering wood resounded from directly behind me, and then I did scream, because that meant it was on the porch.

I'm going to die, I'm going to die, I'm GOING TO DIE, I'M GOING TO

A guttural sound unlike anything I've ever heard in my life came through the door. I could liken it to the lowing of cattle, but that would be wrong. I could say it was like the growling chuff of big cats, but that would be wrong too. It had elements of the snarl of a wolf, but that would do this sound injustice beyond measure. What I can say was that it contained frustration, and dismay, and sadness all at once. It went on for several long, loud, terrifying seconds, and then it abruptly stopped.

I sat where I was, my ass wedged against the door, all my muscles tensed as though I might spring from my hiding place to run. But where could I run? Where could I possibly hide from the creature that came from the darkness of the woods to call on me?

There was the sound of rending wood, the whole cabin shook with the force of it, and then

CLUMP, CLUMP, Clump, Clump, clump…

I don't know what came over me then. Perhaps it was that human instinct to *see*, to *know*, that took over, but I stood then and ripped back the curtains to look at the creature exiting my little retreat. I gasped when I saw it, a hulking black shape hunched over, melting back into the woods as it moved. To call it *tall* was an understatement, as it was at least thirteen feet high, but the antlers that splayed out above its head made it even taller than that. Its limbs—Arms? Legs?—were like tree trunks, thick, bent, twisted. It used one arm—Paw?—to push aside the limbs of a live oak, and stepped through them with another *clump* of its heavy—Paws? Hooves?—feet.

It must have known I was watching, must have, because then it turned, ever so slightly, to look back. I was utterly paralyzed to look away, and in the gloom I saw two moons

Eyes, those are its eyes, its eyes, its

shining silver as it briefly regarded me, small and frightened and soft and human, from the shadows. Then it turned away, the tree branches snapping sharply closed behind it, and was gone.

EIGHT

"*C*HOO*,*" LAURIE SAID quietly, running the tips of her fingers over the splintered boards of the steps. "I just don't know, Ms. Shaw. I just don't know."

She stood, hitched her belt, and shielded her eyes so she could look up at the torn gutters hanging in metal tatters above us. "You say it *rubbed* against these? Nothing fell on them, like a tree branch, heavy enough to break these boards?"

"Do you see a tree branch? Nothing fell," I confirmed, smoking furiously. "It rubbed against those *before* I heard the boards snap. They snapped when it stepped onto them, not from anything falling."

Laurie rubbed her mouth, thinking. "Well, I'm sorry to say I can't think of a single animal in these woods that could cause this sort of damage. Early?"

I turned to Earl, who'd observed Laurie's inspection with uncharacteristic silence, and found him gazing intently at the shredded gutters. He roused when Laurie said his name. "Yuh?"

"Can you think of anyone who'd want to do damage to your property like this?"

"Nary a soul."

Laurie turned her sharp eyes to me. "How about you?"

Dane. Dane would do this. I shrugged. "No. Nobody knows I'm here except my mom and dad, and they'd just barge in, not smash the stairs."

"Good. Good. Hm." Laurie stood with her hands on her hips, chewing her bottom lip thoughtfully. "OK. The only thing I can

49

think to do is go back to town and report this to Wiley, as well as my boss. If it *is* an animal, it's much more dangerous than we thought if it's trying to get into houses. Maybe rabid, though we haven't had a case of *that* going on six years now. If it's *not* an animal, whoever it is, he's plenty pissed off and has a jump like Michael Jordan." She looked pointedly at me. "You gonna feel safe out here alone, or should I ask Wiley for a detail to stick close by?"

The thought of being watched by cops made my skin crawl more than the thought of the creature coming back. "I think I'll be OK. It just scared me, is all. You said to call you if anything else happened, so I did."

"You did the right thing." Laurie slapped her hands against her thighs. "Well. Seems I can't do much more than I have already. You need help cleaning her up, Early?"

"Nah, I've got 'er. Few boards and some nails and she'll be good as new. Gonna have to call Chris about them gutters, though."

It wasn't until he mentioned the gutters I realized they were talking about the cabin and not me. "Can I help at all?"

"Sure," Earl said, his eyes now glued to the hole in the stairs. "Let me get Laurie back and gather m'tools. It'll do you good to get some work in after that scare."

Earl was back in less than an hour, a little trailer hitched to his four-wheeler with building supplies inside. I'd spent the entire time sitting on the porch, gazing out at the woods, enthralled with the idea that it might come back in the daytime when I could really see it. The shock of seeing it in shadows had faded by now, and the idea that I may see it again simultaneously frightened and thrilled me. The instinct to *see*, to *know*, is stronger than fear, always.

It took a little over an hour to fix the stairs with the two of us working. When we were done, we were both sweating despite the cold, and I went inside and got us each a glass of Crystal Light. When I came outside, Earl was standing in the grass, staring out at the woods. He grunted his thanks as he gulped down half of his and belched. I sat down in the rocker, and he leaned one hand on the porch railing, still gazing raptly at the tree line.

I didn't like how quiet he'd been. He seemed off, somehow, and I needed something to fill the quiet besides the wind rustling the leaves. "So do you think I need to be on the lookout for a rabid bear?"

"No, I don't," he said, not looking at me. "No, Miss Claire Shaw, I do not."

"What do you think it was?"

He looked at the busted boards sitting in a pile, then up at the gutters hanging like loose teeth above us. "Dunno. Something mighty big, that's for sure."

"Earl," I said carefully, "it kinda seems like you want to tell me something."

He heaved a sigh. "That obvious, am I? Shee-it. Pardon my French."

I chuckled, but Earl wasn't smiling when he turned to me. "Down where you're from, I'm sure you've heard all kinds of stories about swamp monsters since you were a kid, right? Honey Island monster, the Rougarou, things like that?"

"Yeah," I replied, a feeling of unease in the pit of my stomach. "There's even a Rougarou exhibit at the zoo. Big papier-mâché werewolf with shell teeth and light bulbs for eyes. It's tucked behind a wall so you can't see it until you turn around and he's just *there*. Used to scare the shit out of me when I was little."

"Yuh, I guess it might," Earl nodded. "I ever tell you my great-great-grandad was indigenous?"

I furrowed my brow, thrown by the abrupt subject change. "No."

"No, I guess I wouldn't have. I got a letter when I was eighteen telling me I had enough Native blood in me to live on the reservation up yonder if I had a mind. I declined, my thinking being those folks had had enough big, dumb white guys taking up their living space to last a lifetime. But I have some cousins who do live out there, and I've visited often enough. It's a nice piece of land, very open, with every sort of living arrangement on it from trailers to mansions." He took a long swig of his Crystal Light, then looked into it thoughtfully, scratching his chin. "Laurie's older cousin Anthony lives on one of those plots of land, and it was his brother Tommy who called me. This was before Laurie married into my family, mind, and I'd appreciate if you didn't bring up to her that I told you this story. She'd think I was going Cocoa Puffs, if'n yer follow me."

"I follow," I said, extremely aware that Earl was choosing to open up to me, someone he barely knew, and I'd do well to not take that trust lightly. "What did Tommy call you for?"

"The reservation grows some a'their own crops, keeps their own animals, and the like, so as you can imagine, it's a pretty dang big plot of land. About nine, ten years back, though, they started having some trouble. Nothing major at first. Some plants got trampled, few stalks of corn got et up, things like that. It was autumn, almost harvest time, so they figgered it was some a'them deer that roam around out here. Back then there was a sight more of 'em, and they was always showing up on people's land, eating their plants, having their tussles over who got the hottest girl, you know. But it was little damage. Easy to fix. Can I have more of that pink lemonade you got? Talkin's thirsty business."

"Sure, of course," I said, and went inside to get the pitcher. I brought it with me and poured him another glass.

He gulped down three swallows and smacked his lips. "Thank you kindly. Now where was I?"

"Deer ate some of the crops on the reservation."

"What they *thought* was a deer," he said, holding a finger in the air. "Until the hens started going missing."

I grimaced. "Deer don't steal hens."

"Nor do they eat them. Tommy himself found some blood and feathers behind one of the coops, and at first they thought mebbe it was *two* animals, a feisty deer and p'raps a hungry fox. But they have these dogs, see, that are trained to look after livestock. They steer the cows away from the trees, alert the farmers to intruders, like that. The folks on the reservation made the decision to leave these dogs out at night after the hens was kilt, you know, the thought being that they'd bark if anything came out of the woods like they was trained to do. Two days later, five a'them dogs was found dead and mutilated at the edge of the woods. Nary a one a'them barked."

I was chilled. "That's...impossible. Five of them? And not one made a sound?"

"Yuh," Earl nodded. "Tommy called me that day, told me about it. Said when he found them, they looked like they'd been squashed flat, almost like they'd been run over by a tractor, but there were no tire tracks. Just big, deep impressions in the earth under each smushed dog."

I thought of the scooped-out earth in the path from Earl's house to mine. Thought of the divot beneath my bathroom window. I shuddered, my arm hairs raising with gooseflesh.

"I'm an experienced hunter and tracker, I guess I don't have to say, so Tommy asked me if I would mind helping him and some of the reservation folks search the woods for any sign of what done it. I'll admit, part of the reason I agreed was just to see what happened to those dogs, but when I got there and saw it with my own eyes..." Earl shook himself, miming shivers. "Disgusting. No animal deserves to have that happen to 'em. So I went out with Tommy and a few other guys to go have a look at the scene of the crime, so to speak.

"I don't have to tell you, we didn't find much. There were those impressions in the dirt, mind, but they looked like no animal tracks I'd ever seen before, and there were no others leading to or from the spot where whatever it was caved in those dogs. We decided we'd go as a group into the woods, then spread out in four directions, have a little looky-loo and see if we could figure out where this thing was coming from. Tommy reasoned if we knew where it denned, we could figure out a way to either contain it or kill it, if we had to. I was all for killing something that could do what I'd seen done, but Tommy was less keen on the idea. He told me—and I'll never forget the way he said it—he said, 'Earl, some things must be understood instead of killed.'

"Well, I certainly did *not* understand, as will be evident in a moment. We traipsed around those woods all gat dang day, turning up neither hide nor hair of that thing. Until…" he trailed off, looked out at the woods, at the sun turning from afternoon to evening. He was so still and quiet, so lost in the past, that when I reached out and touched his elbow, he startled.

"Fuck's *sake!*" He shouted, clutching his chest. "Pardon my fuckin' French, but God *damn it,* woman."

"I'm sorry, I'm sorry!" I said, holding up my hands in truce. "I just…you've got me on the edge of my seat. Literally. And you just sort of…left me there."

"Ain't you ever seen a man collect his thoughts before?"

I smiled. "Most men I know are idiots, so there's nothing to collect."

He gaped at me for a moment, then let out that big belly laugh that let me know I was forgiven. "In that case, no, I don't guess you have. I didn't mean to leave you hangin', Miss Claire, but this next part is…I guess *heavy* is a good word for it. And parts are so plumb crazy I don't rightly believe them myself. I'll try to tell it all to you fast as I can, but be patient with me, Claire. I'm an old slob and I ain't got quite the language of the educated. OK?"

"OK," I smiled, urging him to go on. "No judgement from me."

"Thank you kindly. It was nearly night when we decided to head back to the reservation, and Tommy was plenty discouraged. He was sure we'd find some sign, but all of us, all day, found diddly squat. When we got back, all of us were present and accounted for except a guy named Dave who was known to slip off and smoke the funny grass when he was supposed to be doing work, so we wasn't worried. We just sat there talking about what we'd found—or rather, not found—when we heard Dave start to scream from in the woods.

"I'm not a fast man, I don't need to tell you, but that night I ran fast as anything, bringing up the rear of a knot of men running toward the sound of pure-d terror coming from in them trees. Thought I was like to die, keeping up with those fellas, but Dave's voice got closer, so I pushed as hard as I could, breathing like a freight train the whole dang way. We all had flashlights, so when we found him kneeling in the dirt with a gash down his face and his clothes all bloody, we cast them around, looking for the thing what had done it to him. We couldn't see fuck all—pardon my French—and Tommy knelt next to Dave, speaking in their Native tongue. I couldn't understand any of it, but then Tommy asked, 'When'd he go?' and Dave raised one trembling hand to point into the trees, mumbling an answer fast and low.

"The other guys were busy searching in every direction, so I took it upon myself to walk closer to where he'd pointed. If whoever had done this hadn't left too long ago, and it sounded as if he hadn't, they'd still be struggling through the thick underbrush and I'd see 'em." Earl rubbed his chin, smoothing

55

his moustache thoughtfully. "I remember thinking 'it's a man, it's a man, and we can catch a man no problem,' because if this was a *man* problem and not a wild animal, men can be identified and apprehended. But it wasn't a man. Not at all."

"What was it?" I asked, my skin still crawling thinking about the enormous shape turning its silvery eyes to look at me before disappearing into the trees.

"It was…" Earl faltered. He set his cup down and plopped heavily onto the boards of the porch (but not as heavily as my nighttime visitor) as though relaying the story was as difficult as living it. "Claire. I need to say before I go on, that I'm not saying what *I* saw and what *you* saw are the same thing at all. I couldn't possibly know. But hearing you describe what came out of the woods last night, and seeing *that*—" he gestured toward the broken boards on the ground and the dangling gutters, "—with my own eyes gave me the shivers like you wouldn't b'lieve. I'm not *saying* the same thing is in both stories, mind, but I wonder. I wonder."

I patted his knee affectionately. "I know, Earl. Please tell me."

When he went on, it was in a hushed voice I'd never heard him use, as if he were afraid of who—or what—might hear his confession. "I only saw it for a moment, mind. And only from the back. But it was huge, tall as a telephone pole, so black that it swallowed the light of my torch, and it *creaked* as it stepped deeper into the woods. No, that's not right." He shook his head. "It didn't *walk* away. It melted into the trees. As though it was one a'them. And then it was gone and I was just standing there with my mouth hung open and my flashlight dropped at my feet."

"What did y'all do then?"

"What'd we *do*? We went home. Dave calmed down and let us lead him back to his house, and he smoked himself stupid while we all rehashed our unfruitful trip into the woods."

"Didn't you tell them what you saw?"

Earl scoffed. "Tell them what? That I saw a monster turn into a tree? They'd have laughed me right off the reservation."

"But Tommy said…"

"Don't tell *me* what Tommy said," he replied, annoyed. "I was the one who was there." Seeing the shocked look on my face, he softened. "My apologies for that outburst. It ain't your fault I didn't—and still don't, to be honest—know how to explain what I saw in the woods that night. But I'll tell you something else."

He leaned in conspiratorially and I leaned forward too, so that our faces were nearly touching. "*Dave* couldn't tell anyone what he'd seen either. After that night, he didn't come to any of the council meetings or group activities on the reservation anymore, things Tommy said he'd dearly loved doing. He was, at heart, community minded, even if he was a pothead. But after that night in the woods, all he did was set up in that trailer of his and smoke dope. Wouldn't come out, wouldn't let nobody in either, even when Tommy came by to tell him the attacks had stopped. Tommy banged on that there door for many minutes, he said, and got nothing from inside, not even a 'go away.' He found this plenty suspicious, so he called up Wiley to come help him get in."

"Wiley?" I asked. "The same cop who came out here the other day?"

"The very same," Earl said. "Wiley tried for a response and got goose egg same as Tommy, so he kicked in the door, thinking maybe Dave was in trouble. But, as it turns out, the trouble had passed for old Dave."

My eyes went wide. "He was gone?"

"Dead," Earl said flatly. "Hung hisself. Wiley once showed me pictures of the crime scene, seeing as I was involved, asked me to help make sense of what had happened to Dave. He'd heard about the woods, see, and figgered it had something to do with why he'd found this fella strung up in his house by his own hand. So I looked. And oh, was it horrible. Before he killed hisself, Dave had taken to his own chest with a knife—carved a word, red and deep into his own chest. Then I understood, see, that what Tommy said in those woods wasn't 'When'd he go.' No. That word was carved deep into Dave's chest, and I felt afraid all over again."

My eyes were like dinner plates, my muscles quivering. Here was the answer I sought. The name of the beast that had come to call. "What did it say?"

Earl swallowed, a click in his throat. "It said 'wendigo.'"

NINE

I N THE SHOWER, with no music on this time, I pondered what Earl had told me.

Wendigo.

As soon as he left—which he'd done reluctantly only after I promised to call him if I heard so much as a groan from the woods, *and* with the insistence I take his high-powered work light—I looked up the word. The wendigo was an Indigenous folk legend, a shape-shifter that lured people into the woods and drove them mad, caused them to kill their fellow tribe members. It was also the explanation for why some long-ago Natives went cannibal if left alone in the woods too long. We had words like *exposure* and *mental illness* to account for that now, so the wendigo was treated as nothing more than a fireside story to scare kids. There were descriptions of what a wendigo looked like, but they were vague and jumbled, no one tribe agreeing with another about what its true form might be. The general consensus was that they were bigger than a man, sneaky shape-shifters, and capable of disappearing shortly after passing on their curse. Drawings of it ranged from a delicate forest spirit to a slavering monster. This was one instance when the Internet was singularly *un*helpful despite a wealth of information. A tendril of nerves rose up from the pit of my stomach as I mulled this over. Earl's story had chilled me in a way that the hot water couldn't reach. I scrubbed myself down quickly, eager to be out from behind the curtain and back where I could see the entirety of my surroundings.

From on the vanity, my phone chirped out the first few bars of Billy Joel's "Only the Good Die Young," the ringtone reserved for my mother, and I startled so hard I slipped. My feet squeaked and squalled over the porcelain of the tub, and I caught the rim in just enough time to avoid going face-first into the fixtures. The phone went silent for a moment, then rung again. I groaned in frustration, swearing under my breath. The last thing I wanted right now was to talk to Marilyn Shaw, but it looked like I was going to have to.

"You can wait till I'm clean, Ma," I said out loud, and then phone fell silent and stayed that way, as if she had heard me.

I did my best to hurry through the rest of my shower, but when I was finally dry, hair wrapped in a towel and pajamas clinging to my damp skin, I picked up the phone to see several texts in a row.

MOM 7:15 p.m. *Where are u??????*

MOM 7:16 p.m. *I've been trying to call u honestly Claire why r u avoiding me????????*

MOM 7:16 p.m. *I keep calling r u OK*

MOM 7:19 p.m. *CALL ME!!!!!!!!!!!!!!!!!@!!!@@@!!!*

I sighed so deeply my back popped, and steeled myself for this inevitably tense conversation, then hit send on the call button under the word MOM. It rang only once before she answered.

"*Claire?*" She practically shouted, as if anyone else might be calling from my number. "Is that you?"

"Yes, Mom, it's me."

"Oh thank *God.* I thought one of those country bumpkins might have kidnapped you and taken your phone."

"Nope, I was just in the shower." I put her on speaker phone and began toweling off my hair. "The people out here are really nice, actually. The guy who rented me this place is super friendly. I like him a lot."

"I'm sure he likes you a lot too," she said suspiciously, her voice dripping sarcasm. "You want to stay away from those country clods. Nothing but high school dropouts and meth heads up in *Homer*."

"That's not true," I defended, but I knew I'd get nowhere, so I left it at that. "So what was so important that you needed me right away?"

"I need a *reason* to want to talk to my only daughter now?"

I sighed. "No, I just…I was in the *shower*, and now I need to make dinner. You texted so many times, it sounded like it was urgent."

"Well, it's not, now that I know you're safe," she said in a triumphant way that made me think *safe* meant *going to answer me no matter what you're doing.* "If you're interested, your father has decided that he's going to retire next year. I thought you *might* like to know, but maybe you don't care."

"That's great news, Ma. I'm sure he's really excited about that."

"As excited as he gets about anything these days," she said, pointedly letting me know without saying that I was the sole reason my father didn't experience unbridled joy anymore. "He says it's more *practical* to retire, so that someone can always be home if you need it."

Unbidden, that song came back to me. *My daddy was a railroad man, killed a mile and a half from here—*

"I don't need someone to take care of me."

"That's what I said, but he insisted this was the way. He said that you would be more willing to accept help from *him* rather than *me,* but I don't know about that. You're willful no matter *who* you're dealing with, so I just don't know. And then Dane said that—"

"Wait." I cut her off, ice in my veins. "Dane? You talked to Dane?"

"Well, *yes*, Claire," she sighed in that long-suffering way that meant I was being especially dense. "He's your husband, after all."

You caused me to weep, you caused me to moan

61

"*Ex*-husband," I corrected, my throat closing like a fist. "When did you talk to him?"

"He calls a couple times a week. Am I supposed to be rude and *not* answer?"

Shock spread through my body in a hot wave. "Yes, you fucking well *are* supposed to not answer the calls of the man who beat the *shit* out of your daughter!"

"Oh, Claire, *language!* There's absolutely no call for this kind of hostility. He was *acquitted.*"

You caused me to lose my home

"Yeah, he was, but he still *did it*, mom!" I sank down onto my bed and put my face in my hands, tears coming hot and fast now, but I kept myself quiet. If she knew I was crying she'd scoff at my emotions, and then I'd cry more, and she'd win. Like Dane won. Anger rose like a tide in my throat.

Better luck next time, sweet cheeks

"Claire? Claire, are you still there? This damn thing better not have hung up on m—"

"I'm here," I moaned morosely, coming up for air, my voice miraculously empty of the tears streaking my face. Then a horrible thought occurred to me. "Mom. This is important. Did you…did you tell him anything? About me leaving?"

Little girl, little girl, don't lie to me

"What, tell him about you running away? Not much. I told him you went to that little hick town after quitting your job, and he agreed that—"

I hung up. I could hear no more of her through the whooshing sound of the fury in my ears. She'd told Dane where I was. My hands clenched into fists in my lap, my eyes scanning the cabin that had brought me so much pleasure when I first walked in and realized it—and the woods that surrounded it—was mine for a while. Looking at it now brought me no enjoyment whatsoever. My retreat was now a prison.

TEN

THE REST OF that evening was a blur of anxiety. My mother, that bitch, had told my abuser where I was, which meant, I knew, that eventually he'd come calling. It was his nature. We'd been divorced over a year, he'd won against me in court, but he wouldn't be able to resist the urge to further lord over me the hold he had, and always would have, over my life. He very likely dressed it up as concern for my well-being to my mother, casual questions regarding what I'd been doing since the trial, and my whereabouts. He knew, also, that I was essentially alone out here, and for him, that would be too much temptation to ignore. If he came—as I knew in my heart that he would—it would be to "ensure my safety" (a term which generally meant that he needed to make sure I wasn't talking shit about him behind his back, even to people he didn't know). And if he found I wasn't behaving myself, if I was taking "unnecessary risks"? Why, even with the status of ex-husband, he was duty bound to correct me until I flew straight again. To save me from myself. I toyed with the idea of leaving, lighting off into the night and running away for real this time, dropping the key and an apology into Earl's mailbox, getting in my Saturn, and bolting to God knows where.

But that would mean walking through the woods at night, by myself—*in the pines, in the pines, where the sun never shines*—with all of my things weighing me down. If either Dane or the thing that had come calling the previous evening found me out there like that, I was toast. I opted to stay this last night, reasoned that I had no idea when Marilyn had told Dane where I was.

He'd potentially had *days* to make a move, and hadn't yet. The odds of him showing up tonight were slim, but I still checked to see how many cabins were for rent in Homer. There were dozens. I relaxed enough to stave off a panic attack and went about collecting my things for the next day's exodus. I *would* be running, just not tonight, in the dark.

I sat on the couch and flipped through Netflix, settling on old *King of the Hill* reruns for background noise. I wasn't watching; I was thinking. What excuse could I give kind, helpful Earl about why I was leaving? Did I owe him an excuse at all? I thought I did, even though it felt like covering up more of Dane's wounds in an effort to hide them. Then again, I might *have* to tell Earl what was going on, because if Dane showed up, who knew what he might do? I didn't think Dane could take Earl in a fair fight, but if he had the element of surprise, as he so often did? Well.

"Lord knows it's worked for him before," I muttered, rubbing my left cheek where so many sucker punches had landed.

I thought I was done with this. I thought it was over, I thought, stuffing yesterday's jeans into my duffel bag.

I felt like weeping, but there were no tears left, it seemed. At least not right now. If I was lucky, if I left fast enough and cut all ties, maybe there never would be again. My tank was full enough to get me deep into Texas, and as long as I shut my phone off and got a new number there, one that couldn't be tracked and that nobody knew, I could move west until I felt like stopping. Hell, I might be able to make it to California and hop on a plane if my funds held out (I figured I'd empty and close my bank account when I got to Texas as well, just to be sure) and take myself to Canada, maybe even off the mainland.

I sat down on the sofa, my brain buzzing like a hive of angry bees, and forced myself to lie down, covering myself with the quilt and pillowing my head on my arm. I didn't think I'd be able to sleep, keyed up as I was, but at some point during the episode where Dale thinks he has rabies, I fell asleep. My doze was fitful, my dreams harrowing.

I dreamed that I was back in Dane's house, the one he still lived in with all the furniture I'd picked out, all my dishes, our wedding pictures framed on the walls. He had me by the hair, his sharp, skinny fingers wrenching my head back and forth by the scalp as he screamed.

"*You worthless bitch!*" He shouted in my face, spittle flying out to burn my eyes. "*You filthy fucking cunt whore! I'll fucking kill you for this!*"

I couldn't remember what I'd done to deserve this, had no idea what he was screaming about. I knew only that his wrath was as it always was: violent, painful, immediate. If he said I deserved to die, then I did, and there was no questioning his judgement. I tried to twist away, but he yanked me back, throwing me onto my back on the floor and launching himself to kneel over me, pinning me, smacking down my protective hands.

"*You*," he said, leaning down, his handsome face, contorted in rage, bare centimeters from my own, "*you* are going to learn your lesson about running from *me*." He put the hand with the wedding band on it behind my head, cupped it almost lovingly. "You *belong to me*. And once you've had your lesson, you're going to show me with your mouth and your dirty fucking *cunt*, exactly how well you retained what I taught you."

He drew back his fist and my heart screamed. My mouth, as always, was unable to comply. And then, in the way of dreams, time slowed. The arc of his fist moved at a snail's pace, the drool on his bottom lip swung in immeasurably small increments. I opened my eyes slowly, hardly able to believe my luck. And then, suddenly, I was no longer lying on the warm, beige carpet of our living room, but on a cool bed of moss and dirt.

I glanced around me, fearful, but able to move at normal speed. I was in the woods, the trees rising around me like gentle giants, protectively shielding this display of human weakness from the world. I scrambled out from beneath Dane, who didn't so much as twitch, stuck as he was in the molasses of the dream. I stood, brushing leaves and dead grass from my jeans.

A soft sound from my left made me turn, and that was when I saw the deer. It was the same deer from my afternoon at the waterfall, his huge black antlers hands pointing to heaven, his heavy body moving gracefully as he approached me. He got so close that I could smell him: musky, alive, the scent of a creature that belonged outside, that lived in the sun, silvery creek water and the pleasant rot of fallen leaves. The smell of freedom.

"Buck," I said, my voice muffled to my ears. "What are you doing here?"

Is this what you are? I felt his voice more than I heard it. It was the creaking of branches, the susurration of wind through dead leaves, the trickle of river water cascading down in a flood.

I glanced back at Dane, still crouched, with his fist moving incrementally down to where my face was moments before. "It's what I was."

Buck nudged me, bringing me back to him and his black, feral eyes. *Do you wish to be more?*

I gulped back tears. "Every day of my life. I'm always so afraid, Buck. I'm so…so *tired* of always being afraid."

Buck's head bobbed understanding, his antlers clacking. He nuzzled me with his wet, velvety muzzle, his hot breath chuffing against my arm. Then he turned, walking away from me. I couldn't move to make him stay, much as my heart ached to see him leave. It only seemed right that such a majestic creature would abandon me and my sad life and my rabbit heart.

I. Gift

As he made it to the tree line, the waterfall appeared at his feet, its splashing clear and so loud, so loud.

When Buck turned his head to me, his eyes were no longer the deep black of a deer, but two moons, shining silver in the gloom of the trees. *Then come and see.*

I woke with a shout, drenched in sweat, breathing hard, my scalp still stinging and my veins singing with fiery blood. But there wasn't a trace of fear anymore. I knew what I needed to do.

ELEVEN

"**O**W, *FUCK*," I grumbled when I barked my shin on a broken tree branch lying in the path. It was extremely dark in the woods, the dense foliage blocking out the weak glow of the stars on this moonless night, and I'd left my flashlight back at the cabin. I didn't need it. My feet found the path towards the waterfall all on their own, even with the visibility being near zero. I rubbed at the bruise forming on my shin and walked on. The wind kicked up, and I rubbed my arms with my hands, hoping the friction would make me warmer. I may not have needed the flashlight, but I did wish I'd had the sense to put on my jacket.

When I woke from my dream about Dane and Buck, I'd felt the pull immediately. It was like the air had been charged with electricity and a magnet planted in my belly, a magnet pulling me out here. It ached, impossible to ignore, so I'd given in and set out, my head a dreamy fog. I was almost there, I could feel it, that heavy, not unpleasant feeling of *drawing* in my body getting stronger the more I walked. Soon I would be at the waterfall. Soon I would shed all that I had been. Soon I would become more.

I came to the clearing just as I had the last time. One minute I was in the dense trees, sightless and lost, scrabbling over that huge dead log, and the next I was in the clearing with the moss-covered boulder illuminated by starlight, the rush of the water louder in the stillness of night than it had been during the day. And it *was* still, I realized. Aside from the sound of the waterfall, there were none of the usual night noises. No owls, no creatures scuttling in the underbrush, hardly a breeze to speak of, so that even the trees were silent. It was as if the forest was holding its breath, waiting for this nocturnal communion to commence.

I walked up to the river, holding myself and shivering— *we'll shiver the whole night through*—staring out into the forest. The crack of a branch made me spin around and squint into the dark, seeking the source of the sound.

I climbed up onto the boulder and addressed the silence. "Buck? Are you here?"

There was nothing for a moment, no movement, no sounds. Then there was, and my heart leapt.

A chuckle like the snapping of twigs came from all around me. *"Buck." I like that. I have been called many names before. Wendigo. Skinwalker. Furfur. Jotünn. But never something so endearing as "Buck."*

I spun around in circles, quaking in the gloom, searching for the voice, which seemed to come from everywhere and nowhere. "Where are you? I can't see. Come out where I can see you."

Are you afraid? There was the crunch of gravel in the question.

"No," I said, surprised to find that it wasn't a lie.

There was a pregnant pause, a consideration in the quiet. I could *feel* a decision being made in the crackling electricity that flowed through me, and then Buck stepped into view.

Stepped is the wrong word. What actually happened was that two of the trees in front of me began to split, their boughs and their trunks winding together to form a hulking shape so black it swallowed the stars, the topmost limbs winding together to form the crown of supplicating antlers, while the earth and rocks below lifted themselves up to form the legs and hooves of the thing I knew as Buck. Stones gathered and floated into the air, crunching together to make a shape not unlike a deer skull, which settled gently onto the stump of a neck. Buck, twelve feet, antlers to hooves, and now fully himself, took two booming steps toward me and stood, two silvery moons swirling into existence within his sockets to peer down at insignificant me.

And now? The voice was soft, hopeful, the cascade of water down mossy stones.

I stared up at him, this ancient forest god that had seen fit to give me an audience. "No."

Buck reached out one hand, easily as big as my entire body, the claws branches. I put my small hand in his and he creaked-snapped until he was on one knee, an elegant suitor with a proposal to his love. His eyes were now level with mine and I was mesmerized, gazing into the light of the moon brought right to my feet, the glittering depths full of promise. *Then I have a gift for you. If you will have it.*

I leaned forward, placing my free hand on his skull to stroke his beautiful head. Buck groaned with pleasure at the gentle touch, probably the only gentle thing to happen to him in a millennium, his joy the sound of ancient cypress trees bending in a hurricane. I pressed my lips to his smooth forehead, my body against the cool rocks of his skull. "I accept, Buck. Gratefully."

TWELVE

I STRETCHED IN THE morning sunshine, loving the delicious way my muscles unwound. I sat up on the boulder, letting the sun on my skin warm me. The cold snap had disappeared in the night, leaving a heat behind that I knew would rise in time with the sun. I collected my clothes—they were scattered everywhere—and got dressed, splashed my face with freezing water from the stream. When at last I began the trek back to the cabin, I did so floating in a thoughtful cloud of wonder.

I hummed to myself tunelessly, admiring the beauty of the woods, really looking at the trees with new eyes and catching details for the first time. There seemed faces etched in the bark of oaks and willows, curious dryads that marked the passage of a lone girl making her way through their midst. A red cardinal lit on a jutting stick nearby, tilting its head this way and that, before swooshing down to snatch a bug out of a pile of dead leaves with their green turning gold and brown at the edges. The bird flitted out of sight to enjoy its repast elsewhere. Here was a cluster of foxgloves gathered around the trunk of a huge old elm, the pink speckled bells swaying gently in the breeze. Something scampered—*rabbit*, I knew—in the distance, its feet leaving furrows in the dirt as it hustled to put itself out of my path. I wouldn't have harmed it, but it didn't know that. It was just doing as instinct dictated it must, same as anyone else. And everywhere, everywhere, was light and warmth and life. I'd never felt so close to the earth, so much a part of this great *whole* called existence. I was almost sad when the cabin came into view ahead

71

of me, did not want to give up this feeling of blissful surrender and oneness.

It's with me no matter where I go now, I thought, smiling. *I am part of it, and it is part of me.*

I patted my pockets, half hoping I hadn't dropped the keys by the waterfall, half hoping I had so I could take another happy stroll through nature with myself. But no, there they were, in my left front pocket, and I dragged them out, sticking the key into the door.

"What the fuck are you so happy about?" Said an all-too-familiar voice behind me.

I couldn't help it. I cringed. Then I turned slowly, my neck creaking, to see Dane standing there, big as life and twice as ugly, at the break in the forest where the path let out. Blocking my escape route. He stood with his legs set apart, hands in his pockets, his traditionally handsome face holding a trace of that indulgent smile I always hated so much.

"I waited for you," he said slowly, dangerously, "all night long. I slept on the porch of this dump. Where were you?"

Little girl, little girl, don't lie to me

I turned to face him, my heart speeding up. "I don't think that's any of your business."

And oh, he was advancing now, step by careful step, the way a wolf moves towards an unaware rabbit in the snow. "None of my business? I was worried sick about my wife."

"Ex-wife," I corrected him.

He stopped, his face a moue of surprise that I, ever the cowering hare, should correct the wolf so readily. But then he smiled again. Took another step. "Feisty today. I like that. It suits you. How did you get such brave new confidence?"

He was at the steps now, the toe of one shiny loafer on the bottom step I'd helped Earl fix a hundred years ago. I swallowed, gripping my keys between the fingers of my right hand. "I think you should leave, Dane."

"Oh, you do, do you?" He said with his eyebrows raised as he stepped down on the stairs, lifting himself closer to me. "Why is that?"

"Because I don't want you here. That's enough of a reason."

"Were you fucking someone out in the woods, Claire?" The question was abrupt, angry. "Is yer big ol' hyuk-hyuk bumpkin gonna stop filling you with his inbred spunk if I'm around? Is that why you want me gone?"

Tell me where did you sleep last night?

"So what if I was fucking someone else, Dane?" I shouted at him. I narrowed my eyes at him and leaned in, a big grin plastered on my face. "Fucking a dead tree stump would be more of a thrill than your *limp fucking dick,* you worthless, wife-beating shitbag." And then I reared back and hawked a huge gobbet of phlegm in his face.

He stood there, gaping, shocked, motionless, my spit sliding down his cheek for about three seconds.

"You…you…you…" he stammered, wiping the chunk of lung butter off his face with disgust.

And then he lunged. He came up the second step with a roar and grabbed me by my neck, shoving me against the door, my head whacking the wood so hard I saw stars. He shook me by my throat, roaring incomprehensible words, the sound of his violence loud in the quiet woods. He brought a knee up and into my stomach so that I wheezed in pain, choking on my need for air while the fingers of my left hand scratched and clawed at his hands, my feet scrabbling for purchase as he thumped my head over and over against the door.

He's finally going to do it, I thought. *He's going to kill me right here and now, and no one will ever find me because he'll dump me in the woods.*

And on the heels of that thought, another. The thought had a voice like stones toppling down a mountainside, like trees cracking from the tidal rush of a mudslide, like fire burning furiously through miles of woods, hungry, ancient, filled with crimson rage: *NO MORE.*

"N…no *more,*" I choked out around Dane's fingers. I brought my right hand up in a fist, the keys like porcupine quills, and drove them with all my force into his furious eyes.

In the pines, in the pines, where the sun never shines

He yowled in pain, releasing my throat to clutch his bleeding, wounded face and ruined eye, the keys dangling from his socket. Something ran from the popped eye that looked like yellow jelly, splattering his polo shirt. I fell in a crouch, tearing breaths of hot air into my lungs, before leaping with all my strength at his legs. He toppled backwards with a shout, and oh, I was on him then, screaming with all my might as I pummeled him, tore at him with my fingers gnarled into claws. His head cracked hard against the ground as he fell. He tried to cover his face, but I grabbed his left hand and held it, mashing the key in his eye further home as I inserted the ring finger that still wore his wedding band into my mouth. I bit down hard. He bellowed in pain, and the blood spurted into my mouth in a salty red river of pleasure. He tried to hit me back with his free hand, even landed a few weak blows, but he was discombobulated from the fall and all the sudden pain. I felt nothing, nothing at all except the singular pleasure of spitting his severed finger back into his fearful face.

I hit him square in the face two more times, dizzying him further and ceasing his fighting. Then I leaned in close, my gore-streaked face centimeters from his. His still intact eye was glassy with fear, his breath stank of it.

"I'm going to teach you a lesson," I growled, and my voice was not my own, it was that of a monster, a god, the voice of wildness and freedom, freedom, at last, freedom, "and then when I'm done, I'm going to test you to see how well you've retained what I've taught you."

We'll shiver the whole night through

In the end, there was no test. He couldn't very well tell me a thing after I tore his tongue out with my teeth and swallowed it.

THIRTEEN

"Y OU SURE I can't say anything to get you to stay?" Earl asked as he helped me hump my bags into the hatchback. "I hate the idea that you're going on account a'what I told yer t'other day."

"It wasn't that at all," I reassured him. "In fact, I'm leaving for a *good* reason. I did what I set out to do when I came here."

He rubbed a forearm across his sweaty brow. "And what was that?"

A vision of Dane's body (what was left of it anyway), chewed through and dumped in a deep hole I'd spent all day yesterday digging, my stomach heavy with his meat, flitted over the surface of my mind. I'd slept the rest of the day after that, curled up on the boulder by the river. I knew no one would ever find his bones where I'd hidden them. Well, maybe the scavengers, but that didn't matter. I laughed. "I'm free, Earl. Finally free of everything that's been weighing me down for such a long time. It's time to go home and reconcile the rest, start my new life."

"Well..." he said, a look of concern on his face. "I suppose that's alright then."

"You're darn tootin', it is."

The clouds on his face broke and that sunny grin emerged. I loved him a little then, this big man with his calloused hands and soft heart, who had no idea how much he'd actually helped me, and never would. There was no way to explain the gratitude I felt, so I opted to throw my arms around him and hug him tight. He hugged back, rocking us both, laughing.

"Best let go a'me, Miss Claire," he muttered, "lest Lilyanne think yer tryin'a snatch me away."

I let him go and held him at arm's length, grinning broadly, knowing that he would never find any evidence that Dane had been there at all—*his body was never found*—and he'd be safe. The dumb fuck I called my ex-husband had known better than to take his own car, had had an Uber drive him to Earl's house and leave him there when no one else was home. A couple months from now, if there was an investigation at all, the local law would determine he'd tried to find me and decided to take an unsafe path through the woods and gotten lost, died somewhere of exposure and been picked apart by the fauna within. People got lost in these woods all the time, after all, even locals. And Dane was no local.

"Promise you'll be careful," Earl said, fatherly in his concern for me. "And you let me know if you ever decide to come back here for a visit. Cabin's always open."

"I promise," I said, though I knew in my heart I'd never be back. I slammed the hatchback and went around front, slipping into the driver's side. "Thank you, Earl."

He scratched his head. "For what?"

I smiled. "Everything."

I beeped my horn as I drove away, and Earl waved. I turned on the radio and drove very fast down the interstate, singing along with Led Zeppelin of whispered tales of gore, howling hoards, and tides of war. My phone vibrated in my lap, and I glanced down, saw MOM, and groaned. I let it go to voicemail, pulled off at a rest stop to smoke, and called her back.

"So you're screening my calls now?"

"Sorry, Ma," I said around the butt, and inhaled deeply. "I was driving."

"Are you smoking, Claire?"

"Yeah."

There was a beat of shocked silence. "Well. I don't know who I raised if you're doing *that*. Did I hear you say you're driving?"

"Yep." I flicked ash at my feet and gazed across the parking lot to the woods beyond, their verdant depths no longer daunting, but enticing, full of promise.

"Where are you going *now*? Some other hick town to *find yourself*?"

"Nope," I said, stubbing out the butt on the bottom of my shoe and rolling it into a ball. "I'm headed back. And when I get there, I'm gonna pack my stuff and move out. Probably live with Candace, but certainly not with you. That arrangement doesn't work for me anymore. It hasn't since I was a kid."

"But—"

"No buts. I'm moving out and you have no say in what I do anymore. Is that clear, Mom?"

I could hear her working up a sob, but it did nothing to me. Where there used to be an ache of mixed sorrow and guilt, now there was clarity so sharp it stung, but my eyes were clear, tearless, dry. I didn't need her. I didn't need her tears or her guilt.

No more, that voice whispered again, and this time it was the wind whipping through the trees, the finality of an animal thudding to the ground, felled by a hunter's bow.

"If that's how you choose to hurt me, so be it. You're your own woman. But…will you be home in time for dinner tonight, at least? I suppose you could deign to have one more meal with us, couldn't you? You know I hate waiting."

"You won't have to wait," I replied, walking back to my car. "I'll be home in plenty of time to eat."

And it was true. I would be home in time to eat, but it wouldn't be Marilyn's Swedish meatballs I devoured. I would tell them both what my new boundaries were, and if they didn't listen, well… My stomach rumbled. I was hungrier than I'd been in years.

II.
DOGS FOR SALE

And the train it won't stop going
No way to slow down

– Jethro Tull, "Locomotive Breath"

ONE

I DECIDED TO WRITE this under something like duress. My name is Liam Doherty, I'm thirty-one years old, as native of a New Orleanian as one can possibly be. My therapist, Mindy Yang, tells me that this writing exercise will help me order my thoughts and come to terms with the most god-awful year of my life, and get me some closure—whatever that's worth in a thing as open-ended as this. I confess I haven't written a blessed thing besides a Facebook post in going on ten years, so I don't know how well this is going to work out. What I do know is that my older sibling has been a ghost in my head since I left middle school, and I'd very much like it if that ghost would go quietly back to its grave where it belongs.

I don't just want this for me. For Lyric too, and all the pain she carried with her in her heart and mind. All the pain she caused in retaliation. I'd like to believe she's somewhere out there, living happily, whole again, but I know in my heart that isn't true.

Still, I'd like to believe it.

I suppose I should tell you—whoever may read this missive of misdeeds and miscalculations of childlike judgement, if I ever decide to show it to anyone at all—what my life was like as a kid before all this happened. My parents were the late Bill and Megan Doherty, as happy a couple as you could want. I got my mother's looks—the thin frame and large, blue eyes—but my dad's thick, curly mop of blond hair and his crap eyesight that earned me Coke-bottle-thick glasses by the tender age of nine. They doted on me from the start, Mom working tirelessly with me, her baby

81

boy, so that by the age of three and a half I could read whole story books aloud to them and their friends when they came by for dinner. They were dead proud of that, as any parents would be, and I was proud of me too. They fostered in me a kind of quiet self-assurance that is so hard to come by in the very young, encouraged me to think for myself, and cheered me on with such vehemence that I never questioned whether or not I was loved.

As I grew, I was a total bookworm, reading far above my level and testing into the advanced classes in just first grade. My grades were always stellar, with the extremely rare C on particularly difficult tests that did nothing to keep me off the honor roll every semester. I was a quiet kid, some would say shy even, not at all prone to the wildly rambunctious proclivities of other boys my age. I was more interested in the affairs of the adult world, being an only child, and sometimes had trouble relating to people my own age, preferring older kids as companions. I had very few friends, but the ones I did have were excellent stock, good kids my parents approved of wholeheartedly. I never got into a single ounce of trouble my whole life.

Until Lyric showed up, that is. A lot of things changed with her arrival, not the least of which was the near immediate departure of every single one of my friends. I was utterly alienated by my unwillingness to dissociate from her, and kids I knew as friends began to distance themselves as though a stench clung to me from being related to Lyric. My parents' attitude toward life in general changed as well. They became two people who carried themselves as though they were decades older than their years, exhausted from lugging the weight of a hard and tumultuous life. They still loved me, I still felt it, but even they seemed to get a whiff now and then of whatever the kids at school smelled on me. I became even quieter than before, turning inward to avoid dealing with the hurt of this sudden, drastic change. My grades were still good, and I wasn't a disciplinary problem, but the pall hung over my life just the same, guilty as I was by mere association. I clung to my books and my interior world even harder, the complex topography of love my wilderness to navigate.

Lyric was prone to doing and saying strange things, things that often started as a joke and ended up deadly serious (at least, as far as she was concerned). I remember once, she told a bunch of people at school that she was in love with a bridge, specifically the Bywater overpass. I think at that point, it was just so she could laugh at people's confused expressions. She made it Facebook official one day, in this silly post that had Lyric's face and a photo of the bridge conjoined by little pink hearts. I knew she had made the bridge's profile with a dummy email, and it was just Lyric being in love with herself in a spiteful attempt to stave off loneliness with false bravado. At the time, I thought it was pretty funny, her doing all that work at taking the joke so far, but looking back now I know it was the heralding trumpets of the end. I know this because, three weeks after her Facebook announcement, when I asked her if she was ever going to take it down, she wrinkled her nose as if I had said something completely idiotic.

"Why would I?" she asked me.

I shrugged. "Because it isn't real."

"Pfft," she replied, waving me off. "Says you. I'm happy where I am."

Lyric had always been an oddball. Even when we were kids, she'd say weird things like, "I think maybe my throat is filled with wires today" and compulsively use a flashlight to look for them in the mirror down the black hole of her gullet, or ask questions like, "Do you think the roaches in the kitchen scream for us to stop before we hit them with a shoe?" if one got in the house and Dad squashed it. It never bothered me much, I suppose because I'd grown up around her, and thus whatever strange things she said never fazed me. I'd just nod or answer the questions best I knew how.

Lyric, for her part, seemed relieved to have had a brother like me who was also her friend. As you could probably guess, Lyric had issues keeping friends. She was certainly boisterous and outgoing enough to *make* friends, but *keeping* them was a much harder task. People get tired and used up when constantly confronted with frenetic energy like that. They burned out pretty quickly on Lyric's brand of clingy, possessive friendship. Lyric also had a nasty habit of totally taking down anyone who disagreed with her, and people tended to disagree with Lyric's take on the world quite a bit.

"Eventually I let my guard down," Lyric confided in me one day, her voice miserable and on edge from a recent spat with a girl she had perceived as safe to open up to, "and then they always abandon me. They say things like 'this is too much to deal with,' or 'you need to see a doctor'—like I haven't seen every fuckdamn doctor in New Orleans seven times apiece—and then it's bye-bye, so long, too bad, so sad for me. Except you, Liam. You never left."

And Lyric was right about that, I never had left, even though, looking back now with my adult eyes, that love hurt me in so many ways. But we were family, so even if I had a choice, it would have made things difficult. Plus, without Lyric, I would have been totally alone, seeing as my friends kept their distance those days.

Lyric was my dad's kid from his first marriage, the one he often told me had been a mistake to tie himself to legally. It was a story old as the hills, he said, but that didn't make it easier to live with. He'd gotten the prom queen, a girl named Maggie Sellers, pregnant before the end of their senior year, had done what he thought of as his due diligence and married her the minute they graduated, in a little family-only ceremony at the courthouse. They convinced themselves they were in love, and that fate had spoken. My dad was determined to do right by Maggie, his love, and had stepped up to be a dad, abandoning the idea of college and putting himself immediately to work.

"Don't make my mistakes," he told me solemnly, sipping his beer and staring at the muted television. "It was a bitch to backtrack with school and all. Always use protection, and if you do have an accident, you tell us. We'll always help you, son. We want you to succeed." He squeezed my shoulder. "With me and your mom at your back, you can't fail."

Lyric was born shortly thereafter, and the problems began. The newlyweds fought a lot, had hardly any money, seeing as my dad was fresh out of high school, and Lyric's mom had what we now know as postpartum, but back then was just called being a shitty mom.

"I was doomed from the jump," Lyric always said when making any mention of her early life. "Mom's brand of crazy ran deep."

It did indeed seem to run deep, because when Lyric was four, Maggie scooped her up out of her bed, packed the sleeping Lyric into the family's only car, and drove away. The police found the car at the railway station, parked sideways in two spots, but no sign of either Lyric or Maggie. My dad spent six long, excruciating years trying to find the two of them. In the first two years of that time, he'd met and married my mom (a PI hired to find his wayward family members) and had me. I remember him being up late some nights, on the phone with my mom, his gruff, sleep-infused voice grumbling out questions as he chain-smoked in his office, thinking I was asleep. They'd mostly given up by year six of Lyric's mom's disappearing act, had indeed stopped any active investigation. He'd even considered holding a funeral for them to give everyone closure.

But then one night, when I was six, there was a small knock at the front door. When Dad opened it, he'd sat down hard in the doorway, hands over his mouth and eyes unblinking, so surprised was he by what was on the other side. It was Lyric, and only Lyric, dirty, with matted brown hair and dark, hollow eyes, holding the handle of a pink, battered rolling suitcase. She had her thumb in her mouth and a badly tattered stuffed rabbit in the crook of her elbow. He ran outside, certain that he would see Maggie making her retreat, but there was nothing. Just his daughter, returned to him looking so worse for wear that it was heartbreaking.

He was, of course, happy to have Lyric back, safely at home, and welcomed her as part of our family. I remember that Lyric barely spoke the first year she was home, except to me. Her voice was quiet, thin and raspy as though from disuse. If I got scared at night, Lyric would climb in my bed and tell me stories in that husky voice until I drifted back into sleep. But never, ever about what happened to her in the years that her mother had spirited them away. Whatever mistrust Lyric had of adults due to that time didn't extend to me, the brother she loved instantly, easily as breathing, but about that no one could get Lyric to speak. It made my mom and dad plenty worried, so they put Lyric in therapy.

"Never took," Lyric would say proudly to anyone who might be listening. "I know what I know, and I ain't gotta tell *nobody* what I know if I don't want to."

I suspect whatever happened to Lyric in those years is somewhat to blame for what happened later. Somewhat, but not all. A lot of it was just the sad story of someone with mental disease so virulent that it overshadowed who they were, and made them into something else entirely. But some of it, the worst and best parts, I can find no rational explanation for, and it is because of those parts that I'm writing this now. My sincere hope is that once it's written in black letters on white paper, reasonable explanations will bob to the surface like corks on a fishing line. I think, however, that hope is unfounded.

TWO

I T STARTED WITH a flyer on the bulletin board at Gladstone, the school we both attended. Lyric was an upperclassman, a junior, but I was still in middle school. I was glad that my older sibling was in the same building as me, Gladstone going from the nubby little Pre-K kids all the way to seniors in high school that snuck out at lunch to smoke behind the coffee shop across the street. My parents liked it because Gladstone's classes were small enough that every child got individual attention. I liked it because it meant that Lyric was close.

Lyric was in another section of the school, but it was still a relief to have her nearby. By that time I was a reedy, pimply preteen who, although I was nearly a head taller than anyone else in my class, was so skinny that I often got picked on or harassed to the point of assault. Brendan Randall called me a skinny pussy more times than I could count, either before or after he knocked my glasses off my face, whichever took his fancy that day. Not when Lyric was nearby, though. The other kids were afraid of her, for the insane things she said, as much as her intimidating appearance. She'd chopped off her hair at the beginning of the school year, so it laid in a greasy, uneven shock of bright cerulean across her forehead. She had homemade piercings made with hot needles and safety pins, and a stick and poke tattoo of the middle finger on her bicep that even I had no idea from whence it had appeared. Lyric disdained the clothes our parents bought her, instead choosing to dress in secondhand clothes that bordered on rags, claiming she preferred clothes with character. I agreed they did have that. But, as with many things about Lyric, I suspected that this was just another holdover from whatever had happened in those years away with her mother. Old habits are often difficult to break, but a feeling of closeness to someone who's gone is even more difficult, because we have to choose to sever it ourselves. And Lyric never would, because she claimed this was all temporary, that her mother would show up soon enough to claim her, and this nightmare of normalcy would be over.

Still, it was good to have her enormous presence so close, because if by chance someone *did* pick on me, it was as if Lyric had in her a homing beacon for it. Once, when Tommy Childress (a boy who used to call himself my friend) punched me in the mouth to get a comic out of my hands, Lyric appeared as if summoned by my blood hitting the concrete, and shook Tommy with immense ferocity up and down till he yelped.

"If you don't give my brother back his comic," Lyric had snarled, punctuating every few words with a shake, "I'm going to take your dead body down to the swamp and sell your bones to the old witch who lives there. She'll give me a dollar for every pound of bones I bring, and she'll know I'm coming, because I gave her my blood to use for scrying."

Tommy had given back the comic book, tears in his eyes, and run away.

"Thanks Lyric," I said as she dabbed my mouth with the corner of her shirt. "But you didn't have to lie like that. He was plenty scared already."

Lyric's face screwed up in the funny way it did when she was puzzled by a statement, a look usually reserved for our parents. "Who said I was lying? That woman owes me ten dollars and she lives right outside town in the swamp."

"But...there's no swamp nearby." I stooped to pick up my glasses, tucked the comic in my armpit, and rubbed the sweat-greasy lenses with a corner of my shirt. "Not one that's worth talking about, anyway."

"The one in here is deeper." Lyric tapped a temple. "One day I'll take you to meet the witch in the swamp. You don't believe me now, but you will. Mom will take us, and you'll see it too."

At that point Mr. Dagle, the principal, showed up, so I couldn't ask what that might mean. Lyric got three days' suspension, we both were ordered home early, and my dad got plenty mad when he came to pick us up. Dad mumbled his way to the front seat, and Lyric and I got in the back, she turning her eyes placidly to the window and watching the scenery go by as my dad fumed. I half expected smoke to rise from his ears, he was so pissed off.

"All the shit you pull," he said gravely, shaking his head. "The shit you fill your little brother's head with. You told that Christing Childress kid you were going to sell his *bones,* girl. I'll be damned lucky if his parents don't come after us." He glanced at me in the rearview. "I want you to know, Liam, I'm not mad at you."

"I know, Dad," I replied. I was my parents' easy kid, quiet and reserved with good grades despite my status as an outcast, and the fight really hadn't been my fault. "But you shouldn't be mad at Lyric either. She saved me from that kid who would've hit me more if she hadn't stepped in."

Lyric squeezed my hand, her eyes never wavering from outside the window.

"Well, she could have gone about it in a way that didn't bring us more shame than she has already."

"Shame?" Lyric spat. "What do you know about shame? *You* should be ashamed you aren't more grateful I saved Liam from an ass-beating. I think you should apologize *and* thank me."

"And I think you need to go back to Dr. Shetland." Dad took a sharp right towards home, his hands gripping the wheel with white-knuckle ferocity.

"Can't fix what isn't broken," Lyric replied in a sing-song voice, gazing out of the window. "Besides, Mom took me there. To see that woman in the swamp, not the fucking *hospital*. I saw her with my own two eyes."

"Well, what did you see?" Dad queried wearily, ignoring her swearing.

Lyric stiffened. "None of your business. You couldn't possibly understand, anyway. You're too closed off to see it right. Liam isn't though, huh, bud?"

She winked at me. I thought it prudent to stay silent, my lip aching still from the punch, and merely nodded, squeezing her hand.

Dad sighed. "Don't you think it's possible, even *probable,* that your very sick mother told you a story about some drug dealer she took you to meet? That you don't know what you saw, if you even saw anything at all? Maggie was always—"

"You think my eyes lied to me? No." Lyric frowned, her hand coming up to briefly cup her left eye, then shook her head as if clearing it of our father's words. "No. I know what I know. You aren't gonna convince me I'm crazy, and you're not gonna pay someone *else* to convince me, either. Fuck Dr. Shetland and his useless *pills* and *noise.*"

And so it was. Lyric did not go back to therapy, would still not tell anyone about the time she spent ferreted away by her mother, and my parents continued to sulk about a child they couldn't understand. It may have continued that way forever—who knows?

If not for that fucking poster.

DOGS FOR SALE!! it said in large, green letters above a blurry photo of ten puppies. They appeared to be big dogs, perhaps German Shepherds, their chubby black and tan bodies sleeping in a pile on soft bedding. SIX LEFT!!! CALL MARK!!!!! was at the bottom, with a phone number listed below.

Lyric and I were walking through the hall, on the way out of school, when she stopped and gasped, staring at the poster.

I stopped too. Lyric had her hand over her mouth, her chin quivering, eyes wide and wet. I looked over at the poster, squinting, trying to see what she saw that was so terrible. "Lyric? What's wrong?"

"What's wrong? *What's wrong?*" She marched over to the bulletin board, shouldering kids out of the way, and smacked her index finger right over the M in Mark. "This! This is what's wrong!"

I squirmed uncomfortably. Lyric was being loud, and people were starting to take note. Already three kids had stopped to watch the school's resident crazy person lose their mind. I adjusted the straps of my backpack and hunched my shoulders, willing them to look away. "It's just an ad. For if someone here wants to get a puppy. Seems like a guy has a bunch of them."

"Oh, you *would* think that." Lyric laughed sarcastically. "You sound like Dad."

"It's just a—"

"It's disgusting!" She screamed, her voice high and glassy, with an edge of fear to it. Now all conversation in the hallway ceased, everyone turning to look at Lyric, who, upon noticing their stares, growled and tore the ad down. She crumpled it in her fists, ripping and smashing it until it was a pulpy grey ball, then slam-dunked it into the trash. She then stalked away on legs like stilts, children parting like the Red Sea to let her past without being touched by this seething red mass of human misery.

I ran to catch up, my backpack bouncing painfully against the small of my back, and finally came alongside Lyric as she passed through the gates of the schoolyard and into the street. I could see that she had been crying, the tears leaving clean rivulets on her dirty cheeks, and, wisely, decided to remain silent for now. Silence came to me much more easily than it did to Lyric, and I employed that gift more often than was probably healthy back then. Lyric, on the other hand, was prone to sudden, violent displays of fervor about seemingly random things, something that I knew I would never be able to fathom as long as I lived. It was a fool's errand to ask, also, and more likely to cause a fight than to get any answers. I'd seen the rage Lyric would dole out onto our parents in heaping spoonfuls, the days-long whirlwind of screaming and thrown objects that would culminate in a week of silence, Lyric locked in her bedroom listening to loud music and refusing to come out even to eat.

I walked with Lyric in companionable silence until we reached the train tracks that bisected St. Claude, the red lights above flashing to indicate a train was coming. Lyric stopped, watching the metal hulk of locomotion lumber past at a creeping pace, her face unreadable as she squinted into each open boxcar door. The tears had stopped by now, and Lyric swiped at her cheeks, turning the dirt into black war paint beneath her eyes.

"We rode the trains, Mom and me," Lyric said suddenly, her voice unusually quiet. I was shocked. She rarely spoke about her mother, and I got the distinct impression that this was going to be a confession I needed to hear. "There's a language to riding trains, y'know. You learn to read the markers for safe places to sleep, places where people will feed you, yards where the cops are lax and don't check for stowaways much. Mom and me, we rode all the way up the coast to Pennsylvania." She laughed. It had a hollow quality I didn't much like. "The wind almost knocked me out the door a time or two, till Mom taught me how to feel the motion of the train. Like riding a wave."

She watched the train a few moments more, saying nothing, eyes distant. I was about to say something, when Lyric blurted out, all in a rush, "Then there were worse people, y'know, the ones who hated us just for *existing* on that train, who wanted to make slaves of us. Sometimes they'd use money we desperately needed as a weapon to buy us for a night. Sometimes after they bought us, they'd trade us around, letting other people know they had us using their secret language to communicate among all the sickos who wanted a single woman with a little girl. But mostly they would pull us down off the cars and tell us in so many ways that we were less that human as far as they were concerned. Called my mom a bitch for putting a kid in a situation like that. And then—" Her voice broke, thick with tears. She cleared her throat. "Mom is coming back for me soon, see Liam? I hate it here. More than I hated what those people said about me. About Mom. More than how they treated us. She knew who I was and *respected it*, unlike Dad. I'm so sick of having even my *thoughts* disrespected." She toed the rocks, head down, not looking at me anymore. "Mom is coming back for me, I know it. Soon. She told me in a code only I can read. She taught me how when I was really little. I can read the messages in the edges of books, the paper—she likes the paper, says it's a constant in an insane world—the ads that are around town on bulletin boards." She nodded. "Yeah. Those too. She's coming back. I know it. I thought you might want to know it too. In case, you know, you wake up one day and I'm not there."

The train passed and we were finally free to cross. I pondered what Lyric said for a minute, chewing my lip. "You don't want to stay with Dad and Mom?"

"She's not *my* mom," Lyric responded ruefully. "She's *your* mom."

"She loves you, though. Takes care of you."

"She does *not* love me. I'm a burden to her. To Dad, too. They don't get me like my mom did." She sighed. "As for taking care of me, how? Sending me to doctors who don't believe me, think I'm crazy, give me pills that never work, or stuff me in a ward with drooling idiots who can't tie their shoes without having a meltdown? Nuh-uh. It's better I'm out here." Lyric breathed deeply the crisp autumn air. "Better for me. Better for Mom. She can't see me when I'm in a ward. Blocks her out."

We turned onto our street and began walking toward the river. This was the most I'd ever heard Lyric talk about her mother in all the years she'd lived with us, but that wasn't the most distressing part. Even in my child's mind, I knew that nothing good could come of Lyric being in an agitated state. But also, unlike my parents, I knew better than to openly disagree. I'd seen Lyric medicated. The pills *did* work, because on them, there was no talk of secret messages on bulletin boards. On them, Lyric was usually much more sedate than she was now, which I suppose is why she didn't like them. To Lyric's mind, the pills were blocking out all the signals, and the signals were abject reality.

"If she's coming, I hope your mom comes soon," I said awkwardly, not knowing what else to say.

Lyric shot me a dark look as she dug out her keys from the vast pockets in her jeans. "Trying to get rid of me, Smalls?"

"No!" I shot back fiercely. "I love you. I wish you could stay forever. But…but you…you don't want to be here, so…"

"Relax, I'm fucking with you." Lyric laughed, pinching me lightly on the arm. "You're a great brother to a fucked-up weirdo like me." She ruffled my hair, something which usually annoyed me but right then made me laugh with relief, and smiled. "What do you say this fucked up weirdo makes you a snack? PB&J with a banana in the middle?"

I grinned. "Fuck yeah."

At that, Lyric busted out in a great big belly laugh, a rare occurrence, but which always made my heart grow three sizes if it was directed at something I did. Looking back now, I think this was the last time she laughed like that.

THREE

THE NEXT COUPLE months after the incident with the poster were like hell. Lyric, utterly convinced her mother was imminently returning from the nether into whence she disappeared, fought back against absolutely everything my parents wanted her to do. Schoolwork was ignored, personal hygiene went out the window, chores were shirked and neglected. The last thing on the list I took upon myself to rectify, my reasoning being that Dad wouldn't really notice if Lyric bathed less or her grades were worse than they already were, but he *would* notice that the trash piled up, and that would cause more contention in an already wire-taut household.

The poster went back up at school at intermittent times, presumably because Mark (whoever he was, probably someone's uncle) was a breeder. There were always different puppies in the picture at any rate. Any time Lyric saw one, she tore it down, and would remain agitated for several days afterwards. One time I came into her room to tell her dinner was ready and I saw her sitting cross-legged on her bed, crying silently, one of the posters in her hands. It had a worn and folded look, but I had no idea why she'd kept one, let alone that she had one at all.

She looked up when she heard me knock on her half-open door. She swiped the tears off her flushed cheeks and gave me a wan, tired smile. "Hey kid, what's up?"

"Mom said dinner's ready." I shuffled my feet, wanting to know what she was doing, afraid to ask.

The curiosity must have shown in my face, because she crooked a finger at me, beckoning. "Come in. Shut the door."

I did as I was bade and crossed over to her bed, sitting beside her. She pulled me into a hug, her bony arms wrapping around me as though I were a delicate thing that might break if held too close. I glanced at the poster. "You hate these posters. Why did you take one?"

"Evidence," she said simply, her voice clogged with recently shed tears. "This one was different from the others."

"How?"

"See this?" She tapped a few small lines of text below the photo of the puppies.

I leaned over and read aloud, "Two males, yellow, four females, brown, black, spotted, white. They look like Labradors to me, maybe crossed with something else."

"The *picture* is of labs, yeah. But the *words* mean another thing entirely." She lowered her voice to barely a whisper. "You remember I told you my mom taught me how to read the hidden messages in things? This is one of those things." She heaved a shaky sigh. "Mark is a bad, bad man."

"Why?" I asked, hoping for a straight answer, knowing I'd get no such thing from Lyric.

"Liam," she replied, her eyes distant and her voice heavy with sorrow, "there are terrible people in this world. Awful. They'll chew you up, spit you out, and fuck your corpse after you're dead. I hope you never meet any of them, but I'm afraid you might. Promise me something."

"What?" The anxiety was rising by the second.

"Promise me that if you ever meet someone, and you get even a *hint* that they're not who they say they are, you'll run as fast as you can away from them. Anyone who even seems a little bit off. And then, when you're safe, you come and get me, and I'll deal with them. I don't care how far away I am, if you call out to me, I'll hear you, and I'll be there as fast as lightning."

It was on the tip of my tongue to tell Lyric that *she* was acting pretty fucking off, but I held my peace. It would only have alienated more a person who felt at odds with the entire world already. "I promise."

Lyric smiled, looking much less tired and more herself, even though her eyes were still red from crying. She kissed my cheek gently. "Good boy. Now let's go eat before Dad pops a gasket."

FOUR

THE FOLLOWING WEEK, Lyric got into a fight at school. Not a bad one, but enough to earn her a suspension and get her grounded by Dad. Apparently, a girl at school called Mandy Hamilton had teased Lyric about her clothes, told her she looked and smelled like a dirty hobo. Lyric had promptly told her and her friends they could go fuck themselves, something Mandy didn't like. Mandy and her gaggle of friends were known to bully underclassmen and people who even seemed to be less than middle class, so none of that interaction was surprising in the least. But Mandy didn't like to be talked back to, so later that day they followed Lyric to the bathroom and, while Lyric was sitting in one of the stalls, Mandy had hurled a used tampon over the door, which landed on Lyric's face.

Mandy and her friends had laughed, and Mandy said, "There. Now you smell better, you fucking hobo. I hope your druggie mom is proud."

Until that point Lyric had taken it all on the chin (the tampon, quite literally), and would have been content to just yell obscenities back, but the comment about her mother was the straw that broke the camel's back. Lyric had come out of the stall a whirling blur of fists and teeth, blacking Mandy's eye and attempting to shove the tampon down her throat. Mandy's friends left her and ran to get the principal, who came in the find Mandy cowering in the corner of the bathroom, hands up to ward off the hail of blows coming from a screaming Lyric.

And, of course, Mandy had no idea why this was happening, a claim which her friends backed up. And, of course, Lyric was the school psychopath. And, of course, Dad was less than receptive to the wild story Lyric told of being brutally mocked and assaulted in the school bathroom. She was, after all, an unreliable narrator, even of her own spotty history.

Lyric got a one-week suspension and a three-month grounding, something she felt was wildly unfair. And maybe it was. But this was a hostile crescendo in a months-long stint of bad behavior, and my father had no idea what else to do. She wouldn't take meds or go to therapy, and violence in our house was strictly prohibited. Lyric pretended this didn't faze her, but I could tell from the set of her chin and her wounded eyes that it hurt to not be believed at so crucial a juncture. She was more fragile than anyone besides me realized, and more sick than she let on, as became evident later that night.

"I told you, that skinny bitch attacked *me* first." Lyric pushed her green beans around with her fork, slouched in her seat at the dinner table.

"Maybe we'd be more inclined to believe you if you didn't always make up such wild stories, Lyric," Mom said curtly, taking a neat bite of her potatoes. She'd been on the phone with either the school or one of her friends all afternoon, trying to sort out exactly what had happened. She looked tired.

Lyric growled in frustration. "I wasn't talking to you, *Megan*."

"Enough," Dad said, and pointed his fork at Lyric. "You won't take that tone with her. You *will* be respectful of my wife in my house. I don't care what happened, frankly. You made a bad choice either way. Megan is right."

"'*Megan is right*,'" Lyric scoffed. She slouched lower in her chair, her chin now nearly level with the tabletop. "Nobody in this house cares about me."

"Wrong," Dad replied. "We care very much. We just..." he looked up at the ceiling as if the way out of this conundrum may lie there. "We just don't know how to help you." He began ticking things off on his fingers. "You won't bathe or wear any clothes we buy you. You won't keep up with school. You don't do chores and your room is a pigsty. You refuse to go to the doctors that—"

"I don't *need* doctors!"

"—that may be the *only* people who can give us real answers." He sighed. "And now you do this terrible thing, which, I might remind you, is gonna cost us more that reputation. We have to pay that girl's medical bills. We'll be lucky if her parents don't sue us." He tented his fingers under his chin. "What would *you* do about this, in our position? Just say, 'Yeah, that's fine, just keep on doing what you're doing, kiddo, you'll grow out of it'? No." He shook his head. "No. Unacceptable. You're grounded until further notice, and you *will* be doing *all* of the things you've been neglecting until it becomes habit. And you're *going* to go back to Dr. Shetland."

"What?" Lyric dropped her fork and sat up, looking to me as if to confirm this. I shrugged. My parents hadn't told me anything about their plans. "But I said I don't *want* to go to a—"

"It's not up for discussion. Your first appointment is tomorrow."

Lyric whimpered, tears welling up in her eyes. Her mouth opened, but no sound came out. She cleared her throat, but her voice was husky when she spoke. "You really want to help me?"

"We really do," Mom said, trying to be gentle.

"OK." Lyric's eyes were everywhere at once, a caged animal that finds it is locked up with its natural predators. "Then you can help me find Mom."

My father rubbed his temple. "Lyric. I told you—"

"No, I mean it." She turned to face my mom, her expression one of wild hope and desperation. "You. You're a private investigator.

You spent years looking for me and her. You must have found *some* indicators of our patterns and the places we went. You must know *something* about where she may have gone after she left me here. Right?" She leaned forward, her shirt dipping into her mashed potatoes as she reached across the table for a lifeline. "Right?"

My mom made a small, trapped sound. She disliked direct confrontation with Lyric, especially when she had her blood up. She looked from Lyric to her husband for help, reaching over and grabbing his hand. "Bill…should I…"

"It's OK, Megs," he said, patting her hand. "I'll tell her."

"Tell me what?" Lyric looked back and forth between them, her brows furrowed. "Tell me what?"

Dad took a deep breath, then glanced at me. "Liam, you might want to leave for this."

"It's OK," I said. *I'm here for every other fucking thing, might as well be here for this too.*

In truth, I wanted to stay and hear whatever it was they had to tell her because with Lyric, knowing was half the battle. I could help better if I knew everything, I could diffuse her in her own language, but for that I needed every piece of information available to me, no matter how much it hurt to be present for the telling. It didn't occur to me until now, writing this down after years of therapy, that that is a trauma response in children who live in explosively abusive households, and that I was employing this tactic not only to help my sister, but to keep myself safe.

Dad gave me a considering stare, stroking his moustache thoughtfully. I stared right back, hoping I looked as adamant as I felt. Finally, he put his hands up in defeat. "Alright. Have it your way. But this isn't going to be pretty."

"Tell me *what?*" Lyric demanded again, her voice shrill.

Dad sat back and folded his arms. "If you think we didn't look for Maggie when you showed up on our doorstep, you're wrong. Once we knew that *you* were alive, we knew she must be as well, and we made it our business to try and find her. We reasoned she was in town, and we were right. I saw her myself not a week later. But that was the last time." He cleared his throat. "Megan found her, really. She found out that a very…odd woman and an unkempt child had stayed at a motel outside of town, and that the woman had come back alone one night, which raised suspicion with the staff, who reported it to the police. Megan went there and discovered that she'd bolted after the cops questioned her, so we thought that was that and she was gone. We were wrong."

Lyric's face was baffled, still. "But…but you said you saw her."

"I did." Dad nodded. "Five days later, I left the house for the first time since your arrival, to go get some odds and ends from the grocery store. Maggie was outside, crouched behind the big maple out by the street. I was shocked, to say the least, by her appearance. She…she was no longer the girl I married so long ago, and certainly not anyone I'd be comfortable to call a mother."

He stopped briefly, hitching a sigh. I noticed that he'd never once said Lyric's mother's name before tonight. "Honey, she looked bad. Maybe you couldn't recognize it, as little as you were, but I could see it right away. Her clothes were rags, her skin had that sallow, waxy look that people get when they've lived hard lives and done too many…erm…made bad choices. But her eyes were the worst. They had the glassy, crazed look that wild animals get when they're terrified, like they might bite if anyone touched them. She saw me come out, and she ran. Took off like a shot. I chased her, of course, calling for her to come back. I thought… I thought I might be able to help her, as stupid as it sounds now. I really *wanted* to help her. But that thought was gone in a split second, because she dove into a car with two men in it, and they sped right off. Then she was gone, really gone this time, and we never heard of her in town again."

"You said you looked for her," Lyric said flatly, a dazed expression on her face.

"We did. I took down the plate number, gave it to Megan, and we started the search. We got a hit now and then in some far-flung place, but after a month or two, the trail went cold. We had you, poor little you, to tend to, and we had to drop it. For your sake. For all our sake." He shrugged. "The way I figure it, either she doesn't want to be found, or she passed away. She was not a well woman, Lyric. I think she did one good thing, though. She left you here with us rather than drag you down whatever path she was on."

"Dead?" Lyric's voice went small, as though she'd drunk the potion in *Alice in Wonderland* and it had only affected her vocal cords. "My mom…is not…dead."

"Honey," Mom said, trying to reach her through her daze with that gentle mothering tone reserved for extremely delicate times, "Bill didn't say she was. Just that you have to accept it as a very real possibility with someone like that."

"No," Lyric said, shaking her head so violently her hair flopped back and forth. "No. Impossible. Mom would never leave me. Never. She told me she wouldn't ever, ever—"

"But she did, sweetheart." Dad's voice was full of pain, loss, sorrow of having to deliver such terrible news. "It's awful, what she did. How she took you away from us. How she left you. In her right mind, no, she would never have left you. But she wasn't in her right mind, not then. And she *is* gone, no matter what the reason is. We're only trying to help you, because we love you."

"If y-you l-l-loved me," Lyric stammered, tears coursing down her cheeks now in fat rivulets, "you w-wouldn't be sitting here t-trying to convince me that the *only* person who *ever* really understood m-me is *d-d-dead*."

She abruptly pushed away from the table, her chair legs squalling against the floor, and ran from the room. I watched her go, my heart aching for her, listening to her feet stomping up the stairs and her door slam behind her. Moments later, muffled music played, a sure sign she was crying.

"May I be excused?" I asked. "I'm not hungry anymore."

"No." My mother and father said in unison.

"Son," my dad said in that way that meant he thought he was about to impart wisdom to me, "leave her be. She has to grieve, and it's better if you aren't in the way when she gets to the anger portion of the process."

FIVE

"**W**AKE UP." SOMEONE shook me roughly in the dark. I mumbled sleepily, turning over. Another rough shake came from my back this time. "Come on, dummy, wake up and tell me goodbye."

"Huh?" My eyes flew open, and I rolled over. Lyric was crouched by my bed, her face half lit by the moonlit coming in through the window. "You're leaving?"

She nodded. "Yeah. I got to."

I rubbed my eyes. "What time is it?"

"After midnight. *They* took forever to go to bed."

"Why are you leaving?" I thought I knew already, but I had to ask to be absolutely sure.

"Because my mom isn't fucking dead, and I know exactly where to go to find her." She pushed her backpack to the side and pulled the folded advertisement for puppies out of her pocket. She tapped it with one finger. "This. This tells me where."

I sat up, already concerned but growing more frightened by the second. "You think your mom is hiding at that guy's house?"

"No, not *hiding there*, you goober. She's watching him. She watches for these kinds of things, you know. She tries to save them if she can." She smiled, making her face into a grinning skull in the half light of the room. "I've seen her do it. And because *I* know about this fucking pervert, *she* knows about him too. She wouldn't want me near something like this, so she's definitely in town, probably has been for months." She tutted. "I was just too distracted to see it."

My brows furrowed. "Lyric, that doesn't make any sense. What's he doing? How would she know?"

"Shh," she whispered fiercely. "You're gonna get me caught if you don't keep your voice down. I can't say any more without you being in danger too, but I wanted to say goodbye."

"How will you even find this guy?"

"There can't be *too* many freaks like him in this zip code, right? Someone will know. I know the right people to ask."

Her eyes were terrifying, too wide, too wet. Everything about her screamed madness, and I was suddenly very afraid for what might happen to my sister if she left our house alone that night. Best case scenario, she was picked up by the police as a runaway and caused a whole heap of trouble for my parents. Worst case, she found the guy who was selling dogs, and knocked on his door in the middle of the night. He would probably be confused, hostile, and Lyric's questions about a woman he didn't know might cause him to get riled up. Worse still, when she found out he knew nothing about her mom, *Lyric* might get riled up. Then, only God knew what might happen.

I threw my covers back, my decision made. "I'm coming with you."

"No you're not."

"Yes I am."

"Your Mom and Dad will have a conniption fit if they wake up and we're *both* gone." She smiled wryly. "Me, they don't give a fuck about. You're their perfect baby boy. They'd fucking kill me if I let you get involved with this dangerous shit."

"I'm coming," I whispered resolutely. "If you try to leave without me, I'll just follow you. You can't stop me."

"Liam—"

"Then I'll be out wandering around alone at night," I said casually, picking at the edge of my blanket. "And you'll be responsible."

Lyric blanched and I smiled. I knew then that I had her. She would never in a month of Mondays let me roam around New Orleans alone at night. She sighed heavily. "Fine. Have it your way. But when my mom shows up, we're bringing you back home before we leave for good. Deal?"

"Deal." I was in my shoes in a flash, the two of us tiptoeing past my parents' room and down the stairs.

Outside, it was hot and still wet from the afternoon's rainstorm, the puddles reflecting the streetlights and the little frogs screaming in the shadows. Not a soul was anywhere nearby, not even any cars were on the street at this hour on a Wednesday. Lyric carefully shut the door, easing it into its casing so it wouldn't snap shut and give us away. She shook out her keys and locked it softly, then turned to me, pointing left to indicate where we should go.

We didn't get far. Later, I would find out that my dad had gone to bed but lain awake, mulling over the conversation he'd had with Lyric at dinner. He felt guilty for dashing her hopes, and had gotten up to go and check on her, perhaps try to console her. He'd heard her rustling around in her room muttering to herself, saw through the crack in her door that she was wildly stuffing things into her backpack. Before she'd come out, he'd ducked back into the bathroom. As distracted as she was, she didn't even notice him as she crept into my room to wake me up. He heard what she said and decided on the best course of action right then and there. He waited until we were down the stairs and away before calling the cops.

The first squad car rolled up right in front of us as we rounded the corner, lights on, but no sirens.

"Fucking run!" Lyric screamed, and turned on her heel, grabbing me by the arm and hauling me after her.

I tried to keep up, I really did, but I was shorter than her by about six inches, and a lot less coordinated. I slipped on the wet pavement and went down, cracking the side of my head against the lawn of our next-door neighbor, a flash of lightning going off behind my eyes. Lyric made an agonized sound and doubled back, trying like hell to pull me up off the ground when the second squad car came around the *other* corner.

By this time, one of the cops from the first car was out, calling to us as his partner mumbled into her walkie. "Hey, kids? Your parents would like you to go back home, now. Lyric? Can you hear me?"

Lyric crouched over me protectively, one hand under my armpit and the other on the grass, tensed and ready to run. "I'm not going back."

"Liam?" The cop said to me, still advancing. "You OK?"

"I'm fi—" I tried to speak, but found blood in my mouth. I ran my tongue around and found that not only did I have a big gash in my mouth where I'd bit the inside, my front tooth was broken. My head pounded in time with my heart, and my left arm, which I had landed on, was scraped to hell and back. I spat out blood.

The cop saw and stopped moving. He spoke into his walkie. "We've got injuries. Call the parents out."

"No!" Lyric shouted, springing to her feet. "No, you can't make me go back there! They told me my mom is dead and she's not, that I'm crazy for thinking she's alive! They want to put me on pills! They want to make me an addict like…like…"

"Young lady, your parents do not want to turn you into an addict." He was close enough now that I could see him past the red-blue swirl of lights, and I saw a stocky, fortyish man with silvery hair and kind eyes, hands upraised and nowhere near his weapon, a man begging an angry child for peace. "Nobody wants to hurt you. They want to help you. *I* want to help you. My name is Jonathan, and I'm not gonna let anybody hurt you or your little brother. OK?"

Lyric spun, saw the officers creeping up from behind. Turned again to see Officer Jonathan's partner and my parents in a huddle by the squad car. She was hyperventilating, her breath coming in wheezy gasps, her hands clenching and unclenching into fists as she danced from foot to foot.

Jonathan took another step forward, was now only about five feet away from where I sat on the grass, the seat of my pajama pants soaking up rainwater and my body throbbing in various ways. "Liam? Would you like to get up and go back to your parents, bud?"

"Only if you promise not to hurt her." I didn't realize until that moment how close to tears I was. Whether they were tears of fear from what was happening, or relief that this had not been allowed to go too far, I couldn't tell.

"No, son, we're not gonna hurt her." He had the kindly voice of a favorite uncle, the one who would play any game you wanted if you ate all your dinner.

Lyric let out a contemptuous, "Ha."

Jonathan turned to her. "It's true. Your dad said you would very much like to find your mom, is that right?"

Lyric stopped moving all at once, became very still. Her eyes narrowed, the frightened rabbit being replaced by the cunning serpent. "Yeah?"

"What would you say to some help?" Jonathan ventured another step forward. Another. He was right in front of me now, only a foot or so away from Lyric. They held each other's eyes as he spoke. "I am willing to personally put my own hours into helping you figure out where she is. My off time, that is. That means you'll have all the resources available to the NOPD behind you. I've even got friends in other states that work in law enforcement, and I'm sure they'd be happy to help you too."

Lyric considered this, the fingers of her right hand working, stretching, fiddling. "What's the catch?"

"No catch. You let this young man go back to his parents, and you come with me into the house so we can discuss what our next step is in finding your mom."

Lyric took a step toward him, until there was only an inch of streetlight between them, her face upturned to his. "I am never going back there."

I don't know where she'd kept that knife, only that suddenly it was there, a dark line in that inch of light between their bodies, and Officer Jonathan grunted as it sunk through the Kevlar and into his belly. Then the rest of the officers swarmed them, and I could see no more.

SIX

I THINK I NEED to explain, for the sake of my narrative, that all these things happened over a long period of time. Lyric really *didn't* talk about her mother very often. Most times when she did it was offhand remarks that were inconsequential. She rarely spoke about it in any real way, and would retreat to sullen silence more often than not after a bout of brief discussion. She lived with us for many years before the notion that her mom was coming back overtook her reason, and most of the time, she was pretty normal. We did brother-sister things like movie nights, holed up in her room eating too much candy, took family trips to museums, the zoo, the aquarium, whatever. She liked animals, the cinema, all meat pizza, and video games, all things she would share with me because I was her favorite person. She was only odd enough to catch the notice of other people who didn't know her like I did, couldn't dismiss the strange stuff she said as just being one part of her. I know, given the subject of my writing, that it may seem like it was an all-the-time thing, but it wasn't. And she was never, ever that violent, even on her worst days. She might threaten, or rough a lower classman up some in my defense, but it never went past that. That's what made the incident with Officer Jonathan so horrible and shocking.

It was something of a miracle that Lyric didn't end up in juvie—or worse, actual prison, seeing as she was seventeen and the charge was aggravated assault with a deadly weapon—but Officer Jonathan made the extremely empathetic decision not to press charges. He got a six-week fully paid leave of absence to recover from his wound, and Lyric got to spend three months in a mental institution for troubled teenagers, governed by the inimitable Dr. Shetland. My parents went to visit her, sometimes together and sometimes just my dad, but I was never allowed to see her. It was probably a protective measure on their part, her being so unpredictable and me being so obviously swayed to her side like I was, but it felt like a punishment for trying to help her. No matter how many times they talked to me about that night— and they did quite a lot—they couldn't wrap their heads around why I would go with her, in the middle of the night, on a fool's errand to find someone who was most likely dead. They couldn't understand that I was as protective of her as they were of me.

I spent three long, lonely months going through the motions of school, homework, chores, eating, but the whole time all I thought about was Lyric. Not that they'd know it. My grades stayed good, and they never asked how my nonexistent social life was going. They assumed I was fine. I was, after all, the kid they didn't need to worry about. But every night I cried myself to sleep, wrapped around one of Lyric's T-shirts. I even tried beaming her messages with my mind, until I remembered she said she couldn't receive them when she was in the hospital. It felt kind of silly to even try at all, but what did I know? I was just a kid worried for his sister's safety in a place she made sound like a nightmare. It didn't seem fair after all she'd been through, to hide her in a place like that, and since my parents wouldn't take me along to visit, I had only her descriptions to go by.

Christmas came and went without her. I opened my gifts, trying hard to appear excited and grateful for the sake of my parents, but there was the empty spot near me where Lyric always sat to open hers. There weren't even any presents for her under the tree. All those had been taken to the ward in which she was kept, sent unwrapped because the nurses had to check every single thing to make sure nothing could be used as a weapon or an instrument of self-harm. After I finished with my gifts and thanked my parents, I went upstairs to my room to put them on my bed. From beneath it, I pulled out two messy packages wrapped in bright green paper and tied with silver ribbon. Inside one was a Dream Theater CD, a band I'd recently gotten into and wanted to share with my sister. Inside the other was a necklace I'd made myself using string and tireless effort, in all of Lyric's favorite colors: red, yellow, purple, green, electric blue. In secret, I'd gotten one of the girls at school, Stacey Biglio, to teach me how to make them, how to tie the knots it was comprised of, and I'd made two. The other, much shoddier, first attempt in Lyric's colors hung around my own neck under every shirt I wore. I suppose it was yet another attempt to feel close to her when I wasn't, to connect. I slipped into her room and put the gifts on her bed, confident they'd be there when she got home. Neither of my parents ever went in there anyway.

Finally, after what seemed like forever to my child's mind, she came home. My dad got the call on a Friday morning, the doctors saying she would be ready for release that afternoon at 2 p.m.

"Liam," my dad said, pulling me aside after he got the call, "I know you're excited to see her again, but we need to talk about expectations."

I looked up from my breakfast, chewing on the microwave pancakes Mom had given me to eat before school, tucking the feeling of exhilaration back as best I could. "Yeah, Dad?"

"Your sister," he began gravely, "did something absolutely unconscionable to be put away like this, you understand that, right?"

"Yeah." It was an understatement, but I agreed it hadn't been a strictly necessary step in her escape.

"And you understand she wasn't in her right mind?"

"Yeah."

"Good. Good." He stroked his moustache and took a deep breath. "The doctors have spent the last three months working with her, getting her therapy, getting her medicated. She's still your sister, but she's…different now. She doesn't talk like she used to. She's lucid. But she's also less aggressive, less exuberant, and easier to keep a handle on. She's not the person you knew. That may be scary to you at first, because up till now you've only known her as the charging force that drove the action of this household by causing turmoil. When you meet this new Lyric, it will take some getting used to. OK?"

"OK…" I said carefully, not liking anything he was telling me. *New Lyric*? What had they done to her? Had she been right about the hospital, the horrors it held?

"What we need from you," my father said, tenting his fingers in front of him, "is cooperation. She's on a whole heap of medication, but most of it is temporary, to ensure she stays stable. If you see her denying it, hiding it, or in any way *not* taking it as prescribed, we need you to tell us right away. If you find she's acting like she used to, that means she isn't taking it, and you tell us immediately. She won't be in trouble," he added when he saw me open my mouth to speak, "but she *will* be strongly encouraged to take it. It's a stipulation of her release, both from the hospital, and to keep her out of jail. You want your sister to stay out here, with us, right?"

I nodded. I knew what "strongly encouraged" meant. It meant "forced". So Lyric was forcibly on medication and coming home to a place where that force would continue. Not only that, I was expected to behave like one of her jailers. I had a bad feeling about that but kept it to myself.

"I bet you do. I bet you missed her plenty, huh?"

"Yeah." I poked my pancakes with my fork, suddenly not wanting the overly sweet nothingness of empty carbs. I wondered if my mom thought when she gave them to me that they would soften the blow of what my dad had to say. They didn't. Not at all.

"So, what are you going to do to help us keep her with the family and out of the hospital?"

"I'm going to help make sure she takes her medication."

"And?"

"If she does or says anything weird, I tell you immediately."

"Good boy," my dad said, ruffling my hair. I pulled back from the affection, and he frowned. "Something wrong, bud?"

You made sure Lyric wasn't herself anymore. You changed her so you could be comfortable, and you took all her hope away. You turned her into a shell. I swallowed my too-sweet bite of pancake. "No. Just anxious to see her, I guess."

Dad smiled. "She'll be home by the time you get back from school."

"I can't skip it and come with you?"

"No, son," Dad said, shaking his head. "You don't want to go to that place, even for a minute."

Well then how come it's OK to send your daughter *there for months?* I wanted to ask but decided against it. Fighting would do no good. It was better to keep it in and stay in his good books. Not for myself, but for Lyric.

School was difficult that day. I kept fucking up, getting things wrong, looking out of the window when I should be doing classwork. I just couldn't concentrate, knowing that Lyric would be back before I got home, wondering what would happen after that. I watched the clocks in every classroom get closer to two by the hour. My dad would leave no later than 12:30 to account for traffic, would likely arrive at one in order to sign off on paperwork and talk to the doctors about how to handle Lyric's first day home. He would gather her things, such as they were, at about 1:45, putting her bags in the car so that all he had to do was load her in and drive away. Would they let her walk to the car herself, or did they make you use a wheelchair, like at the regular hospital? Would she be happy to see Dad there, or would she cry and beg not to go home? Would she be there enough to bathe herself before she left, or would some kindly nurse give her a sponge bath? And—the biggest question—would she remember what had happened, or would this experience, like those with her mother, become yet another thing we never talked about?

By the time 3:15 rolled around, I was less human boy and more a mass of frenetic anxieties. As soon as the bell rang, I practically jumped out of my chair, knocking it over in my haste to get out of the concrete prison and away. It was raining, but I didn't care. I didn't even use an umbrella, just ran through the rain, gunning for home with my clothes sticking wetly to me, my heart pounding and my mind buzzing with one singular purpose: home, and Lyric.

I got back, shaking water from my hair and shivering despite the heat, and dumped my backpack at the front door. My dad was in the foyer already, apparently waiting for my return, his arms crossed and his face an expressionless mask.

"Is she here?" I asked hopefully, trying to move past him into the living room, where I could hear the television playing *The Fairly OddParents* at low volume.

He put a hand on my chest to stop me. "She is. Remember what I told you. She's much different than she was when she left, so don't say anything—and I mean *anything*—about the night she went away. No questions about the hospital. Are we clear on that, son?"

So. It *was* to be added to the pile of things we didn't talk about after all. I nodded, more to get him out of my way than any sense of real agreement, and he studied my face. Hunting, I suppose, for my true intent. I simply looked back at him, resolute and eager. He *would* let me see my sister, whether he thought I deserved to or not. He seemed satisfied that I was telling the truth, that I wouldn't assist in causing a ruckus, and stepped out of my way.

The lights in the living room were dim, the windows glowing softly because of the clouds, casting barely any light at all. The TV shone bright colors, and strange shadows leapt everywhere. I could see Lyric's hand lying limply over the arm of my father's easy chair, and towards that hand I walked. I came around and saw her for the first time in months. Her hair was clean and brushed back, the faded blue gleaming in the light of the TV, her face slack and dreamy, her eyes flicking back and forth as she watched the screen, her body folded into a loose ball and her bare feet on the leather cushion.

I cleared my throat. "Lyric?"

She peeled her eyes from the screen, her head turning slowly until she looked up to face me. A smile crept over her face, a more serene expression than I'd ever seen her wear before, untroubled and genuinely happy. "Hey, kid. How you been?"

Her voice was rough from disuse, quiet, unnervingly normal.

"OK," I replied, tears welling up. "Better now that you're home."

She put out her arms and I went to her, climbing into the chair with her. She scooted over to give me room, wrapping one arm around me and using the other to pull my legs into her lap. The affect was like that of holding an infant, so careful were her hands. I leaned my head into her chest, holding her back, inhaling the medicinal hospital smell that clung to her, the smell of her body beneath it. Normally, I would feel I was too old for this, be embarrassed by the idea that someone might hold me like a child that needed comforting, but right now I didn't care at all. She stroked my hair and soothed me while I cried, her voice distant and floaty, my relief in equal parts to the fear and pain I felt knowing I couldn't ask any questions about what had been done to her. There would be time for questions later, in secret, away from the watchful presence of my father. For now, there was only this, and this was all I wanted.

"You made me a nice gift," she murmured, her breath tickling my ear, and reached into her shirt to pull out the necklace I'd made her. "You picked all the best colors."

"They're your colors," I replied, squeezing her. I pulled out my own necklace to show her. "They're supposed to be friendship necklaces, Stacey said, but…"

"We're better than friends," Lyric said, leaning her hand closer so that our necklaces touched. "We're family. Real family. And that means you're stuck with me forever, my good dude."

I cuddled closer, tears rolling out and pattering down on her shirt. "I think I can live with that."

SEVEN

T HE NEXT COUPLE months were peaceful, however uneasy the peace was for my part. The end of the school year was coming up fast, and I had projects out the wazoo, which kept me busy. Lyric was also finally participating in school, and set about asking for extra work to make up for lost time from her (extremely surprised) teachers. The two of us passed like ships in the night most days, never really getting a chance to talk, which my parents seemed to think was for the best. Lyric had even asked to get a summer job, something Dad said he'd think about if her grades were good enough. I spent most of my time writing essays and making PowerPoints for last minute assignments, and Lyric, more often than not, stayed behind after school to use the library.

She'd stopped saying and doing all the things that had been problematic for our family. She never even said anything about her mother. At first, this bothered me quite a lot, because who was this new person inhabiting the body of my sister? What was her goal? I often wondered if it was an act, but in those first months she was heavily monitored, and I'd personally watched her down her medication so many times that eventually even that notion faded into the background. I stopped feeling like a spy sent to watch her every move and started to feel more like a good brother who didn't *need* to watch his sister's every move. It seemed it was over. All the pain, the violence, the ranting, was all gone now, leaving behind only a sweet, apologetic girl who was trying desperately to make things right.

And the thing was, it was working. Her grades improved drastically. She no longer fought with Mom and Dad about anything. She did her chores and her homework, and even set about apologizing to Mandy Hamilton and her family. Even my friends had begun to drift tentatively back towards me, so great was the change in Lyric. Chris Summers invited me to his house for a pool party, and high-fived me when I'd agreed to come. Suddenly, after a long drought, I had weekend plans with people who liked me again.

But, as with all good things, at least those in my life back then, it came to a terrible end.

A week before school let out, I walked to the library after the final bell to see if Lyric wanted to leave with me today instead of staying behind that Friday afternoon. I was eager to tell her about Chris Summers, excited by all the possibilities the weekend now held. The hallways were mostly deserted save for a few stragglers and the maintenance man, Mr. Charles. He waved as I walked past, and I smiled to him, waving back with two fingers. It felt good to finally be acknowledged again, to feel like part of the world instead of an outsider. My sneakers squeaked on the cracked linoleum all the way to the big glass double doors of the library.

When I went in, Ms. Thomas, the librarian, also smiled warmly at me. "Hello, Liam. Here to do some research, or just to get your sister?"

"Just Lyric today, ma'am," I said, and pointed to the coffee can of Dum-Dums on her desk. "Can I steal one of those?"

"Absolutely. Take one for Lyric, too." She extended the can to me. "She's been working so diligently for two weeks on this essay she's writing. Really in-depth stuff. I'm very proud of her."

"Thanks. I'm proud of her too." I took two—a watermelon for Lyric and a root beer for me—and unwrapped mine as I walked to the back where the computers were, popping it in my mouth. The sweet taste flooded my tastebuds, filling me with its small pleasure. I saw Lyric at the last table, books spread out around her, papers in stacks, hunched over newspaper clippings with her tongue protruding from the corner of her mouth.

"Hey, Lyric," I said sotto voce, so as not to incur the wrath of Ms. Thomas. "Got you a sucker."

She looked up, her eyes wide and startled, and quickly covered the newspaper clipping with her palm as though there were sensitive information printed on it instead of what appeared to be an article on a farmers market opening.

"Oh, thank fuck, it's only you." She relaxed, but kept her hand over the article. "Whatcha got?"

"Watermelon." I produced the Dum-Dum from behind my back. "Your fave."

She reached out and took the sucker, but didn't open it. Instead, she just stared at me, her eyes searching my face, as though looking for some indicator there of what my intentions may be. I knew that look. Something was wrong. I felt a sinking feeling in my gut, and my head began to swim, the sarsaparilla flavor in my mouth suddenly nauseatingly sweet.

I sat down at the computer chair adjacent to hers, sweat beads beginning to form on my forehead despite the chill of the library. "So…what's your essay on?"

She tapped her fingernails thoughtfully on the newspaper article, her eyes flicking over my face, her brows cloudy. "Why do you want to know?"

"Because I'm interested." This wasn't good at all. I could feel it, like electricity in the air.

"You never come to see me at the library after school. Did Dad send you to check up on me?"

The question caught me off guard. "What?"

"Liam," she said slowly, as though I might be an extremely dense toddler, "it's important. Did Dad send you?"

"No," I sighed. "I just…I finished all my end-of-year projects yesterday, so I finally had time. I meant to come sooner, but with everything going on, I just…couldn't. I'm sorry I didn't."

She squinted at me for a moment, chewing on her lip. It made me tense up, that scrutinizing look, as though she were searching my soul instead of my face. It felt like the way people stared at us the day she'd lost it over the poster on the bulletin board. Then it seemed she made a decision, and shrugged. "OK. Apology accepted."

I relaxed. "Are you gonna tell me about your essay now, or grill me some more?"

"No more grilling," she laughed. "Mr. Raymond gave us the topic 'problems in the US and potential solutions' for our Current Affairs exit essay, which is just, like…there's so many. Poverty. Trans rights. Reproductive rights getting fucked. I thought about doing child trafficking, but figured that would be a little gruesome for a junior year social studies class, so instead I settled on homelessness in the United States. Specifically, how the homeless population gets around, which I know a bit about, y'know. I started researching statistics for transient arrests near railways stations—ages, sexes, stuff like that. And then I found this."

She rifled through the stack of papers and came up with a computer printout of an article from a paper called *The Missouri Herald* dated August 16, 2019. The headline read "Transient Woman Arrested in Multiple Injury Robberies," alongside a blurry black and white photo of the woman in question. She was difficult to see, as one officer's hand was mostly in the way of her face, but she was turned to the camera, her mouth open and the cords of her neck standing out as though she were screaming.

Her hair was long, matted, wild, her clothes mismatched and dirty-looking even in grainy black and white.

Lyric tapped the photo. "That's my Mom."

My head snapped up. "What? How do you know?"

"Read the article." She slid the paper closer to me. When I made no move to take it, she let out a groan of frustration and took it back, reading quietly aloud. "'At nine o'clock p.m. the Priam County officers at last arrested a suspect in a series of violent robberies that have plagued citizens since last month. The suspect had multiple IDs on her person and has not yet been accurately identified by police. They are, however, looking into her being a suspect in the vandalism done to the home of Mr. and Mrs. Alexander Linch, a local foster family to two transient children. It is likely that the suspect tried to break in and "rescue" them, as she put it, by breaking into their bedroom late on the night of 10 August. The suspect likely came in on one of the many trains that...*blah, blah, blah.*' You see, Liam? You see?"

I didn't see, but my old friend silence tapped me on the shoulder and bade me hold my peace.

"This means Dad was wrong. This means she's alive. My mom is alive." Her voice was high and giddy, exuberant, her eyes filled with a sickly light I knew all too well. She practically bounced in her chair as she spoke. "It means that she's coming back for me, just like I said. I just couldn't see it after Dr. Shetland doped me up."

"But you've been taking your meds," I said, my face numb. "I've seen you do it."

"Did you?" Lyric said slyly. "Did you really?"

I shifted uncomfortably in my chair. "I *thought* I did."

"People see what I want them to see. Hopefully Dad is as blind as you are, even with those big, honkin' glasses y'all wear."

I knew I shouldn't feed into this. It was delusion, pure and simple. The woman in the picture could be *anyone*, after all, but there was no telling Lyric that. She'd convinced herself, yet again, that what she saw was absolute truth, a truth no one else could possibly see. Because, of course, she had stopped taking her meds right under our noses. It was safer to play along, because if I did, she'd eventually tell me her plan, and maybe once I knew what it was, *then* I could bring it to Mom and Dad. Lyric would see it as a betrayal, of course, and likely never speak to me again, but it felt necessary to protect her from herself. Especially after what had happened with the cops the last time she got a bee in her bonnet about finding Maggie. "So…what did you find out? And what are you going to do?"

She smiled in a way that made me think of the shark from *Finding Nemo* when he found the two helpless little fish swimming in his territory. "That would be telling secrets. Not here. Here they can see me. Through these." She tapped her brow bone next to her eyes. "I'll explain on the way. Walk me home."

Suddenly I very much wished that *I* could hop on a train and disappear, so that I never had to go home again. No course of action seemed right or safe or good. I watched her carefully gather her things, putting papers neatly into folders, stacking books so that they fit into her bulging backpack, my heart sick with distress. Lyric was off her medication, probably had been for some time, and I hadn't even noticed. Nobody had. Perhaps we'd become complacent when she was less of a whirlwind of bullshit paranoia, or maybe none of us had *wanted* to see. I knew I should tell my parents immediately, but somehow, that didn't seem in the cards. I felt—wrongly, I know now—that this was my mess, and I was going to be the one to clean it up.

Once we were out of school and walking home, the sun hot and the air roughly the consistency of lukewarm soup, Lyric started talking.

"I know you feel like this is your fault," she said, pulling me up short. "Don't look so surprised, dude. It's all over your face."

"Lyric, I'm so—"

She held up a hand. "Save the apology. You've done nothing wrong. It was Bill and Megan who sent me to...*that place*...so this is more *their* fault than anyone else's. You've done nothing except be a great baby brother, looking after your crazy sister, and I very purposefully mislead you. So I'm really the one who should be apologizing to *you*. You had no idea what kind of place Bill and Megan locked me up in, because they never let you visit. Probably so you wouldn't see and get upset, which I guess I get. But don't worry. Your hands are clean."

It was on the tip of my tongue to say that *her* hands weren't clean either, that Mom and Dad hadn't *sent* her anywhere. The state had decided where she would go after she stabbed that cop, and nothing anyone said would have swayed that decision. True to form, though, all I said was, "It's OK."

"The things that they did to me were horrible." She spoke in a quiet, choked voice, not looking at me. "It wasn't just medication and stupid group therapy where we talked about feelings, but there was that too. It was long stretches of time locked in a room all by myself, screaming and crying to be let out, sleeping on a bed with round corners and no sheets or pillow. It was...it was torture, sometimes. Electroshock. Freezing water baths where they put me in the dark to 'experience my past as present,' as Dr. Shetland put it. But the worst part? One night I went to sleep and didn't wake up for two days. Two whole days of nothing, pretty early on. When I did finally wake up, my head ached and my eyes burned like fire, and that's when I knew."

"Knew what?"

She took a deep, shaky breath. "That they'd put cameras in my eyes. So they could monitor my movements, at first, I think, but then when they let me out, so they could help the sick fuck who's hiding behind those posters." She grit her teeth. "The medication did double duty. One, it's to keep the cameras operating smoothly. Lithium is a heavy metal, y'know? Has to be that. It also keeps me docile, a willing participant in the demise of little kids, and made me forget about the operation. I go to school, and they can see all the kids through the video feed from these cameras, right? And that's how he chooses. Through me. He must be *loaded*, to be able to buy off the doctors like that. So I stopped taking the meds, and voilà, they can't see anymore. And my memory of what they did is restored."

It was insane, what she was saying. Impossible. Maybe some of what she relayed had actually happened to her, the electroshock and the sensory deprivation tanks, but this part? No. My heart was pounding, and my mouth was dry, so acute was my terror. "Who…who are you talking about? Who's doing this?"

"Isn't it obvious?" She fished the folded poster that advertised dogs for sale from her pocket. "And now I know where he is. I figured it all out just yesterday. I'm going tonight, and I'm gonna confront this sicko about everything. You can come with me if you want, but remember, he's plenty dangerous if he can pay off doctors to do this to me just for knowing he exists."

"What about your mom?" I squeaked, struggling to breathe around the weight of my fear. "I thought you were trying to get her attention?"

"I already have it." She tapped her temple. "Been in communication since I stopped taking the meds that dulled my senses. And she's so *strong*, Liam. Like you wouldn't believe. She'll be here."

"When? When is she coming?" I thought wistfully of the pool party I now knew I would not be able to attend, never in a million years.

"Tonight."

"How? Mom and Dad are watching you like hawks. We'll never be able to get out." I hated that *we* with every fiber of my being. I hated knowing that I was going to go through with this, again, without hesitation.

"I think I can manage a little surprise for Bill and Megan, don't worry. Like I said, with or without you. I would appreciate you not ratting me out, though, if you decide not to come."

I said, "I'm coming."

I don't know why I thought my presence would make any difference in the outcome. Maybe I thought I could stop her. I know now that nothing could have, no matter what. Maybe I thought I could at least *help* her stop herself. But no, that would also be wrong. The truth is, I was too scared to say anything but yes, too caught up in my own feelings to realize what kind of danger I was putting myself in.

At home that night, Lyric was the model daughter. She took out the trash, did her homework, and showered, all before dinner. She even helped prepare the food, putting our plates before us with a flourish. At dinner she sat up straight, complimented Mom in her cooking.

"Well, thank you, but you helped too," Mom said, smiling. "You also deserve a round of applause. I hardly had to do anything with you by my side."

"How's that project for school coming?" Dad asked, forking some green beans into his mouth.

Lyric sawed a piece of chicken slowly in half with the table knife, the only kind of knife she was now allowed to use. "Going swell. I'm actually almost finished. Just a few loose ends to tie up.

Liam is helping me figure out how to put them down in order, right Liam?"

She smiled and winked at me. My Mom's chicken parmesan hung like lead in my mouth, was instantly drained of any appeal it once had. I forced myself to swallow around the lump in my throat, almost hoping I would choke so this would all be over faster.

EIGHT

T HE REST OF the evening I spent floating around in a haze of anxiety and terrible anticipation. Lyric had not let me in on the plan, something I now think was done to give me plausible deniability if things went south, which I knew even then they were bound to do. Medicated Lyric was predictable, even-tempered, and light. Unmedicated Lyric was a speeding plow that bowled over anything in her path, unpredictable, volatile, a rolling bomb. I knew only that she thought she was onto something that would bring her mother back, and it had something to do with that fucking guy selling dogs and his fucking poster.

I brushed my teeth mechanically after my shower, then smoothed my hair down with my comb, staring at my distorted face in the steam-slicked mirror. I know they say that human beings can't stay in crisis mode for long, but that entire evening my heart had been thudding painfully in my chest, my limbs so numb I kept dropping things. I fumbled the comb and it clattered to the floor. When I bent to pick it up, things went wavy, the world tilting on its axis. I closed my eyes and breathed deeply the steamy, greenhouse air of the bathroom, willing the shaky feeling of nausea to subside.

Lyric said it would be tonight that we enacted her grand plan, so I didn't bother with pajamas this time, I simply put on the clothes I'd worn to school. I was hyperaware that I was choosing to participate in this, that whatever calamity befell us, I was to have a hand in it. If someone got hurt, if *Lyric* got hurt, it would partially be my fault, premeditated, and then I'd end up the same as her. I wasn't too young for juvie, after all, and certainly not too young for the courts to stuff me in the hellish place they'd put Lyric. My breath came hard and fast, thoughts of my immediate, extremely bleak future crashing around, smacking into one another, each new horror jostling for the top spot.

It was all too much to bear. I pushed myself up off the floor, yanking the bathroom door open and gulping the cold air that immediately hit my face, determined to go downstairs and tell my parents everything. They'd be angry at me, sure, and so would Lyric. She might even hate me forever. But that notion was nothing compared to the unknown of what Lyric had planned for that man with the dogs, and infinitesimal compared to the horror of what might come after. I bounded down the stairs to the living room. Mom was on the couch, on her side, asleep in front of the TV, her head pillowed on her arms, breathing slow and deep. Dad's back was to me, but I could see his arms on the arms of the chair, and so toward him I went.

"Dad?" I asked as I came around. "Dad, I have to tell you some—"

I realized as I came around that he was *also* asleep, his head tipped back and his eyes shut, a line of drool coming from the corner of his mouth. He was snoring lightly, his chest moving up and down in the rhythm of deep sleep.

"Dad," I whispered, glancing over my shoulder to check that Lyric wasn't anywhere nearby. "Dad, wake up." I shook him once, twice. Harder the third time. "Dad? Dad. *Dad!*"

"He's not waking up for a while," Lyric said behind me. I whirled and there she was, leaning in the doorway of the kitchen with her feet crossed, eating an apple. "I made sure this time. Him and Megan both."

"What did you do to them?" My voice quavered, broke.

Lyric smiled, walking over to where I was. "Nothing permanent. It's amazing what you can do with a couple glasses of wine and some ground up Valium." She toed Dad's leg, watched it flop back bonelessly. "Dr. Shetland was good for something after all."

"You drugged them?" The tears were coming now, falling down my cheeks. "Why did you do that? What if you overdosed them? What if they die?"

"I didn't overdose them, promise. They won't die. And you know why," she growled. "I don't want to end up in the nuthatch again before I can get the fuck out of here. And I was afraid *you* would have a change of heart this go-around. "She took a bite of her apple, examining me in the half light from the TV. "Looks like I was right."

"But…but…Lyric…they're…I wasn't…" I was blubbering now, and I knew it wouldn't change anything. I knew she wouldn't be swayed by my tears.

She let out an exasperated sigh. "I had faith in you. I thought you wanted to help me."

"I *do*," I said, swiping at my eyes. "But…"

"But nothing. Help or don't. I'm leaving in five." She pointed at me. "But if you stay behind, and the cops show up, I'll know it was you. And I will never, ever forgive you. I'll never speak to you again as long as I live, *if* they ever let me out of that hellhole of a hospital. I won't have a brother anymore. You understand?"

I nodded, my face contorted in anguish. Yes, I understood full well what my choices were. The way I saw it, I had three options. First option, stay here and do nothing, wait till my parents woke up (if she was telling the truth and hadn't overdosed them so they never would), hope that I could explain what was happening and that they understood, then let them handle it. This option required a lot of waiting and hoping, and still might land me in juvie or worse. Option two, I stayed behind and called the cops, risking immediate arrest and Lyric's wrath when she found out what I'd done. This option terrified me just as much as option three, which was following Lyric on whatever misadventure she had planned, and hope that at some point I would be able to either escape or call for help somehow if needs be.

"I'm still coming," I said miserably, sitting down next to my dad's chair and taking his warm, limp hand in mine.

"Awesome," Lyric replied, as though I'd agreed to go to the movies with her instead of on some dark errand. "I got his keys off him after he passed out, so I took the money out of the safe, plus some other useful stuff. Now Mom and I'll be set when we finally blow this pop stand." She patted my dad's sleeping face. "Old man was finally good for something. I'm gonna go take a piss then we'll be on our way." And with that she left the room, ruffling my hair on the way out.

You must understand, I was still a child in many ways, only thirteen. I thought like a child, reasoned like a child, and all of my options were fraught with pitfalls I wanted quite desperately to have an adult navigate for me. It was too much to ask a thirteen-year-old boy to surf the waters of his older sibling's white-rapids psychosis in the canoe of his own budding maturity, with only his wits as an oar. I was doomed to capsize no matter what I did. But while she was gone, as soon as I heard the bathroom door close, I had an idea. It was my saving grace, as it turned out.

I made sure she was gone, listening for her to start peeing. When I heard it, I jumped up and began to wedge my hand between my father and his chair. His head lolled to one side as I struggled with him. He was a big man who filled the seat end to end, so it was difficult. I jostled him, shoving him to one side with my left arm, trying to make room, trying get the fingers of my right hand into his front pocket. I got my index and middle in, only, and fished desperately around until I found it: the edge of his phone case. I wiggled it, hearing the toilet flush, my sweating fingers slipping on the smooth case. The tap started up, and Lyric sang under her breath as she washed her hands.

"Come on, come on," I whispered, scissoring my fingers around the edge of the case, pushing my father's bulk to one side and tugging frantically, until finally—oh God finally—the phone slipped up and out of his pocket. I dropped his weight and hurriedly stuffed it into the front pocket of my hoodie, sitting back down and taking Dad's hand in mine just as I heard her footsteps on the stairs. My pulse banged in my ears, and I prayed she wouldn't notice the sweat on my hairline or that my Dad had moved from his previous position. Minute details, yes, but when she was like this, she saw signs in everything, so she very well might notice that a drugged man's head was turned to the opposite side it was when she left the room.

"Hooooo, boy, I needed that," Lyric said as she came into view, shaking the water off her hands. I saw that she had also grabbed one of her oversized hoodies, the black one with the pirate flag emblazoned on it in red, as well as changed into a pair of dark blue jeans. "You OK, kid? You look a bit peaked."

I swallowed hard, trying to think of what to say.

I must have looked like a deer in headlights, because her face softened, and she put her hand out to me. I took it, allowed her to help me up. When she put her arms around me, I felt like throwing up.

"Don't worry," she cooed, stroking my hair and scratching my scalp lightly with her nails, "nobody is going to get hurt that doesn't one hundred percent deserve it. And it'll only happen if he doesn't do the right thing and give them up." She held me out at arm's length. "Do you believe me?"

I searched her face, saw nothing there but honesty and madness. "I believe you."

"Do you trust me?"

"I do," I lied.

Her dark eyes with their blown pupils roamed over my face. I was sure then that she'd see the lies I just told, that she'd leave me here, maybe hurt me. But her purpose was clouding her judgement, I suppose. Or maybe it was her love for me, her need to be loved *by* me, that made her leave whatever she saw alone and simply nod. She let me go and crossed to the front door, picking up her backpack and slinging it over her shoulder. "Let's go."

NINE

Outside it was balmy, the air so thick with moisture we may as well have been swimming instead of walking. Cockroaches swarmed the garbage cans left out for tomorrow's pickup, scuttling out of the way of our sneakers. It wasn't exactly late, only about 8:30 p.m., so we still saw people here and there puttering around their front yards, coming home from work, and the like. Lyric waved and smiled to everyone she saw. She'd told me that if anyone asked, she was the dutiful big sister walking her little brother to the corner store for Friday night snacks that they would gorge on during a movie night. I wished that were true. I wanted to be home, cuddled under her duvet watching *Nightmare on Elm Street* and housing Twizzlers, not sweating into the crotch of my jeans and feeling sticky with heat and anticipation.

She talked while we walked. "I know you're worried. I can tell just from how you're walking with your hands in your kangaroo pouch. Those uptight shoulders tell a story."

I try not to think about my father's phone, which I was pressing against my body. "I just don't like being left in the dark, is all. You're being really cryptic."

"All will be revealed, sport," she said cryptically. "What's important is, I found the guy, and he's definitely a creep. His Facebook is wide open and all he ever talks about are his fucking *dogs*. And get this: he lives right by the tracks. It's too easy to put together."

"Not for me."

135

"Of course, not for you. You haven't lived the way I've lived." She took a right at the train tracks, following them past the businesses and crossing into the neighborhood on the other side. "You'll see when we get there, though. You'll see more than you ever wanted to."

"What's in your backpack?" I asked, needing to know, afraid to know.

"Supplies," she said airily, waving a hand. "Clothes and shit. My mom is coming tonight, right after this is over. I'm sorry to say you're gonna have to walk home alone, bud."

That was the least of my worries.

After that, there was little to say. She obviously wasn't going to reveal her big plan to me, and I wasn't going to get it on my own. I followed her through the dark, waving my hands to keep termites off me as we walked through a swarm, stepping around puddles that might be ankle breaking potholes in disguise. It felt like we walked for hours, but it was really only about thirty minutes before she stopped in front of a two-story brown house with wood siding and a small lamp illuminating the front door.

"This is the place." Lyric sounded nervous, and her fingers worked around themselves. She shook her hands and reached for me, and I took her sweating hand in mine. "Ready?"

"I guess."

"Pull up your hood."

I did as instructed, and she did the same, then began pulling me toward the front door with its peeling whitewash. I could hear sounds from within, small yips that could only be the sound of many puppies calling for their mother. Lyric swatted a gecko away and leaned her thumb against the doorbell. It screamed inside, a harsh metallic bray that resounded through the interior. Nobody came to answer it.

"Maybe he isn't home," I ventured, hoping that was true, that Mark was at a friend's house this evening and we'd soon abandon this and go home ourselves.

Lyric pointed over the porch railing at a beat-up Chevy, parked askew. "He's home."

She pressed the bell again, holding it down, letting it screech inside. There was a muffled curse from within, the heavy sound of angry feet coming towards us.

"I'm coming, I'm coming, let go of the gat damned bell!" There was the sound of turning locks and Lyric relented, just as the door was pulled open. A white man with more stubble than clean face stood in the crack, his faded, beady blue eyes squinted and a frown on his face. He was wearing a tattered wife beater and khaki shorts, his sallow skin hanging in shiny folds where it was exposed. He took the two of us in and growled, "Well? What the hell do you kids want?"

Lyric smiled. "I'm here about a dog."

"A dog?" He peered at her suspiciously. "Young lady, it's after 9 p.m. I don't show puppies this late at night. Now get the fuck off my property and come back in the day like a normal person."

He made to shut the door, but Lyric was quicker, putting her palm on it before it could shut all the way. "Please, sir. My brother has wanted his own dog for a year now. I'm looking for something really particular, too, and I was told you were the guy to see. I want a brunette female, blue eyes. Young as you can get it so we can train her right. We walked all this way. Please."

His jaw worked, annoyed. "Like I said, come back tomorrow. Make a fucking appointment like everyone else."

"I have money." Lyric let go of my hand to shove it into her pocket and produced a wad of rumpled bills. Mom, I knew, kept a coffee can stuffed with money for emergencies, and it was the only place I could think of that would provide Lyric with this much cash. "There's more in my backpack. A lot more."

The old man eyed the money. "Blue eyes, you said?"

"Yes, sir." Lyric's voice was honey. "Female. Brunette."

"I may have what you're looking for." He scratched his chin. "Come in, I guess. But this is not how I like to do business, missy. Not at all."

He opened the door wider, and Lyric smiled at him, stepping over the threshold. "Thank you, sir. Coming Liam?"

Unhappy, I followed her inside. Mark's house was musty with the smell of animals and old newspapers, dank and mildewy. The wallpaper was yellow, more from tobacco smoke than from any actual shade. Small pink flowers patterned it. A television blared from a room we passed on the left, the light from the screen making large, strange shadows leap on the wall. The floor had about a foot of dirt on it, and I kicked a dust bunny out of my way as we followed him deeper into the house. He led us towards the back, through a kitchen that stank of unwashed dishes and old man farts, to a room at the back with a closed screen door. From within I could make out the small whimpers of many small animals, could hear the scratch-scratch of many tiny claws.

"You may be in luck," he said, "my chocolate lab bitch whelped not four weeks ago, and her litter is a lovely mix of shades." He opened the door, and the sound of puppies grew louder. "Can't promise their eyes will stay blue, but there's one or two of 'em that might be exactly what you're looking for."

I looked in and sure enough, a panting brown dog was lying on a soft dog bed surrounded by six squirming puppies all fighting hungrily for a nipple. The mother dog's ears perked up when Lyric and I stepped in, her tail thumping on the ground. I crouched and picked up one of the squeaking balls of fur, relieved that there were indeed puppies here. It squirmed in my grasp, and I stroked its fat little body, soothing it. I looked up at Lyric, and my blood turned to ice.

Her face and body had gone rigid, her eyes wide, her mouth twitching at the corners. Her hands came up and twisted into her hair, a whine escaping her throat. She whirled on Mark. "Where are they?"

"Who?" Mark asked, his face scrunching in confusion. "These are all the puppies I have available right now. I'm sorry if they aren't what you wanted. If you tell me exactly the breed you're looking for, I can get you in touch with—"

"I don't want your fucking *puppies*," Lyric seethed. "You know goddamn well what I'm talking about."

Mark glanced at me, then back at Lyric, wary now of this angry girl he'd allowed in his house. "I'm sorry, miss," he said, his voice a low crackle in his throat, "I don't."

Lyric put her backpack down on the ground, unzipped it and rooted around inside, then suddenly, there was a gun. I recognized it as my dad's gun, the one he kept locked in the safe for emergencies, the safe that needed keys he kept with him at all times. Apparently, one of the *useful things* she'd found had been my dad's Ruger. She pulled it out and stepped forward, aiming it directly at the old man's face. Mark yelped, doglike himself, and took a step back. "Hands up, Mark."

Everything around me seemed to move at half speed, the colors all standing out as heavily lined as a comic book. I saw Mark, his sallow face littered with white stubble and pitted from acne long gone since his teenage years. His white hair stood up with bedhead as though he'd been given an electric shock—I could even see that he'd been lying on the left side of his head when we'd woken him from his snooze in front of the TV. I saw the wallpaper, those tiny flowers a riot of pinks and reds, the leaves a delicate green over the yellow background, framing him as his gnarled and blue-veined hands began to move upwards, his rough palms coming up with agonizingly slowness. His eyes gleamed, those eyes the color of faded denim that had once belonged to a man in his prime, but now spent their days in the grizzled mass of wrinkles that was an old man's face. The puppy in my arms squirmed, its hot weight against my chest like a stone, its breath panting like the bellows of a little engine. And Lyric, my sister newly liberated from her confinement, stood before him, her cheeks pink with the rush of her blood, her hair swept back, grinning with all of her teeth bared, the gun aimed with murderous intent, looking for all the world like some criminally misguided angel of vengeance. I was dimly aware that I was making a high keening sound in my throat, and I wanted very much to scream *stop, stop this right now!* But no words would come.

Mark did as she said, fingers splayed, his face a mask of fear. "Now, miss, we can work this out if you just let me—"

She cocked the gun, the click loud even over the cries of the dogs. Mark went silent. I cowered on the floor, clutching the puppy to my chest.

"Mark," Lyric said calmly, too calmly. "I'm going to ask you some questions, and you better know the answers. Question one: Where are the kids?"

Mark looked to me again, but I was no use. I couldn't even move I was so scared. "I don't…I don't have any kids. I'm single. I was never even married. Hell, I never even fathered a bastard. There aren't any kids in this house."

"Yeah, sure, that's why you sell 'dogs' every few months, right?" *Dogs* was in air quotes, dripping with sarcasm. "Admit it. You live by the tracks for the same reason all old men live there. You take advantage of the women and children who ride for free, because you think they're less than human. You call them 'dogs,' and you use those fucking posters to advertise to other perverts that you have them. Just like they did to me and Mom when we rolled into the wrong town. Admit it, Mark. Come clean. And you *used me* to spy on them before you picked them out. You and Dr. Fucking Shetland. Didn't you?"

Mark was crying now, the gun inches from his face wielded by an obviously disturbed person who wouldn't be deterred. "I don't know what you're talking about. I'm…I'm sorry that happened to you, I truly am, but that's not what I'm doing." Fat tears rolled down his face. "I just sell puppies sometimes because I have a few good breeding dogs." He risked pointing to the dog on the floor and her brood. "You can see them. The boy is holding one himself. Please. Please don't kill me."

Lyric glanced at me, at the dogs yapping, and made a sound of frustration. "You're telling me there are no kids here?"

"No!" Mark insisted. "I never even have kids *over!* I don't even *like* kids! All I do is sell *dogs!*"

"So…so she's…she's not coming?" Lyric said in a small voice, her arm holding the gun falling an inch as she began to shake. She turned her head to face me. "My m-mom isn't coming? I was wrong?"

"Yeah, you were," I said as gently as I could, still terrified and pressing the squirming puppy to my chest. "But it's OK. Put the gun down, and we can go." I looked to the man trembling, knock-kneed, in front of us and looked at him pointedly. "Right, Mark? You'll let us go home?"

Mark looked from me, to my sister, and back again. He nodded hesitantly. "S'right. You put that gun away and I'll let you kids leave. Won't even tell nobody you was here."

"See?" I said, standing up, placing the puppy back down with its mother. "Mark is gonna let us leave. We can go home and pretend this never happened. You'll be safe, and you won't have to go back to the hospital. I promise."

Lyric was crying freely now, confusion, hurt, and anguish playing over her face like clouds on a sunny day. Her hand trembled, the gun clattering in her grip, still aimed at Mark, who was crouching now, trying to get out of the way. From outside, a horn blatted as the 9:30 train came rumbling past the neighborhood, making the walls of the house shake and rattle. Lyric stopped crying all at once, her head tilted, listening to it as it began to roll slowly past. Her body tensed. Her hand steadied. When she looked back at Mark, her eye was so cold and clear, she was like a different person—a gunslinger in a long-ago western, ready to make his final showdown.

"No," she said, so quietly I could barely hear her over the din. "I know what I know."

"Lyric—" I began, but it was too late. She shoved me backwards and I fell into the wall, trying to catch myself and hearing a snap as my wrist went. I yowled in pain, scaring the dogs.

Lyric advanced on Mark, who turned to run, but she was younger, faster. She pulled the trigger once, twice, three times, deafening me. The first shot went wide, hitting the wall behind Mark, making him *and* the dog yelp as plaster showered down from the home left behind. The dog shot out from the little room and under my feet as I was beginning to get up, knocking me back to the floor with and *oof.* My wrist let out a war cry as it banged against the door casing. The second shot hit Mark in the shoulder, blood, meat, and bits of bone spraying in a fan on the wall, spinning him around. He screamed and came forward, and that put him right in the line of fire. Lyric squeezed the trigger once more with Mark's face only about a foot away, his eyes round and glassy with fear. The third shot hit him in the neck, arterial spray splattering both Lyric and me as his head rolled back from the force of the shot. I was a screaming, but I couldn't hear it, only feel it, as I scrambled backwards, trying to get out of the way of the red gushes that spurted out. Mark grabbed at his throat, gurgling, sliding down the wall as his eyes rolled back in his head and he lost consciousness forever.

Lyric's expression was serene, a stripe of blood like war paint covering one side of her face, her eyes emotionless as she watched Mark twitch his last. She turned to me, saw me trying to press myself into the wall to get away from her, and smiled. She dropped the gun and put her arms out.

I pushed myself up from the ground, my wrist screaming, and shouldered past her. She let out a surprised yip and grabbed at my hoodie, nearly choking me as I wrenched out of her grasp and away. She called after me, but I couldn't stop, wouldn't, tears and snot coating my face as I powered through that moldering house and out the front door. I thought maybe she'd shoot me then for trying to desert her, but no more shots came. I nearly fell as I leapt down the stairs and ran into the street, only then remembering my Dad's phone in my pouch. I pulled it out as I charged down the street, towards the tracks, away from Lyric, who was calling my name, close—too close—behind me.

I hit the EMERGENCY CALL button and heard the ring as I ran, trying like hell to keep my wrist held close to my body.

A woman's voice answered. "911, what is your emergency?"

"My sister," I gasped as I turned the corner and saw the train still rolling slowly across the tracks, "She's…she's got a…a gun… she…she killed…Mark…"

"Your sister killed someone, is that right?"

"Yes…yes…she's…she's not…" and then I stopped. Half a block away, coming from the railroad tracks, a woman stepped into view. Her hair was long, matted, her clothes mismatched and dirty, but even from a distance, I could see the resemblance. I didn't think she'd seen me yet, so I ducked into the space between two houses, my heart pounding.

"Are you there?" the 911 operator asked, her voice tinny in my ears.

"Yes," I whispered "but my sister won't be for long. We're on Mazant by the train tracks. My wrist is broken. Hurry."

I hung up, unable to continue speaking. My arm pulsed furiously, the swelling already purple and black with broken blood vessels. I crouched against the side of the house, leaning on the

143

wall of my hiding spot for support as Lyric's mother drifted into view. She was taller than I'd expected, slim like Lyric, and when she glided into focus, I could see it on her face. The resemblance was uncanny.

"Mom!" Lyric said from a distance, her running feet resounding on the pavement. She entered my frame of vision covered in blood spatter, her backpack bouncing against her. She still held the Ruger loosely in her right hand. Her mother put her arms out and Lyric ran into them, hugging her mother fiercely and laughing, really laughing. "You came."

"Of course I did, darling," her voice was melodious as she cupped her daughter's face. "I can always hear you calling. The time just needed to be right. Does anyone else know what you did tonight?"

Lyric glanced into my hiding spot, and I thought I might faint. She held my eyes for a moment, smiling, triumphant, then turned back to her mother. "Nope. Free and clear. We should probably go, though. People do still call the cops in this neighborhood."

"Yes." Her mother took Lyric's hand, and they began to walk away, the sound of the train passing louder now. The horn blatted.

Before they disappeared from view, Lyric turned to me and mouthed, *I love you.*

And then it was all too much to bear. I slumped against the house, sweat dappling my forehead, hissing through my teeth as I propped my arm up on my knees. It throbbed in time with my pounding heart, my head swimming with agony and everything I'd just witnessed. The world began titling this way and that, sickeningly, and as soon as I heard sirens in the distance, I remember thinking *it's over, at last, it's over, I survived,* before my body gave up the ghost and I passed cleanly out in a stranger's side yard.

TEN

T HE NEXT FEW days were a blur. I stayed in the hospital all weekend, not just because of my arm, which required surgery to patch up, but because my parents were *also* there being treated. As it turns out, Lyric had given them just a few too many Valium, but because of my near-unconscious ravings in the ambulance, the police had gone to our house and broken down the door, which ultimately saved them both. According to the police, the doctors, and my parents, my actions that night were heroic, but I felt differently. I still kind of do, all these years later. I didn't want to talk to anyone, especially not the detective who came to my room with balloons and cookies my second day in a hospital bed. Lyric was long gone, so none of it seemed to matter.

I did, however, request to see the news when I finally woke up from surgery. My parents were there already, both in hospital gowns and trailing IV poles, and they exchanged a worried glance. But ultimately, my dad turned on the TV and let me watch.

"It was a veritable house of horrors," the anchorman on location at Mark's house said into a microphone. "Mark Hazlet, sixty-four, had two upper rooms in his home where he had been keeping seven children, ages four to ten. The parents of these children are now being sought for questioning in—"

I turned it off. I had seen all I needed to see.

The detective in charge of the case, a guy named McNulty, popped by on my last day in the hospital.

"Mr. Hazlet died of a gunshot wound," he told me, as if I didn't know, his fingers constantly twirling the pen he was holding while he talked, his other hand gripping his notepad in case I said anything interesting. "Very serious indeed. Liam, do you know where your sister is?"

"She's with her mom," I said promptly. "I watched her go. The police were pulling up just as they walked away. Did any of them see her? Did they see Lyric's mom?"

My parents exchanged worried glances while McNulty wrote down what I said, but he never followed up. And my parents, well, they'd just as soon never speak of what happened again if they could help it.

And that's what happened to me in the worst year of my life. My sister, Lyric, for all her madness, had been right on the money about the man behind the poster that screamed DOGS FOR SALE. It was hard to wrap my head around at first, and so I took to therapy like a duck to water. I felt guilty. Guilty for the violence, yes, but moreso for not believing her. For not believing in her. Her mother *had* been alive, she *had* come for Lyric, Mark *had* been trading children for money, likely for years. She was right about everything, and the world was a much more horrific place for it. What else, I often asked, had she been right about? Every therapist I ever saw tried to convince me that I hadn't seen what I'd seen, that Lyric had stumbled upon Mark purely by chance, until I finally stopped talking about it at all. I know what I know.

I have looked for her since then. Sometimes, there are signs in an advertisement, or a poster, even the paper, to indicate where she and her mother might be. I like to think they look for me too, the same way, that Lyric hears me when I call out for her with my mind. I think she does.

I only saw her one other time. I think, even now, it's too dangerous for her to fully come back, no matter how much she might want to. But she *does* check up on me, I can feel it. And that one time, I saw her.

It was when I was eighteen, right around my birthday, the summer before I went to college. I was petrified at the idea of going away to school—I got accepted to UCLA, and it seemed *so far away*—and had been calling for months for her to give me some sign it would all be OK. I scoured the paper, online publications, lost pet posters, everything, but I found nothing of her to comfort me. I spent the summer packing my things and saying goodbye to friends, trying so hard to be who I needed to be, I felt, in order to succeed. I laughed when called on to laugh, smiled when I was supposed to, but I didn't really feel it, because Lyric wasn't there to share it with me. She would have been twenty-three by now, sneaking me into bars and sharing in my achievements, and everything felt utterly empty without her.

My parents objected to me taking a train to California. They said a plane was faster, safer. But I didn't want a plane. I wanted to ride the rails, feel close to my sister as I embarked on life's next great journey. So I boarded the train at the station downtown, and I was away. The journey was long, but I had a window seat, so I watched the scenery change as it went by, from swamp, to plains, to hills, to desert.

We stopped just outside of Vegas, somewhere near Route 66, and there she was, standing on the platform. She was older, skinny as ever, in cutoff jeans and a shirt with no sleeves, her hair orange now instead of blue, but it was her all the same. She smiled at me and waved. I waved back, through the glass. She came closer and I pressed my palm to the glass. She did the same. She mouthed, *I miss you*, and I wished like hell I could hear her voice. Tears came and I mouthed, *I miss you too.*

She fidgeted, looking over her shoulder. She said, *I wish...*but didn't finish the sentence. She just looked sad.

Come with me, I motioned. *I'll pay.*

She shook her head. *I can't.*

The train started moving. She blew me a kiss, waving furiously as the train pulled me westward, out of her sight forever.

But maybe not forever. It's been a long time, true, but she's still out there. I know it. I *feel* it. College taught me a lot of things, but the most important thing I learned at school, I learned from a bum who rode the rails to get to California. He lived by the dorms at UCLA, and no matter how many times the cops chased him off, I brought him back. Because he taught me to read the language of the rails, the signs for safe houses and places to eat, how to tell a good place from a very bad place. And then I taught myself to read the signs like Lyric did. I taught myself to see things her way. I'm not scared anymore. I know what I know.

I stayed in California after school. I bought a house near the train tracks. I studied, even after I graduated, and I finally found what I'm looking for.

The poster says PUREBRED PUPPIES, WHEAT ALLERGY. They're all over the poles by my house. The best part? There's an *address.*

I know Lyric is coming. I can hear her every night, now that she's closer, and she's so proud of me for figuring this out. We'll do this together—fight against evil and scarper off onto a train. We'll be free, at last, with one another. I can't believe I was ever so afraid. We'll be heroes, even if no one ever knows it. She forgives me for not understanding. She's glad that I finally do.

We know what we know, and no one can take that from us.

III.
PROFESSIONAL
MONSTER

You can love a monster; it can even love you back.
But that doesn't change its nature.

– Eliza Crewe, *Crushed*

ONE

"**YOU WANT SOME?**" Koda asked as he tore into a huge hunk of red meat, the blood staining the soft, light brown down of his muzzle and streaking his massive paws crimson.

Brian wrinkled his nose. "No thanks. You're not supposed to have that anyway."

"It's not like it's *human*," Koda scoffed, ripping another piece off with his fangs and sucking it in with a *schlorp*. "It's lamb. You like lamb."

He dangled a flap of meat inches from Brian's nose, the gristle shiny and wet. The smell was tantalizing, fresh, but Brian put up a hand and pushed it away, pulling his TV tray with its plate of mushroom risotto closer. "I'd prefer not to."

"Suuuuure you would, bud."

"I really don't want any," Brian insisted, watching Koda smack and crunch his way through a leg bone from the corner of his eye while taking another bite of his risotto. He waggled his fork at Koda's muzzle. "Why are you like that?"

Koda shrugged one shaggy shoulder. "Feels good. Moon's close, you know?"

"I know," Brian grumbled, suddenly not hungry anymore. He wished he could be more like Koda, who felt comfortable in his own skin no matter what shape it took. When Koda was a man he was tall and lithely muscular, with long, curly brown hair and lean, feral features the girls went nuts for. As a wolf, he was huge, as dark brown as his hair, with bright amber eyes that screamed madness, intimidating enough that no other males had ever challenged him as long as Brian had known him.

No girls ever see him sitting on the couch in his underwear, stuffing his face and watching reruns of Is It Cake, Brian thought wryly. But even *if* girls saw Koda in his natural, relaxed state, he would somehow get away with it, pull it off in a way that made him seem interesting and cute, as opposed to slovenly and crass. Koda got away with a lot of things.

Brian didn't have any such leeway. Women didn't respond to him much, whether in his man form or as a wolf. He was a wiry, bespectacled man with dark auburn hair and blue eyes, a bit on the doughy side, and as a wolf he barely rated above average in size. His grey fur wasn't thick and lustrous like Koda's, his limbs not nearly as strong, his eyes nowhere near as striking. In short, he was little more than just a bigass dog. He shifted uncomfortably in his chair, watching Koda as he ate his way through what seemed like a herd of lambs.

"But you know we aren't supposed to shift forms at any time except during the moon."

"Uuuuugggghhhh," Koda groaned, leaning his head back against the wall in exasperation. "Bro, we've been over this. I fuckin' *know* I'm not supposed to change *outside* any time other than the full moon. And I'm not. I'm inside my fuckin' house. If the Bureau wants to kick our door down because I wolf out where *literally no one but you can see me,* then so be it." He paused, licking blood off the pads of his claws. "Unless *you're* gonna snitch on me."

"But the Bureau guidelines say that—"

"The Bureau guidelines can sniff my shit and call it Funfetti," he grumbled, and turned up the volume on *Is It Cake* with one giant elbow, so as not to gore the remote.

So that was that.

Brian scraped the last of his risotto from the bottom of the bowl and pushed his tray table away so he could bring it to the sink and wash it. He hated dirty dishes piling up almost as much as he hated Koda sitting on the couch in wolf form, mashing the springs out of shape with his bulk and leaving hair everywhere. He scrubbed the bowl down, picking at flecks of dried sauce with his fingernails. He knew Koda was as likely to leave the bloody paper of his lamb on top of the bin lid as he was to put it inside, and he frowned.

"There's gotta be *order* to things," he said under his breath, rinsing the bowl and putting it on the dish towel with the other drying dishes he'd unloaded when he got home from work.

"What?" Koda called from the living room.

Brian winced. He'd forgotten Koda's hearing was sharp as a tack on a normal day, in his wolf form quadrupley so. The wolf heightened every sense.

Stuck in my own head again, he thought morosely. *At least here he can't hear me. Fucking Bureau. They're the reason I'm stuck here with him in the first place. Fucking stupid werewolves, taking most of my life out from under me.*

And it was true. Brian had become a werewolf two years ago, when a rogue wolf had escaped custody for a traffic violation, of all things. The werewolf who'd made him, Malcolm Tate (Brian had made sure to look him up), had gotten involved in a rear ending for which he was at fault (surprise) and run from the police (double surprise). To escape capture, he'd turned into a wolf and gone bounding into the park, thinking he'd hide. Brian had been taking his evening walk, his headphones in, and Tate had heard his feet and gotten spooked, coming out if the bushes to attack whoever was coming up on his hiding place. He only realized *after* he'd bitten a chunk out of Brian's arm that this person was in sweats and not a uniform, and ran off into the night. He *was* apprehended eventually, and due to the attack was sentenced to ten years at a correctional facility specializing in the keeping of wolves. Brian had gotten a trip to the hospital, where he remained unconscious until long after Tate was arraigned, and a subsequent visit from an Agent Christian Agus from the Bureau of Werewolf Relations. Brian healed fast, but his life had changed forever. There were rules for werewolves these days, seeing as their population had exploded about thirty years back, and the BWR enforced them in order to keep the peace.

There were some good things about the BWR's existence. For instance, they supported and enforced a werewolf's right to work, fought against discrimination, and monitored the well-being of anyone who found themselves recently turned. Their rules invited order into a chaotic plague that otherwise would have been a daunting task tinged with shame and steeped in blood. But those selfsame rules made it difficult for people like Brian to live normally, which was the only thing he really wanted to do.

Be licensed to work, and chipped so they can always make sure you're where you're supposed to be. No turning into your wolf form any time but the full moon. No purposefully biting humans to make more werewolves. No cross-species mating. No eating of human flesh at any time. Werewolves must live with other werewolves.

That was the gist of it all, really. Brian understood the last rule, even if it irked him to no end. The idea was to put checks and balances in place. A human being was always in danger with a werewolf, no matter how docile they might be, but another wolf would be able to take them down if they started acting feral. The cases of feral werewolves had gone down significantly in the last five or so years, but that didn't make it *safe* for them to live with humans. They tended to put the wolves in pairs of a strong, established wolf (Koda) and a weaker, newer wolf (Brian), ostensibly to ensure that the weaker of the two would learn something from his compatriot on how to fit in with werewolf society.

So far all I've learned is that this dude needs a fucking babysitter, Brian thought as Koda shouted at the TV around a mouthful of food.

Still, it wasn't as though he didn't *like* Koda. He liked Koda just fine. But cohabitating with him was sometimes more difficult than keeping a jumpy dog in a bathtub full of ice water while everyone around him threw firecrackers. The house belonged to Koda, though, and as Agent Agus had told him several dozen times, there were no other spots open for new tenants. So here Brian stayed.

There were, of course, benefits to the Bureau's rules and regulations. Brian had been afraid when he was first bitten that he'd lose his job at the insurance company he worked for, but Agent Agus had ensured that wouldn't be so. Not only that, Brian's unique status among his coworkers earned him a higher pay grade working at handling the homeowners insurance for werewolves specifically, which was a class all its own. All Brian had to do was pass the Bureau's licensing tests that deemed him safe to work with humans, get the tracker chip put in his neck, and he became the token office wolf. Suddenly he'd found himself more interesting to coworkers who'd barely spoken to him in his ten years at Crimm and Baker.

On that note, Brian needed to plan out his wardrobe for the next few days. Wednesday night was the full moon, the time at which the shape change was hardest to control, and the only time he was allowed to go to work in that form. It was genuine agony to try and keep the wolf in on moon days, which the Bureau was well aware of, but he was required to wear more than just his fur. On moon days, C&B allowed him to wear anything he liked, and he'd purchased three 4XL T-shirts and three pairs of big and tall sweatpants for just these occasions. He passed through the living room unnoticed by Koda (who was licking the butcher paper with his long, pink tongue) and went to his bedroom at the back of the house.

Brian thought of his bedroom as neat, certainly neater than the rest of the house, an oasis of calm in the chaos of life. His bedsheets were navy blue, plain, and tucked squarely in, the navy duvet covering them just so, and the soft, down pillow placed at just the right angle. His bookshelf was arranged by author's last name and the subject: cookbooks on top, then historical nonfiction, then fiction at the bottom. The spines stood in regimented rows, soldiers ready to be employed against the greatest enemy, Boredom. The desk beneath his window (the curtains of which were a matching navy to his bedding) that held his computer and another small shelf of books dedicated to fixing computer problems was also tidy, every errant soda can or wrapper put in its place in the bin next to the desk. Yes, Brian thought of his spartan living space as neat. Koda called it pathological.

He moved to the closet on the other side of his bed, switching on the lamp on his bedside table (also primly neat) as he went. He rifled through his closet sorted by color and occasion, looking for the sweats, unable to find them. It had been Koda's turn to do the moon laundry last time, so it was possible they were still sitting in a heap on the laundry room floor. Brian sighed.

"What's up, pup?" Koda said behind him, and Brian yelped, spinning around. Koda was back in his human form, evidently chastised by Brian's earlier protestations, and was leaning with one shoulder on the doorframe, blood smeared all over his mouth, licking his fingers, completely nude.

"Don't call me that," Brian said half-heartedly, as he always did. "It's demeaning. And put some pants on."

"Sorry, sorry," Koda said, not sounding sorry at all. "What's up, *Brian?* Is that better?"

"Much. You don't happen to know where my moon sweats are, do you? You were supposed to wash them last time."

Koda pressed sticky fingers to his mouth and thought, evidently not in any rush to get dressed. How he could manage to look so at ease naked and covered in blood, Brian couldn't fathom. "Well, I *did* wash them, if you're thinking I shirked the *one* chore you gave me. But it's possible they ended up bundled in with mine. You wanna check?"

The thought of going into Koda's disaster of a room gave Brian the heebie-jeebies. "Could you look for me? My office requires me to wear clothes on moon days, even with all the fur."

Koda snorted. "I don't envy you. My boss lets me go *au natural* on the days I'm wolfed out. He says I work better like that." He toed the carpet, suddenly bashful. "He also says he wishes I was like that all the time, because it's when I actually get shit done."

"A win for you."

"A win for *him*, really," Koda replied gloomily. "He doesn't know what it's like to be outside under all that fucking fur. I'll go look for your stuff right now. You want to watch *Stranger Things* later? There's a new season out."

He sounded so hopeful that Brian felt genuinely guilty saying no. Koda was in the same spot as he was, thrust together with a roommate he didn't choose, and was trying, in his way, to make the best of it. "I will if you shower and put on some clothes."

"Oh, shit, I didn't even realize," Koda laughed, looking down at himself. "Sorry for putting my dick in your face, buddy."

"It's fine. My clothes?"

"Right, right, right." Koda backed out of the room and disappeared, leaving a smudge of tacky, rapidly oxidizing blood on the doorframe.

And who, do you think, is going to have to clean that? Brian sighed and went to fetch the paper towels and Lysol.

TWO

"A NOTHER MEETING THAT could have been an email," Summer muttered from behind him, making Brian jump.

He dared not turn around, lest he call attention to himself, but said over his shoulder, "Yep."

Summer tittered *sotto voce* laughter behind him, and that was it, Brian could no longer pay attention to his boss, Mr. Weeks, or the presentation the man was giving regarding the software for their new account with Lloyd's of London. He saw Evan Laverton, sitting three chairs away, raise his lip at the both of them in disgust, but Brian didn't care. He'd made Summer laugh, and that was enough. Brian had never had many office friends, even before the bite and his whole life changing, but afterwards people had more of a tendency to avoid him once his status as Office Curiosity had worn off. It stung some that people he'd known nearly a decade now jumped out of the way when he moved too quickly down the corridor for their liking, but part of him was glad, hungry even, for that reverential fear he inspired. He hated participating in office politics, disliked the games one had to play to ensure the work day went smoothly. Now he didn't have to. Now he could do his job and go home, and no one ever plopped their busy work on his desk anymore, expecting the meek assistant underwriter to do their jobs for them. He could even totally ignore loudmouth blowhards like Evan Laverton, who wore gold pinky rings and made it a point to tell everyone he had *two* BMWs.

And then there was Summer Landry. Oh, Summer. She was a relatively new hire, only with C&B for two months now, and seemed to want to make it her business to be friends with every single person in this office, Brian included. When she found out he was a werewolf, she hadn't even looked afraid. Her small, heart-shaped mouth had parted in a soft, interested smile, and she'd stood by his desk asking questions for thirty minutes. She'd been caught up in meetings the first full moon she was there, and so hadn't yet seen his wolf form, but told him she was determined to see "the sweet pupperino" this go around. She shifted in her chair behind him, and Brian caught a maddeningly sweet whiff of her perfume.

To say he was charmed by her open enthusiasm for knowledge (as well as her curvy figure, wide doe eyes, and wavy blonde hair, don't forget those) was an understatement, and he got a huge case of nerves any time she talked to him. She seemed to revel in his flustered answers, teasing him for being so uptight practically every time they talked.

"You gotta loosen up, Bri," she'd said a few days ago when he stammered over questions about a million-dollar account they both handled. "You're gonna give yourself a heart attack, being all pent up like that."

She was right, of course. He *was* too pent up. It was only made worse by the approaching moon, and the fact that he could smell her body beneath that perfume, her sweat and her skin, and hear her heart beating, slow and steady, in her chest. He wiped his mouth, afraid that someone near him might have seen him drool.

Finally, at long last, Mr. Weeks called the meeting, and everyone was allowed to file out for lunch. Brian lurched for the door, trying desperately to get away from Summer and her smell, glad for the moment that people moved for him automatically now, allowed him to pass unhindered as though he might bite at any moment. He burst through the boardroom doors, made a beeline for his desk, and grabbed his lunch, speeding towards the exit.

"Where are *you* going so fast?"

Brian stopped, closed his eyes. *So close, yet so far away.*

He turned, and put on his most professional smile. "Summer. I was just heading out for lunch."

Summer smiled, her red lipstick reminding him of Koda tearing into lamb's meat. Her hair was pulled back in a bun today, showing off the angles of her face. Her blouse was sailor-neck, the same red as her lips, her pencil skirt showing off just enough of her curves and her low heels pleasantly complimenting the shape of her calves. Brian swallowed *very* hard but kept his smile firmly in place.

"Lunch for one?" She asked coyly, a hand coming up to smooth hair that needed no smoothing. "Really, Brian, it's like you have no friends."

"So how about that deal with Lloyd's?" He piped up, too loud, too fast.

Summer looked taken aback. "Uh…it's great. Really. We're gonna get so much more international business dealing with them."

"Yeah…yeah…" As always, Brian felt the rising shame of awkwardness flood him, as with any length of time spent in her presence. She was just trying to be nice, he knew, to be his friend, but he felt weak around her, unable to just let things *be*. He wished more than anything in these moments that he was more like Koda, that there was more *wolf* in him. "I, uh…I gotta go. Only an hour for lunch, and I gotta pick up…I gotta get, uh…"

"Look," Summer said quickly, putting a hand on his chest. Brian stilled, somewhat shocked by the sudden, overly familiar touch of her fingers on his shirt. "I don't want to make this weird, but I have a…a favor…to ask you."

The feeling of her hand, so warm, so inviting, so alive, was almost too much to bear. "S-sure. Anything."

Idiot, he thought. *Way to sound like an eager little puppy.*

"So, tomorrow is the full moon, and I've never worked with a werewolf before," she said quietly, dark lashes lowered, as though this was a shameful confession. "I was wondering...do werewolves like...do *you* like...um...treats?"

Brian's mouth hung open for a moment, then he burst out laughing. Summer took that hand away and smoothed her clothes, laughing also.

"Not *dog* treats, no," Brian replied, wiping tears from his eyes.

She smacked him lightly on the arm. "I wasn't gonna bring you a fucking Milkbone. I meant like...are there any foods that you particularly crave?"

"None come to mind." The thought of asking her to bring a raw, dripping side of beef was out of the question. "Though we do get hungry as hell on the day of the moon. Like...bottomless kind of hungry. Anything with meat in it, we want it, even if as people we're vegans. But anything works, as long as there's a lot of it."

"Maybe lasagna?" She asked hopefully. "I make really good lasagna, and I can put extra beef in it."

"Lasagna sounds amazing," he replied, the smell of her excitement dizzying. *The better to smell you with, my dear.*

"Then I'll make a whole one, just for you." Her bright green eyes glittered with resolution.

The better to see you with, my dear. "You really don't have to trouble yourself."

"But I want to!" She blurted, and now she was the one who was too fast, too eager, too excited. "I mean...I want you to...I want to make a good impression, I guess."

Brian squinted. "You said you wanted a favor. This sounds more like *you* doing *me* a solid."

"Oh. That." Again her hands came up to rub against her outfit. Brian could smell that her palms were sweating, but enjoyed the sight of her running her hands over her hips just the same. "I wanted to know if—if it isn't too rude, that is—I was wondering if you'd be willing to let me…um…touch your fur?"

That pulled him up short. "You want to…pet me?"

"No, no! You're not a pet!" Her hands were up again, flitting birds gesticulating her point, high color on her cheeks, embarrassed. "I've never been this close to one of you…oh, I don't mean it like *one of you*…and I never had a chance to really *feel* what it felt like to…not that I want to feel you up or anything, I just…oh, I'm making a mess of this, aren't I?"

"Not at all," Brian replied, grinning, his heart beating harder now but in a good way. If his tail had been in place, it would have been thumping the walls, he'd be wagging so hard. "It's OK. Really. You're fine. I think that the exchange of one whole lasagna for a light petting session is extremely amenable."

Summer turned bright red, her green eyes large, but she was smiling again.

"OKthanksseeyoutomorrowbye," she said in a breathless rush, then turned on her heel and practically skipped away to lunch.

Brian watched her go, mystified as to what had just occurred. Was this all he'd have to do to get closer to her? Agree to eat extra beefy lasagna? Being touched by Summer Landry, though, that would be the *real* treat. That was the thought that had him salivating.

The better to

THREE

"YOU SAID YOU'D eat her lasagna and let her give you half a handjob!" Koda howled, rocking back and forth with laughter on the kitchen floor.

"Yeah, maybe I could have worded that part better," Brian chuckled. Normally, Koda laughing at him this way would bother him, but tonight he was on cloud nine. "But at least I'll get to finish the lasagna."

Koda roared laughter, slamming his fist on the floor. He gulped air, unable to hold in his mirth. Brian grinned from ear to ear as he sautéed garlic and onions for the chicken stir fry that would be tonight's dinner. Tomorrow night at this time he and Koda would be arriving at The Paddock for full moon activities with the other werewolves, hunting their dinner by starlight. But tonight was just Tuesday, and what a happy Tuesday it was. Brian wasn't even excited about the hunt. He was excited about Summer, about his lasagna, about the feel of her fingers travelling through his fur.

"*A light petting session,* my fucking *God,*" Koda wheezed. He grabbed Brian's leg suddenly, his expression falling grave. "Man, if you don't turn this into a way to get laid, I'm gonna be so disappointed in you. I'll revoke my friendship, I swear to Christ."

"You know I can't do that. She's human."

"So?"

"It's *forbidden,* Koda. Maybe you like bending the rules, but I just…can't."

"The rules aren't the only thing you wanna bend," Koda said gleefully, up in a flash and dry humping the table, putting on a high falsetto. "*Ooooh, Brian, yes, knot me, knot me, you're my good boy, Brian, eat my lasagnaaaaa.*"

"Cut that shit out," Brian said, but he was smiling through his blush. "I'd literally split her in half."

"Yeah you would!"

"No, dude, *literally*. She's…so tiny compared to wolf-me. She'd die. I can't do that with her. Besides, if we so much as *kiss* I run the risk of infecting her, and then I'll get charged with illegally creating another werewolf. And I'll bet that she doesn't know about any of that, because she's never worked with one of us before. It would be…dishonest. A breach of trust. Or something."

"Man, you are such a buzzkill." Koda slumped into one of the kitchen chairs. "But yeah, you right. Does seem kinda shitty to do that to somebody who doesn't know what they're fucking with. The chicks I've banged all knew the risks."

"*Koda!*"

"What?" He shrugged and spread his hands. "Girls get horny too, dude. And some of them are *mad* kinky. I'm doing them a service, trust."

"But the infection spreads by—"

"I *can* read, you know." Koda tugged one of his curls and watched it sproing back. "I did my research *long* before I started involving other people. Infection by saliva exchange in kissing is really fucking rare, and when I fuck, I always wear a rubber. I don't bite even when they ask me to, and some of those weirdos *do* ask. I always say no. I might be a big, bad wolf that attracts horny milfs in my area looking for a thrill, but I'm a responsible monster. What can I say?" He rubbed the back of his neck and smiled shyly, almost self-consciously, an expression that didn't look at home on his face. "I'm equal opportunity nasty."

Brian sighed and added the chicken to the wok. "Yeah, I guess you are. Responsible, that is. I just would hate to see you catch a charge for that."

Koda put his chin in his hands and batted his lashes. That cheeky look *did* look like it belonged on his face. "Aw, you love me."

"I wouldn't go that far."

"Man, you don't go far *enough*. You need to get laid, big time. I'd do it myself if you were into dudes."

"Thanks. I think."

"You should be honored, motherfucker. I've got premium schmeat, served piping hot all day long. Speaking of—what's for dinner? I'm starving."

FOUR

Brian was gathering his things to take a shower, his skin itching like mad, when his mobile phone rang—"Ride of the Valkyries," which meant it was Agent Agus from the Bureau.

He picked up on the third ring. "Mr. Agus, how are you doing this evening?"

"Mr. Hersch, a pleasant evening to you," Agus replied, not answering Brian's question. "Tomorrow is the full moon."

Straight to business, then. Brian grabbed a washcloth from the pile of unfolded laundry on the sofa. "Yep, same as it is as every month."

His joke, like his question, went unheeded. "Do you need transportation to The Paddock?"

"Yes, please. Koda and me both."

"I'll put you two down for transport. How are things going with Mr. Kodalis and yourself?"

"Pretty well." He stole a glance at Koda, who was in the kitchen, washing dishes in his underwear and singing along to music playing loudly out of his phone. "He's a good guy."

"I ask because we've had issues housing folks with him before."

They make him sound like a difficult rescue. Brian rolled his eyes. Koda may be a pain in the ass to live with sometimes, but Brian still felt protective of him when it came to Agus and his endless questions, only in part because now they were the same species. "Like I said, he's great."

The click of a keyboard came through the speaker. "Good news. You're sure you have no complaints?"

166

"Nary a one." Brian lowered his voice. "You don't have to call me every month, you know. I'm handling this whole thing much better than I was a year ago. Largely thanks to Koda. I appreciate it, but I'm fine."

"Standard procedure is to call once a month to check on the welfare of new lycanthropes, for the first three years." Agus spoke like he was reading lines off a cue card. "You've still got…" there was a rifling of paper, "…fifteen months left of that time period. And Matthew Kodalis was something of a wild card for a long time. Real pain in the ass for the Bureau when he was getting his kicks in. We generally place newer lycans with older, more experienced ones, and he's been around for twelve rowdy years, causing all kinds of trouble. You're there to temper *him* as much as he's there to help *you*. Soon enough you'll be the mentor, with a younger lycan in your charge, don't worry."

Brian hadn't been worried, and said as much. He found himself feeling defensive of his roommate, hated the idea that Agus called him a *pain in the ass*, as well as the insinuation that he'd be made to leave. "But I'd rather *not* ditch Koda, if it's all the same. Sure, he's a bit…thrown off…sometimes, but he's easy enough to live with, once you get to know him, and gives me my space. I like it here." He scratched an itchy spot under his chin and found a patch of fur bristling out. "I'm not sure I'm qualified to mentor anyone, either."

"Be that as it may, this is the way of things," Agus replied gruffly. "Tomorrow night the bus will arrive at 6 p.m. sharp. Be outside with Mr. Kodalis, or they'll pass you up. And we wouldn't want that."

"No, we wouldn't," Brian agreed.

Agus rung off without so much as a goodbye, leaving Brian to stare, mystified, at his phone. *What a weird fuckin' guy.*

"Who was that?" Koda called from the kitchen.

167

Brian was, as always, astounded by how good his hearing was. "Agus," he called back. "We've got a ride tomorrow night."

"Good, cos I'm not fuckin' walking. Shit's too far out in the sticks."

FIVE

THE CHANGE ON the full moon is never easy. The first time is the hardest, as with many new and troublesome things. The first time, the change is painful, often incomplete, and happens the moment that silvery moonlight hits the skin of a newly made werewolf. At this most vulnerable time, the cursed is at his or her most likely to go on a rampage, even with all the medications that science has come up with to combat it. After that first change, though, things get simpler, easier to predict. Every subsequent full moon, on the night before the moon, the person afflicted feels as though they'd been struck by a particularly awful cold, their body a mass of aches and pains, their skin feverish, prickly, bathed in a cold sweat. Food doesn't taste right, but they're hungry as if they haven't eaten in days. Sleep is difficult, restless, plagued by strange dreams of running, hunting, tearing into supple flesh with fang and claw. They awake in the morning a beast too big for the bed they went to sleep in, unable to change back until after the night has passed and the moon begins to wane. As it was for the rest of the cursed, so it was for Brian.

"Ouch," he said gruffly when his head hit the ceiling for the umpteenth time this morning. He rubbed between his ears with one giant, furry mitt, annoyed. He'd been up with the sun, unable to lie still any longer, and kept bumping his bulk clumsily into things left and right. Even after almost two years, he found it difficult to navigate this shape and was as painfully awkward as a beast as he was as a human man.

"Found them!" Koda called from the hallway, and ducked down into Brian's room to hand him his clothes. "Sorry. They weren't where I thought they'd be."

"Are they ever?" Brian tugged his shirt over his head, then sat down on his protesting bed to pull on his sweats. Koda, ever the exhibitionist, stood hunched and watching in the doorway, his amber eyes flicking this way and that. "Are you just gonna stare at me or what?"

"No," Koda replied, but kept watching. "I just wanted to say… well…I hope everything works out for you today, man. With that Summer chick. I really do."

Brian stopped dressing, surprised. Koda rarely said things like that, and the words were so genuine that Brian was touched. "Thanks, Koda. Truly."

Koda studied his feet shyly, wiggling his toes, his claws clacking on the door skirt. "If any of us mangy assholes deserve a shot at happiness, it's you. You always keep me pointed straight, and you're a good dude. So…have fun today, for me. OK?"

"I will." Brian glanced at the clock. "If you don't hurry up, you're gonna be late. Again."

"Oh, *fuck!*" Koda growled, then stomped off and out of the house, slamming the door.

He's better than he gives himself credit for, Brian thought, chuckling to himself as he gathered his work things.

He couldn't possibly fit in the car today, so he did was he always did on moon days, and walked. It was a very nice day, albeit a bit on the hot side, with big, puffy clouds and birds singing everywhere. Brian saw other wolves making their work commutes, in ones and pairs, some clothed, others not, and waved happily to each of them as he passed. Some waved back, others merely glared their displeasure at the grinning wolf bouncing his way to his office job in sweats and a T-shirt. The wind blew in his face, bringing the smell of cooking food from breakfast places, the dark brown smell of Starbucks coffee, and the equally good stench of a dead opossum rotting in someone's back yard. Brian's mouth watered. A brief desire to roll in it flitted through his mind, but he pushed it away. Today was no day for the pleasant stink of rot. He was extra fast on moon days, his back haunches powerful enough to leap to the gables of buildings if needs be, so the walk that would have taken human Brian twenty-five minutes took wolf Brian a paltry ten. He was panting by the time he pushed the elevator button to go up to six, but he was happy.

He hummed to himself as he readied his desk, adjusting his chair and his headset to accommodate for today's shape. A few early officemates stared from behind him, watching the werewolf get ready for work. Usually their stares irked him and made him feel like a zoo exhibit, but today all he had to think about was Summer and her excited eyes, her tiny hands that would rub through the fur he'd brushed 'til it gleamed, her softly parted pink lips and wide green eyes sparkling as she hung on his every word, and the irritation melted away like butter in a hot pan. The rest of the office could step right up and ogle him up close and personal for all he gave a damn. Today, *nothing* could bother him.

"Brian, Brian, you ain't lyin'!" intoned the voice of Paul Murdoch, his cubical mate, from behind him. Paul was edging on fifty but was a pleasant sort, short and bordering on chubby, balding, with tiny, rimless glasses, and nothing but nice things to say. His wife Cathy always sent fudge along at Christmas (which Brian couldn't eat, but never said so), and Paul played Santa in the annual office White Elephant exchange. He was one of the few people in the office Brian actually liked instead of tolerated, and he'd done this play with Paul enough times to know what came next.

Brian grinned and spun around in his chair, catching Paul's fake punch deftly in one enormous paw. "Gotta be faster than that, Pauly Wants a Cracker."

"Ah, you're just quicker when you're all fuzzy." Paul shook his hand rapidly, pretending to be hurt just to get a laugh, which he received. Then he sat down at his desk and began getting his things ready for the day. "How's tricks with you, kiddo? Anything new?"

"Not since yesterday," Brian replied, the same as every day. Then it occurred to him. "Although..."

Paul stopped rooting around in his desk and turned around, eyebrow raised. "Although what?"

Brian perked up his ears, scanning their surroundings for any sign someone might be nearby, listening. Not even a peep. He gestured for Paul to lean in, and when he did Brian whispered, "Summer Landry is bringing me a whole lasagna today."

Paul's grin was more wolfish than Brian's. "Alright, kid, *alright!* Look at you, landing the prettiest gal in accounting."

"It's not like that," Brian assured him. "She's just...never worked with a werewolf before, and I think she's curious about what we're like."

"I think she's curious about more than that," he replied, bopping Brian lightly on the knee with his fist.

"Maybe, maybe not. Even if she *was,* it's not like I could—"

"Werewolves aren't *allowed* to mix with human women." The snide, jeering voice of Evan Laverton came over the partition seconds before he came into view. Evan was the antithesis of Paul: young, athletic, with a thick head of black hair, and a fuck-you attitude that won him no personality contests. In short, he was a total asshole who absolutely hated Brian, taking any opportunity to mock him. Brian mentally admonished himself for being so wrapped up in Summer that he hadn't heard this dickweed coming.

Whether he hated Brian for being a werewolf, or simply for existing, Brian didn't know. He bristled, his pale grey fur standing up in hackles down his spine. "I was human once, too, you know."

"But not anymore," Evan sneered. He examined his buffed and manicured fingernails, pretending to be casual. "You gonna be a good little doggy and play nice? I'd hate to have to call the dog catcher."

Brian held back the growl trying to rise in his throat, unable to speak, just staring daggers at Evan. Paul noticed and stood, clapping his hands. "Well! It's 8 a.m. on the dot. Time to get to work, huh, fellas?"

Evan looked up from his nails and met Brian's gaze, held it there, completely unafraid. He knew as well as Brian did that there was nothing a werewolf could do in situations like these. Too many wolves had been fired from perfectly respectable positions because they raised their voices too loud on a moon day, on the grounds that it created a hostile work environment. What it really meant was that the people who worked with them were afraid to have a werewolf go feral and kill everyone around them, but that sounded too much like discrimination. There were laws against lycanthrope discrimination, but there were no laws against firing a hostile employee. And assholes like Evan, who weren't afraid in the slightest, would exploit that prejudice just to be a dick.

"Yeah," Brian said, his eyes never leaving Evan's. "I've got a lot of work to do."

Evan barked out a laugh. "Just make sure you don't miss the peepee pad in the men's bathroom, OK, Fluffy?"

He turned on his heel and strode away, whistling "Stray Dog Strut." Brian hated that fucking song. When Evan was out of sight (but not earshot), he shook himself vehemently as though he'd been dunked in brackish water and was trying to get it off. He took several deep breaths, eyes closed, willing himself to let it go. Slowly, slowly, his fur began to lie down, his blood to cool. Slowly, the boiling anger reduced to a simmer, and Brian sat back up, brows knit in contemplation. Maybe Evan would always be an asshole, but that didn't mean Brian had to be a monster.

You're a professional, he thought. *Now act like a goddamn professional.*

"You OK, Bri?" Paul asked, genuine concern in his voice.

"I'll be fine," Brian said, forcing a smile. He made sure not to show any teeth, certain that if he did, it would look like a snarl. "It's a moon day, and I'm having lunch with Summer Landry. Nothing can get to me today."

SIX

"**A** RE YOU READY?" Summer asked brightly.
Brian had prepared himself for this lunch since last night.
Given himself a pep talk at his desk for the last hour, getting
hardly anything done and accidentally hanging up on a client
(twice) in the process. He'd prepared himself to sit near her,
smelling her perfume and her skin so close to him on the day
when his nose was at its most sensitive. He had steeled himself
for the inevitability of her touch gliding over him, and reserved
the strength to use restraint if she tried anything else. He had
expected all of this to be the most difficult thing he'd ever done
in his entire life.

What he hadn't expected was the picnic basket.

"Where...uh...where are we going?"

"Wow," she replied, "your voice sounds *way* different as
a wolf."

She giggled in a way that sent pleasant shivers down his spine.
He swallowed. "Uh...yeah, I guess it does. So...are we...going
somewhere?"

"Welllllllll," she said, suddenly hesitant, fidgeting with the
gingham blanket laid on top of the basket, a self-conscious smile
touching the corners of her mouth. "I thought that maybe, given
your current, um, state, that you might be more comfortable
having lunch out at the park. You know, some fresh air? The
break room is so tiny, but I checked the weather this morning
and it said it's gonna be nice out, so..." She held up the basket
with some effort.

"That looks heavy," Brian said as if in a fog. "Give it to me."

Summer handed it over, looking up at him, hopeful. "Does this mean you'll come with me?"

She couldn't see it, but a flush was creeping into Brian's cheeks. He surreptitiously gripped the end of his tail with his free hand, stopping the wag from knocking everything on his desk down. "Yes."

"Yay!" She laughed and clapped her hands.

Brian thought in that moment he'd probably kill a mailman a day if it meant she'd look at him like that when he did it. He followed her out of the office like a good boy and they began their walk to the park. She huffed trying to keep up with him even though he was walking his slowest, and about halfway there he had an idea.

Don't do it, he thought. *You're going to cause a scene.*

But his mouth had other ideas. "Seems like you're having trouble keeping up."

"Oh…you know…" she panted, her face flushed and forehead beaded with sweat. "Not…too much…"

"Would you like me to make it easier on you?" He stopped, looking down at her.

She stopped too, her green eyes curious. "How?"

"It's a surprise," he grinned, showing off his fangs. She didn't flinch. That was good. "But you have to give me permission to touch you."

She let out a nervous giggle, hands coming up to smooth her blonde hair held back in a red headband, looking very much the part of Red Riding Hood facing down the Big Bad Wolf. "Hm. Do you promise not to make it weird?"

"Only as weird as you asking to pet me."

She smacked his hip, which was about as high as she could reach, and laughed. "OK. I give you permission to touch me."

This is a bad idea, he thought as he bent and swept Summer Landry literally off her feet with one tree-trunk sized arm. She screamed, but it was an excited scream, full of surprised pleasure. He plopped her down on his shoulders to straddle his neck. "Get comfy and hang on tight, OK?"

She settled in, her bare—*ah, fuck*—thighs pressing gently on either side of his neck, leaning in to press into his fur and hold on. She screamed again when he started to walk, squeezing him tight, and Brian's tongue flopped out in a doggy grin of intense pleasure, his tail wagging for all it was worth.

The park was fairly empty that day, and aside from a few mothers and their toddler-aged children on the playground and an old codger feeding pigeons from a bench, the wooden copse of trees by the lake was uninhabited. Brian knelt on all fours in the shade, bending so that Summer could slide—*oh my word, oh my god*—down off his neck and light onto the grass. He crouched, brushing leaves and dead grass from his sweats and watched her stretch, her back to him, his body thrumming with needful desires he couldn't fulfil. The piggyback had been a great idea and a terrible idea all at once. Great because Summer was thrilled, smiling ear to ear as she unpacked the blanket from the basket and spread it out for them, kicking off her flats to dig her pert, tiny toes into the grass, bad because it had left Brian with a raging hard-on that was difficult to cover in sweats when one possessed a dick like a dog. He could still smell her all over him, the scent of secret places he couldn't allow himself to think about. He opted to sit before the picnic was spread out and tuck his paws in his lap, looking over the lake and hoping he looked pensive instead of lecherous as he willed his erection away.

It wouldn't be so bad if it wasn't a moon day, he reminded himself. *Tomorrow you'll feel much differently about this whole thing than you do now.*

But somehow, he didn't think that was true, because the sight of Summer scootching toward him with a giant Pyrex dish full of something extraordinarily meaty and delicious didn't *just* make him horny. That he could write off on the moon. The *other* feelings—like the one of hope, the one of joy, the one of *rightness*—couldn't be as easily pushed aside. He took the Pyrex and peeled back the tinfoil, the smell of beef and ricotta cheese hitting his nose and making him salivate.

"I'm sorry it's not hot," Summer said, uncertainty in her voice. "I had to make it last night and put it in the fridge and the microwave in the break room isn't big enough to—"

"It's fine," he chuckled, wiping his chin with the back of his paw. "Clearly I appreciate it. Sit with me?"

She folded herself down next to him, primly tucking her skirt around her knees as though she hadn't just been splay-legged around his neck, and watched him eat. The lasagna was gone in minutes, and he smacked as he licked the Pyrex clean.

"Whoa," she said with some fascination, "I didn't think my cooking was *that* good."

"It's excellent." He held up the empty dish, clean as a whistle. "Obviously."

She tittered, pleased with herself. "I take it you don't have a partner that cooks for you."

"Usually I do the cooking."

"Really?"

"Really. My roommate isn't...well, let's say he's not as domestic as me. He helps a lot in other ways, but his cooking leaves something to be desired."

"Domestic, huh?" She arched one eyebrow, looking him up and down. "You look plenty wild to me."

He smiled, musing. "I guess I don't look very domesticated, huh? Not like this, anyway." He held up his paws, inspecting them. "It *is* pretty wild looking, now that I think about it. I suppose I still just think of myself as Brian Hersch, middle-aged assistant underwriter, and not like...this."

Summer leaned in, her shoulder brushing his bicep—*sweet Lord*—and pressing against him. "How long have you been like this?"

"Too long for my taste." He sighed. "But really, only about two years. The werewolf that got me is in jail and everything, but he really changed the entire scope of my life. One day I was a normal, average dude with normal, average dude problems, and now...Now I've got the Bureau watching my every move, a weird roommate who works in construction and has a penchant for nudity, and once a month I'm stuck being a monster for twenty-four hours."

"I don't think you're very monstrous," she said quietly.

He allowed himself to look at her then, her eyes so green and lips so rosy pink, her small human body quivering, rabbit-hearted, next to his. But was she afraid? No. He could see in her face only a kind of curious reverence, the same way a person might look if they came across a wolf in the woods and knew to just be quiet, be still. She reached out one of her tiny, beautiful hands. Hesitated.

"Go on," Brian said breathlessly, his belly full of her food, his eyes full of her face, his nose full of her scent. "I already said you could."

Summer stood—*the better to reach you with, my dear*—and put her hands on either side of Brian's muzzle. Leaned in.

SEVEN

"**D**ID SHE CUM?"
"Don't be gross, Koda."

Koda held up his frankly enormous paws as if to say *don't shoot the messenger*. "I know you aren't about that life, man, I'm just joking around."

"She kissed my nose and scratched me behind my ears. She didn't climb on my dick."

"OK, then did *you* cum?"

"*Koda*."

"I know, I know, sorry, but she did a little more than *light petting*, don't you think? The way you tell it, she basically had her face buried in your crotch." He leaned back in his seat, looking over his shoulder. "Hey, you think Rhonda would be down to bone? She keeps looking at me and I'm itchy as *fuck* for some pussy."

"Why don't you go ask her?" Brian said absently, the bus with the top cut off that the Bureau used to transport lycanthropes to the secure location referred to as "The Paddock" bouncing him around. Koda got up, ostensibly to see if Rhonda was interested in some moonlit fun, and left Brian, at last, to his thoughts.

Koda was right, the light petting session Brian had agreed to had been a bit more than that. Before she'd even started, though, Summer had leaned in and planted a soft kiss on his wet, pebbly nose. That had certainly disarmed him, and after that he was putty in her hands. She'd gone (nearly) everywhere with her hands, stroking his ears, under his chin, down his back, hiking up his shirt to scratch his stomach and admire the rows of muscles on his abdomen with soft fingertips, liking the various textures of his body and saying so over and over in a small, high voice that had been music to his ears. She'd laid across him in the sunshine pressing her face to his stomach fur and inhaling, needing to known what he smelled like, had kissed the pads of his palms and fingers just to feel them against her mouth, then pulled a promise from him to meet her for dinner the night after the full moon. And with her body draped across his, her sweaty hair in both their faces, and her eyes screaming *lust* when she bit her lip, how could he be enough of an idiot to say no? It was all too much, too fast, and he knew deep down in his soul that this was going to cause a world of trouble.

Still, though. Still. He glanced behind him and saw Koda nestled in the same seat as Rhonda, his arm draped around her, whispering in her ear. Koda caught his eye and gave him a thumbs-up. Brian returned the thumbs-up, then turned back to look at the scenery whooshing past, allowed his nose to take in every smell coming off the freeway—exhaust, a dead deer, melted rubber, greenery—trying to expel the scent of Summer from his mind. It wouldn't go. He wished he was like Koda, so at ease and happy with himself exactly as he was, so confident that what he was doing was the right thing. Or, at least, confident he wouldn't get caught.

I'm a responsible monster.

Brian thought before today that he was *also* a responsible monster, but this thing with Summer made him less sure of that by the second. He was putting her in danger just by entertaining this second meeting, even if he was in his human form when it happened. A werewolf is a werewolf, no matter what shape it's in, and his spit was every bit as damning whether the bite was from the wolf or the man. Not that he intended to bite her—*the better to eat you with, my dear*—but what if she tried to kiss him again, not on his nose this time? What if she *did* want to fuck, as Koda thought she did?

There's no "what if" about it, he thought, feeling simultaneous chagrin and a buoyancy the likes of which he hadn't experienced since the accident that had left him a lycanthrope. That Summer Landry might *want* him, want to *be with him,* in either shape was a tantalizing fantasy indeed to entertain. But also a dangerous one. Mostly because it invited hope of a thing that could never come to fruition and was sure to leave one or both of them damaged and heartbroken.

The bus crunched up the road to The Paddock doors, to the whoops and shouts of its passengers. The gates stood, twenty feet high and surrounded by electrified barbed wire, mute and malicious, lights in the guard towers blinking orange in the dark, briefly illuminating the men that stood up there.

Koda came up and slid back next to Brian. "They got this shit from *Jurassic Park*, I bet you any money."

"I'm not taking that bet," Brian replied, because it was true.

The Paddock was immense, sprawling acreage in the wasteland of New Orleans East, bought solely for the purpose of allowing the werewolves living in the Greater New Orleans area a place to roam on the full moon where, to be succinct, humans weren't. The land was surrounded by twenty-foot fences, electrified barbed wire, and soldiers that patrolled armed with silver bullets, just to be absolutely sure no wolf was tempted to leave before the morning sun turned them back into doctors, office managers, and bartenders. People could be reasoned with. A moon-drenched werewolf, Brian knew from experience, could not. The guards and the bullets seemed harsh until you remembered that each and every wolf on this bus would lose him or herself to the siren song of that tidal pull in a little less than two hours. The bus driver spoke to the guard at the gate, who pushed a button inside the guardhouse, and the doors swung inwards. Koda began humming the *Jurassic Park* theme song as the bus trundled through.

One good thing about The Paddock and the quarantine it implied: a wolf had room to stretch his legs. Brian did just that as the bus drove away, crouching on all fours to lift his leg on a tree. Nobody minded. The others—and there were at least four busloads for this area alone—were doing similar things, some marking territory, some tussling, some sniffing each other hello. Their group was fairly large, but not *that* large, considering how overpopulated and violent New Orleans was—there were maybe fifty folks, all told, all adults. Brian shook himself and trotted over to Koda and a group of four others, the only one Brian knew by name being Rhonda. She was a secretary at a financial consulting group by day, but tonight she was bedecked in sable fur that held swirls of gold, a light smattering of grey on her muzzle.

"Oh, hey, Brian's here. Briaaaaan," Koda said expansively, "you know Rhonda."

"Sure do."

"And this is Allen, Mike, and last but not least, Patricia, Rhonda's roommate." He winked. "She's new. This is only her first time at The Paddock."

"Welcome," Brian said, sticking out a paw to the pretty, pale white wolf with icy eyes that took it gratefully and shook. He was glad she was new and would still greet him this way. He didn't think he'd ever get used to sniffing butts.

"Charmed," she said, her voice bubbly and sweet. "I'm really glad Koda is here. He was the first one to say hi to me at the group meeting. I thought I'd never make friends like this." She gestured to herself. "But he proved me wrong."

Brian turned to Koda, shocked. "You go to group meetings? You?"

"Calm down, dude, it's not like it's AA," Koda said, bashful, rubbing the back of his neck and not meeting Brian's eyes.

"It's a Bureau thing. For new wolves who just went through their first change. I think of it as unrequested community service for all the hell I put them through as a teenager."

The other wolves laughed along with Brian and Koda, who warmed well to being the center of attention. "OK, OK, shut up," he said, waving a paw. "I'm not the important thing. The important thing is that we all make Patricia feel welcome, like they say at the meetings. Brian?"

"Hm? Me?"

"Yes, you. Why don't you show her around." And then Koda was squishing them together, shoving them off in the direction of the woods, grinning like a fool. "Let her get a *feel* for the place. You follow me?"

Brian thought he did, all too well considering subtlety was not Koda's strong suit, and he nodded. He looked from Koda, to the others, down at Patricia and back again. They all looked at him expectantly, but Patricia genuinely looked nervous. Mentally, he sighed. It wouldn't do to reject outright someone so new to lycanthropy. He had been in her position once, and kindness had meant the world to him. Better to pass on the favor and simply decline anything that wasn't strictly platonic than to hurt her feelings at this most delicate time. He turned to Patricia and offered his arm. She shyly slipped hers through his, looking much relieved, and they started walking.

"This place seems really chill," she said, gazing at all the wolves gamboling in the weak moonlight together as they walked. "Everybody is really laid back. This wasn't what I expected at all, especially when I saw the guys with the guns."

"The guys with guns are just a contingency. And don't let this fool you," Brian said, tipping his head towards the antics of the other wolves. "The moon isn't even a quarter of the way up yet, and the guards haven't even released the sheep. Once the moon gets to its apex, things start getting a little crazy. Folks get feisty, get a little more aggressive, get hor—"

Horny, he thought, swallowing hard. *I was about to say horny. Jesus Christmas, get it together.*

"So where are you from?" He asked, opting to change the subject.

"Here. Well, really, the Seventh Ward. Born and raised."

"And how did you come to be…here?"

She sighed deeply. "My ex-boyfriend and I were attacked waiting for the bus to go into the city. A wolf was mad he got a boot put on his car. My ex tried to help him, but, well…let's say he wasn't into it. Now he doesn't have his freedom *or* his car, and I'm stuck like this till I die."

"Ex, huh? He, uh…make it?"

"Yeah, he did, thank God. Not a scratch on him. We thought we could make it work afterwards, but I got bit and he didn't. And when he saw *this* come outta my skin, boy was he surprised."

"Surprised you turned into a werewolf after a werewolf attack?"

"No," she said, smiling mischievously. "Surprised because usually, I'm Black."

Brian gawped at her for a moment, then doubled over with laughter. Patricia was laughing too, the two of them falling over each other in their mirth. He hadn't realized how tense he really was, how much he desperately needed that laugh. Brian wheezed and thumbed tears from the corners of his eyes. "Yeah, yeah I suppose that *would* come as a shock."

"Enough of a shock he decided to move to Colorado in the middle of the night right after that first time," she chortled. "Some men just can't handle change. Not that it would have worked out anyway. They don't…the Bureau, that is…they don't let us fraternize with humans, do they? Once we're like this?"

Brian thought of Summer pressed against him in the sunshine, the feel of her nails trailing down his abdomen as she breathed him in. "No, they don't."

Patricia heaved another long-suffering sigh. "Then I guess my dating life is back to nil. Typical."

"Nah," Brian replied, putting his arm around her shoulders. "Just give it some time. Give *yourself* some time. Priority number one is getting in tune with yourself, figuring out what you need and what you want from this new life you've got. Give yourself permission to go slow. You'll get used to being a werewolf in no time, and then everything else will fall into place."

Like Summer's legs fell around my neck.

"Trust me," he said, letting Patricia's arm go, "it'll only get easier from here."

Liar, liar, tail on fire

He walked Patricia through a good bit of The Paddock, his hands clasped firmly behind his back, trying like hell to chat about inconsequential things while Summer cavorted through his mind. Patricia oohed and ahhed at the woods and the little babbling brook that ran through it, marveling at the sheer expansiveness of the place that the Bureau provided its charges ("Just for us!" She'd squealed, like it was Christmas). She told him about her family ("Five generations of Johnsons in one miniscule zip code."), her job ("Nobody expects the Lawyer Wolf's Precision!"), but Brian's mind was always elsewhere. The moon would be fully risen in less than an hour, and all he could think about was his date—a real date, dinner and everything!—with Summer tomorrow. He would have to scrub extra hard to get the musky dog smell off of him, and choose his wardrobe carefully. Maybe a night in the woods, howling with the others, was exactly what he needed to be cool enough to get through it with positive results.

"—back to the others?"

"Huh?" He snapped back to the here and now, saw Patricia caught in moonlight, looking beautiful as anything with the breeze ruffling her fur. "I'm sorry, I was miles away."

"That's OK," she said, smiling warmly. "I'm feeling a bit distracted, myself. I was saying, it's getting close to moonrise. Do you think we should go back to the others?" Her lashes lowered and she wrung her tail in her paws. Brian thought of Summer saying, *I don't think you're very monstrous.* Or...should we stay put?"

Brian swallowed hard and tried to look innocent. "I think that...seeing as it's your first time here...you should see exactly what it's like for everyone else. So you don't feel like the odd wolf out. It really is something when we're all together under the moon."

One ear tipped back in mild disappointment, but she put out a paw. "Then walk a lady back?"

"Absolutely." He took it and led her back to the huge field where most of the others were gathering in an excitable mass of fur and hormones. He could practically *smell* that the moon was reaching the tree line, feel its imminence like electricity in the air. Koda was wrapped around Rhonda, who playfully nipped at his mouth while he held her around the waist. Others were doing the same with their partners, some were scrapping with one another, much less gentle now, their bodies charged and ready for the fun about to commence. Soon the guards would release two dozen sheep. There would be a hunt, a feast, a communion of body and spirit for the lycanthropes watched by men carrying silver bullets, ready to put them to rest if they got too exuberant. Brian both loved and hated this part, the anticipation before the loss of control.

We do this to keep everyone else safe, he thought, his golden eyes flicking over every face in the crowd. Everyone near Brian had an expression of mixed excitement and nervousness, ears tipped back and tongues lolling, panting in the heat. *We do this so that most of the time we can pretend we're normal. Respectable. So we can hold jobs and find love and buy groceries at Whole Foods. But we aren't normal. We do this to protect other people from what happens to us once a month, so we don't accidentally make any more like us, because it's a curse. But mostly, we do this because it feels good to not be responsible for keeping ourselves under control for the safety of those around us. Even for just one night.*

And then, all at once, everyone stopped. Their heads turned in unison to the sliver of light peeking over the treetops, furred bodies quivering with excitement, noses twitching in anticipation. Patricia squeezed his hand so tightly her claws dug in, and that was good, that was fine, because Brian's head was full of silver light, so bright it was nearly painful. Someone began to whine, the whine drawing out into a howl as the moon made her arrival in her silver chariot, and then another, another, until they all had their heads tipped back, howling with their hearts and souls as well as their throats. And then, then everything was movement and wild hearts and hot breath and the gong of instinct pounding in veins that thrummed with dark red blood.

Brian was running, bounding, his skull so full of that joyous silver light he thought he might burst, loving the way his muscles carried him, not caring if he was leaping in circles like an overactive puppy, just reveling in the being *present,* here, powerful in this shape, on this night. He saw Koda rutting Rhonda in the dirt, his teeth at her throat, their bodies moving in unison, and thought, *Summer.*

His body resounded with the sweet heat of that thought, his hips bucking, and when had Patricia gotten under him this way? It didn't matter. All that mattered was the heat and the feel of his claws wrapped around her throat, her tongue (Summer's tongue?) thrust deep in his muzzle, the bright spark of *here,* and *now,* and *Summer, Summer,* everywhere, *Summer.*

The better to eat you with, my dear. And then the last vestiges of human thought left him for the night, replaced by the silver dagger of the moon.

EIGHT

T HE ALARM CHIMED out "Steh Auf" for what seemed like the hundredth time this morning. Brian groaned and smacked his phone, silencing Lindemann's pleas for him to *get up*, already. He pulled the pillow over his (now extremely human) head, silently pleading with the morning to either go away or wash clean the hazy, disjointed memories of last night.

What the fuck did you do, you uncontrollable piece of shit?

But he knew. He always knew, far too late to stop it from happening, what the beast had done in his absence as soon as the moon was in view. It came back to him in flashes, as it always did. He remembered being with the others, the howl, seeing Koda fucking Rhonda, and then...

Then you ruined anything you might have had with Summer, he thought miserably, *because you were horny, and Patricia was* there. *You absolute fuckup. You massive piece of dog shit. You irredeemable dumbfuck.*

"Hey, Bri," Koda's voice came from the doorway, a husky whisper. Brian imagined his throat was sore from all the howling, just as his was. "You got the day off too?"

"No," he mumbled from under his pillow.

"Well, then you're gonna be late, my dude. I mean, later than you already are." When Brian made no move to get up and out of bed, Koda sidled closer, apprehension in his voice. "You OK?"

Brian groaned, throwing the pillow away. "No, Koda, I am most certainly not OK."

Koda nodded, and came to perch on the edge of the bed, his hands clasped lightly together. "Is this about last night with Patricia? And that Summer chick?"

For someone with little to no common sense, his perception is keener than he'd ever admit. Brian sighed. "No. Yes. I...I fucked everything up."

"Kinda like waking up with blood on your hands, isn't it?" Koda asked quietly. "Losing control like we do."

Brian sat up, immediately awake. "You feel like that too?"

Koda smiled sadly. "All the time. It's part of why I go to meetings, to tell new people they aren't alone in this shitty, post-moon feeling. There's rarely an afterglow, just...heavy bullshit that feels unforgivable. There's always little pieces missing, moments—*important* moments—that only come back in a jumble, sometimes not at all. It's the part I've hated since I was sixteen years old." He chuffed out rueful laughter. "It was part of the reason I left home so early. My parents didn't know how to help me. Shit, *I* didn't know how to help me. Every full moon I was making people I love take their lives in their hands, and it was a gamble as to whether or not I'd remember what I did in the morning. But if you're worried about what happened last night, my dude—" he shook Brian's leg lightly, smiling, the dutiful big brother, "—you didn't do anything you should feel bad about. Patricia was as hot 'n' ready as a Little Caesars pizza, and it's not like you and Summer are *dating*."

"I know," Brian replied, slightly taken aback by Koda's revelation. He rarely showed much beyond the surface to anyone, and Brian thought he'd be wise not to take it lightly. "I mean, in my head I know that. It just...it feels like I used her. Patricia, I mean. And I didn't even use protection."

"Ehn, don't worry about that. Patricia is on the pill." Koda looked pointedly at Brian. "Ask me how I know."

"You didn't."

"I did. My dick is basically a welcome mat, homie. And I'm telling you, you did nothing wrong. She needed it as much as you did, just for different reasons."

"Even if I'm not interested in anyone except…you know?"

"Yeah. Even then." Koda swept his hair over one shoulder, finger combing it thoughtfully. "But you didn't use anyone, my dude. Patricia mentioned to me at the last meeting that she was looking for something casual, a hookup, y'know, someone to ride out the full moon with. Said she wanted to 'explore the options within the community.' She's the only wolf in her neighborhood, lonely, but real sweet, and definitely not looking for anything serious." He chuckled. "I'd say she used you more than you used her, if I'm honest. She won't get in the way of anything you're trying to do. If you're trying, that is."

Brian relaxed. "That…actually does make me feel better. Thank you, Koda."

"My pleasure, dude. You want to help me eat this gallon of goat cheese and cherry gelato?"

"It's seven thirty in the morning."

"Don't put that bad juju on my day off. Besides, after last night, I need all the carbs I can get to fuel back up after all the fu—"

Brian's phone rang. "Ride of the Valkyries." Which meant Agent Agus. He exchanged a panicked look with Koda, then hauled himself into a sitting position and picked up the ringing phone gingerly, as though it were a snake that might bite him. He looked at Koda, questioning. Koda's face was stricken—the Bureau never called this early unless something was wrong— but made a *go on, go on* gesture with his hands. Brian delicately clicked the green *send* button and put the phone to his ear.

"Good mo—" The words stuck in his chest. He cleared his throat, tried again. "Good morning, Agent Agus. What can I do for you?"

"Mr. Hersch," Agus said loudly, his voice echoing as though he was somewhere big, concrete, not his office. Agus was in the field, which meant trouble. "There's been an incident at your place of business. May I ask you a few questions?"

NINE

" ...**A**ND THEY FOUND his headless body up on Floor 6, completely dismembered. Whoever it was tore Paul's *arms off* before he was even *dead*."

Brian sat at his cubicle, a sick feeling in his stomach, staring at Paul's empty chair. Paul was never walking in again to groan his way down onto that chair, never again going to say *Brian, Brian, you ain't lyin'* before throwing a soft fake punch for his deskmate to catch. Brian's hearing wasn't as good as Koda's, but it didn't need to be. The whole office was buzzing with the news: Paul Murdoch was dead, and a werewolf had killed him. That much they had right. What they had *wrong* might not just cost him his job, but his safety.

The facts were these: Paul had come back to the office last night alone to put in a renewal for an account he'd forgotten about, trying to get it in before the midnight deadline, but he'd never made it inside. He'd been accosted in the parking garage, his assailant biting out his throat then leaving him for dead. A cleaning lady on her way out had found him at approximately midnight, already long dead in a pool of his own congealing blood, and placed a terrified call to the Bureau. Agents had immediately descended on the place and gone to work cleaning up the scene, tagging evidence, and trying to find the culprit. There were no cameras in the garage, and Brian was the only werewolf on staff at C&B, really the only one in the *building*, so naturally Agent Agus called him this morning to confirm his whereabouts on the full moon. Brian told him about The Paddock,

193

his story immediately corroborated by Koda, and later Patricia, so Brian had been cleared of any suspicion, however tenuous in had been. The agents were still downstairs in the garage, taking photographs before the blood got washed down the drain by their cleanup crew. All this hullabaloo would be over by lunchtime.

But they don't know any of that, Brian thought, listening to his coworkers' embellishments of Paul's death. *They just know I'm the only werewolf in the building.*

And he'd been late today. A missing werewolf directly after a werewolf attack? It may as well be a conviction as far as they were concerned, forget his ten years with the company *before* his lycanthropic adventures. He bounced his leg, hating this situation, saddened by Paul's death, nervous for his own future. He spent most of the morning like that, trying to stay busy and failing, fumbling his way through phone calls, writing emails that barely made sense because his mind was so far from his work.

At eleven o'clock, a familiar voice came from behind him. "Hey, brochacho, you left your lunch on the counter."

Brian whirled around, his nerves flaring up again. "What are you doing here?"

"You forgot this." Koda held up his lunch sack by way of explanation, but looked concerned. "I may also have come to check on you."

"Why?"

"Uh, because the guy you sit with was eaten and you're a werewolf in an office full of humans who, like, jump out of your way when you sneeze. I thought that would be self-explanatory. And I told you, I have the day off."

"First of all, he wasn't *eaten*," Brian said in a harsh whisper, "he was just *killed*. Second, do you think that a *second* werewolf in their midst is gonna make the folks around here more or less likely to string me up by my balls?"

"I, uh…I admit I hadn't thought that one through," Koda said rubbing his mouth. He put the lunch sack down on Brian's desk. "Anyway, I brought you this. So maybe less attitude and more gratitude."

Brian rubbed his face with both hands in frustration. He wanted this over as fast as possible, so he could go back to hunching miserably at his desk until the rest of the office forgot he existed. "Thanks. Can you go now?"

But Koda wasn't leaving. He stood with his hip against Brian's desk, that worried look plastered all over his face. Brian knew that look. It meant Koda was ready to be there for him, which was nice and all, but now wasn't the time. The big, handsome dork even had the nerve to look hurt that Brian didn't want to chat about this *right now*, during work hours, and call even *more* attention to the wolf among the sheep.

Then, to make matters worse, Summer came around the corner of his cubicle just as Koda opened his mouth, tears streaming down her cheeks. "Oh, Brian, I'm so *sorry*. I was held up in meetings all mor—" She stopped short when she saw Koda. "Um…hello."

Koda raised a hand in salute. "Ma'am."

Brian groaned inwardly. *He's gonna make this weird.*

Summer's eyes flicked back and forth between the two of them. "Brian? Is this a…a friend of yours?"

"Summer Landry," Brian said, voice dripping with discomfort, "This is Matthew Kodalis, otherwise known as Koda. He's my roommate. Koda, this is Summer."

Koda put out one of his large, calloused hands, and when Summer took it, he pulled it to his mouth and kissed her knuckles, keeping eye contact the whole time. She blushed and delicately took her hand back, and gave him a flustered once-over, taking in the sleeveless Iron Maiden shirt and the skinny jeans tucked into boots, the long hair and dark eyes.

Please do not let them hit on each other in front of me, Brian begged the universe silently.

"Brian told me a lot about you," Koda said, breaking the silence. "He really likes your cooking."

Summer smiled warmly back at him. "And Brian told me you're a total weirdo. You really live up to the hype."

Koda laughed, folding his arms. "We aim to please at Kodalis Incorporated."

Summer turned her attention back to Brian, and he felt as if a knot in his chest had finally let go when she threw her arms around him.

"It's just so awful. He was your friend." She was crying again, all at once. She buried her face in his collar, leaving behind mascara. Brian didn't mind at all. "And it was a *werewolf*, so of course people are being absolutely *shitty* about it."

"Don't worry," he said, patting her back and trying for a smile, trying to comfort her even in his misery. "They'll get over it. I'm in the clear. I told the Bureau where I was last night already, so I'm not even a person of interest to them anymore."

"Really?" She looked to Koda for confirmation.

"That's right," Koda said, nodding. "He was with me all night, and was heavily corroborated by several others."

Brian thanked him with his eyes for not mentioning Patricia by name. Koda smirked.

"Oh, but what will happen if people start being nasty?" Summer fretted.

"You mean what if people suddenly wake up and realize the office *feral* isn't just some old lady's little lap dog?" Evan appeared around the corner, smirking. He looked extra asshole-y today, with his hair slicked back *American Psycho*-style, and a blue pinstripe shirt with gold buttons.

"It wasn't me, Evan," Brian growled, his voice low and bordering on dangerous. Nobody pushed his buttons like Evan, and Evan knew it." And I don't appreciate the insinuation. You don't have to like me working here, but you can't just walk over and accuse me of murder."

Evan scoffed. "I suppose next you'll tell me I can't prove you and Summer here were having a cute little affair yesterday under the willows, huh? Made for some excellent portrait shots, I assure you."

That stopped Brian in his tracks. He knew Evan was a dickhead supreme, but the thought that he'd followed them, had *watched* them, maybe taken *pictures* at a time when he and Summer were so vulnerable and open with each other? Brian felt the prickling of fur beginning down his spine, felt the creak and slither of claws itching to push out from his nail beds. This was going to be bad. Not just *fired* bad, but *help, help, police* bad if Evan didn't fuck off. Soon.

"Shut the *fuck* up, Evan."

Evan stared, mouth agape in the ringing silence that followed. "What…did you just say to me?"

"I said," Summer replied, taking a step forward, her shoulders squared and her jaw set as she looked him right in his beady eyes, "shut the *fuck up*. Nobody here wants your shitty attitude. Not today."

Brian shot a look to Koda, whose eyebrows were in the stratosphere, then back to Summer, who stood quivering, a full head shorter than Evan, one hundred and eighty pounds of pure fury.

"You can't talk to me like that," Evan said, but all the bravado had left his voice. "Especially since he brought another *mongrel* in to back him up. With two of them around, we'll all be dead by closing. You…you can't…I'm…I'm…"

"These mongrels," she replied, folding her arms, her body a wall between Evan and the two shell-shocked werewolves behind her, "are more man than you could ever hope to be. And they're *not* dangerous. Brian has worked here over a decade. He hardly ever misses a day! You've taken off six days this month alone, when we really needed you. And Koda was sweet enough to bring his friend the lunch he forgot *on his day off.* When have *you* ever showed that sort of kindness, Evan?"

"I was…I have…" Evan stammered. He looked from Summer's angry face to Brian's surprised one, to Koda, who was now grinning fit to split.

"I think you better leave," Koda said, "before you get your ass handed to you by a woman half your size, and the mongrels are forced to get scrappy."

Evan's face was a war of emotions, going from shock, to anger, to disbelief in seconds.

Brian came up behind her and put his hand on Summer's shoulder, the heat of her small, human fury emanating into his palm. "Leave."

Finally, Evan let out an exasperated noise and said, "I don't have to take this shit."

Then he whirled and stomped off, ostensibly to go ruin someone else's day. The three watched him go, barely waiting till he was out of earshot to start snickering. Summer turned to Brian, swiping more tears out of her eyes. "I'm sorry, I don't know what I was thinking, talking to him like that. And it'll probably land on *you.* But I just…I hate it when people treat werewolves like they're…they're somehow *less* human because of their affliction. And on the day you lost your friend. It's caveman behavior."

"Sorry?" Koda said, laughing and leaning against Brian's desk. "Are you kidding? That dude that bathes in Axe body spray deserved to be nut-checked straight to hell. You're a down-ass bitch, you know that?" He pulled her into a bear hug, Summer's laughter muffled by his chest as he rocked them side to side rapidly before twirling her out so that Brian had to catch her to stop her from falling. "I'm not saying you're a *bitch*. Just...that was awesome."

She leaned her head against Brian's chest, the light, fruity scent of her shampoo filling his nostrils, and all he could think was, *Thank you, Koda.*

"It's OK," Summer said, smiling like she'd just won a blue ribbon at the spelling bee. "I know what you meant. I just hope I don't get Brian in trouble."

"You won't," Brian said, squeezing her shoulders and making her meet his eyes. "And he's right. People don't usually stand up for us like that. It was very brave of you."

"You think so?" Her eyes sparkled with mischief, as she leaned in. "I think Evan shit his pants a little."

Oh, he loved that look. "I think so too. Though...we do potentially have another problem."

"What's that?"

"Well...I mean...the attack has obviously left people a little raw, and things are likely to be tense in town tonight once the report hits the news that the person responsible was a werewolf. I know we had a date tonight, but..." he stuffed his hands in his pockets, unable to touch her now, looking down at his feet, hoping, praying, needing her answer to be good but knowing it likely wouldn't be, "I understand if you don't want to go out in public with me later for dinner. Most people act like...Evan... when these things happen, and I tend to hide out for a few days afterwards, especially if we're with our human friends. So.

You know." His cheeks reddened. "Staying in is probably safest for me. For you too."

Summer leaned back, tapping one delicate fingertip against her bottom lip thoughtfully. She shrugged. "OK. Then we stay in."

Brian's head snapped back up. "What?"

"We stay in. You told me you cook, and you owe me one after that lasagna." That mischief was back in her eyes again and oh, the urge to kiss her slow and deep when she looked like that was so difficult to tame. "Just give me your address and I'll come by later. Say…seven?"

"Uh…" he faltered, "S-sure. Seven."

"Hell yeah, dinner party!" Koda said, punching the air and squeezing Brian around the shoulders. "Summer, you like paella? He makes a bitchin' paella."

TEN

P^{ING.}

Brian picked up his phone, looking at the text from Koda.

KODA: *Where the fuck is saffron?*

Brian typed back, *With the McCormick spices. The other brands never have any.*

There was a brief pause, in which he assumed his roommate was rummaging through the spice racks, and Brian turned back to the paella recipe. He was nervous. More nervous than he'd been in a long time, for many very valid reasons. The most pressing was that very, extremely, impossibly soon, Summer Landry would step over the threshold and be in his home. He and Koda had cleaned the house in a whirlwind of activity when Brian got home from work, emptying the trash, folding clothes, vacuuming, scrubbing the kitchen floor. He was surprised to find out Koda had also cleaned his room during his afternoon off, nearly unheard of, and the normally chaotic mess with only a clean path to his bed was now spotless. They didn't often get visitors, especially not human ones, and Brian could smell in Koda's sweat that he was anxious too. Koda wanted this to go well the same as he did, which Brian thought was sweet. Now it was just a question of making dinner delicious enough to impress Summer so much that she stayed for the rest of the evening.

Ping.

KODA: *I fuckin found it. Goddamn, this shit's expensive. Worth it, tho!* ☺

Awesome, now get back here so we can do the damn thing, Brian responded. *And don't forget the ice cream.*

KODA: *Aye, aye, Captain!*

Brian paced, going over the plan in his head. He had a little over an hour before Summer arrived. By then, the paella should be mere minutes from being done, provided Koda didn't get stuck in traffic. The kitchen table was freshly cleaned, devoid of discarded mail, and they'd all sit down to eat together. After dinner, Brian would surprise her with homemade blueberry crumble (already cooling on the counter) and vanilla ice cream, and they'd retire to the living room (vacuumed, tidy, with a peach scented candle lit to dispel any lingering doggy odors) to watch the movie he'd rented at Redbox on the way home. He'd agonized over which film to get, and finally settled on *The Lighthouse*, a thriller with Robert Pattinson and Willem Dafoe. Hopefully Summer hadn't seen it yet, and *hopefully* she scared easier during films than she did when confronted with a nine-foot werewolf. After the film, Koda had promised to feign exhaustion and leave them alone together, at which point Brian hoped to—

"Ride of the Valkyries" sounded from his left. Brian let out a frustrated groan, and answered, trying not to let the annoyance come through in his voice. He hadn't done anything. When would the Bureau leave him to fuck alone already? "Agus, what a pleasant surprise. What can I do for you this evening?"

"We found some new evidence," Agus said, sounding exhausted. "After a long and somewhat troublesome search, some footage was recovered I need to ask you about."

"Footage?" Brian's brows knit together. "But the parking garage doesn't have cameras."

"It doesn't. The poboy shop up the street does. They put in the cameras after a robbery six months ago, sounds like, and these things are state of the art. They captured an extremely clear fifteen seconds in which the lycanthrope in question emerges from the garage and runs towards the camera, then turns and disappears from view."

"OK..." Brian said slowly. "You know it isn't me. So what are you calling for?"

"I want you to take a look at a still we got. Texting it to you now."

His phone buzzed and Brian opened the text window, peering at the photo. A hulking wolf with haunted, hungry eyes was stepping off the curb, his face covered in gore. "Got it."

"It's a male," Agus went on. "Dark grey, black stripe down his back, white underbelly. Much darker than you, if you think I'm implying all lycans look alike. Approximately ten feet, three hundred or so pounds, beefy fucker."

"I'm still failing to see what this has to do with me."

"Well, yes, I suppose you would. We looked into it immediately, and absolutely no tracking chips pinged in that area during the full moon. So he's likely new, and he's definitely unregistered. Do you know anyone who might have showed up in the last month or two, who may be operating as an unregistered lycanthrope? Possibly with a connection to your workplace, or that building in general?"

Brian's blood went cold. "No. No, I don't know anyone like that."

"If you hear anything, would you keep us informed?"

"Absolutely." He thought of Summer. How new she was. How fascinated she'd been with his body, his shape, his scent. The thought of another wolf roaming nearby, finding her alone in the dark, her thinking at a distance that it was him...

"Thank you. You have a good night now. And Mr. Hersch?"

"Yes?"

"Be careful out there. A wolf like this, well, I can't emphasize enough how dangerous he'd be if confronted by another of his kind."

ELEVEN

S UMMER ARRIVED JUST on time. Which was good, because *Koda* had arrived just on time, saffron and ice cream in hand, so dinner was ready minutes after she got there. She exclaimed over Brian's cooking and laughed when he blushed. She asked a thousand questions of the two men at the table with her, about their lives, about their work, about their condition. She seemed to have no shame at all in asking about lycanthropes, had in fact listened to their answers with rapt attention, her eyes sparkling with curiosity. Brian couldn't remember the last time he'd felt so accepted by a human being, let alone a woman, and found himself utterly relaxed in her presence by the time he brought out dessert.

"Mmm," she'd moaned with her eyes closed, rolling the first bite around in her mouth with obvious pleasure. "Brian, this is *fantastic.*"

Koda shot him a lecherous look, which he'd tried to ignore, but he felt his blood pressure rise just the same—and definitely not in anger. Quite the opposite, in fact. After dessert, she accepted his invitation into the living room to watch *The Lighthouse,* and cuddled up next to him on the couch, her head nestled into the crook of his arm, her shoes discarded so she could tuck her feet under a cushion. The film was somewhat more sexual than Brian had intended, but she responded with enthusiasm just the same, holding his hand and squeezing it during the tense scenes.

As the credits rolled, Koda yawned loudly, and said, "Oh, man, I'm wiped. I think I'm gonna hit the hay. You two kids have fun. Nice to see you again, Summer."

They watched him make a beeline for the hallway and disappear without turning on the lights.

"He's not very good at being anything but obvious, is he?" Summer said softly, maddeningly close to his ear.

Brian chuckled. "No, he's not. But he's a really great wingman."

She chuckled, her breath tickling the hairs on his neck and making them stand up. "Great wingmen are hard to find."

"Yes, they are." And then he was looking into her eyes, seeing that desire etched across her face, and he swallowed. "Summer...I...don't know if we should..."

"Shh." She pressed a finger to his lips and he smelled sweet blueberries, vanilla, *her*. "I know. OK? I've been reading since the day I met you, figuring this thing out. I can't catch what you have through kissing, unless you bite me. You won't bite me, will you, Brian?"

The better to eat you with, my dear.

His voice sounded far away in his own ears. "I would never."

"Then I'm safe." She smiled, her eyes glittering in the half light. "As for the rest...we're just gonna have to be extra careful. Can you be *extra* careful with me?"

He could. He would be so careful he'd wear a full body hazmat suit to fuck her if that's what it took. "Since you met me? You mean you're not...you're not just interested in me because I'm a...a..."

"No. That was just a jumping-off point." She narrowed her eyes, looking sly. "That was my excuse to get to talk to you."

He smiled tentatively, hardly able to believe it. "So...even if I wasn't a wolf...?"

"Even if you weren't a wolf."

And then she was on him, straddling his lap and pulling him close, her tongue invading his mouth and tasting of sweet cream and heaven, her hands in his hair, tugging, grinding, pressing closer. He responded in kind, his hands everywhere at once, his body screaming for more, more touch, more taste, more *skin* as he gripped her ass with both hands and she moaned into his mouth. Forget what he had done last night with Patricia. It couldn't possibly compare to this. Forget the feeling of the fucking moon filling him, because Summer was the *sun*, and she was so hot for him he could smell it. She was heaven and this was it, they were finally here together and—

Koda cleared his throat from the doorway, rapping his knuckles lightly on the wall. Summer pulled off Brian, immediately returning to her spot on the couch and smoothing her clothes, and he nearly groaned with the loss. He turned to Koda, annoyed, but when he saw the expression on his friend's face, the annoyance melted away.

"Uh, I hate to interrupt you guys, but…" he faltered, his face pale, his eyes too wide and panicked for Brian's liking. "You should turn on Channel 7."

Brian fumbled for the remote, finally getting it, and flipped it to Channel 7 News. A pretty Hispanic anchorwoman in a bright blue blazer held a microphone.

"—earlier this evening. Witnesses say the deceased, Patricia Kelley, age thirty-two—"

A photograph of a smiling black woman proudly holding up a law degree came onto the screen. Brian and Koda exchanged a look of baffled dismay.

"—continued to be a pillar of the community despite her affliction. Sources say Kelley was on her way back from the library when the attack happened. It appears to be a lycan on lycan attack, the other lycanthrope fleeing the scene before he or she could be ID'd. Witnesses say—"

But Brian wasn't listening anymore. His ears rung, his pulse pounded. "Koda. Was that...?"

Koda sat down heavily in the doorway, his face in his hands. "Yeah. It was."

"Did you know her?" Summer asked gently, putting her hand over Brian's.

Know her? Course I knew her. I fucked her last night under the full moon and my spunk is still inside her and now they're gonna come looking for me because there's a connection. A real one, this time. He nodded, his face tingling and numb. "Yes, I did."

"Oh no, Brian, I'm so sor—"

Someone pounded on the front door.

TWELVE

THERE ARE LAWS against the discrimination of lycanthropes, that outline everything from the right to work, to due process. The powers that be like to say these laws are infallible, but they are not. They don't stop individual law enforcement officers from getting an extra kick in the ribs on a detained and shackled werewolf, and they certainly don't stop certain places from losing paperwork and making detainment take ages longer than it has to. So this part of the change had been with Brian also, as he found out the night they picked him up at his home for his connection to Patricia Kelley.

"When is Agent Agus coming?" He hollered through the bars at the knot of cops laughing and eating fried chicken. He hated that his mouth was watering, but he hadn't been fed in two days, had had nothing but metallic-tasting water since the paella with Summer. It seemed an eternity ago. "Agent Christian Agus, with the Bureau of—"

"Shut up, mutt," one of the officers shouted back. He was broad and gruff, bald with steely grey eyes that said they'd like it very much if Brian would get rowdy so he could use his special taser reserved for lycans. "He'll be here when we *say* he can be here. In the meantime, I invite you to enjoy the service and the scenery, but shut the fuck up while you do it."

Brian slid away from the bars and sank onto the bench. There were only a few other scraggly looking guys in holding, but they were in the other cell, far out of his reach, as per regulations. The one good thing was that he had this cell to himself, and could be alone with his racing heart. Two days. Two days he'd been here, and used his one phone call to get in touch with Agus, who said he was on his way. After forty-eight hours of waiting, Brian didn't think he'd ever come. He curled up facing the wall, hot tears that wouldn't fall no matter how hard he tried pricking his eyes. He dry sobbed his way into a light doze plagued by nightmares.

In it, he watched from outside himself as he got up and opened the door. The police yanked him out of his home and piled on top of him, smashing his face into the concrete so hard it bled as they cuffed him. Koda was yelling his head off at them, but they weren't listening, and the last thing Brian saw as they stuffed him into the car was Summer's horrified face. Her fists were clamped to her mouth and she was crying, saying his name over and over, but he couldn't hear over the sound of the sirens as the cops drove him away. And then it repeated itself. He went to the door, opened it, and…

"Mutt!" A sharp voice came from behind him, followed by the clang of a night stick against the metal bars. It was the same cop who had told him to shut up. Brian cringed. "The zookeeper is here. And lucky you, he's got a lawyer with him."

"Who?" Brian sat up, his head muzzy.

"Some guy named Aggie?"

"Agus." Brian was alert now and got up to walk toward the officer who was unlocking the cell. He stuck his wrists out (*be a good boy,* he thought) so that the second officer behind the first could put shackles on him. "You said he has a lawyer with him?

"Don't get too hopeful," the steely eyed cop growled. "You still might not get out of here alive. I've always wanted to put down a feral, and what was done to that girl? Let's just say someone was a bad dog." He leaned very close to Brian's face, so close he could smell olive salad from his lunch muffaletta on his breath. "And you behave on the way to the conference room, or zap-zap. Capiche?"

"Capiche."

Brian allowed himself to be shoved down the hall past the bullpen, his stomach in queasy knots. He needed now to show no outward signs of aggression, no emotions whatsoever. He kept his face a careful blank until he was led into the little room with the wall of one-way glass and saw Agus sitting with a harassed-looking man in a brown suit rifling through the papers in his open briefcase.

"Mr. Hersch," Agus said, his voice as neutral as could be. "This is Damon Kent, your lawyer."

Relief flooded Brian's system, and he all but collapsed into the chair across from them, sticking out his hand. "Nice to meet you, Mr. Kent."

"Pleasure," Kent said distractedly, ignoring the hand in favor of continuing to dig through papers and putting them in order, not even looking at Brian.

Agus waited until the officers shut the door behind them, then leaned in and whispered, "I paid them off to ensure no one is on the other side of that glass, but how long they'll uphold that bargain is anyone's guess. You're getting out today, Brian, that much is certain, but I need you to answer our questions quickly, thoroughly, and one hundred percent truthfully. Can we do that?"

"Absolutely," Brian agreed, nodding vigorously. He was thankful for Agus, for Kent, for having people, regular people, on his side today. He wondered wistfully what Summer was doing right now, if she was worried about him, if she cared.

"Excellent. Kent?"

Kent sat up straight and finally looked at Brian, his hazel eyes sharp and keen. "Mr. Hersch, you knew Ms. Kelley, correct?"

"Correct."

"What was the nature of your relationship?"

The question made his stomach do a flip. The taste of bile crept up the back of his throat and lingered there. "I just met her on the night of the full moon. There wasn't a relationship, really, but you could say we were acquaintances."

"Do you have unprotected sex with all your acquaintances?"

"No," Brian said, slightly offended. "It wasn't like that. She... we kinda just needed it. The full moon does things to lycans, and it was just a one-time thing."

"I'm well acquainted with what the full moon does to lycans, Mr. Hersch. That's why we're here at all. Had you spoken to Ms. Kelley since the full moon and your, erm, sexual escapade?"

"No."

"And Summer Landry, who is she?"

His heart sank to hear her name in Kent's mouth. "A friend from work."

"Just a friend?"

"Yes," he said, blushing mightily. "That's all we're allowed to be, right?"

"Yes, but that hasn't stopped others. Including, if I may be quite blunt, your roommate, Mr. Kodalis. So, one more time, is there anything going on with Summer Landry we should know about?"

He thought of her straddling him on the couch, her tongue exploring his mouth, and the taste of blueberries and vanilla. "No. Nothing."

"Alright." He scribbled something down. "Now, about Mr. Murdoch. Did you know Mr. Murdoch was going back into the office on the night of his murder?"

"No, I didn't."

"So you couldn't have made mention of it to anyone?"

212

"No."

"Did *he* make mention of it to anyone?"

"How would I know that?" Brian asked, spreading his hands. "If I didn't know he was going, I wouldn't know if he told anyone else either.

"That's true." More scribbling. Then he set his pen down and folded his hands on the table, his sharp eyes meeting Brian's. "Mr. Hersch, we find ourselves in a very delicate position. You, quite obviously, are not directly involved with either of these deaths. And yet, you are. You knew both victims, and that raises some suspicious questions about what exactly this unregistered lycanthrope is getting out of the deal."

Brian narrowed his eyes. "What are you saying?"

"I'm saying," Kent said quietly, his gaze never wavering, "that it seems someone has a vendetta against you. Can you think of anyone that may be angry and unhinged enough to do something like this, particularly to you?"

"No," Brian said immediately, but his empty stomach churned. "I told Agus before that I don't know anybody who even comes close to fitting the bill for something like this. As far as I know there are no other werewolves in the building, and I'd be able to smell them at the very least. I wish I could help more—God, do I wish—but I'm as in the dark as you are."

Kent gave him a calculating look for a moment, as if deciding whether or not this was the truth. Brian did his best to look as sincere as he was. Finally, Kent nodded and began collecting his papers, evidently done talking.

"You'll be free to go in no time," Agus said, then surprised Brian by reaching out and patting his hand, a stoic look on his craggy face. "But you're going to need to be very careful for a bit till we figure this out. And don't leave town. It'll look suspicious, and you'll end up right back here." He frowned. "Or worse."

THIRTEEN

WHEN BRIAN WAS released two hours later, Koda waiting for him in the lobby, long legs stretched out, feet crossed, hands tucked in his armpits, head leaned back against the concrete. Koda jumped up when he saw him, and when he hugged his roommate fiercely, Brian noticed the dark stubble all over his cheeks and chin.

"You look like shit," Koda said affectionately.

Brian gave a weak smile. "You don't look much better. Have you showered since I got picked up?"

"Can't shower if I slept here, can I?" Koda stuffed his hands in his pockets, his cheeks flushed. "I couldn't stay home. It was too quiet. So I came here and…waited."

"That was very sweet," Brian said, squeezing his friend's arm. "You really didn't have to do that."

"You'd have done it for me." Koda shrugged. "Besides, before the cops told her to go home, Summer made me promise to look out for you and keep her posted on what was going on."

Summer made him promise. Brian's heart swelled. "So you got her number?"

"Well, yeah, but it wasn't like *that.* All she wants to talk about is you. I told her you were getting released but she hasn't responded yet." He glanced behind him at the window with officers behind it. "Can we get your shit and go? This place brings back bad memories."

"Yeah. Let's blow this cop stand."

III. PROFESSIONAL MONSTER

His phone and belt—the only two things he'd had on him to confiscate when he got pulled from his living room and into this concrete hellhole—were returned to him, and he signed off on the last piece of release paperwork, still getting eyeballed by the big, bald cop. He and Koda at last went outside and Brian squinted in the mid-afternoon sunshine. Being stuck in lockup was disorienting, time moving at a snail's pace with no difference in the light, day or night, so he was actually surprised when Koda told him Agus had been there since this morning. Koda drove them home, careful to stay at exactly the speed limit lest the police find more reasons to harass the two lycanthropes inside. Brian's phone was at ten percent, but he saw he had a slew of texts from a number he didn't know. Most were from the night of his arrest:

9:57 p.m. *Hey it's me*

9:58 p.m. *Summer. It's Summer. Sorry. I made Koda give me your number. I hope that's OK.*

10:31 p.m. *I know you can't get these right now but I wanted to reassure you that I know you didn't do this. It's dumb you're even a suspect. I'm not going to abandon you.*

11:04 p.m. *How long is this supposed to take? It feels like it's been too long. Idk tho I've never had a boyfriend that went to jail lol*

11:04 p.m. *Or a werewolf boyfriend*

11:04 p.m. *Or a werewolf boyfriend who went to jail*

11:07 p.m. *Sorry for rambling. Koda says you're still in lockup and it might be a while. Maybe when you get out we can celebrate. Just the two of us ☺ ❤*

And then one from this morning:

6:50 a.m. *Koda said you get to go home today. Let me know when you get out ❤. The office is weird without you in it.*

Boyfriend? He thought, no longer worried about the last two days. *Boyfriend. She called me her boyfriend.*

"What are *you* smiling about?" Koda asked, making a right onto their street.

A giddy grin spread across Brian's face, all the turmoil of the last two days sloughing off him like an old lizard skin. "It appears I have a girlfriend."

"Far fucking *out!*" Koda exclaimed, smacking the wheel. "Hell yeah, you do. I could *feel it* in her texts that she wanted you bad, but in like, a romantic way. My *man!*"

Brian chuckled, leaning his head back and looking out at the sunshine as Koda pulled into the driveway and killed the engine. He practically floated into the house, uncaring of anything that wasn't Summer. He knew he *should* feel bad right now, but how could he when she used the word *boyfriend?* He whistled in the shower, washing the stink and grime of NOPD off of him.

I'll go see her today after work, he thought. *I'll take her for coffee, tell her all about jail, and she'll clutch her chest and sympathize with me, and we'll laugh, and I'll be her boyfriend. I'll tell her about what Kent said and she'll be shocked, worried, maybe want to take care of me. And I'll let her, yes, I'll let her pull me close and kiss it all away. Then we'll walk home, and I'll be such a good boyfriend that I offer to stay the night and keep her safe from the bad wolf out there.*

He bounded out of the shower and padded to his room where his phone was charging. He sent off a quick text, to the number he now had saved as *Summer*.

2:15 p.m. *Hey, just got home. Obviously not coming into work today, lol. You want to meet up after close and chat?*

For a moment, almost directly after, chat bubbles appeared beneath his text, then disappeared.

Ah well, he thought, *she's probably in meeting. I can wait. I'm patient as the trees. The better to wait for you, my dear.*

He got dressed, wincing as he pulled his shirt over his head, then rubbed at the bruise left behind by the poking of that asshole cop's night stick. They hadn't been kind to him there, not at all, but Agus and Kent had worked their magic, and now he was free, free to be with Summer as her *boyfriend* and free to fill the roaring void in his stomach. Fill it he did, eating two heaping helpings of leftover paella and gulping down ice cold Cherry Pepsi, mentally giving the finger to the cops who roughed him up and left him hanging. He burped, yawned, the exhaustion of the last two anxiety-ridden days finally catching up to him. His eyelids were heavy, his body sluggish after all the food. He checked his phone. No response yet.

I'll call her after work, he thought, *but for now, I think a nap is in order if I'm going to take her anywhere later.*

He trundled back to his room, waving to Koda, who was reclining on the couch eating the last chunks of blueberry crumble sprinkled over the remnants of the tub of vanilla, and collapsed into his bed. For a few hours, Brian knew no more, his sleep as heavy and dreamless as a Mardi Gras drunk.

When he awoke, it was dark outside. He frowned, squinting at the window, and checked his phone; 7 p.m. on the dot, with no text from Summer. A worm of worry began to nibble around the edges of his brain.

She gave up on you. She abandoned you. Because it's too much to love a monster, too much to ask. Being arrested was the last nail in the coffin.

But that couldn't be right. She said herself that this was not her plan, that she believed he had been falsely accused. She'd been eager to hear from him. So what had changed?

He called her phone. It rang six times, then went to voicemail.

"Hi, this is Summer Landry, leave your message at the beep."

He hung up.

Something's wrong. And hope springing eternal, on the heels of that: *Maybe she left her phone at work by accident.*

He hauled himself up and went to Koda's room, knocking.

"Enter."

Inside he found Koda hunched over with a pulled-apart keyboard in his lap, digging out broken wires and snipping them off. He didn't look up. "Hey man, you're awake."

"Koda, when did you hear from Summer last?"

Koda stopped what he was doing and looked up at Brian, his face serious, picking up on the worry coming off Brian in waves. "About eight this morning. Why?"

"Can I see what she said?"

"Sure." He felt around the bedclothes for his phone, found it under one of the myriad pillows there, and tossed it lightly into Brian's cupped hands. "Code is 122391. Have at it."

Thank Christ for his total disregard of boundaries, Brian thought, tapping in the code and pulling up the text app. Summer's texts were right at the top and Brian opened them, scanning the conversation for clues. At lot of them were inane, the expected replies in a conversation of two people worried about the same thing:

I hope they're treating him OK. I hate that this is happening to him at all.

Have you heard anything else?

When do you think he'll be out?

Keep me informed.

But the last text, the one that came in that morning, was much more concerning.

8:03 a.m. *I hope he gets in touch soon. I need to know everything that happened. Plus, today they fired Evan (that prick who called you guys "mongrels" the other day), and he's basically losing his mind.*

Brian's mouth went dry. He fished out his phone and pulled up Summer's number, hitting send and putting it to his ear with a shaking hand.

"Please pick up, please pick up," he muttered.

Koda was watching him closely and stood, coming closer. "Dude, what is it? What happened?"

Brian shook his head, listening to the ring and hoping that Summer would answer. But she didn't. On the fifth ring, someone *did* pick up, but it wasn't her. There was the sound of heavy breathing, but no voice.

"Evan," Brian said carefully, trying like hell to keep the panic out of his voice, "please let Summer go."

"Why should I?" Evan replied, his breathless voice full of malice. "This place terminated me like trash because of you. It only seems fair I terminate *her* because of you too."

"What happened, Evan?"

"What happened is the big boss didn't like that I was, to put it his way, 'creating a hostile work environment' by telling people here that it's fucking mongrels like you who make it unsafe." He chuckled darkly. "I showed *him* a hostile work environment."

Brian's blood went cold. "What did you do, Evan?"

"I didn't do *fuck all* but follow my instincts," he shouted, "the same as the fucking feral who did this to me!" He took a deep breath, and when he spoke again, his voice was calmer, more measured. "He snuck up on me, you know. Outside of my own home. He fucking *bit me*, the prick, and now I'm stuck being this way for the rest of my life." He let out a choked sob. "He was my fucking *neighbor*. I went to see what all the noise was about one night, and he leapt on me the moment I walked into his back yard. I had no idea he was a mutt till then. You scum should have to notify people when you move in, just like any other predatory trash."

"Please let Summer go. She didn't do anything to you." His voice was high now, too full of emotion. He took a deep breath, and said again, "Please."

"I'll let her go, sure. *After* you come down here." Evan's voice was low, dangerous, full of the promise of violence. "I want you to watch when I take everything away from you the same way your kind took my whole life away from me."

"Where are you?" And there was the resolve he'd needed. He would go wherever Evan was, confront him, win. He would save Summer or die doing it.

"I think it's only fair we get this done in the same place it started. Don't you?" And then the line went dead.

Brian took a shaky breath, then turned to Koda, who was putting on his shoes. "What are you doing?"

"I'm coming with you. That dickhead has Summer, and he's at C&B, obviously."

"Koda, it's too dangerous. I'm going alone."

"Like fuck you are." He stood, his face set and stony. "Two against one is better odds. And I didn't *ask*. I'm straight up telling you: I'm coming with you."

Brian's shoulders slumped, but he felt immense gratitude towards his friend, so willing to put himself in danger just to help. He felt words were inadequate to express his feelings, the mixture of fear, apprehension, and relief that he wouldn't have to do this alone, so he merely nodded, resolved.

"Excellent," Koda said. "Now let's get this fucker."

FOURTEEN

I T WAS DARK when they arrived at the building where C&B was housed, the light of the waning gibbous moon shining bright over the still streets. They parked a block away and crept toward the building in human form, not wanting to rouse suspicion from the people in the neighborhood (or Evan, wherever he might be hiding). The pavement was still baking up heat from the day, and they were both sweating by the time they reached the high-rise. They decided to take the stairs in favor of the elevator, which was noisy and old, so as not to announce their arrival to their foe before they were ready to confront him. Brian led the way, with Koda at the rear, their ears on high alert for any sound that may come from any direction, their bodies quivering with anticipation of extreme violence.

In the car, they'd come up with a plan. They'd sneak up to the sixth floor and split up. Brian would enter from the big glass doors in the front of the office, and Koda would use the maintenance entrance at the back that was near the management offices. Evan would expect Brian to come alone, and be surprised by the entrance of Koda, who would come up from behind and take him down before he could do any damage to Summer.

They hoped.

And if he hadn't hurt her already, simply out of spite.

If he's somewhere near the middle of the office, it'll work, Brian thought, his nerves jangling as he mounted the fourth floor landing. *If he's hiding in the back or—God fucking forbid— in the hallway instead of the office itself, we're absolutely boned.*

But they did have hope. Even if they couldn't get the drop on Evan, the two of them were more experienced at being lycanthropes, which was good. It had taken Brian months to be coordinated in his other form, and he prayed the same was true for Evan. The messy business of being a werewolf was difficult to control at the best of times, and Evan had had no tutor to help him along the way. Then again, unbridled rage could lend a werewolf some distinct advantages, not the least of which was losing control of themselves and becoming a tsunami of unmitigated destruction.

As they tiptoed up the last flight of stairs to Floor Six, Brian glanced back at Koda, wordlessly asking with his eyebrows, *Are you ready?*

Koda nodded, and Brian pushed the creaking metal door open an inch. No one stood beyond the panel of glass doors at the entrance to C&B. He pushed the door open another inch and saw there, just in front of the doors, a splash of dark red blood. He opened it further and revealed the decimated body of one of the cleaning crew, her grey uniform and white apron splattered with crimson, face down in a pile of cleaning supplies. Her right arm had been torn off completely, and rested against the far wall, waving a morbid hello to the two men crouched in the stairwell. Her back was a shredded mass of meat, bone, and gristle. The smell of copper and death hung in the air, thick and cloying. Brian moved to allow Koda a glance out. Koda made a grimace of disgust, his nose wrinkling from the heavy smell of human suffering.

Brian pointed to the front doors, to himself, to Koda, to the back. *I'm going in, you get into position.*

Koda nodded again, but looked pale now. Brian pushed the door open as wide as he dared, Koda slipping under his arm to slink past and down the hallway to the left, sticking to the wall.

When he was out of sight, Brian let the door fall shut behind him with a soft bang. He had to let Evan know he was here, much as he wished he didn't. If Evan was surprised, there was no telling what he'd do. He stepped gingerly over the body of the cleaning lady, careful not to get blood on his shoes as he went towards the big glass doors. They pulled open silently, as always, and then he was inside C&B, inside Evan's den of brutality.

He sniffed the air, let the mingled scents of humans, acrid cleaning products, the tangy scent of garbage from the break room swirl together in his nares, seeking out a particular smell. He heard from his left a small shift of fabric, and then he smelled them: Evan. Summer. Bloodshed. A *lot* of bloodshed. His heart gave a fearful lurch, and he followed the scent, crouched low behind the cubicle dividers, staying out of sight.

"You know damn well that I know you're here." Evan's brutish voice sailed over the dividers, ever the jeering fuckface. "I knew you were stupid, but I didn't think you were *that* stupid, to think you'd sneak up on me."

Brian didn't stand, but crept forward a few more inches. Now he could see that in the pathway between the cubicles there was more carnage, specifically the top half of his manager's head. Mr. Weeks was most likely the person who delivered the news to Evan that he was fired, and he had paid dearly for it. One of his eyes was rolled back in his head, but the other was fixed on Brian, mutely accusing. Brian made an internal apology to him, a man who had never said a cross word to him in all his years with the firm, and steeled himself before standing. As he rose, he saw two more bodies on the ground just in front of Weeks, also spectacularly, gruesomely dismembered, so torn apart that he couldn't even begin to discern who they were. One had on low pumps, so was likely a woman, and that was as good as he could do. The wreckage was just too much. His heart gave a sickened lurch.

Be brave, he thought as he took the three steps that would put him in clear view of his aggressor. *Don't do it for yourself. Do it for Koda. Do it for her.*

He came around the corner to a harrowing scene. The rest of Mr. Weeks and the two unidentifiable office workers were strewn about the office, organs and limbs festooned the cubicles like particularly real-looking Halloween decor, the stench of ripped bowels and splattered blood heavy in the air. Evan stood towards the end of the row where the room opened up into the gathering space, where they put the Christmas tree every year and Paul Murdoch doled out White Elephant gifts. Evan was naked, covered head to toe in gore, flecks of meat and bone stuck to his face, neck, and hands like horrible jewelry. His hair stuck up in wild tufts in the places where it wasn't flattened to his skull by rivulets of blood.

He's been rolling in it, Brian thought, hearing his own pulse in his ears.

But the worst part, the *absolute worst* part, was that Evan was smiling. His teeth were the sharp teeth of the wolf, too big for his still human-shaped mouth, and he grinned an unnaturally enormous grin as he waggled his sticky fingers together. His eyes were bright yellow pools of madness, his face halfway wolfish, his body misshapen. He was only half turned, his body at war with itself as to what it wanted to be. Soon one side would win again, and Brian thought he knew which side it would be. Evan was having too much *fun* to give up and go quietly back to being a man.

"Where's Summer?" Brian said in a voice that sounded stronger than it felt. *And where's Koda?*

Evan barked a laugh. "Worried about your whore?"

"She's not a whore. Where is she?"

"We'll get to that." Evan's voice was businesslike now, a young agent giving a presentation on his newest business model. "First we're gonna talk about you and me, and how things are gonna go tonight. Why don't you have a seat?"

"I'd prefer not to."

He shrugged. "Suit yourself. But you're gonna goddamn well hear what I have to say." He stared at Brian, unblinking, his eyes full of hate as he spoke. His voice was unnervingly calm. "Now, I don't have to tell you, I absolutely *detest* lycanthropes. You mutts get treated like you're a special class all the time, without any due cause. Guys like me get passed up on promotions, jobs, housing, because of you fucking mongrels. But you weren't satisfied with all that, were you? Oh no. You had to start taking our *women* too. The thought of any human woman *willingly* giving herself to an animal like you just…ugh…it absolutely disgusts me; I can't emphasize enough how much. And none of you have the decency to even be *sorry*. You call men like *me* evil for not playing your stupid game, and we have to walk on eggshells, or we lose everything. To *you*."

While he talked, Brian scented the air, seeking Summer's smell of clean, flowers, salt. It was almost impossible to get beyond the overwhelming smell of death.

"You paying attention, mutt?" Evan snapped his fingers.

Brian scowled at him. "Yeah. You hate werewolves."

"I sure do." Evan grinned, human meat lodged in his teeth. "Did she tell you I asked her out on a date her second week here?"

Brian startled. "Summer?"

"Who the fuck else?"

Brian chuffed out laughter. "It never came up."

"Figures," Evan growled, shaking his head.

"Is that what this is about?" Brian asked incredulously. "Summer wouldn't go on a *date* with you?"

"I'm getting to what it's about, you mangy mongrel, so shut your trap." He snapped back. "Where was I? Oh, yeah. Anyway..."

"Then I was attacked, see. I became the very thing I hate. I scrubbed as hard as I could, considered chopping my own arm off *Evil Dead*-style to get the poison spit of that disgusting monster out of me, but it was no use. The deed was done. I tried to kill myself, you know." He paused, as if waiting for Brian to empathize with him, but when he got nothing but a stony stare, he moved on. "It didn't work. I tried *six fucking times*. Can you believe that shit? But they don't sell silver bullets to citizens, because they feel guys like me would take matters into our own hands and rid the world of your plague. And we would, because we're human, and you're not. You're less than human. You're a beast, and God gave man dominion over the beasts of the Earth."

Brian rolled his eyes. "Cute. But now you're one of us. You're *also* less than human, by that token. So, what is the point of all this?"

"Ahh, there's the rub," Evan said, his voice menacing and deeply filled with contempt. "I decided, very recently, what I was going to do with my newfound affliction. If you can't beat them, tear them apart, right?" His grin was impossibly wide, his face shifting, becoming longer. "I'm gonna take as many of you motherfuckers down as I can. The cops or your shitting Bureau can't find me. I'm untagged. And I'm gonna start with you, your bitch, and all your mutt friends. That loudmouth one will be especially fun, I think."

And icy dump of terror filled Brian's stomach. "But you killed Paul. He wasn't even one of us."

"I *am* sorry about that," Evan replied, real sorrow in his voice. "But I could smell *you* on him, and it drove me...temporarily insane. That and the fucking moon. I'd never been a wolf before, you understand. After *that* little fiasco, I worked to control it, and now look at me! I'm doing this without the help of the moon! Look ma, no hands!" He raised his blood slicked hands and let out a shrill, glassy laugh that gave Brian shivers. Then he dropped his hands and heaved a sigh. "Anywho. Not long after, I came upon that bitch you fucked—at the grocery store of all places—and wouldn't you know it? That detestable slut hadn't showered you off her yet. She *reeked* of you, Brian, so away *she* went. I swear you bastards are more grotesque with every new thing I learn. And the cleaning lady, plus our friends here?" He kicked the leg of the corpse in pieces around them. "Collateral damage. Couldn't be helped. At least I made sure they died instead of waking up a walking abomination with *rights*."

Movement caught Brian's eye. He glanced behind Evan and saw Koda in his wolf form, a swirl of darkness melting into the gloom of the offices beyond. He tucked himself into the middle doorway and held a finger to his lips—*shhh*—before flattening himself to the ground and disappearing from view.

Brian looked back at Evan, who was picking his teeth with a shard of bone, looking content as anything to be dressed only in blood.

"Evan," Brian said, his tone as measured as he could make it, putting his hands up in what he hoped looked like a gesture of peace, "there doesn't have to be any more violence today. Whatever it is you think I've done to you, we can work something out. Nobody else has to die."

"Glad you brought that up. I have a proposition for you." Evan pointed a gnarled, claw-tipped finger at him. "Stay right where you are. If you move, this all goes south. Got it?"

Brian nodded, rooted to the spot. Satisfied he would go nowhere in his absence, Evan disappeared behind the cubicle wall. Brian heard the supply closet door open, a muffled scream, and then the rolling sound of a wheeled office chair. Suddenly, Summer was in view, seemingly unharmed, but mouth stuffed with socks taped in place, arms duct taped to the back of the chair, and clothes splattered with blood. Brian hoped none of it was hers. She looked at him with pleading, helpless, questioning eyes brimming with fear.

"My proposal," Evan said, putting a slowly shifting, bloody paw on her blonde head, "is simple. You for her."

Brian swallowed hard, heard a click in his throat. "I don't understand."

Evan gave him a withering look. "Yes you do. I want you, not this foul bitch who stinks of dogfucking. If you agree to let me rip you to shreds with no fighting—something I'd like very much—I'll let her go. She gets to live. If you *don't* agree…well. Let's just say that what I did to these guys on the floor…and walls…and ceiling will look like a mercy by comparison."

He's lying. He's not going to let her go, no matter what I choose. Brian knew this as well as he knew his own name, but also knew he had to feign ignorance, if only for Summer's sake. First order of business was to get her up out of that chair. Maybe then she could run. Maybe then Koda could grab her and get out while he distracted Evan with dying. He thought that maybe, just maybe, his death could be worth it to the two most important people in his life.

"OK," he said, his voice shaking. "I agree."

Summer made a strangled sound of disapproval, yanking herself side to side in her chair, but Evan was grinning. He leaned down, his mouth pressing against her ear as she struggled to get away and said, "You hear that? Your boyfriend is a loyal little lap doggy. Seems lycan trash *does* have feelings beyond fighting and fucking." He breathed in, taking in the scent of her hair.

"I wouldn't have minded making you my little puppy bitch, though. We could have fucked on a pile of bones, like he and Patricia did." He put out his tongue and drug it slowly, wetly up the side of her face, keeping her head still with one twisted hand. "You really are delicious. Too delicious to let you die before I get a taste."

"Stop that," Brian said, anger finally overtopping his other emotions when he watched that malevolent freak lick Summer's face with his swollen, purple tongue. "Don't talk to her like that."

"Wassamatta? Little Rover doesn't like it when other doggies touch his toys?" Evan jeered. But he stopped, stood, took a step away from Summer, wiping drool off his chin.

"She isn't a toy. I agreed to your terms. Now let her go," Brian commanded, feeling the change coming on, his muscles growing, fur sprouting, feeling his clothes rip as he grew, tearing away the pieces with his claws until he stood, primed and ready for a fight. "You said you want me? You've got me. Let her go."

Evan, the insane grin still plastered on his rapidly shifting face, took a step forward as his knees popped backwards in their sockets. "*After.* I want her to *see* how weak you are, so that she never makes such a stupid choice again."

Brian crouched, tense, waiting. "I said *now.*"

"And I said *no!*" Evan roared, his monstrous voice filling the space between them, and flecks of bloody spittle flying with every word. "I am *done* with being told what to do by subhuman dipshits like you! I'm done cowering! Now I can do whatever I want and if I have to go down, *I'm taking all of you ratfucks with me!*"

A metal scream bounced off the walls as Evan snatched up one of the cubicle dividers with a snarl and chucked it at Brian's head. Brian deflected it deftly, but it crashed into one of the windows to the outside world hard enough to spiderweb the glass. Evan howled in rage, and Brian leaped at him, taking him out at the knees, but Evan was fast, too fast for a new werewolf, and soon they were locked in battle, rolling, biting, clawing one another, knocking over dividers, desks, ceiling fixtures as they pummeled one another ruthlessly. Summer scrabbled backwards when the two of them landed at her feet hard enough to shake the floor. Evan pinned Brian beneath him with one gigantic forearm, cutting off his windpipe and leaving him clawing to get away.

"You said you wouldn't fight!" Evan screamed, his eyes wide and ferocious and utterly deranged. *"You're supposed to let me win! You went back on the deal! You know what happens* now, *you stupid fuck?"*

Evan turned his head and lunged towards Summer's face. Brian's heart seemed to stop, and all time slowed as he watched those jaws open wide, the hairy black lips pulling back from pink gums and razor-sharp fangs, watched Summer cringe backwards in a futile attempt to shield herself from the attack.

I'm going to watch her die. I'm going to watch her die, and I can't stop it.

He pushed upward as hard as he could, and Evan's muzzle snapped closed. Summer shrieked, and that was fine, that was good, because that meant she wasn't dead, her head hadn't been crushed by Evan's gaping maw. Then all at once Brian's windpipe was free, Evan's weight lifting off him as Koda barreled in from the left. He shoved Evan clean across the room, biting down on the back of his shoulder, and Evan yowled in pain, twisting his head to try and bite back. The momentum of Koda's leap sent them sprawling across the floor ten feet from where Brian lay gasping, with Koda landing on top, driving the wind from Evan's lungs in a whoosh.

Koda reared back, ripped, tore, then spat a chunk of Evan's flesh directly into his upturned face. "*That's* what fucking happens now, you furry cunt."

Evan was screaming and writhing, trying desperately to get out from beneath Koda, his back awash in his own blood and matted fur. Koda was not only more experienced, but bigger and stronger, and he held the screeching lycan down, pinning the wounded arm up against his back. Brian flipped himself over and got into a crouch in front of Summer, his muscles singing in agony more from the pummeling he'd taken than the bites he'd received.

He reached up and yanked the tape off Summer's mouth. She let out a yelp, but said in a rush, "Oh thank God, thank god you're both here and you're OK, I'm sorry, I didn't know what to do, I'm so sorry, I don't know how I let this happen, I'm sorry, how did I not know that—"

"Shh, it's OK," Brian said gently. "Are you hurt?"

"A...a little..." she replied, her voice quavering and uncertain. "Brian, when he snapped at me, I think he—"

A roar from the right cut her off, and they both turned to see Koda on his back, evidently overturned by Evan despite his superior strength. Then Evan was on his feet, pouncing at Summer and Brian, incoherent sounds of fury emanating from his throat. But Koda was as fast a thinker as he was a doer, and he sat up, grabbing Evan's tail and yanking back, turning the maniacal wolf's attention back to him. Evan screamed and whirled on Koda, his claws coming up to slash, rip, tear at the face of the one stopping him from fulfilling his bloody desires.

"Get her out!" He yelled before Evan fell upon him once more. "Get her out and *run!*"

Evan landed on Koda with all four paws, driving the wind out of him, but it didn't stop Koda slinging a roundhouse punch into the side of Evan's slavering face, knocking his jaw to the side with a loud *crunch*.

Gotta move fast. He won't be distracted forever. Brian spun Summer's chair around so fast, her head snapped sideways. "Sorry."

"Don't apologize, just get me the fuck out of here." She shot a nervous glance over her shoulder at the two wolves locked together in a murderous ball of fur, claws, and fangs.

"Yes ma'am." He slashed the tape with his claws and wrenched it loose, taking care to be more gentle with the bonds that held her wrists. Then he turned her again—gently this time—and nicked the duct tape around her ankles. Koda and Evan were still at it, ripping, clawing, kicking, biting, and rolling this way and that through the office, utterly destroying anything and everything in their path. Keys from keyboards fell like rain and shredded paperwork drifted down like a heavy snowfall, as though the office itself couldn't figure out what season it was. Blood and insults flew from the roiling knot of wolfdom.

Brian ushered Summer away, to the service entrance Koda had used to enter. "You have to go. Right now."

"You're not coming with me." It wasn't a question. He could tell from the look on her face that she knew he'd never leave his friend, and that if Koda failed to kill him, Brian would have to, because men like Evan never stop until they're satisfied.

"We'll catch up to you. Stay safe." He pushed her out the door and closed it behind her without another word. If he was going to die, he would rather not give a heartfelt speech before he did it. The thought was too painful. He bounded back to where Koda and Evan were still fighting, snarling, wrecking the office with wild abandon.

Their hands were locked together, each one trying to force the other backwards. Evan's back was to Brian, and he was screaming to Koda's face, *"You should have just let me kill him, you mangy fuck!"*

Koda didn't take his eyes off Evan, his face contorted in rage and the effort of keeping his place. *"You're gonna have to kill me first, you murdering dickhead!"*

Brian moved as fast as he could, plowing his way through the wreckage, but Koda's feet were slipping, his toes digging for purchase in the sliding heap of broken furniture and computer parts beneath him. Brian got to them and dug three fingers into Evan's wound, pressed his claws in with a wet squelch. Evan howled, but he was undeterred in his purpose, kicking back into Brian's stomach, winding him. Brian doubled over gasping, and Evan brought himself in, toward Koda, blood pouring down his back in rivulets as he pushed his shoulder into Koda hard, hauling him onto his shoulders. Koda struggled mightily, his jaws snapping and limbs flailing for purchase, but it was too late. With a mighty bellow that filled the room, Evan heaved backwards, then tossed Koda clear across the room, towards the shattered window.

"No!" Brian wheezed, helplessly watching as his friend sailed full force into the spiderweb of broken glass. The crash was loud, louder even than Evan's roar of triumph, and then was a split second where Brian saw Koda's expression of shock and dismay before he fell out of sight without so much as a scream.

Wind filled the room, blowing papers everywhere, churning through the office as Evan turned, grinning, his fur ruffled and face a network of scratches. He pointed one long finger at Brian and said over the gale, "After that sucker-punching shit stain, *you* won't be a problem." He took a menacing step forward, and Brian took one backwards. "And then? I'm gonna hunt her down and eat your bitch whole."

The better to eat you with, my dear.

Brian's face was numb with fury and shock, his muscles bunching, ready to spring if Evan took another step forward. "I'm going to tear you apart, you weak-willed, murdering son of a bitch."

"Weak? Me?" Evan laughed. The sound was like nails drug down a chalk board to Brian's ears, stoking the flames of hatred that burned bright in his chest. "I was stronger than your sneaky little mutt friend. And I *bet* you'll be easier to take down than him. Because *you're* the weak one. *You* lose control any time you see a full moon. Me? I'm a fast fucking learner, and I have more control than you'll ever have. I'm just *superior* to you in every way, Brian, Brian, I ain't lyin'. Tear me apart? I'd like to see you try."

"Come on, then," Brian growled, his body tingling with a need to kill, to destroy, to become savage and lost to that savagery. "Let's see what you're made of, fuckbag."

Evan's tongue lolled out, his fangs exposed in a half-snarl, half-jeering grin. "If you insist."

Evan leaped forward, claws outstretched, fangs bared, ready to rend Brian limb from limb. Brian leapt a half second later, coming in low, hoping to land a shoulder to his gut.

He killed Paul, Patricia, Koda, wants to eat Summer, wants to kill me, kill him, kill him, KILL HIM, YOU CANNOT LET HIM LIVE.

They locked together, tooth and claw, blood and bone, rage against homicidal rage. Evan bit the juncture of his neck and shoulder, shaking his head, and Brian wailed, shoving his hand under Evan's throat and digging his knuckles into his suprasternal notch. Evan gagged and let go, and Brian grabbed his ears in one giant paw, yanking backwards hard, then punched him in his throat. Evan wrenched out of his grasp, gasping, and ran for the doors.

"I'm going to kill her!" He shouted over shoulder. "I'm going to fucking make you *watch!*"

"*Coward!*" Brian called after him, scrambling to catch him, but Evan was fast, too fast, and had a lead on him.

Evan reached the glass doors, ripping them off their hinges and hurling them at Brian. He felt the wind of them whistle over his head.

Then the shot rang out. It came from the hallway by the elevator, a loud, ringing *pop* that hurt Brian's ears. Evan's head rocked backwards, his skull exploding outwards in a spray of blood, brain, and bone. He staggered backwards a few steps. Reached a hand up to his forehead, slowly, slowly, as if moving underwater, touched, came away with blood on his fingertips. It took Brian a moment to clock what it was that had happened, it happened so out of the blue. Then Evan turned to Brian, and Brian saw the entry wound, a small, dark circle through his left eye socket, his eye a well a of blood. Evan held out his fingertips, that were rapidly melting back to a human shape. He took one step towards Brian. Another. He said only one word as he stood on shaky legs, alive, somehow still alive, the madness in his eyes replaced by a dim surprise. "Look."

And then his knees buckled out from underneath him. He fell in a heap on the floor, and was still. Brian stepped tentatively over to him, toed his arm. No movement.

"Looks like we got here just in time," Agus said from the doorway.

Brian looked up and saw him standing there with his gun still smoking, Summer by his side. He could have wept with relief. But there was no time for that now. He opted instead to walk forward, and pull Agus into an embrace, his limbs quaking with relief. "Thank you."

"No need to thank me," Agus said, pulling back and dusting fur off his jacket. But he was smiling when he said it. "This little lady was the one who found me downstairs and told me where to go. She was very brave to come back up here after all this."

Brian gave Summer a grateful look, squeezing her hand. He turned back to Agus. "How did you know to come?"

"We've been keeping a close eye on you since the attacks started," Agus said, holstering his weapon, "so when both your chip and Mr. Kodalis' pinged here, we knew—"

"Koda!" Brian exclaimed and ran to the busted-out window through which his friend had fallen.

Don't be dead, don't be dead, don't be dead, he prayed as he leaned out, afraid he might see a red splatter where Koda had landed, and nothing more.

Instead, he saw a small group of agents hustling back and forth in a busy knot, tending to Koda, who was sitting bareass on the concrete with his leg in a splint, swearing mightily at them. He looked more or less human now—*the better to tend your wounds, my dear*—and was waving off an agent who kept trying to touch a flap of forehead that hung over his eye.

"You made it!" Brian called down, a joyous relief flooding him.

Koda looked up, squinting, pushing an agent with a flashlight away. "Get the fuck outta my face and quit blinding me, I gotta talk to my dude. Hey man, *you* made it!"

Brian smiled. "Barely."

"That *sucked!*" Koda replied, but he sounded in good spirits. "Could you bring me my pants? The concrete is a pain in my balls."

FIFTEEN

"THERE WE GO. All patched up." The nurse with bright orange hair whose nametag read "Katie M." said to Summer as she delicately placed one last butterfly stitch on her face. "How's your pain?"

"There isn't any," Summer said, casting her eyes to Brian, who laid in the next bed over, watching anxiously. "Maybe ask him, though. Some of those bites were nasty."

Nurse Katie nodded and turned to Brian. "How about you? A Dilaudid for the road?"

"Yes please," Brian replied. He decided, wisely, to stay silent until the nurse had gathered her wound care supplies and was out of earshot. Agus had asked him to stay mum about what had happened until he could get his lawyer friend back on the phone, so Brian listened intently, waiting to speak with Summer until Katie was out of earshot. Satisfied, he leaned closer and whispered, "Are you sure you're OK?"

"I'm fine, really," Summer said back, reaching up to gently touch the row of stitches on her cheek. "I don't think these will even scar."

"That's not what I'm worried about," Brian said. "Those aren't dog bites you got. You know that now you're…well, you're gonna be…"

Summer smiled. "I know. It means we aren't going to have to sneak around anymore."

"But—"

"Listen." Summer held up a hand to silence his protest. "I'm OK with it. It really isn't a big deal to me at all. You protected me. You stopped Evan from *killing* me, at your own peril. I'm not gonna nitpick that just because you couldn't stop him from changing my life. It was already changed when I met you. Besides," she sat up, adjusting her shirt, "I think I'll be a pretty cute werewolf, don't you?"

Brian stared at her, confounded by her acceptance, her willingness to change her whole life around, forever, for him, of all people. His body felt wrecked, a mass of salted wounds and deep bruises, but for her, it was worth it. He smiled at her, this amazing woman he was lucky to call his friend, and said, "Not just cute. Terrifying in your beauty."

"Oh, shut up, you." She blushed, but now her smile widened to a grin fit to split.

Brian sat back, musing. Their story was indeed that they'd been attacked by an unregistered werewolf, but Agus had given strict instructions not to mention Evan by name, or that they'd been at C&B. The Bureau agent reasoned, perhaps very astutely, that the news getting ahold of the story of an unregistered feral lycanthrope attacking those he worked with—one being another lycan—would cause a degree of panic and set other lycans up for some very specific discrimination in their own places of business. The public at large would not see this as the isolated incident that it was, and would begin painting lycanthropes as territorial terrorists that viewed human life as collateral damage in their war games. Brian thought that *might* be a tad overblown, but agreed it was better safe than sorry. The hospital accepted their story—that they were attacked as a group walking home from work—and Agus had left them in the hands of the emergency team, leaving them to go organize a deep clean and restoration for C&B.

Nurse Katie came back, needle in hand. "I've got a present for you."

"Is it drugs?" Brian asked hopefully, pushing himself carefully into a sitting position, his nerve endings screaming bloody murder.

"Yes! But also," she pulled paperwork from behind her back with a flourish. "Your discharge papers. Once I stick you, you can go down the hall and see your friend in Room Three." She smirked. "He's been a real treat, let me tell you. But a very good boy when we set his leg."

Brian took the paperwork, chuckling. "I bet."

"You two gonna be OK?" Katie asked, narrowing her eyes. "I've been a nurse for twelve years. I'll know if you're lying."

"Werewolves are fast healers," Brian retorted, nodding his head toward the deep gouge in his arm she'd bandaged earlier. "By tomorrow, that'll be almost gone."

"Oh, I know," she said, winking and turning on her heel, presumably to go terrorize someone else with cryptic sentences.

Brian stood carefully, wincing at the pain in his ribs where Evan had kicked him. He wobbled only once, then toddled over to Summer and offered his arm. She took it, and they went in search of Koda.

They heard him before they saw him. "Stop poking me, damn it, I'm *fine*. Haven't you medical dicks ever treated a werewolf before? Jesus."

They rounded the corner and came upon Room Three, its doors flung wide and curtains open, inside of which Koda was surrounded by three doctors each trying to examine his rapidly knitting leg. The bone had already set, and now it was just a deeply bruised area. He was swiping at them half-heartedly when they came close, obviously high on painkillers.

"Bri!" He exclaimed, grinning a doped-up grin, his face a mass of cuts and contusions. "You're a sight for sore ass! Can you *please* tell these *lovely morons* to stop gawping at me like this is the ten-dollar freak show and let me eat my shitty hospital food in peace?"

"OK, guys," Brian said to the doctors, "I think it's time to stop baiting the wolf for a few minutes, so I can talk to him privately. Is that possible?"

The doctors exchanged forlorn glances, but wordlessly filed out. Brian shut the door behind them, pulling the curtains closed so they'd stop gazing in. He took the chair closest to Koda, Summer taking the other. She put her hand in Brian's, and he warmed to the familiar gesture. He put his free hand on Koda's arm—the one not hooked up to an IV—and squeezed. "How you holding up, buddy?"

"I've been worse," Koda grumbled, "but not much. So far, they've given me enough morphine to kill a horse, as much food as I want—even though it sucks compared to yours—and that nurse Katie has proven herself to be a tidy piece."

"Koda," Brian groaned, "you know the Bureau says not to—"

"First of all, you're one to talk," Koda said, his voice slurred and muzzy. "Second, Katie is already one of us. It's strictly legal that I got her number and made out with her about ten minutes ago when she came to check on me."

"You're high."

"As a giraffe pussy, but that doesn't stop it being an accurate rendition of events."

Brian laughed. He couldn't help it. All this death, all this horror, and his friend still maintained his raucous sense of humor. *Thank goodness for small miracles.*

"You know," Summer said quietly, "on the next full moon… I would…like to meet Katie. Maybe we can all hang out? Like a kind of…full moon double date?"

Koda's face went slack in surprise. "Wait, what? You're…? No kidding?"

Summer smiled. "No kidding."

"Well, *alright!*" Koda pumped the air with his fist, winced, then decided on a less exuberant fist bump with Summer. "Welcome to the fold, my girl. You should come to the meetings." He turned to Brian, his face serious. "I promise to keep the welcome mat firmly tucked away."

Brian burst out laughing. Despite all that had happened, things just felt too good, too *right* not to.

"Um, honey?" Summer whispered, "what is he talking about?"

"Don't worry," Brian replied, kissing her gently and patting her cheek. "I'll roll it out for you myself when we get home."

IV.
PRECIOUS CARGO

He thrusts his fists against the post
And still insists he sees the ghost

– Stephen King, *IT*

ONE

1983

"**M**OM, STOP FEEDING him cake," Elise Cunningham, Milo's mother, said, hands on her hips.

"Make me," replied Astrid Schulze, the formidable matriarch of their family. When she leaned in to gently pinch Milo's cheek, her long grey braid swished out from behind her, plopping onto the countertop. She set the second piece of rich chocolate cake in front of him with a smile. "How else would I guarantee he stay so sweet?"

Elise rolled her eyes. "He's not a baby anymore. He needs nutrition beyond cookies, cake, and candy bars."

"You survived just fine," Astrid retorted. "Though maybe I miscalculated by feeding you all those sour balls."

The two women looked hard at each other for a second, before dissolving into giggles and hugging one another. Milo swung his feet, his mouth already full of Astrid's famous German chocolate cake, content to be the small, placid valley between these two mountainous women. They weren't *really* arguing anyway. *His* mom knew better than to argue with *her* mom. Everybody did.

"Do you promise to feed him a healthy dinner at least?" Elise sighed, slinging what Milo thought of as her dress-up purse over her shoulder. His mom was very dressed up tonight, wearing a sparkly black dress with spaghetti straps, heels higher than he'd ever seen her wear before, glittering earrings, and—most surprising of all, it was so rare to see—makeup. Tonight was an important evening for his father, something to do with his "business future," according to his mother, and she'd put quite a lot of effort into her appearance. Milo thought she looked beautiful, had told her so a thousand times on the ride over.

Astrid patted her daughter's bare shoulder. "I'm making baked salmon with a side of ratatouille. Loaded down with vegetables, that dish, and salmon is chock-full of protein. Milo will eat every bite of his portion no matter *how* much cake I give him, won't you Milo?"

They looked to him, his chocolate-smeared mouth and cheeks stuffed like a squirrel hoarding nuts. He nodded his assent, unable to get words out around the sticky confection.

"You see?" Astrid said, crossing over to hug him. "Such a good boy. And if he eats his dinner like he says he will, perhaps another slice of cake."

"Mom—"

"Kidding." Astrid raised her hands in defeat. "You can't blame Nana for trying, though. It's my job to overindulge my only grandchild."

Elise fiddled with her earrings, a nervous habit of hers that Milo's dad, Greg, thought was cute. "And you're *sure* overnight isn't too much for you? We can leave early if we need to."

"What am I, an invalid? It's not too much. You and Gregory have a good time tonight, Leesie. I've got this grandma thing in the bag."

"I believe you." Elise visibly relaxed. She looked at her watch. "Greg should be back any second. Milo?"

"Yes, Mama?" He said thickly, reaching for his glass of milk.

"You be good for Nana while we're gone."

"I will be."

"And absolutely no touching any of her collection stuff, OK? That stuff is strictly off-limits."

"I won't."

"Such a good boy," she said, sounding every bit like her mom. She walked over to him, heels clacking on the tile. Milo loved that sound and wished she'd wear those heels more often, even though their house had carpets on which they'd hardly ever make a sound. She was so tall and slim, so beautiful as she leaned down to give him a hug and a kiss, leaving a red lipstick mark on his cheek. "Nana has our house number and the number at the restaurant, so if you get scared in this big old house, or even if you feel lonely for your dad and me, you tell her, and she'll call us. I'll come get you if you need me. I'm just a phone call away, always. OK?"

"OK," he said brightly, smiling up at her. "But I won't get scared. I'm not a *baby* anymore. I'm nine and a half."

"Practically a man," Astrid chortled, and Elise joined in. "But the little man *is* right. He's not a baby anymore. We'll be fine together, won't we, Milo?"

"Sure will." He dug back into his cake.

Elise stood next to him, looking down, her eyes distant and a sad smile on her face as she stroked Milo's light brown hair. She sighed. "No more baby."

"No more baby," Astrid agreed.

Brrrrrring. Elise practically jumped forward and caught the wall phone on its second ring. "Greg? That you? Yes, I'm ready." She hung up and turned nervously to her mother. "Well, that was him, from the gas station up the block. He'll be here in two minutes."

"Better get going then." Astrid held her arms out and Elise went to her, the two women hugging fiercely. "You're going to do *so well*. Gregory will have that promotion on his desk by Monday morning, you just wait."

# #

"Thanks, Mom," Elise said, sniffling. "Shit. I'm going to ruin my mascara."

"You look stunning, my dear. Don't worry. We'll keep the hatches battened and be here tomorrow morning when you come to pick him up."

"Bye. Bye, Milo."

"Bye, Mama."

And with that, she was gone in a wave of expensive perfume, her heels click-clacking all the way out the door.

Astrid leaned down, her elbows on the table and her face cupped in her hands, mischief twinkling in her eyes.

"Well," she said slyly, "now that *she's* gone, what hijinks should we get into now, my sweet grandson?"

TWO

"READY OR NOT, here I come!" Astrid trilled from the kitchen at the back of the house.

Milo was hiding in the library, his favorite spot in the house. He crouched low behind the overstuffed leather armchair, the soft green blanket that shrouded it arranged in such a way that Nana wouldn't be able to see his feet if she came in. He smiled as he listened to her shuffling through the first-floor rooms, his grin getting wider as he heard her mount the stairs, softly calling his name. As soon as she was up near her bedroom, he would break from his hiding spot, run to base (the ancient potted aloe on the kitchen windowsill), and win the game. But for now, it would pay to be patient.

He sat still for what seemed like hours, staring up at the giant wooden bookshelves that surrounded him, the framed photos on the walls, the paintings. He loved his grandmother's home, had spent countless hours in this room alone, coloring pictures, doing homework, counting books. There were one thousand two hundred and twenty-four of them, to be exact, ranging in subject from children's books, to high fantasy, to manuals for electronics long since out of fashion. He loved them all, but the most curious of them were the ones on the long middle shelf of the case on the farthest wall, the ones under glass. *Those* books, his nana said, were not for children, even though some of them, with their slim, cracked spines and shiny covers, did appear to be children's books. *Those* books, Nana said, were not to be handled by him at any cost.

"They're precious cargo," she often said, a phrase she used to describe a great many of the objects under glass in her home, of which there were several dozen scattered throughout.

He heard a thump and a sigh from upstairs.

I'm not there, Nana, he thought, feeling extremely clever.

A rustle was followed by a creak from somewhere to his left. He risked a peek over the side of the armchair, his eyes scanning the room, but saw nothing.

Nothing, that was, besides the glass case of books, its hinged latch slightly ajar. He looked more carefully around the room, but saw no one. Was this his grandmother's way of drawing him out from his hiding spot? How had she gotten down here from upstairs so quickly?

There was a sound, the slick sliding sound of shiny cardboard on shiny paper, and a book fell out of the glass case and landed, open, on the floor of the library.

Milo frowned. He wasn't supposed to touch any of those books under glass, but this one had fallen out, seemingly on its own. He *could* go get his nana and tell her this had happened, or he could simply come out from hiding and put the book back, close the latch, and *then* tell her what had happened. She might be upset with him for touching her *precious cargo,* but alternatively, she might be proud of him for being mature enough to handle the situation on his own. And then, perhaps more cake.

He made his decision, slipping out from behind the armchair slowly, carefully, so that his sneakers didn't make the floorboards creak and give him away before he'd done his good (but semi-selfish) deed. He went over to the book lying mutely on the floor and saw the bright picture of the brown and white dog inspecting a butterfly He crouched down and picked it up, his fingers feeling the soft, worn pages. He closed it, looking at the cover. *The Poky Little Puppy.*

This was *precious cargo*? This old book about a puppy that noses its way through a garden in the sunshine? Milo's class had read this in Pre-K. He frowned. Surely this wasn't meant to stay behind that glass?

Maybe she put it in the wrong place, he reasoned. *Old people do all kinds of weird things.*

He sat down, cross-legged, and flipped to the front page. In seconds he was engrossed in Poky Puppy's benign little adventure, smiling at the thought of the little dog teaching himself this fun new trick, the trick of exploring the world all by himself. Milo loved the pictures, too, the puppy's big round head and large eyes, his spots, his expressions.

"Milo."

He startled, dropping the book on the ground, and turned to see his nana, standing in the doorway, looking down on him with horror, one of her hands pressed to the center of her chest, the other gripping the doorframe. But she wasn't really looking at *him* with her mouth open and her eyes wide, she was looking at the *book*. She was to him in two strides, swiping the book off the floor and practically leaping to the glass case, working it back into its spot, shutting the case with a *bang*, and firmly latching it.

She stood there for a moment, breathing hard, her forehead pressed to the glass. Then, slowly, she turned around to face him. "Did you open this case? Be honest, child."

The way Nana looked was frightening, how pale and serious she was, but Milo knew better than to try to lie his way out of this. For one, he wasn't a good liar. For another, she would know immediately even if he was. "No."

"Are you sure?"

"Yes, Nana. The book fell out on its own. I was gonna put it back for you, but then...then I...I just wanted to see what was in it." He was crying now, unsure exactly why, but it felt right.

He'd been bad without meaning to, betrayed his grandmother's trust and broken one of the very few rules of her home. "I'm…I'm really s-sorry."

Astrid gave him a calculating look, took in his tears and his smallness, then pinched the bridge of her nose and inhaled deeply. "I know you didn't mean to do this. You're a good boy, after all. I'm just glad you weren't hurt. But if this ever happens again, you come and get me, OK? Do not touch these books. Clear?"

"Clear." He nodded, but then tilted his head in thought. "Nana?"

"Yes?"

"How would I get hurt by a *book*?"

Her shoulders became rigid and she scanned his face, meeting his guileless, curious eyes with her own. Then she relaxed, crouching down to get on his level, her knees popping softly. "Stories are wild things, Milo. They're often only tamed by the pages containing them, and even that sometimes isn't enough. Do you know *The Jungle Book*, by Rudyard Kipling?"

"Yes. The one with the little boy who lives in the jungle with the bear."

"That's the one," she nodded. "When I was a little girl, I fell asleep reading it, the book open on my lap, and dreamed *Shere Khan* was in my bedroom. I had to fight him off to shove him back where he came from. When I woke up, I had bloody, red scratches all over my arms. Deep ones, like they were made by big, black claws."

Milo's eyes went wide. "No kidding?"

"No kidding. These books," she cocked a thumb over her shoulder to indicate the glass case, "are sort of like that. They tell a different sort of story than what's on their pages, and if they're left open too long, or handled by the wrong person, those stories that hide under the words can escape. They *want* to escape. And the stories these books tell are more dangerous than you can ever imagine. Have you ever felt strange, looking at the things I have in the cases?"

"Well…" he ventured, "maybe. That painting upstairs in the hallway? Of the little girl in the velvet dress with the red bow in her hair, holding the dog in her lap?"

"I know the one you mean."

"Sometimes when I look at it, my eyes feel like they're going funny. I feel like if I just looked hard enough, or long enough, I'd see something else. Underneath the painting."

Astrid nodded. "But you can't look too long, can you?"

"No. I always have to look away because I start to get a headache."

"Good," Astrid said pensively. "That's probably best."

"Nana," he asked slowly, curious, "What kind of stories are in the books in the case?"

"Stories of death," she replied, her voice soft, reverent. "Violent deaths. Sad deaths. Untimely, far-too-early deaths."

Milo scrunched his face. "But the one I read was about a dog. The dog didn't die."

"No, the dog didn't die," she repeated. "But someone else did. A long time ago now, but it still lingers, ever present. Waiting. It's under the pages, just like that feeling you get about the painting. And that's why you must never, ever touch those books or anything else I've got under glass in my home. It's important for your safety that you not engage with these objects, as often as you can avoid doing so. Can we agree that this is the best course of action?"

"Yes," Milo said, more confused now than he was before she gave him answers. "But Nana…"

"Yes, Milo?"

"How come they don't hurt you or make you feel weird? You live with them all the time."

"Ah," she said, smiling. "That's because I'm the *right* person to handle these things. They can't hurt me any more than a fly can hurt a lion. Do you understand?"

"Not really."

"No, I suppose you don't." She stood, smoothing her slacks down, and offered him a hand, which he took. "Maybe one day in the future I'll tell you more about this." Her eyes flittered over his face, reading it. "You're conscientious enough already, that you could, perhaps, with the right knowledge, *also* be the right person to look after these things. But only when I'm gone."

Milo squirmed. He didn't like imagining a world in which was gone and he was without her.

"Don't worry," she said, reading his expression, and squeezed his shoulder. "That won't be for a long, long time. Your mother… God, I love her so much, but she just doesn't see things the way I do, the way you do. Never has, and likely never will. One more question: when you were reading, did you hear anything strange? Such as, oh say, breathing that wasn't yours?"

"No."

"Feel sick, cold, anything like that?"

"Nope."

"Excellent. Now, this is important. Did you see anything moving nearby? Or any faces in the glass other than your own?"

"You said you only had *one* question."

Astrid laughed. "So I did. But humor an old lady."

Milo thought. He'd been engrossed in the adventures of Poky, and hadn't been paying much attention to his surroundings. He hadn't even heard his nana coming back down the stairs, and those creaked like all get-out. He shook his head.

"Good. Happy to hear it." And was that relief he saw in her face? "Are you hungry?"

"I could eat."

Astrid laughed her big, jolly laugh, pulling him into a bear-hug, and then everything was alright again. She wasn't mad at him; he hadn't failed her. He hugged her back, breathing in the smell of her hair, her skin, baked goods, happiness.

He looked over her shoulder at the glass case while she hugged him, thinking about what she'd asked. He could see them both reflected, their shadow selves dull, immaterial, ghostly. A blur of motion toward the right caught his eye. He squinted at it, pressed himself to his grandmother, and let out a small gasp.

It was a hand. A small hand, the digits chubby, see-through, and it was pressed against the glass from the *inside*. The palm was flat, the fingers splayed. He pushed back from Astrid and blinked, and the hand was gone.

"What is it?" Astrid asked, concerned, one hand coming up to cup his face and bring his eyes to hers.

"It…it was…" He glanced back at the bookcase. No hand was there, nor anything else besides their reflections. "Nothing."

Astrid looked unconvinced, her brow furrowed and lips pursed tightly. She turned and looked at the shelf herself, scanning it for something, anything, that could have made him gasp that way.

"I think," she said carefully, her eyes still on the bookshelves, "that dinner is nearly ready. I can smell it. Can you?"

Milo inhaled deeply. He could smell the salmon in the oven, the vegetables of the ratatouille, and nodded. "Yes."

"Perhaps, then, it's best we leave this room for the night, my darling." And with that, she turned him by his shoulders and shooed him into the hallway, pausing to close the library doors firmly behind them, then turned the lock.

THREE

"GOODNIGHT, MY SWEET," Astrid said to Milo, bending at the waist to give him a hug and kiss. "Did you enjoy the story tonight?"

"Yeah," he replied emphatically. "I really like Dr. Seuss. I mean…they're kinda *baby* books, but I like the way you read *Fox in Socks.* You do the tongue twisters better than Dad."

She chuckled, smoothing his hair over his brow. "I've had a lot of practice. I read that book to your mother when she was little."

"Really?"

"Really."

"I saw you close it all the way, too."

"Sure did." She wrinkled her nose and smiled, leaning close to his face to whisper, "I won't be letting any stories out tonight. Even though I doubt very much that Mr. Fox and Mr. Knox have anything nefarious up their sleeves."

"I'm sorry," Milo blurted suddenly, "about earlier. Touching your book like that. I knew I wasn't supposed to, and I did it anyway." He wrung the sheets in his hands, the words coming in a rush. "I just…when I saw it was just a story about a dog, I thought maybe it wasn't *that* bad, so I read it and I thought it would be OK, but I upset you and I feel really bad."

"Stop, stop, sweetness," Astrid chuckled, waving her hands. "These things happen. It's OK. No harm came of it, so all that happened was that you learned an important lesson. Which was?"

"Not to touch the things under glass. Come get you if I find one where it shouldn't be, because you're the *right* person to pick them up."

"That's correct," she said, booping his nose with her index finger. "You're such a smart kid. But now, I'm afraid, it's time to rest that big brain of yours and get some sleep."

"OK."

Astrid clicked off his bedside lamp and plunged the guest room into darkness. She kissed him once more on his forehead and slipped out of the room. Milo listened to her slippered feet thwack softly down the hall, heard her partially close the door to her room. Then the television in there switched on and Milo heard the familiar and dramatic opening score of *Tales From the Dark Side.*

He turned over in the dark of his room, scissoring his feet inside the cool sheets, bundling them up around himself until he was wrapped in a cocoon rapidly warming with his own small body heat. The house was quiet save for the murmur of Nana's TV, the tick of the clock next to the window, and the hum of the air conditioner. His mother had been wrong to think he'd be afraid here. There was nothing even remotely scary at his nana's house.

Well. Except for the stuff under glass. And it wasn't even the *objects themselves* that were scary, but his grandmother's reaction to him having touched them. Astrid was a sweet, funny, indomitable woman by nature, but when she'd seen him holding that book, she'd been so pale, so afraid. He'd seen her mad before, even so sad she cried her eyes out (that was last year when one of her best friends passed away) but never had Milo seen her *scared*. And what was with all those questions she'd asked him afterwards, about seeing or hearing anything?

He rolled onto his side, looking out into the hall where the light from Nana's TV played in purples, reds, blues on the walls, and yawned. He felt pretty bad that he hadn't told her about the hand on the glass, but he'd done it for protective reasons. He was sure if he'd told her, she would have called his mom and dad to come get him, and he didn't want to go home. It would make him feel like a baby to leave, and his mom would make a huge fuss about him having touched one of Nana's things when she'd explicitly told him not to. But the biggest reason he hadn't said anything was because he didn't want to scare Nana any more than he had already.

Besides, it wasn't as if anything *bad* had happened.

I'll tell her about it in the morning, Milo told himself, then snuggled down in the covers, inhaling the sweet lavender scent of the bedclothes. He was asleep in seconds.

Milo was at school, doing his favorite subject, art. He was drawing a beautiful picture of flowers, orchids, which looked exactly like the ones on Nana's bathroom windowsill. The pinks were perfect, the little purple dots traveling inwards precisely placed. He was the best artist in the whole world, a child prodigy. His teacher, Mrs. Simmons, was there, her mouth moving and her words inaudible to his ears, but she was smiling. Sun was streaming in through the wall of windows in the art room, and outside his classmates were pressed to the glass, watching the master at work. Milo held up his drawing for them to see, and they began cheering and clapping, faces bright and excited as they pumped their fists for his creation.

All but Bobby Zimmerman. Bobby, a short, freckled kid with Coke-bottle glasses and perpetually unruly blond hair, wasn't cheering or clapping at all. Bobby's face was slack, expressionless, and he lifted his arm slowly, slowly, to point one finger behind where Milo was sitting.

Milo turned to look. Sitting directly behind him, his head buried in his arms on the desk, was a small boy about his age, with black hair slicked with sweat and sticking up in cowlicks. The room around Milo darkened. He glanced back at the windows and saw thunderheads gathering in the sky, blocking out the sun. His classmates were now standing in a motionless line of flat, slack faces, all pointing just like Bobby Zimmerman.

A small squeak brought his attention back to the boy. He was pushing backwards slightly, the chair legs squalling as they dragged backwards. The boy unfolded his arms, and Milo saw white fingers dappled with deep maroon. His heart began pounding as the boy placed those hands on either side of the desk, and pushed himself up, up, his head coming off the desk with a wet *schlorp* that made Milo's skin crawl. The boy had his head leaned forward, his hair hanging limply over his face. Slowly, he turned his head towards Milo, the bones in his neck creaking. One of those pale—too pale—hands reached upwards, gathered the hair in his hand, and pushed it back.

The boy's one eye was so dark it was nearly black, the pupil blown wide, the sclera filled with blood. Where the other eye should have been was a red, pulpy hole, the bones crushed, the juice of the ruined eyeball leaking down his cheek. The boy opened his cracked, bruised lips.

"Ready or not," he croaked, his voice choked and gravelly, "here I come."

He lunged forward, his blood-sticky fingers hooked into claws, his face contorted in killing rage.

Milo screamed, sitting up in bed, sweat rolling down his face, arms trembling. He stared wildly around him, panicked, needing to confirm he was still at his grandmother's house, not back at school, not where that boy with his ruined face and bloody hands could reach him.

"Just a dream," he said in a quavering voice, not at all convinced, his heart in his throat. "Just a dream."

He took a couple of deep breaths, willing his heart to slow, then rolled on his side to reach for the bedside lamp. He stretched, reaching for the pullstring, groping in the darkness for the lifeline of light. As he leaned toward the bedside table, a small, pale hand came up from below, reaching to grab at his wrist.

"*NANA!*" He screamed, scrabbling backwards against the wall, his bladder suddenly painfully full, desperate to get away from the boy, who was here, *here*, in the dark with him. "*Nana, come quick! Please!*"

His grandmother's feet hit the ground and she ran to his room, flicking on the light. She took one look at Milo and crossed quickly to his bed, climbing on, past where the boy would have *had* to have been.

Did she not see him? He grabbed at her nightshirt, crying, inconsolable, and she held him, rocked him, whispered sweet nothings to him as Milo recovered from the shock of what he'd seen.

When he was calmer, Astrid curled next to him, stroking his hair, and murmured, "What happened, my darling? Did you have a nightmare?"

"Yes," he sniffled, "but it was…there was more than that. Someone was in my room."

"What?" She pulled back from him and looked into his eyes. "Who? Who was in your room?"

"A b-boy," he replied, feeling hot tears welling up again. "A boy with black hair and b-bloody hands. His face was all messed up and he…he was missing an eye. He tried to grab me."

"In your dream."

"Yeah." Milo swiped at his nose with his sleeve. "But when I woke up, he was *h-here*, too. He almost g-got me, and I'm *s-s-scared.*"

Astrid clutched Milo to her, her gaze scanning the room, searching. She stroked Milo's back and swallowed hard.

"I think," she said carefully, "that it would be best for you to sleep in my room tonight. With me. Would that make you feel better?" He nodded, and she smiled down at him. "Good. Now gather your things and come along."

He grabbed his pillow and held his nana's hand while she led him to her room, then he let her tuck him in once he was settled. She fluffed his pillow, kissed him, then walked to her enormous cedar armoire, flung open the doors and began rifling inside.

"Ah-ha," Astrid mumbled, and when she turned she had two things in her hand: a small bottle of liquid, and a jar full of what looked like red dirt. "What I'm about to do may seem strange to you, Milo. But it's for your own protection. Even if you think it's silly, will you permit this old lady to do what she believes will make things right?"

"Sure," Milo replied, curious. "What are those?"

She held up the bottle. "Holy water."

She held up the jar. "Brick dust and graveyard dirt."

"And now," she said, unscrewing the lid of the jar and placing both the lid and the bottle on her bedspread, "for the application."

Astrid poured a small handful of dirt into her palm and laid a line of it across the threshold of her bedroom doorway, then stood, dusted her hands, and stretched her back. She put the lid tightly back on the jar, and picked up the bottle. She undid the top and tipped it onto her fingertips, anointing her forehead with it. Then she came to Milo and did the same to him.

"There," she said, closing the bottle. "I think we'll have no more trouble tonight."

M.R. Hauck – Pentacle

"Why? What'll some dirt and water do?"

She laughed. "You'd be surprised what a little dirt and water can do. They are, after all, the basic components of life itself."

"OK," Milo said. He didn't understand, but as a nine (and a half, don't forget that)-year-old, *most* things adults did and said he didn't understand. And now that the shock had worn off and he was safely ensconced in his grandmother's bedroom, with her so close by to keep him safe, he was sleepy again. He nestled down in the covers, his head already heavy and his eyelids drooping.

"Shall we sleep with the TV on?" Astrid asked, getting into bed next to him.

He nodded, but it really made no difference. Milo was fast asleep before Nana even shut off the bedside lamp. There were no more dreams that night, of the boy with the missing eye or anything else. His sleep was a blissful blank.

FOUR

T HE NEXT MORNING, Milo rose early with Nana, the horrible dream about the boy with the smashed eye all but forgotten when she kissed his nose to wake him up. He followed her downstairs (studiously not looking at the shut library doors when he passed them) and climbed up onto one of her high kitchen chairs, hooking his bare feet through the rungs.

"What are we thinking? Pancakes?" Nana asked, and then glanced at the wall phone, frowned, and looked away.

"Yes, please," he said brightly, but the worm of worry had started squirming in his gut. She'd done the same thing with the phone in her room last night after tucking him in, this morning when he woke up, and again right after they'd brushed their teeth. Each time, she got this pinched, worried look on her face that made him antsy.

But when she turned to him, that look melted away, replaced by the doting, affectionate smile she usually wore when she addressed him. "Pancakes it shall be then. Would you go into the larder and grab me the bag of flour while I get set up? All-purpose, not self-rising."

"Okie-doke." Milo slipped down from his chair and crossed the kitchen to the door of the big walk-in pantry Nana called her "larder," and pulled open the door. He glanced behind him and saw that Nana hadn't moved to get the other things she needed for pancakes. She was leaning against the counter, back to him, her hand on the phone. She picked it up, the dial tone low, then shook her head and placed the phone back into its cradle.

She looked out the window, running a hand through her hair, shoulders hunched.

Something is wrong, he thought, but experience with adults informed him that they would never reveal whatever private struggles they held to a boy his age, so there was no point in asking. He turned away from her, left her to her thoughts, and clicked the light on in the larder.

All morning it was like that.

As he ate his pancakes, he glanced over at Nana and saw her looking out the window, pensive, her fingertips always straying to the chord of the phone on the wall. She hardly touched the two pancakes on her plate, the syrup congealing on the porcelain. Afterwards, they collected the dishes, and Nana washed them while Milo dried. Usually he loved this task, the simple pleasure of helping his grandmother, but today it was tainted by an unnamed tension. Her phone rang and she shouted, almost breaking the plate she held in her surprise.

She snatched the phone off the cradle and shouted, "Hello? Elise? Is that y—oh. Wilfred. Yes, hello, good morning to you as well." The hopeful look ran away from her face and her shoulders sagged with disappointment. "It really isn't a good time now, dear, perhaps later? I'd like to keep the line clear. Thanks."

It was still very early when they finished, only 9:30 a.m., and Nana's uncharacteristic quiet was unsettling, so Milo went about entertaining himself. The library was still firmly closed—with good reason, he thought, the boy in his dreams still chillingly fresh in his mind—so he went upstairs to get his sketchbook and colored pencils from his overnight bag. Milo tromped up the stairs, running his fingers over the cool wood banister, and traipsed down the hall to his room.

To get there, he had to pass the painting of the girl in the velvet dress with the little dog in her lap. He studiously avoided looking at her. Still, a tingle ran up his spine as he passed, as though *she* were noticing *him* from her spot high on the pale pink walls.

He hadn't been back in his room since last night. The door was flung open, exactly as they'd left it during their swift night exit, but now the sun was coming through the big window on the far wall, dappling the hall runner and the floorboards in sunshine and the moving shadows of the banana tree outside. Milo peeked cautiously around the door frame, ready to run if he saw anyone, any *thing*, lurking within, waiting to pounce. There was nothing.

He took a deep breath and strode into the room, his hands in fists at his sides, all the hairs on his neck standing up. He couldn't *see* anyone in here, no, but that didn't mean nobody was *there*. The same as the painting, his room now had a watchful quality, as though unknown entities were observing the small boy rummaging through his battered backpack, looking for the tin that held his pencils. Milo was very glad when he had what he came up for in hand, and he could go back downstairs to where Nana was nearby.

When he hit the bottom step he saw her in the den, the lights off and the blinds drawn so that she was in shadow, one hand tucked under her elbow and the phone she kept in there against her ear, pacing back and forth. She let out a small sound—*mmph*—that was part stress and part frustration when she brought the phone away from her face and set it back down with a soft click.

"Nana?" Milo asked, more to let her know he was there than anything else. She was as jumpy as he was today, and he didn't want to add to it by sneaking up on her.

She turned to him, her face crumpled in a nest of worried wrinkles that smoothed when she saw him with his pencils and sketchbook. She smiled. "Did you enjoy your breakfast, my heart?"

"Yeah." He shifted, not wanting to push, but still feeling anxious about the previous night. "When are Mama and Daddy coming to get me?"

The wrinkles returned, deepened. Vanished again like a cloud burned away by the sun. "I don't know. Elise never mentioned a time. Not that I mind hanging out with my favorite guy."

"You think they had a long night?"

"Most likely, yes. Your father wanted very much to impress his boss. I'm sure they were just out late and needed a good lie-in. Your mother was never a morning person, anyway." She came out of the den finally, into the light of the foyer. "Are you going to draw me a picture?"

"If you want." He glanced up the staircase, at the hallway with the girl and her dog, at his room where the boy with the broken face lurked, he was sure of it, hiding in the closet or under the bed. Watching. Waiting.

"Let's not look so glum," she said, putting her arm around his shoulders, leading him away. "Why don't we go outside and draw by the greenhouse? Maybe you can draw the pink hibiscus? Or I could teach you how to draw a mouse in ten seconds."

Milo brightened. "Really?"

"Really."

"OK." He allowed her to take him by the hand and lead him through the house, outside, into the world and the sunshine, to all the smells of hothouse flowers and the swish of elephant ear fronds rustling in the muggy breeze. It was difficult to stay afraid out here, and he felt the tension melting the same way the strawberry popsicle she gave him melted: sticky, sweet, and then gone. It was a perfect day, the sky a blameless blue, and after she taught him how, he drew a hundred mice, perfecting it, making her laugh. He laughed too, because her joy was his, in the way of all young children.

Except that she kept glancing back at the house, as though she were listening for something. Each time the sound did not come to fruition, the furrow in her brow deepened a little more. Each time she got a little less involved and a little quieter. She excused herself twice to go into the house, and while she always came back out with something for him—lemonade, a cushion to lean on that wouldn't be dirtied by the earth—he hadn't asked for those things, so he knew she'd been making calls. And by the look on her face, receiving no answer.

By lunchtime, Milo was nervous. The tension in the air was palpable as he chewed his bologna and Swiss cheese sandwich on the fluffy white bread Astrid baked weekly. It was usually a treat reserved for going to Nana's, the bread so soft and the meat his mom never bought (she said was full of bad fats) so salty and pleasant, a semi-forbidden fruit. But today he could barely taste it.

Astrid paced back and forth, her hands clasping her elbows, her back hunched, looking every single one of her fifty-five years. She'd pause now and then to stare blankly at a wall or door casing, her mouth working but no sound coming out. And always, always delicately touching the back of the phone.

Milo ate quietly, feeling in his gut that now was not the time for questions, that he would do well to be a good little church mouse and not add to whatever she was going through.

Maybe one of her friends is sick, he reasoned. *Mr. Jay is about a thousand years old, and fell down a couple months ago. Ms. Rita has cancer. Maybe she got some bad news and she's waiting to hear back, and that's why she's so upset.*

But none of those reasons explained why his mother hadn't called. Usually he'd have been picked up by now, because she liked to spend Sundays doing what she called "weekday prepping." She did laundry, made a week's worth of work lunches for herself, made sure he was bathed and his uniforms were ready for Monday, cleaned the house. And Milo helped with all of it. Elise Cunningham was extremely big on fostering independence in her only child, so Milo was usually picked up from Nana's, if he'd spent the night, well before noon. But here it was 12:30, with no sign of her. Nana was right, Elise *wasn't* a morning person, but she never slept *this* late. Besides, Daddy would have come if Mama couldn't for some reason, and would likely have taken him to do something like go to the movies if Mama was, say, sick and needed him out of the house.

Milo's stomach did a flip. He gulped down his ice water, pushing the sensation down with the icy chill.

A knock at the door startled them both. Three sharp raps— *bam bam bam*—on the screen door, followed by someone leaning on the bell until it screamed. Astrid clutched her chest, not moving to answer it, breathing hard and fast. Milo put his sandwich down, his heart thumping in his ears, and slipped from his chair to run to her side and clutch her around the hips. She held him right back, her gnarled old-lady hands pressing him to her body.

Once more a knock resounded through the house—*bam bam bam*—and this time Astrid moved. She crouched low and looked into Milo's eyes. "You stay here. OK?"

Milo nodded, but he didn't want to *stay here*, alone in the kitchen, the scare of last night's nightmare still fresh in his bones, while his grandmother stepped out of view, through the sitting room, into the foyer. But she had looked plenty scared, too, and disagreement would have just made it worse. He crept after her, but only into the sitting room, where he crouched behind the overstuffed baby-blue couch to listen.

The screen door creaked open.

"Yes?" Nana's voice. Hesitant. Fearful.

A squawk of radio static, then a man clearing his throat. "Sorry about that, ma'am. Are you Astrid Schulze?"

"Yes."

"The mother of Elise Cunningham, née Schulze?"

"What's this about, Officer?"

Officer. There's a policeman on the porch. Milo squirmed, his mouth hanging open. A real policeman. Here. He risked a peek over the top of the couch and saw him, the officer, a burly, balding, red-faced man with broad, square shoulders and a barrel chest, in his blue NOPD uniform with his badge displayed on his chest.

His moustache, thick and bristly, turned down as he frowned, seeing Milo peering at him from within. He nodded toward the boy. "Maybe we'd better talked outside, Miz Schulze."

Nana glanced back, saw Milo, who ducked back behind the couch. "I told you to wait in the kitchen. Yes, Officer, perhaps outside is best."

The screen door creaked open and slammed shut with a wooden bang, and then Milo was alone. Footsteps down the stairs of the porch and muffled voices told him they moved away from the house, closer to the gate out front. Milo's heart thumped, his stomach turning with its cargo of bologna and cheese—*precious cargo*—and he fought the urge to run outside and scream, *Don't leave me alone with him, Nana, I'm scared!*

But that might raise questions with the officer, ones he couldn't really answer.

The door squalled again, his grandmother shutting it slowly, so that it didn't bang. She closed the front door equally quietly. Milo stood, and saw her standing there, her hands on either side of the frame, her head bowed so that her forehead touched the door, her shoulders shaking.

Bad news, he thought. "Nana? What did he want? Did something happen?"

She turned to him, tears streaming down her pale, stricken face, and held her arms out to him. He went, his legs tingling in equal parts from crouching behind the couch and the pervasive sense of *wrongness* that was flooding him, filling him, with each step forward. She gathered him in her arms, hoisting him off the floor as if she weren't elderly and he weighed nothing.

"Oh, Milo, my love," she murmured into the crook of his shoulder as she swayed. "There's been an accident. A man…going the wrong way…on the highway…" she gulped, sniffled, pressed him close. "They're gone, Milo. They're both gone. Oh, Milo, I'm sorry. I'm so, so sorry."

FIVE

THE WAKE WAS crowded, the stuffy parlor of Crane and Darwin Funeral Home chock-full of people come to see off Milo's mother and father. Milo had no idea that they'd even *known* this many people. He knew some of them—the old people his nana was friends with, parents (and even some kids) from school, coworkers from either side—but most of them were strangers to him, or people he'd met once as a toddler and then never again. It occurred to him that most of his parents' friendships and work relations were a mystery to him, and now they probably always would be. He wandered listlessly past the buffet service table outside the kitchen. There were Tastee Donuts, finger sandwiches, muffins, and sodas out here, as well as some acrid smelling coffee inside the little lounge to the left. People he vaguely knew were all milling around, stuffing their faces absently, talking about his parents, last night's football game, jobs that sounded boring. He spied Nana through the crowd, waving him over, and he changed course to wander numbly to her side.

"There you are," Nana said gently, and pointed to the woman standing across from her, an elderly woman with a jet-black bouffant and red lipstick creeping up into the creases around her mouth. "Do you remember Eleanor? She's the organist at the church your parents went to for Christmas services."

"No," Milo replied flatly. It wasn't as if they'd gone to church often enough for him to think of it as an impactful thing, just Easter and Christmas at his mother's behest. He prayed silently to whatever god attended that church that this woman wouldn't touch him. They'd all been doing it today, these strangers, grabbing at him, putting their grief on top of his, pressing him down with the weight of their stories of his parents, times he didn't remember.

His grandmother glanced back and forth between him and Eleanor, her hands wringing her braid. "Now, Milo—"

"It's alright," Eleanor quavered, her old-lady voice a creaking door in a haunted house. "The boy lost the two most important people in his life. He has every right to be blunt." She put out one of her crabbed, black-gloved hands and put it on his shoulder. Milo could feel how cold her hand was, even through the cloth. "I loved your mother, Milo. Elise always made the choir brownies for Christmas. She was such a lovely woman. And your father drove the bus for us a time or two, after dear Henry got too frail from his stroke. They were two of the best people in the world."

Milo didn't know who Henry was, and frankly didn't care. All he knew was that he wanted Eleanor to take her gloved church-hand off his shoulder, wanted her to stop talking about his parents in past tense, wanted to scream, *Stop talking about them like you knew them! You didn't! They were my parents! Mine!*

He gritted his teeth in what he hoped looked like a smile and nodded, the only safe response.

"Oh, you poor dear," Eleanor said, her fingers digging further into his shoulder, using him as a crutch to bear herself up. "They're with God now, praise Him. God has a reason for everything He does. At least you have Astrid to care for you in their absence. So long as nothing goes wrong, hm?" She reached out her other hand and clasped Astrid's with it, her grip firm. "I'll light a candle for you both."

The statement was too much. Hot tears sprang up in Milo's eyes and his throat began to squeeze shut, his breath coming in wheezy gasps. His eyes fell to the floor, the threadbare red carpets, his shiny new dress shoes Nana had bought him for just this occasion. He hated these shoes, hated the carpet, hated Eleanor and her old-lady voice and her intimation that even though he'd already lost so much, he was doomed to lose more. He wrenched himself from her grasp, turned, and ran from her, from Nana, from the crowd. Let them stuff their mouths, stuff them with food, with stories of grief, with platitudes, and let them do it without him. He wove through the crowd, unheeding Nana calling after him.

Milo pushed through the double doors and into the cool silence of the chapel, letting the doors fall shut behind him with a soft *whumpf*. This place was in stark contrast to the parlor outside. Where out there everything was reds and golds, shabby, close and overcrowded, in here it was cool, both in tones and temperature. In here, plants festooned the walls, and the stained glass up front where the coffins were was all blues and greens. Mary in her blue robe and golden halo looked down beatifically, her hands spread in welcome, a soft smile on her mouth. The sound of the air conditioner was all Milo could hear once he stepped away from the doors, and for that he was grateful. His shoes whispered on the thick, soft blue pile of the rug, and Milo loosened his tie as he walked forward through the dark brown pews towards Mary and his parents.

He trailed a hand over the sleek surface of his mother's coffin (no open casket, no final look, no goodbye). "Hi, Mama." He reached out his other hand and did the same to his father's coffin, uniting them. He'd been their conduit in life, the person in the circle of their arms that united them and made them a family. He felt it only right that he would be so even in death. "Hi, Daddy."

There was no answer. There never would be, ever again.

He backed up and sat down heavily on the deep blue cushion of the pew, his hands folded, and breathed in the smell of the potted plants, the cleaning products, formaldehyde. Elise and Gregory Cunningham were going away today, forever, and they were going to leave their son, the very small Milo Cunningham, behind, above ground with his nana. If he wanted to, he could pretend they were away on an extended vacation. The child grief counselor he'd been made to see had told him that herself. He could imagine to himself that they were somewhere having a great time, maybe the Maldives, the place with the bioluminescent plankton that his mother always mused on in pictures in travel magazines, that she and her husband were swimming in warm waters, getting bored with eating and sleeping late, longing to go back to their son. Then they'd board a plane, have a long flight with bad food, and show up on Nana's doorstep, suntanned deep brown and smiling. He could go to them then, complete their circle, breathe them in deeply, completely, and this nightmare would be over at last.

But he didn't *want* to pretend. That would do no good, be too painful. What Milo *wanted* was to un-happen that night his mother wore her slinky dress and click-clacking shoes when she kissed him goodbye, wanted to undo his father's promotion offer, all of it. Unwind the reel and turn the hateful clock back, until they were regular, poor, happy, together. He wouldn't care if they both lost their jobs and he had to live under a bridge, as long as none of this ever happened and things could go back to normal, being complete. Anything would be better than this empty, sullen ache.

But things wouldn't go back. Not ever again.

What's done is done, his dad would say, *and you can't undo it. All you can do is live with it.*

Live with it. Without them. Today, tomorrow, every day.

The magnitude of it all struck him as he sat alone looking at those coffins, and Milo leaned forward and put his face in his hands. No tears came now, just his hot breath in his own face as he curled in a ball.

"Are you OK?" A small voice asked from his elbow, startling him. He looked sharply up and saw Cassie, looking resplendent in a ruffled baby-blue dress, a black velvet ribbon tying back her coiled brown hair in a neat puff on top of her head. Her hazel eyes were bright and full of worry, but a worry that invited complete truthfulness.

"No," he said simply, scooting over on the pew to make room for her. Cassie was ten, almost a full year older than Milo, a tall girl with an easy smile and a pleasant demeanor. Not only did they go to school together, albeit not in the same class, but Cassie's father and Milo's father played cards together two weekends a month (or rather, they *used to,* he reminded himself bitterly). Milo had spent many a sweet evening hour sprawled on the carpet at Cassie's house, either playing Atari, drawing, or pretending to be whatever Cassie's imagination cooked up. Lately it had been spies, and they'd crept around her house on tiptoe, pretending to gather information on the crime ring their dads were *obviously* a part of. She never once lorded being older over him, had just accepted him as though he were a wayward little brother. Milo liked Cassie very much, felt attached to her in a way he didn't his other school chums. He'd seen Luke and Ellison outside with their parents, for instance, the two guys who were supposed to be his best friends, but who hadn't come over to comfort him, either at his house or outside in the parlor. They had, in fact, seen him, turned an immediate about-face, and disappeared into the kitchen of the funeral home.

Cassie, though. Cassie had come to find him when he ran away. "Did Nana send you to look for me?"

"Nah. I saw how you looked when you walked in here and decided you don't need to be alone right now." She sat down, sighing as the tulle on her dress swished loudly in the relative silence of the chapel. "I hate this fucking dress."

Milo's eyes widened. "Cassie…you're not supposed to swear."

"And your parents are supposed to be alive," she responded. There was no malice or mockery in her voice at all, just the calm assurance of *facts*. It was a plain truth, that she *shouldn't* be wearing her foofaraw, or the noisy dress and saddle oxfords, nor should Milo be wearing *his* brand-new pinstripe suit and uncomfortable patent leather loafers, because Milo's parents *should* still be alive. It the world of *should* and *should not,* that was the most glaring fact of all.

He put his face in his hands, trying to suppress tears, and mumbled, "I don't know what to do. All those people out there… I don't know most of them. They won't stop touching me and telling me about Mama and Daddy, like I don't already know how good they were. Like I don't already know how much I lost. I don't *care* about them, any of those people. I care about Nana, and she just looks so *sad,* and there's nothing I can *do.* I wish it was just me and her today, not all these…these…graveyard ghouls."

Cassie put a warm arm around his shoulders, leaning her face against the side of his head. She was quiet for a moment, just stroking his back and allowing him to feel, and when she did speak again, her voice was careful and kind. "When I'm upset, sometimes swearing helps. I know you think you shouldn't, but sometimes what you shouldn't do is exactly what you *should* do. You can't let the adults hear you, but it feels good to say them all the same, even if no one is listening. *Especially* if no one is listening. You know what I mean?"

Milo nodded. He did know what she meant.

"Why don't you give it a try?"

"Here?" He sat back and pointed at the coffins. "In front of them?"

Cassie shrugged. "They can't hear you. And it can't hurt."

Milo took in a deep, slow breath, looking up at Mary with her blue robe and beatific smile. He thought about his mother in her beautiful dress, kissing him absently on the head, her very last kiss she'd ever give him. He thought of his father, with his easy laugh and kind eyes, teaching him how to bait a hook and making a fuss over him when he cut his finger on the scales of a croaker. His thought of his grandmother, so old already, and about Eleanor's intimation that he would lose her too, in short order. He thought of all the people here today, their pawing at him, their empty words and needy condolences. He thought of his stupid friends turning tail and running when he needed them most. He thought of all this, and the ache to tell his parents about these things inside him, to hear their wisdom and their love spoken right into his waiting ear. And finally, he thought of all the nights he had to look forward to where he'd never get that from them again. He would never hear his mother laugh again, never feel her arms around him. He would never again hear his father sing while he played guitar, his voice deep and clear, or have Greg Cunningham to teach him things about becoming a man. He had lost them, all at once, both of them, for good. That no one else felt or understood this as acutely as he did was perhaps more tragic than the loss itself. It was a horrible weight to force—not ask, but *force*—anyone to bear.

Milo's hands curled into fists. "Fuck this."

Cassie grinned and clapped once. "That's the spirit!"

"Fuck this, and fuck all of them out there. Fuck the police officer who came to Nana's. Fuck Luke, and fuck Ellison too. Fuck the fucking party and the promotion." Hot tears were coming now, his voice rising. "Fuck the guy who did this. Fuck drunk drivers. Fuck traffic for stopping the ambulance.

Fuck the old people who keep *touching* me. Fuck God and His mysterious fucking ways. And *fuck...funerals!*"

He stopped, breathing heavily, his head swirling as though his brains had been caught in a blender. His chin quivered with emotion, his body trembling, and now when he looked at those two coffins, he suddenly understood: he couldn't bury his parents today; his parents were not in there. This funeral wasn't for them. It was for everyone *but* them, those left behind in the shadow of their absent love.

"Do you feel better?" Cassie patted his back, not patronizing, just being a friend.

Milo loved her for it, and leaned into the touch until she gathered him in a hug. "I do."

"Good." They sat in silence, the only sound between them the swish of Cassie's dress as she rocked him. He could go to sleep here, in this cool room, with this easy friendship, his parents within reach, and have none of the nightmares that had plagued him since the news of their death. He floated on Cassie's gentle child's love.

"Milo, are you in here?" Nana's voice broke the silence as she pushed open the chapel door, bringing all the noise from outside with her.

He sat up, muzzy, and looked back at her.

"Oh," she said, smiling in an unsure way at the two of them, an expression that Milo had never seen her use Her eyes darted back and forth between them, a questioning sadness stamped on her features. She opened her mouth, seemed to think better of what she was going to say, then shook her head as if to clear it. "Hello, Cassandra. How are you holding up?"

"Pretty well, Ms. Schulze," she replied brightly, standing up and smoothing her dress. She gestured to Milo, who remained seated. "I saw him come in here, and, well…nobody should have to be alone on a day like this."

"Quite right," Astrid agreed, but her eyes were misty when she turned them to him. "Milo. Service is in ten minutes. Are you ready?"

Milo glanced at Cassie, at the coffins, back at Nana. "I guess so."

"Cassandra, if you like, you can sit by us, then walk with us to the gravesite," Nana said abruptly, as if she herself were surprised by the offer. "If you like, of course, and if your father says it's OK. I think it might do our Milo some good."

Our Milo. He winced. *Fuck being talked about like you're not in the room.*

"Sure thing, Ms. Schulze."

Astrid slipped out of the room, allowing the door to fall quietly behind her with a dull thud, once again blocking all the people sounds from invading this haven of quietude. Milo slumped back down, his lip poking out, hating that very soon, too soon, it would be time to put his parents into the earth together and leave them there, while he'd be expected to go home and entertain people some more with his misery.

Cassie seemed to sense his feelings. She sat back down, her dress rattling, and patted Milo's arm. "Don't worry. I'll hold your hand the whole time. We've got this."

He glanced at her. "Promise?"

"Promise." She threaded her brown fingers through his, their palms meeting in the middle. "I'm here for you. No matter what."

She kept her word. Cassie held Milo's hand all through the sermon—delivered by a priest Milo neither knew nor respected for talking about people he obviously had no connection with—about how everyone in the room was made to lie down in green pastures under the love of God. (*Fuck God,* Milo thought, *fuck Him right to hell.*) She held it when the congregation stood to sing

"Ave Maria" in throaty, atonal voices led by a woman in a purple, too-cheery dress who worked for the funeral home. Cassie held on tight as they made their procession to the graveyard, Nana holding his other hand, the three of them leading the shuffling, winding throng through the city of the dead to the stone edifice with its gaping black maw into which the pallbearers placed his parents' coffins—first his father, then his mother, stacked like bricks on top of one another. Cassie stepped forward with Milo when it was his turn to place a single red rose on each coffin before the priest bade them bow their heads in a final prayer.

Milo didn't lower his head like Nana, Cassie, or anyone else. He stared finality in the face and gave no thanks, heard no platitudes full of the promise of a beautiful afterlife. What life could there possibly be, after something like this?

Cassie's dad—a formidably tall and lanky man named Martin, whose stature belied his humorous and gentle nature, and who was also possessed of the single largest moustache Milo had ever seen—balked at the idea of Cassie riding back to Astrid's house in the limo reserved for family, but Astrid had patted his hand and assured him it was fine.

"She's great comfort to my grandson," she said, her voice hollow and ragged. She looked exhausted in a way Milo was unsure a person of her age would ever recover from. "She's doing what I simply do not have the capacity to do today. I will rebound, and quite soon, but for now I think it's best Milo have someone to talk to that *isn't* me. Don't you think?"

Martin's eyes flicked from the haggard lady in her shimmery black caftan dress, to the two solemn children holding hands, and back again. He ran a hand over his close-cropped hair, the palm rasping against the texture, his other hand on his hip. "We-e-ell...I just don't want her to be any trouble to you, Ms. Astrid..."

"No trouble," Astrid assured him, then reached out, turned him around bodily, and gave him a light shove toward his car. "But we must be going. Guests will arrive at my home any minute, and they'll be hungry."

"I, uh…yes. Yes, alright." Martin looked flustered at having been manhandled by a frail old lady, but complied and headed away through the parking lot, the tails of his maroon sport coat flapping in the wind.

Cassie didn't let go of Milo's hand during the drive, and when he leaned in to put his head on her shoulder, she shifted to accommodate him. Astrid sat across from them, her eyes red-rimmed and distant, dabbing her nose with a balled-up tissue. She watched the two children, a thin, bemused smile touching her mouth at the corners.

SIX

THE HOUSE WAS full of people now, louder than even the funeral home had been, more people showing up for the after-party than the actual event. There was better food than there had been back at the funeral home, Nana pulling out all the stops. Milo hurriedly gobbled down some crawfish étouffée that he was barely able to taste, and then he and Cassie squirreled away to his room. He had no desire to mingle anymore with anyone else, though he did notice that Luke and Ellison had not made an appearance. He wasn't angry, exactly, wasn't capable of real anger at anyone but the Eternal Footman today, but he did make a mental note to avoid them next time he saw them.

Abandon ship, he thought grimly as he and Cassie mounted the stairs.

There was enough daylight that he didn't really need to turn on the lights, but a niggling voice in the back of his mind reminded him of the hand creeping up in the dark to brush against his wrist. He pushed the image away and flipped on the light switch, the glare of the bulbs chasing every shadow as far back as it could go. He wanted light, craved it, needed no darkness, not now, maybe not ever again.

Cassie flopped back on his bed, a tired sigh escaping her as she starfished there, stockinged legs dangling over the edge, kicking slightly. "You've got a cool room."

"It's not really mine. It's just a guest room," Milo replied. He looked around at the low dresser and the closet, both mostly empty, the auxiliary bookshelves, the painting framed on the far wall of watercolor ducks. "Though I guess it's my room *now*."

"You don't think your nana will move into your house in the 'burbs?"

Milo thought. Shook his head. "Nana has lived here since she was in her thirties, my mom said. I don't think she's about to move now."

"Not even for you?"

"Not even for me."

Cassie let out a low whistle, coming up on her elbows. "I guess that makes you a rich boy now."

"I guess so."

"Too rich to hang out wit' us po' chirren in low-class Metry?" She batted her eyelashes and gave a sly smile.

Milo smiled back, and for a wonder, it felt genuine. "Aw, come on. You guys aren't poor. We go to the same *private* school." He paused, thinking. "And I'm *pretty sure* Nana will keep me in there. Hein Academy has great academics—that's what Daddy said, anyway—and Nana isn't the type to rip me away from my friends at a time like this. She'd think it was too much change. Bad for my development, or something."

Cassie considered this, her head cocked to the side. "But your nana is richer than my Dad ever could be. What does she do for work, anyway? It's gotta be something *really* special to have had this giant house all to herself for all these years."

Milo pondered her question. He'd never really thought about Astrid as much more than...well...his nana, but now that Cassie mentioned it, she *did* have a job. His mother had said so many times. Milo had never asked what it was, but there were clues about it that didn't fit with what he knew about work as a whole. His mother and father had office jobs—left at seven in the morning, off by five p.m., weekends off—but his grandmother's job certainly wasn't anything like that. For one, she made house calls, that much he knew for sure. Whenever she talked about her job—which wasn't often, at least in Milo's presence—she talked about going to this person or that person to visit their home. Sometimes she stayed there for only a night, sometimes for several days. There had been one time, two years ago, she'd been gone somewhere in Georgia for two weeks solid, and when she came home, she'd come to Milo's house instead of going back to her own. That had been scary. Her hair had been matted and her eyes wild, she stank as though she hadn't bathed the whole trip, and she raved off and on about a woman in white that tried to get her somehow (it was unclear what this woman might do once she got her), her body feverish and her hands flitting around like restless doves. Milo had stayed in the background while his mother had cared for her, rushing back and forth from the kitchen to the den with hot soup and cold, damp cloths, but he still caught snippets. Whoever the woman in white was, she was one bad motor scooter, and Astrid claimed that the bitch had tried to kill her. It was one of the few times he'd ever heard his nana swear. She had convalesced on their couch for three whole days and nights, sleeping fitfully, moaning, her body arching as though some invisible force bowed her spine so hard it might snap in two like a twig. And when she was awake, the ranting would begin again, unstoppable, utterly mad. She'd only quieted down the morning of the third day, and then fallen into a heavy sleep that lasted until nearly midnight.

There had been something else, though, that had come back with Astrid from Georgia, something more physical than her mental duress over the presence of the woman in white. That first night, Nana had come in, drenched from the storm outside, clutching a handled canvas shopping bag to her chest. She took it everywhere, pressing it to her body, never letting it out if her sight. She'd only let it go when she fell into that solid sleep, and his mother had gently wrested it from her grasp, setting it down next to the end table. When Elise left the room, clicking the light out behind her, Milo was waiting. He crept into the room like a ninja, planting his feet carefully on the carpet so no sound issued forth, and snuck up next to his sleeping nana. She didn't stir, didn't even move, her chest rising and falling regularly, not even snoring. Milo pulled one corner of the bag open and peeked in, curious about what she guarded so jealously. He had expected something shiny, a large chunk of gold, perhaps, an idol of some kind like in the adventure stories his father read to him, its face grimacing hideously and eyes crusted with glittering jewels. He had been sorely disappointed to find there was only a battered, leatherbound book inside. It was dark blue, but worn almost grey at the corners, its pages tattered and dog-eared, a frayed red ribbon stuck between them. He'd let the bag corner drop, disappointed. It was a boring find, not even worth further examination.

But now, thinking back on Nana's reaction to *The Poky Little Puppy* (and the boy in his dreams, don't forget *him*), he wondered. He wondered.

"Whatever her job is," Milo replied, "I don't think it means I'm gonna have to change schools."

"That's good news. I've been thinking about it all day, you know."

"What?"

"What I'd do without you. How sad I'd be if you just suddenly switched to some hoity-toity uptown school for rich snots and left me behind. If you moved on to a whole new life." She sat up, smoothing her skirt nervously. "Guess I don't have to tell you that the thought made me plenty sad."

Milo's heart fluttered, and he felt heat creep into his cheeks. Suddenly the room seemed *too* bright, the light to starkly reveal his wave of pleasure at the idea that Cassie might miss him if he were gone. He tugged at his tie, loosening it, feeling breathless. "Uh…that's…thanks."

"No problem," she said, flapping a hand at him dismissively, either not seeing or ignoring his flustered state. "So what's there to do up here?"

I'd like very much to kiss you, we could do that, was the first thought that rose, unbidden, in his mind. He cleared his throat, rocked on his heels and said, "Um…there's a TV in Nana's room, if you want cartoons. I've got some board games in the closet. I think my Dungeons & Dragons manual is in my backpack, but that takes a little setting up…"

Cassie blew a raspberry. "Bo-ring."

"Well, what do you want to do that's so great?" He snapped, suddenly defensive. Cassie looked at him with a mixture of hurt and surprise, her hand coming up to her chest. He willed himself to be more calm, took a deep breath, and tried again. "Sorry. It's just that…all my stuff isn't here yet. We haven't even had time to go back to the house, with all that's been going on. It's only been a week and I haven't…I haven't been playing much. Just staring at the TV, or the walls, or…"

Or into the mouth of eternity.

Cassie tapped her chin. Then, light came up into her eyes and she hopped off the bed. "I forgot! I have something in Dad's car you might like! Stay right here. I'm gonna go get it."

"OK," he said to her retreating back. Girls were such weird creatures. One minute they were making fun of you, the next minute they were excited to show you something. Milo shook his head. *I may never understand them.*

Cassie was back less than five minutes later, brandishing a rectangular board game box in front of her. "Phew! I thought I'd never get past Ms. Astrid with this, but she got pulled away by some guy right as I came up the stairs!"

Milo eyed the box she set on the ground before him. On it, five smiling kids had their hands on a little heart-shaped thing set on a beige board with black letters and numbers on it. In the center of the board was a picture of a conjoined sun and crescent moon.

"Ouija, the Mystifying Oracle," he read aloud from the cover as Cassie snicked his door shut behind her, "'Amaze your friends! Hours of fun!' I thought you said board games were boring?"

"They are," she said simply, dropping cross-legged down across from him and pulling the box to her. "This isn't a board game, but it *is* a board. A *spirit* board."

Milo eyed the box suspiciously. "A what?"

Cassie let out an exasperated sigh. "It lets you talk to dead people. Spirits. My cousin Tyrone gave it to me last week, and I snuck it with me when dad wasn't looking. I thought...you know..."

She blushed, and Milo knew immediately what she'd thought. His parents were gone from this world, and Cassie thought this cheap particle board and plastic doohickey with the clear lens on top would somehow allow him the miracle he'd craved at the funeral home. It couldn't make them not dead, of course, but it would make forever seem less lonely.

It can't possibly work, he thought wryly. *If it's sold to kids as a toy it's probably crap.*

True enough, but the seductive power of knowing for himself rose up in him all the same. He pointed to the plastic doohickey. "How does it work?"

"That's the planchette. You put it on the board, here, by where it says 'goodbye,' and we each put two fingers on it, here...

and here, see? Then we ask it questions." She set the board down on the carpet and put the planchette in place, placing two of her fingers in the correct spot. "And then, if someone's around, they push the planchette around and spell the answers."

"And that's it?"

"That's it."

"What if..." he hesitated, feeling foolish even entertaining this, but the question nagged at him just the same. "What if nobody's around?"

Cassie pursed her lips. "Someone is *always* around, white boy. Ain't your family ever teach you about the other side?"

"You mean the West Bank?" Milo grinned and did his best Godfather impression. "Are they gonna make me an offer I can't refuse? Make me go against the family?"

Cassie smacked his arm. "Haha, very funny. No, I mean like... heaven and stuff."

The boy, his mind whispered, *the boy with his caved-in head.*

"Not really." Milo shrugged off the shiver that coursed down his spine. "My mom didn't believe in any of that, I don't think. I only remember going to church a couple of times, and thinking it was a great story, but not very realistic."

"That sucks, then, because you're about to learn something about the other side *real* quick." Cassie reached out and grasped both his hands, pulling him forward to put his fingers on the planchette. She rested hers delicately on the other side. "Now ask a question."

He had expected to feel silly putting his fingers down on this beige hunk of plastic, but now that they were on it, he didn't feel that way at all. There was a tingling in his fingers like mild electricity, a low voltage battery that ran up his arm. It felt *right*, somehow, to be in this room with Cassie, to try and open communication with the other side. There was a heaviness in the air as though the entire room were holding its breath for something. What, he didn't know. But something.

And if it doesn't work, you're gonna feel like an asshole for thinking like that.

Milo sighed. "What do I do now?"

"Tyrone said you gotta open up *a window of communication*."

"What's that mean?"

"It means ask if anyone's here, dummy."

"You said someone was always here."

"Smart-ass. Just ask."

Milo looked down at the shiny board with its black, gothic letters, its neatly printed scrollwork on the sides obviously made in a factory somewhere with millions just like it, a never ending stream of portals to the other side. He pictured a factory worker on his smoke break getting pulled aside by a tweedy man in a checkered suit and being told, "You forgot to put the portal in the last twenty-five units! We'll be *ruined!*"

Milo smirked at the image. There was no magic here. Just a toy like any other toy, a thing for kids to play with and nothing more.

But Cassie thinks it's real, and I can't hurt her feelings after she's been so nice to me today.

He took a deep breath, shifting a little. "Is there anyone here?"

Silence. The clock on the wall ticked five long, quiet seconds.

"Hello?" Milo tried again, looking down at the board. "I said, is anyone here that wants to talk?"

It won't move. Cassie will be disappointed, but it won't move. Her cousin probably moved the planchette himse—

The planchette jerked. Milo pulled back, but Cassie stopped his hand with her free one. "Don't break the connection! Quick, ask something!"

"Are you…" Milo's voice broke. He cleared his throat. "Do you want to talk to us?"

This time, the planchette moved immediately, sliding smoothly over the gleaming surface of the board to land with a small squeak over the word YES in the top left corner.

Milo's mouth went dry. "Cassie...are you moving it?"

Cassie opened her mouth to speak, but before she could, the planchette swerved wildly across the board to land on NO.

"We've got one!" Cassie squealed, her eyes bright. "We've really got one!"

"Where are you?" Milo blurted, before even he knew what he was going to ask.

The planchette glided down to the letters and began to spell, very slowly.

"H," Cassie said aloud. "E...R...E. Here, it says here!"

Milo's heart sped up. He thought of the boy, yes, the boy who could be lurking in the shadows waiting to pop out and grab him again, but more than the boy, he thought of his mother. His beautiful mother in the last dress she ever wore could be here in this room, right now, crouched next to him. There was a feeling of *settling* directly to his right, of *gathering*, the carpet pushing down as though an invisible weight had been placed there. That feeling of electricity got stronger, the little hairs on his arms beginning to rise and the bulb in his lamp flickering minutely.

"Do you see that?" he asked Cassie. There wasn't a fleck of spit left in his mouth.

Cassie, pale as pale could be, with the eyes of a spooked horse that smells lightning in the air, nodded. A shudder that was equal parts pleasure and fear ran through Milo's body. He reached up with his free hand and touched the air over the indentation in the rug. It had a thick, meaty quality like he imagined touching a cloud pregnant with torrents of rain might feel.

It's working. It's really working.

"Mama?" He said in a small voice, desperate to confirm what he felt in his heart. He was dimly aware of another feeling in the room, behind the static charge that made the hairs on the back of his neck stand up like he'd rubbed them against a balloon. There was a darker feeling too, one like sticky pools of molten tar. A sucking feeling that could pull you down if you weren't careful where you put your feet. "Mama, is that you?"

The planchette didn't move for several agonizing seconds, and Milo's heart sank. Why wouldn't she answer? Surely she wanted to talk to him as badly as he wanted to talk to her? He held his breath. Then the planchette moved, and he let it out in a long wheeze, watching it glide much more slowly now, as though it were underwater. At first, it seemed to make its way toward NO, but hovered just on the outside of the corner before giving another of those lurches and sailing over to YES.

"Mama," Milo whispered, feeling tears course down his cheeks to spatter on his hands. He smiled, totally unselfconscious of this outpouring of emotion. "I miss you. I wish I could see you again. Is that possible? Do you know?"

The planchette swirled momentarily, bobbing like a seagull floats on a wave, then headed back toward the letters below.

C
O
M
I

"Milo!" Nana's voice snapped them both back to reality. A squall of wood told them she was on the first step of the stairs.

"Hide it!" Cassie said suddenly, taking her fingers away from the planchette and scrabbling to find the box. The indentation on the floor disappeared immediately. Milo wailed to see it go, feeling around for the presence he had felt there only moments before, but it was gone. He hung his head. Cassie snapped her fingers in Milo's face when he didn't move to get up, but merely sat staring at the place where it had been. "Earth to Milo! Help me hide this or Ms. Astrid is gonna be *big mad*."

Milo shook himself, the thought of his nana's wrath on this of all days trumping the loss he felt for not being allowed to continue speaking to his mother's spirit. He grabbed the board and planchette, shoving them in the box, and Cassie slid the top on it. Once packed, he slid the box way, way under his bed and out of sight just as Astrid opened his bedroom door.

"Ah, there you both are," she said, her eyes narrowed. "Why was this door closed?"

"I needed some time away from the noise," Milo lied. "Cassie kept me company."

Astrid tilted her head. "I was born at night, but not *last* night. What were you two doing?"

Milo opened his mouth, but found he had no answer. He looked desperately at Cassie, who saw his predicament and took over. She looked Astrid in the face, laced her fingers together, and dug the rounded toe of her saddle oxford into the carpet. "You promise you won't be mad?"

Astrid looked taken aback, but recovered, folding her arms and looking indulgently at the child. "I promise."

"We were swearing." Cassie spread her hands as if to say *ya caught us*. "I thought a few fuck-yous might make him feel better. I shut the door so nobody would hear us saying bad words and get upset."

Astrid's mouth was an O of surprise for a few seconds, but then she surprised them both by starting to laugh. It was one of those big belly laughs that double a person over, and when she came up, she was wiping tears from her eyes and nodding. "Oh, yes, a few fuck-yous do indeed help at times like these. I'm thankful you had the sense to shut the door, otherwise the old-school crowd might think our Milo had knocked a screw loose."

Milo and Cassie exchanged a glance, smiling. *We got away with it! We did!*

Why it was something they had to get away with, Milo couldn't guess, but he was more than happy to go when Astrid held a hand out to him. "Come on, my darling. We need to say goodnight to our guests. You too, Cassandra."

"I just have to pee, then I'll be down," Cassie said back.

"Alright then. Don't dally, though. Your father has been ready to leave for an hour, I think."

Milo let Astrid whisk him downstairs. He shook hands, gave hugs, even allowed the old ladies to kiss his cheek with their dry, papery lips and chalky lipstick. None of it mattered. He'd talked to his mother, he really had, and Astrid hadn't found out. More than that, he knew the word that was being spelled when they were interrupted *had* to be COMING. His mother was coming. Coming back, for him. He didn't know how that could be possible, but he *did* know his mother never lied while she was alive, so she wasn't about to start now. The thought buoyed him as what seemed like the five hundredth old lady pressed her sallow lips to his skin. He glanced back only once, right as they got into the living room, and watched Cassie sneak back out of the house with the board. She gave him a thumbs-up on her way out.

SEVEN

T HAT NIGHT, WHEN everyone had gone home, Nana took Milo into the kitchen and made them both cocoa. She never used powder and steamed milk like his mother did, but instead used special melting chocolate, cream, and vanilla, carefully warmed in a saucepan on the stove. It was usually a Christmas treat she made him just once a year, but it seemed today was special enough to warrant eschewing that tradition.

She set his mug in front of him and tumbled in a handful of marshmallows, then sat across from him with her own mug. "Today has been difficult on you."

It wasn't a question. Milo nodded, staring glumly at the marshmallows melting in his cup. He took a slow sip, the creamy mixture spreading over his tongue and warming his body, but not his heart. That, he feared, would never be warm again.

"Did Elise ever tell you what I do for a living?" Astrid asked, seemingly apropos of nothing. "Did she ever mention to you what growing up around my work was like?"

Milo shook his head. Took another sip. He was tired and didn't feel like talking—especially about his mother, it hurt so much—but said, "She told me she would tell me when I was older. She said it was nothing a kid should ever grow up knowing about."

Astrid winced at that, her hands shaking as she took a thoughtful sip of cocoa. "She was, perhaps, right about that, and I'll honor her wishes as best I can. But you must know this: in my line of work, you quickly learn that not every closed doorway is closed forever, and that roads we've been taught to see as marked *One Way* are often anything but that."

"I don't understand," Milo sighed, ready for this conversation to be over.

"No, I don't guess you do," Astrid agreed. "But no matter. What I wanted to tell you is that I made a decision today. I won't be taking on any more projects. I'm retiring." Milo looked up, startled, and she smiled. "You need me more than any client ever could, so from now on, I'll be a stay-at-home grandma. Is that alright by you?"

"Alright?" He asked, brightening. "Nana, that's *great news!*" He jumped down from his chair and went over to hug her, squeezing tightly. "Are you sure? Really, really sure?"

"I'm sure."

"You *promise?*"

"I promise," she said, doing the sign of the cross over her heart, tears glimmering in her lashes. "No more traveling. No more late nights. No more sad cases that make my old bones ache with the weight of it all. Just you, me, and our little life together."

"Thank you, Nana," he said, grateful to this marvel of an old woman he was related to by chance of birth alone. How lucky he was to have someone who cared so much for him. He yawned enormously and she chuckled. "Sorry. I'm just so tired."

"As well you must be." She nodded. Then Nana cocked her head, a different kind of smile playing on her face. She looked at Milo curiously, folding her hands on the table before her. "I wonder if maybe you'd like me to read to you tonight?"

He smiled back sleepily. "I'd love that. A story?"

"No, not a story. A poem. A very famous poem from back when I was a girl."

"Do I know the poem?"

"Probably not. But you will after I've read it to you, won't you?"

He laughed. "I guess I will."

"Bring your cocoa with you to the library. Take care not to spill on the rugs, please." He did as he was asked and trailed behind her to the library, holding his mug in both hands in front of him like his life depended on it. She walked into the dark as though she had night vision, then she indicated to the chair she'd gotten that was his size. "Pull that up to my chair, would you? And do put on the light."

Milo placed his mug on the side table next to Nana's chair, clicked the switch that brought them from shadows to soft, warm light, then went to drag his own tiny armchair over to the other side of the table. He grabbed the sheepskin blanket from the back of her chair, wondering at the luxuriousness of the thick pelt, then wrapped himself in it before sitting.

A squeak brought his attention back to Nana, who was standing at the bookcase with the glass section open, her fingertips sliding over the spines of the books within. Milo gasped, sitting bolt upright and pointing. "You said not to touch those! That they're dangerous!"

Astrid laughed. "I said in the *wrong* hands, they're dangerous."

He sat back heavily. "And yours are the *right* hands."

"That's correct. In my hands, not *all* of them are dangerous. Some are just powerful, like the one I'm looking for. Ah!" Astrid slipped a slim, blue, leather-bound volume out from somewhere near the middle and shut the case behind her. "Here we are."

She held it up for his inspection. He squinted, bleary eyed, at the cracked and discolored cover. What appeared to be a large water stain was on the front, as though someone had once rested a sweating glass of ice tea on the cover near the center. "Looks like a book."

"A *special* book," Astrid amended with a chuckle, sitting down in her chair next to him. "This book was once owned by a woman whose name was Clementine Williams, and it has been great comfort to me off and on in the eleven years I've had it in my possession."

"Is Clementine famous?"

"No, not at all." Astrid began flipping through the pages. "She was a very ordinary woman. A nurse, in her time. This was her favorite book of poems, and there's one I think would be particularly fun for a boy your age. If I can find it, that is. Hmm… oh. Here we are. Are you ready, Milo? Quite comfortable?"

He nestled down in the blanket, pulling his feet up into the chair until he was little more than a fluff ball with eyes, so cocooned was he in sheep's wool. "Ready."

"'*Little Orphant Annie*,'" Nana read aloud, "by James Whitcomb Riley:

"'Little Orphant Annie's come to our house to stay,

An' wash the cups an' saucers up, an' brush the crumbs away,

An' shoo the chickens off the porch, an' dust the hearth, an' sweep,

An' make the fire, an' bake the bread, an' earn her board-an'-keep;

An' all us other childern, when the supper things is done,

We set around the kitchen fire an' has the mostest fun

A-list'nin' to the witch-tales 'at Annie tells about,

An' the Gobble-uns 'at gits you

Ef you

Don't

Watch

Out!'"

Milo giggled, then yawned again more deeply. Listening to Nana read was nice. The poem itself was silly and spooky (in an innocuous way) at the same time, and he made a mental note to share this with Cassie around Halloween. She certainly would like it, he thought, with its bouncy verses and the bits about the goblins. His eyelids drooped. Slipped shut. Lay heavily against the murmur of his grandmother's voice.

And then he was dreaming. It was dark, nighttime, moonless, the drizzle beginning to turn into a downpour that couldn't wet him as he ran down the two-lane blacktop toward the overturned car in the road with its wheels still spinning and its horn blatting. There was oil pouring from the car, but no. Not oil. Blood. Blood pooling rapidly, filling the street, running toward the gutter, and what was that sound? A voice?

Help me! Help me, oh please, I have a son! Someone help! A pale arm flopped out of the wreckage, the twitching fingers grasping at the sky.

Milo tried to run faster but the air was like pudding, his feet sucking to the earth and immobilizing him. He was crying, he could feel it. If only he could get to her, his mother, help her, save her somehow, if only he could—

Now why you want to go and look at a thing like that, honey-baby? That's nothing for a child to be lookin' at. A dark hand came around and turned his face to the speaker, and suddenly Milo was face-to-face with the most radiantly beautiful Black woman he'd ever seen. Everything about her, from her dazzling smile full of straight teeth, to her twinkling hazel eyes, to her dress the exact shade of sunshiny days cried out in joy. He stopped trying to fight his way to the car immediately, the grip of the road on his shoes loosening as he turned to face her more fully. She crouched until she was eye level with him, her wild hair tickling him so he giggled. *Tell you what we'll do instead. You come with Ms. Clementine, honey, and we'll have us a good time. The mostest fun, like the poem said. Sound good to you?*

She stuck out one hand, the smooth palm upturned. Milo knew just by looking at it that it would be as warm and inviting as the rest of her. She smelled like honeysuckle and cinnamon.

Sounds good to me, he replied, and took her hand in his.

It was just as warm as he imagined.

EIGHT

1984

T HAT FIRST YEAR passed in fits and starts, time alternately dragging and flying by in whirlwind chunks, as Milo began to navigate a world in which he had no parents. The doldrums of the end of the school year were hardest, when his pain was at its most fresh and the wound still leaking around the edges, but he was given special dispensation from Mrs. Adams, the principal, who sniffled sadly when she told him he'd be graded on a curve if need be. He knew Mrs. Adams thought she was helping by giving him this reprieve from pressure to perform, but he absolutely hated the subtext such an offer held, unspoken: *You are obviously broken and in need of charity.* As it turned out, Milo hadn't needed the curve, had, in fact, aced every exam, but while he was still extremely exhausted by grief and loss, he held on to that day of the funeral, when he'd spoken to his mother through the Ouija board. He'd begged Cassie to bring it over again, but she'd stalwartly refused.

"Tyrone took it back last week," she'd told him in the lunch line after he'd pleaded his case for the fiftieth time. "He says it's more dangerous than he thought."

Whatever that meant.

Then summer rolled into town grinning like a madman, hot and muggy and carrying with it a suitcase full of thunderstorms. Nana enrolled Milo in camp through the Jewish Community Center, and for eight of summer's twelve weeks, he was busier than God listening in on the Sabbath services. He hardly thought about the funeral anymore, or the accident that had caused it, and the distraction of playing constant games, doing crafts, and swimming twice a day with sixteen other sweaty, rambunctious boys his age helped to dull the knife-edge of loss that was forever stuck between his ribs. Here, nobody knew anything about his parents. Nobody even asked. The counselors didn't treat him like some wounded thing that needed rescue, and the kids treated him like nothing more than just another boy. *This* was the respite he'd needed all along, to be treated, simply, like the child he was. He made friends easily at camp, and many days that summer Nana's house was filled with the raucous sounds of boys roughhousing, a sound she minded not at all as long as they were careful about her *precious cargo*. All of them seemed, instinctively, to take her very seriously about those things, and none of them tested the boundaries so much as once.

Cassie came over a lot too, though never when the boys were over. Milo had asked her over once when they were there and she'd wrinkled her nose. "And play gross war games with a bunch of stinky boys? No thanks. No offence, Mi."

Milo hadn't taken offence. He rather preferred keeping Cassie separate from the rest of his friends. It wasn't embarrassment. It was the clean, lovely fact that being alone with her, just the two of them reading under the trees out back, drawing, playing games and laughing, felt better than the idea of sharing her with the others. He had a notion one or two of them might pick on him for being friends with a girl, which didn't bother him, but he *also* had a notion they might try to pick on *her*, which *did* bother him. So he kept his camp friends and his school friend separate, and enjoyed both sets of people completely.

When school began again in the autumn, he was glad despite all the fun he'd had. Nana enrolled him in basketball after Milo hounded her into the ground about it. He'd grown two inches over summer, and he knew he'd be good. He was. The coach made him their point guard, and the team went on to win many games under his leadership. It was only little league, and Milo knew it, but still—it was something to be proud of. Before every game, he turned to his right and whispered into the air, "This one's for you, Mama."

He made new friends through basketball, too. Luke and Ellison still avoided him like the plague, but that was alright. Harry, Dwayne, and DeShawn had replaced them, and these boys were of sterner stuff. They never asked once how he was holding up, how long it had been, was he still having nightmares, et cetera, and that was good. He didn't *want* to tell anyone that sometimes he still woke up screaming from dreams of the bloody wreck that played in slow motion, that the last image was always his mother's head rolling to a stop in front of him, one eyelid drooping, the other eye mutely accusing. He said this to no one, not Nana, not Mrs. Adams (who had finally stopped looking at him like he might be a sick dog whose illness may be catching), not any of his teammates.

No one, that is, except Cassie. Their friendship, always easy to begin with, had deepened considerably over that year. She'd stuck with him every step of the way. She'd held him while he cried, listened with interest when he spoke, encouraged him when he felt stuck and unable to move forward. Milo bloomed under her gentle guidance, and felt for her a love he'd never experienced before. It wasn't *romantic*, exactly, but it wasn't like the love he felt for his family, either, and it was so much more than just friendship. It was its own beautiful feeling, one he guarded fiercely, and protected with his whole heart.

"You wanna walk me home?" Cassie asked as she caught up to Milo after the last bell of the day. "My dad said this morning that he'll drive you uptown so you don't have to ride the bus for two dang hours if you do."

Milo grinned at her. "Sounds great. Those bus seats make my ass hurt."

"What little ass you got, beanpole."

"We weren't all blessed with the bubble butt like you."

"Blessed with the…" Cassie stopped and bent double, laughing until tears squirted out. The heads of other students whipped around to see who had said something so funny. Patricia Hinkle rolled her eyes and turned away. Cassie came back up for air at last and bumped Milo with her hip. "You're hilarious, Mi."

Milo hooked his thumbs into the straps of his backpack and smiled the whole walk to Cassie's house. It was only about three blocks, which was the only reason her dad let her walk at all, and she talked a blue streak the whole way. Milo nodded along, with no desire to interrupt. He loved listening to Cassie talk—about her classes, her new uniform skirt not being soft enough for her liking, the cracked sidewalk being a *city problem,* anything. Being near her was one of life's great joys, and he soaked up every second. It gave him as much, if not more strength, than whispering over his shoulder at the basketball games did. Because Cassie was real, solid, a physical emblem of goodness, and whatever stood by his shoulder (if anything even stood there anymore, if anything had at all) was so much smoke and mirrors. He didn't have to *convince* himself Cassie was there. She just was.

And she aims to stick around, he thought, listening to her chatter about the family of squirrels that had taken up residency in her backyard, watching her hands gesticulate while she spoke. He thought she looked very beautiful, but said nothing. It was better, he thought, to allow the warmth of a fire to wash over you in silence, than to yell to the flames about how warm they were.

When they walked up to Cassie's house, Martin was already outside, delicately pruning the birds of paradise that sprouted along the front garden, trimming off the dead heads of flowers and tossing them in a pile on the lawn. He heard them coming and rose from his crouch, still in his work clothes, and put his fists against the small of his back to stretch it out. He smiled down at them from his great height, his teeth very white in his deeply brown face. "Hey kids."

"Hey Dad," Cassie responded brightly, and went over to hug him. Martin swept her up in his arms as though she weighed nothing, and she laughed. She smacked lightly at his shoulders. "Put me dowwwwwnnn. Making me look like a baby in front of Milo."

"Aw, Milo don't think that, do you?" The jovial giant asked him, winking slyly over his daughter's shoulder.

"No, sir," Milo said, winking back.

Martin laughed. It had a lilting quality Milo loved. Ages ago, in another life, Martin had been part of a brass band where he'd sung backup and played the trumpet. He and Milo's dad had played in a jazz band together in high school, which was where they'd met. He'd even played for the kids a few times, drawing out notes so long Milo was sure he'd had extra lungs hidden somewhere. That was before he'd worked with Greg Cunningham at the stock brokerage firm, had a daughter, and lost his wife in short order. He had been Cassie's sole provider, and provide he did. Milo had only a vague notion of what a stockbroker did, but he knew in his dad's case it meant his hours had been flexible enough to pick him up from school every day, and that they'd had money to spare. He assumed that was why Martin had taken a chance on working with his father instead of sticking to the increasingly unreliable music scene—high risk, high reward, his dad would have said. Martin no longer played loud, raucous, late-night music under hot lights to sweating, gyrating crowds, but the music never seemed to be done with him. He hummed a little as he held Cassie, rocking from side to side in a little extemporaneous two-step before spinning and setting her down lightly on the grass. Cassie laughed and kicked her feet till they hit solid ground.

"I suppose you'll be needing a ride home," he said, reaching his fist out to Milo, who bumped it with his own.

"I suppose you're right."

Martin laughed, big and loud, rocking back on his heels. "Well then, I *suppose* we best get going before traffic becomes a killer-diller and you ain't home till dinner time. I sure don't need Ms. Astrid mad at me, uh-uh, no *thank you*."

Milo chuffed out a laugh, but he knew what Martin meant. Nana was a formidable powerhouse of a woman at any time, but when she was mad, it came off her in waves, like a pulse of electricity, even if she was smiling. She rarely showed anger and never even yelled, but you could feel it all the same. It wasn't a sensation Milo (or anyone else, for that matter) relished.

He climbed into the back of Martin's Cadillac DeVille, tossing his backpack on the floorboard and buckling himself in. Cassie climbed in on the other side, her backpack stowed away in her house already, and smiled at him. Martin got in front and started the Caddy up with a roar of its finely tuned engine, backed carefully out into the street, and away they went. He turned on the radio as they hit the interstate, making conversation impossible (the Caddy had great speakers as well as a fine engine), and tapped along on the steering column, bobbing his head to the music. Milo looked out the window at the cars whizzing by, his chin propped in his hand. The speed at which everything moved thrilled him, but not as much as being in the back seat with Cassie. Even without any conversation, her presence was a comfort he could feel all over his body like a tingle.

Something warm touched his other hand. He glanced down and there, having snuck across the soft upholstery like a silent spider, was Cassie's hand on top of his. Milo felt his face immediately redden. He looked to Cassie, but her eyes were fixed on the window, and she didn't turn. But he could see from her side profile that she was smiling. He wound his fingers in hers experimentally, and her hand opened to his, allowing the extra contact. This time he *was* tingling all over, his synapses firing so fast he felt sure his light-headedness would turn into a faint. A stupid grin broke out onto his face.

Martin cleared his throat and Milo looked up, startled. He could see Cassie's father's eyes in the rearview mirror, and they too were smiling. Martin shook his head slightly, his shoulders shaking in an unheard chuckle, and turned his eyes back to the road.

Feeling as though this was some sort of blessing, Milo held Cassie's hand the whole way home, and he couldn't help the feeling of mild disappointment that cropped up when they pulled up to Nana's house.

"We'll watch you till you get inside, Milo," Martin said when he snapped off the radio. "You've got your keys, right?"

"Right here." Milo jingled them as he shouldered his pack. "Thanks for the ride, Mr. Johnson."

"My pleasure, son."

"See you at school tomorrow," Cassie called from the rolled-down window as Milo mounted the sidewalk.

He turned to her and waved, his head still swimming from her prolonged touch. She waved back and smiled brightly, making his heart light up like a Christmas tree. He turned the key in the lock, his mind drifting once more around the idea of what it might be like to kiss her, how her lips would feel pressed against his own.

"Nana, I'm home!" He called into the cool dimness of the house, throwing a final wave to Mr. Johnson to let him know he was in safe. Martin waved back, the Cadillac's engine revving as he pulled back into the street and away. Milo noticed with no little pleasure that Cassie was still watching him, popping up in the rear window to give one final wave, even as the Caddy disappeared from view. Milo shut and locked the door, feeling very warm despite the air conditioned coolness of the house. "Nana? Are you home?"

A silly question, really. Of course she was home. She always made it a point to be here when he got back from school, saying that even when his mother was little, she despised the idea of "latchkey kids" coming home to an empty house. He dropped his backpack by the door and rubbed his arms. A lot of the downstairs lights were off, but that didn't mean much. Astrid often opened the blinds during the day, claiming natural light was better than electric on sunny days, and today had, until recently (Milo had seen the mounting thunderheads in the distance as they whizzed down the interstate) been a very sunny day. Now, though, it was somewhat overcast, those grey clouds piling up outside adding to the gloom in the house, and Milo squinted upstairs, looking for light. Seeing none, he moved into the den, letting his eyes adjust to the low light. The room was still and silent save for the amiable ticking of Nana's ancient grandfather clock, which was now twenty minutes away from sounding its four p.m. *bongs*, the gold pendulum swinging its constant arc back and forth. On the overstuffed paisley couch by the window slept Mingus, Milo's cat—a present for his tenth birthday, the only thing he'd asked for—the pale orange fur of his sides rising and falling in deep sleep. He heard Milo coming and let out a surprised, questioning sound—*prrt?*—blinking sleepily at his boy before stretching and yawning expansively. Mingus hopped down and trotted over, rubbing himself against Milo's legs and *waow*-ing with his rusty little voice.

Milo leaned down and stroked the cat absently. "Where's Nana, Mingus? Do you know, buddy?"

Mingus let out another crispy-sounding *waow*, then flopped on the floor, making biscuits in the air with his little pink toes.

"Thanks, that's a big help." Milo straightened back up, thinking. *Maybe she's in the tub.*

But that was also unlikely. Astrid showered first thing in the morning every single day, a habit that she said woke a body up better than any coffee or tea. Perhaps she was outside doing work in the greenhouse, then, and lost track of time. But no. Nana set kitchen timers for *everything*, and had never once not been present the very moment he got home.

Milo thought suddenly of the old lady at his parents' funeral.

At least you have Astrid to care for you, as long as nothing goes wrong, hm?

His stomach dropped as though he'd swallowed a heavy stone, all pleasure from his ride home with Cassie's hand in his washed away in one drenching, icy wave.

"Nana?" He called again, his voice breaking. He moved through the dark den, past the library doors, into the narrow hallway that went under the stairs, Mingus at his heels. The kitchen door was closed, but a light gleamed underneath, spilling shadows on the walls. Mingus began nudging the heavy door with his head, as though trying to hold the door open for his friend despite his small size. Milo moved forward, his legs numb, and pushed the door open a crack with one sweating hand, Mingus squirting through the crack as soon as it was big enough for him to get inside.

She's dead, she's dead on the floor, you're alone now, they're all gone, you're alone, she's de—

Astrid was sitting at the kitchen table, her face drawn and her hair hanging loosely around her face. Her long-fingered, elegant hands were wrapped around a steaming mug of black tea, one thumb tapping delicate patterns on the handle of the mug. Her eyes were distant, unblinking, her mouth working as she chewed at her lower lip. Mingus was under her chair making loud requests for either food, attention, or both, but Astrid paid him no mind.

"Nana," Milo breathed, relief pushing back the icy waves of terror like the warm hand of God pushing apart the Red Sea so that reason could once again walk the floor of his mind unhindered. Of course Nana wasn't dead. She was healthy as ever, even her doctors said so, in remarkable, sturdy health for her age. She'd assured him she wasn't going to the other side of the veil for a long, long time. And Nana always told the truth. "Nana, I'm home."

"Hm?" Astrid said, her voice distant. She turned her head towards the sound of his voice, her eyes following a few seconds after. She stared at Milo for a few seconds, uncomprehending, but then all at once her attention seemed to focus on the here and now. She blinked rapidly a few times, then smiled thinly at him, holding out her arms. He went to her and she embraced him, kissing the top of his head before holding him at arm's length. "Hi, honeybunch. Sorry, I was just…How was school?"

Her hands were like ice blocks on his shoulders, even through his clothes, despite having been wrapped around the hot mug only moments before. It was not a comforting feeling. "It was OK. Mark Dillinger got in trouble for writing swears on the bathroom stall doors on the second floor."

She laughed, leaning toward him. "What swears did he pick, do you know?"

Milo nodded, a mischievous smile on his face. "I saw them before Mr. Charles scrubbed them off. He wrote 'Mr. Peters Sucks Big Fucking Cocks' on one, and 'Pissfuck Dickhole' on the other one."

Astrid clapped her hands, her head rocking back as she laughed. Milo laughed too, all his tension gone, forgetting for the moment how those hands felt on his shoulders. When she managed to get herself under control, Nana wiped a tear away, her shoulders still shaking. "Those are very good swears. I'm sure Mr. Peters is thrilled to have been included."

"Oh, he was. Two weeks detention's worth of gratitude."

She chuckled, shaking her head. "It's a thankless man who doesn't recognize a creative force when he sees one. One day he'll see Mark's work in an art gallery and regret it. And what about you? Anything interesting happen to *you* today?"

Milo thought about telling her about Cassie walking with him, about how he felt when she bumped him with her hip, about holding her hand and the feeling like he was going to explode in a good way, but decided against it. He wasn't sure what any of it actually meant, and didn't want Nana (or any other adult) ascribing a spin to it that wasn't there. Or, at least, one he wasn't *sure* was there, even if he *kind of* wanted it to be. For now, those were memories and feelings that were just for him. He shrugged. "Not really. Just a boring day at school."

"Funny," she said slyly, leaning her chin into her palm and examining his face with her large, thoughtful grey eyes. Those eyes danced with merriment, were the eyes of a much younger person, shrewd, calculating, full of fun. Those eyes saw *everything*. "You don't *look* like you had a boring, normal day. Are you sure there's nothing you want to tell me?"

Milo shifted under her penetrative gaze. "I'm sure."

Astrid said nothing for a moment, merely looked at him, measuring him with those eyes and taking him in. What she saw there, he had no idea, but from the way she was looking, he knew she could sense a change in him. Probably knew more, in fact, than he did himself. She squinted a bit, blinked, then turned her gaze back to her mug of tea.

Milo relaxed, watching her take a sip. It was something akin to relief that he felt when her eyes finally turned away, and he was much chagrined by that feeling. It wasn't like he was afraid she'd see something bad—he had nothing at all to hide—it was just that when she looked at you that way, you felt like she could see into your secret heart, where all your innermost workings lie stark naked to those questioning grey eyes. Like she was reading your diary right in front of you. He decided to move the conversation away from himself, away from that dangerous territory. "Did *you* have anything interesting happen today, Nana?"

Astrid pulled up short mid-sip, spilling tea out onto the table and her blouse, where it spread and darkened on the white fabric. She swore quietly and put the mug down. "Paper towels, dear."

Milo rushed to the sink and pulled three paper towels and brought them back.

"Thank you," Nana muttered, placing two down on the table where tea flowers began to bloom as the towels absorbed the liquid, and used the third to blot the stain on her blouse. She tutted. "Well, this is ruined."

That was the wrong question. Milo swallowed, a click in his throat. "I'm sorry if I said something to upset you."

She flapped the towel at him. "No, no, it's not *what* you said, just...well. I suppose you surprised me, is all." She shot him a look that was part observation, part question. "You have a habit of asking exactly the right question at exactly the right time.

Most people only get it right by chance, but you...you, I think, get it right as a matter of course."

He made a face. "What does *that* mean?"

"It means I think you're quite a bit more sensitive than you know." She put the towel down and scooped up Mingus, stroking him, talking in the baby voice people reserve for small children and animals. "But never mind an old lady's ramblings, eh, little boy? It doesn't matter. No, it sure doesn't." The cat settled into her lap as she petted him, looking back up at Milo and dropping the cat-voice. "It appears I'm going to have to go back to work."

"Work?" Milo blurted. "But I thought you were done with it?"

"I thought so too," Astrid replied, a small, sad smile touching her mouth, "but it appears it is not yet done with me."

"But...but..." Milo couldn't articulate the range of emotions he felt at her words. There was sadness, a balky sort of defiance against the facts, disappointment, and anger. Yes, anger, in a great, nettling tangle around everything else. His grandmother had promised him, on that night following the funeral, that she wouldn't go back to work, not ever, and it appeared that promise had been made to be broken. Hot shame rose into the cracks of his heart, bubbling like lava, that he had thought himself more important to her than whatever her work was. Not like she'd tell *him* what she was doing, oh no, she—

"I can see you're upset by that," she said softly, reaching over to cover his hand with her own. He pulled away from the touch. She looked hurt, but tucked her hand back into her lap just the same. "I assure you, my darling, if this could be done by anyone else, I would hand over the responsibility immediately. But there is no one else. Just me. And for that, I am deeply sorry."

Milo frowned, staring at the space between them on the table, not trusting himself to look into her eyes lest he start crying. He didn't want to cry in front of her today, didn't want this new development to overshadow the pleasure of holding Cassie's hand in the backseat of her father's Cadillac. "But you promised."

Astrid sighed. "I did, and that's the part I'm most sorry about. I shouldn't have promised something like that, knowing that the world has a way of making a person break them with the back-bending call of duty. I wish more than anything that it wasn't so, that this responsibility wasn't mine to bear." She spread her hands out on the table, her long, ringed fingers splayed. "I always hated breaking promises. To your mother, when she was a little girl, and now to you. I fear those broken promises were why she was so reluctant to talk with you about my work. There's nothing for it now. I must go, and you must stay."

Milo's stomach lurched unpleasantly, and then he *did* look at his nana, searching her face. She looked old and tired, her eyes downcast, her wrinkles deeply set in her face where her brows drew together. "Where are you going? Is it far away?"

"No." She shook her head. "I have to go to Lafayette, which is only about four hours from here. Close enough that if you really need me to come home, I can."

"How long will you be gone?"

She shrugged, hugging her elbows. "That, I don't know. Perhaps as little as a couple of days, maybe as long…" Her voice broke. She swallowed hard. "Maybe as long as a month."

"A *month*?" Milo cried, feeling those tears behind his eyes again, burning and heavy as his heart. "But that's…that's *so long*. What about exams? What about basketball practice?"

"You won't be alone, of course," she said so quietly he could barely hear it. "Tabitha and Chester have agreed to come stay with you while I'm gone."

"Aw, *shit*." he spat.

"Language," Astrid said mildly, but he could see the swearing wasn't even remotely bothersome to her. Her mind was elsewhere.

"Why does it have to be *them?*" Milo hated the whine he heard in his voice, but couldn't help it.

It wasn't that he *disliked* Tabitha and Chester, just that they weren't ideal. Tabitha was Nana's housekeeper, a tall, reedy woman with buckteeth and a great cloud of frizzy, iron-grey hair she kept swept up in a severe bun on top of her head. She had a habit of wearing dresses that looked like they were pulled directly out of the fifties, and a "children should be seen and not heard" attitude to match. She liked Milo fine—the way all employees "liked" their employer's children, he thought—but always seemed to look down her beaky nose at him. Her husband Chester, by contrast, was a portly man with a stomach tight and round as a basketball under his shirt, a double chin, and watery mud-colored eyes behind his owlish spectacles. His hair, of which there wasn't much, stuck out in yellowish-white tufts from the sides of his head. He had a jovial, loud voice and melodious English accent that Milo enjoyed listening to while he told him stories. Chester was Nana's accountant by trade, but took great joy in being an unofficial member of the family, and had taken pains every year since Milo was a baby to ensure he picked Milo a gift he'd enjoy. The couple constantly bickered in a genial way with one another, a thing Milo thought was perhaps customary in couples who had been married a long time, but the tiffs rarely ended in anything but a haughty "hmpf" from Tabitha when Chester lapsed into unaccustomed silence. In short bursts, they were comical, kind (if standoffish, for Tabitha's part) people that Milo looked forward to seeing when they came alone or as a pair. This time, however, he was less than thrilled.

"There isn't anyone more capable of taking care of your needs, and the needs of my home." Astrid looked out the window at the rain beginning to patter onto the glass. "This place needs people in it who know how to care for it, and you need people who know you well enough to get everything done for you that needs doing. The Beckenhams know how to do both with ease."

"Why couldn't I stay with Cassie?" He burst out, the anger bubbling to the surface. "Didn't you ever think of *that*?"

Astrid turned round to look at him, a shocked expression on her face. "Milo, do you not understand that this was short notice? That I couldn't *possibly* ask Martin to undertake *more* responsibilities than he already has, at the drop of a hat? How unfair that would be to him?"

"*It's unfair to me!*" Milo shouted, and now the tears came, slipping hot and heavy down his cheeks and making rivulets on his skin before spattering onto the table top. "It's all unfair to me! You broke your promise, and now you're leaving me with those... those...*weirdos! It's bullshit!*"

Astrid was silent for a moment, her head cocked, musing on what he said while Milo stood before her, fists clenched, shaking with rage and breathing in choked gasps. She tapped one long finger on the table, thinking, her expression unreadable. Finally, she seemed to rouse herself, her shoulders set back and her spine straightening, her eyes becoming as stony and fixed as the thin line of her mouth. Now, she didn't look the least bit penitent, not the soft, sorry woman he'd come home to find slumped in the kitchen. Now she looked exactly the way she really was— formidable, decisive, immovable in her purpose. Her eyes blazed as she looked down at him, and her voice, though measured, carried both threat and promise in equal measure. "I understand you're upset. I agree with you that this isn't the ideal set of circumstances. I have tried to be kind and set things up in a way that will benefit you in my absence, as well as make it easier on me to be away. I have given my word to people in need that I will help them, and on that I will not renege based solely on the whims of a selfish boy who knows nothing of the larger picture.

I *will* be leaving, and you *will* be staying here with Chester and Tabitha, no matter what you may think about the fairness of that arrangement. Life is, you'll find, rarely fair. I *also* do not want to be doing what I must do, understand that—you are not the only one who feels these things acutely. Your emotions are understandable, but I will not allow you, my flesh and blood, to sit here swearing at me in my kitchen as though you're a toddler having a tantrum. Do I make myself abundantly clear, child?"

Milo took a step back. The anger was being rapidly replaced by a new feeling, the feeling that he'd messed up badly and perhaps could not go back from this. "B-but…"

"But nothing." She cut him off with a wave of her hand. "Do I make myself clear? Yes or no."

His cheeks reddened as if he'd been slapped, the heat dipping below his collar and to his chest. "Yes."

"Good. Now go to your room for fifteen minutes and think about what we've talked about. If you have a change of heart, my darling, come down so I can tell you goodbye properly without all this unnecessary drama. If you haven't changed your mind, don't come down until you do. Yes?"

"Yes."

"Good. Go on, then, my love. I hope you come down soon."

He had trudged morosely through the house, making it all the way to the third stair before he heard Nana let out a sob from the kitchen, and his heart—which until now had felt sorry only for himself—gave a little pang for her. He shut his door quietly behind him and climbed on his bed, sitting down cross-legged with his chin in his hands to think, just as he'd been bade. Thunder grumbled outside, its proximity a warning that the evening would surely be a wet one.

She has a job to do. It's how she makes enough money to afford this house. It's how she keeps you at your school with your friends

315

instead of at the public school up the road from here. He scratched at his chin, picking a small scab there. *And it's just her now.*

Yes, that was all true. Astrid (and Chester Beckenham, to some degree, being one of Nana's oldest friends) was the only one of his immediate family left, and she had a job that more or less had made sure she could be home with him for an entire year since his parents' double death. His father's parents were both long in the ground. Pappy Cunningham had died when Milo was around five—the memories Milo had of him were shadowy and grainy, amounting to little more than a handful of snapshots in the family album. MawMaw Cunningham had gone even before that, of a fast-acting cancer. Nana's husband had passed when Milo's mom was a baby, in a factory accident, and somehow the young woman with a baby girl had managed to survive in a time when being a single mother was as good as a death sentence. It was possible Elise's reluctance to speak on Nana's line of work had stemmed from being shunted off on family or friends while her mother was away for an indeterminate time, but what of that? Adults did what they could to survive, and the career afforded Astrid and her daughter a life of plenty that meant she never had to remarry to keep them afloat. And now, at last, it had come to pass again that they needed the money that came with that career, and Nana was doing her best to ensure that it didn't become a burden to anyone else, or strain Milo's friendship with an extended stay under Cassie's roof. That was all. Surely, that was all. If you looked at it that way, he was being very silly indeed trying to hold her to a promise she'd made when they were both raw from loss and not thinking clearly.

Is that all it is, though? He asked himself, tugging a string on his comforter, unravelling the edge. *Why won't she just tell me what she does? Is it something she's ashamed of?*

And, on the heels of that, *Is it illegal?*

He pondered these questions as meticulously as his age allowed, and decided it didn't matter. Nana was a whole person, with thoughts and feelings and, yes, secrets, and that was alright. Milo knew she'd never do anything to put him in *danger*, no matter what else was required of her from time to time, so that meant no, she wasn't doing anything illegal. Whether she felt shame or not about her job was none of his concern unless she chose to tell him about it, and that was that. Besides, his dad had talked about his job all the time and Milo only understood about a quarter of what it all meant. He was sure whatever Nana did would be more of the same, when you got down to it. He didn't know it, but this was his first mature thought, his first experience in *adult* reasoning, and it passed not with a bang, but with a growl of nearby thunder.

When he felt enough time had passed, he went back downstairs to the kitchen, to find Nana standing at the bay window looking out at the gathering storm with Mingus in her arms. When the cat saw Milo, he *waowed* loudly and began struggling in Astrid's arms. She turned, dropped the animal lightly to the ground, then looked up at Milo as she brushed hair from her cardigan. Her eyes had a mixture of fear and wary hope in them that broke Milo's heart.

"I'm sorry I yelled," he said, his voice thin in his own ears with contained emotion. He wanted more than anything for this gentle woman to stop looking at him as though he were a dog that had bitten once and may again. "And I'm sorry I swore. I know you have a job to do, and I know it's important to you—and our family—that you do it, so it should be important to me too." He looked down at his sneakers. "Just…"

Astrid crossed the room and put a hand on his shoulder. The other she used to tilt his face up to look into hers. "Just what, my darling?"

"Just…promise you'll come back safe. As soon as you can."
He tried for a smile. "You're really important to me, you know."

Nana enfolded him in her arms, hugging tightly. He hugged
back just as fiercely. "I'll be home, safe and sound, the very second
I am able to complete my work in Lafayette. This is a promise
I can definitely keep, that can never, ever be broken. Come hell
or high water."

NINE

TWO HOURS LATER, the Beckenhams were at the house, and Astrid was kissing Milo goodbye.

"Don't forget your project for Ms. Gordon is due Thursday," she said as she gathered her bags in her hands.

"I won't."

"And the stew in the crock-pot should go onto 'warm' at seven. Remind Tabitha for me, would you?"

"I will."

"Well," Astrid breathed, her bags and umbrella in her hands, her rain slicker buttoned neatly and her rain boots on. Outside it was pouring already, and would only get worse in the next couple of hours. Milo's only comfort was that Nana said she was driving out of it as soon as she turned west. "It seems everything here is in order. Got a kiss for your old Nana?"

Milo did. He stood on his toes and kissed her on both cheeks when she bent down, making her laugh. His heart ached, hearing that laugh. He waved to her from the window when she drove away, and she beeped the horn twice in response and then was gone.

Now Milo sat at the coffee table in the living room, doing his homework before dinner, under the watchful eye of Chester and Tabitha Beckenham. Tabitha was sitting primly in the armchair under the lamp, her ankles crossed, knitting on her lap. Chester was sprawled on the couch, legs akimbo, sipping a glass of Nana's Glenfiddich 18 Year with a lone cube of ice swirling around inside. He fidgeted quite a bit, which kept distracting Milo from his work, his jumpy movements punctuated with a grunt or a sip of his drink. The grandfather clock let out a soft *bong* to signal the half hour and Chester said, "oh!"

The living room lapsed into silence, save for the ticking of the clock and the clack of Tabitha's knitting needles working rapidly back and forth. After the fifth time Chester went "ooh!" for no apparent reason at all, Milo sighed and put down his pencil. "Everything OK, Mr. Beckenham?"

"Right as rain, lad, right as rain," Chester replied, although he didn't look it. He blinked rapidly several times, his eyelids twitching as his red-rimmed, muddy brown eyes swiveled this way and that around the room. Thunder boomed outside and Chester let out another yelp. "Speaking of, it sounds as if the storm is picking up. I hope Astrid made it somewhere dry to wait it out."

Milo, who had been thinking the same thing, nodded. He knew Nana would do everything in her power to stay safe so that she could be home soon, including stopping at a diner or truck stop if the rain made it too difficult to navigate the road. He knew because she'd promised him.

Chester let out another "ooh" and Tabitha sighed, temporarily setting down her needles in her lap. "Chez, would you *please* stop starting at shadows? It's going to be a very long week if you're jumpy as a cat."

Her accent wasn't nearly as melodious as Chester's. The vowels were deeper, the tone more nasal, especially when she sniped at her husband. Milo sat back and gazed at them both, taking them in. It occurred to him that this was the first time he'd been alone with the two of them for any length of time, and the differences in them were stark. "You're from different places."

Chester startled him with a great *haw-haw* of laughter. "Quite right. You've a keen ear on you, I see."

"Are you from London, Mr. Beckenham?"

"Ha! Nothing so grand as the capital, I'm afraid, no—" Chester replied, taking a swig of his scotch. He pointed to himself and then his wife. "I'm from Wimbledon, and Tabby is from Hook."

Milo jigged his feet, thinking. "Wimbledon. The place with all the tennis?"

Chester grinned, showing off a set of teeth yellowed from years of smoking filterless cigarettes, a pack of which poked up from the pocket of his polo shirt. "The place with all the tennis, yes, the very one."

"What's Hook famous for?"

"Absolutely bloody nothing." Chester spread his arms in mock supplication when his wife tutted loudly. "Sorry, sorry, but I can't help the truth, dear. Hook is nothing but a smudge on the map with a train station in it." He turned his attention back to Milo. "Idyllic views, it has in places, mind—great, lovely hillsides, sweeping green fields outside town—but it's never going to be famous for anything unless someone born there does something to *make* it famous. And even then, they'd have to leave to get themselves a name."

"*Honestly,* Chester," Tabitha sniffed, shaking her head, "you act as though I came from some…some…*hick* town."

"What an American thing to say, my love," Chester mused. He shrugged, draining the glass and looking balefully into the emptiness left behind. "Doesn't matter. We're New Orleanians now."

Milo watched him haul himself off the couch, groaning all the way, and cross to the bar Nana kept on the far wall. It was a lovely piece of furniture with beautiful decanters of all shapes and sizes, and glasses for every type of drink you could want slid into a rack above, with a mirror set at the back. Last month, in curiosity, Milo had opened the top of the decanter Chester was pouring from and taken a whiff. He'd immediately put the stopper back in, gagging at the sharp, acrid odor of the scotch. It didn't seem to bother Chester, though. The man hummed as the liquor *blub-blub-blubbed* its way into his glass, his eyes shifting this way and that, his posture stiff despite the merry tune in his mouth. He sniffed loudly, cleared his throat, then cast around, looking for the stopper.

"I know Nana's known you since before I was born, so I guess you've lived here a long time."

Chester jumped at the statement, slopping scotch onto the bar. "Oh, dash it all," he mumbled, grabbing one of the bar towels to wipe it up. His hand was trembling as he did so. As he wiped, he said to Milo, "Ah…yes. Yes, we've been here a long time. But not since before you were born, I don't think. Maybe about five years? Six?"

"Six," Tabitha said, her voice flat. Milo turned to look at her and saw that she hadn't returned to her knitting, her face as pale as a sheet.

"Yes, six, thank you, dear." Chester stopped fumbling with the rag, plugged the decanter, and turned away from the bar to make his way back to his seat. He didn't look at Milo as he moved, his mouth twitching right along with his eyes as he rapidly blinked. He sat with a great *whoompf*, spilling more scotch onto the back of his hand as he did. "But we've known your nana a good deal longer than that."

"How long?"

"Full of questions, are you, young sir?" Chester asked back sharply, but then his voice softened. "Ah, well, I don't doubt that you are. That horrible business with your parents, being stuck in this…this house…with all these…" he fetched a sigh. "We met your nana when I was twenty-four and Tabby was twenty-two. So that makes it…oh…well over a decade, maybe more, that we've known the wise and eminent Astrid Schulze. We met her in England, when—"

Tabitha made a warning sound in her throat and both Chester and Milo looked at her in unison. She was still pale, dark circles showing under her eyes, and she curtly shook her head. "No, Chester. No."

"Well, what d'you expect me to—"

"Nana's been to England?" Milo piped up, eager to get on with the conversation. He could already sense it might be an important one, the things unsaid as important as the ones uttered. He just had to listen. Listen, gather, learn.

"Oh, yes, yes, she's been to England, all right. And a great many other places besides, I'd warrant." Chester rubbed his chin thoughtfully. Abruptly, he said, "Let me ask *you* something, Milo: is there, in this house, a painting of a little girl with a dog? Wearing a—"

"Velvet dress," Milo finished for him, nodding. "Yeah. It's upstairs, across the hall from my bedroom."

"Is it, now?" Chester's eyebrows raised, his eyes comically large and inquisitive behind his glasses, his index finger tapping the cupid's bow of his lips. "Interesting choice of placement for her, across from a child's room. Very interesting. And you're sure it's the same painting as I described? Not just something similar?"

"Her dress is dark blue, and she has a bow that's red. Her hair is really long and curly, the same shade as the dog on her lap. She's got blue eyes, though. And it…feels weird to look at it too long." Milo scrunched up his face. "I don't look at her if I can help it. If you don't believe me, I can show her to you so you can see for yourself."

"Oh, I have no desire to see her again, dear lad, but thank you. I'd rather not reopen that particular can of worms." Chester said in a dreamy, disconnected voice. "I believe you."

Tabitha let out a choked sob, her knuckles pressed to her lips, and looked wistfully up the stairs, her free hand coming up to touch the little silver crucifix on a chain that lay against her chest.

"Don't even think it, Tabby," Chester said darkly, never taking his eyes off Milo. Tabitha immediately turned away from the stairs and focused on the knitting sitting limply in her lap. Chester took a deep breath and let it out slowly, his cheeks puffed out, blowing his liquor-laden breath at Milo. "We bought that painting at an estate sale when Tabby and I moved into our first house. In Hampstead, that was. Just us and... and our little girl. Elizabeth."

Tabitha let out a choked sob. "Chester, no."

Chester ignored her. "We bought it for seven pounds, at an estate sale, but the price was so much higher than that in the end. Yes it was. Elizabeth—she was only five, mind—was fascinated by the thing. Insisted we put it in her room. We saw no reason not to. She would sit with it for hours, talking to it, playing tea party with it, or just gazing at it. Once I walked in on her standing in the middle of the room, slack jawed, glassy eyed, just...staring. She was only half dressed, the top of her pajamas still clutched in her hand, her chest hitching up and down like she was dreaming. I shook her a few times, scared as I was to see this, trying to rouse her. When she finally came around, she only turned her placid blue eyes to me and said, as if in a dream, 'Hi, Da.'

"I hated the damn thing after that. Didn't trust it. Tabby felt the same, but Elizabeth insisted we let her keep it. Said the girl in the painting was her friend. She screamed bloody murder when I took it down off the wall, intent on chucking it in the bin outside. She cried and held onto my leg and begged me not to do it. Her little face was so full of real sorrow, you see, lad, but something else as well. Anger. Brutal, intense anger, like she'd hate me forever for getting rid of her friend like this. You may find out in your lifetime, you may not, but it's agony to be a parent and have your child look at you like that. So I...we...let her keep it. We conferred on it, Tabby and me, about whether it was prudent, but aside from a slight feeling of uneasiness and distaste, we couldn't pinpoint a really solid reason to force Elizabeth to give it up. Tabby was all for taking it away when she was asleep, but I felt that was a dirty, underhanded way of dealing with it, so it was me who made the final call and allowed it to stay.

"But then...then, about a month later...Elizabeth... disappeared. In the night, you see, with no trace. We put her to bed one night, kissed her goodnight and tucked her in, and in the morning she was just...gone. Her nightgown was still in the bed, and her Teddy, even her hair ribbon still neatly tied in a bow—but of our little girl there was no trace. All the windows and doors were locked securely, none were unsecured, nor were any broken. It was a complete mystery. You can imagine—or maybe you can't, you're too young—what kind of stress, shame, and horror this caused us. Our child, vanished! We scoured the countryside, put up fliers everywhere, involved the police, everything. We were utterly distraught. Our only daughter, missing."

"Weeks went by," Tabitha said suddenly, startling Milo. Her voice creaked like rusty hinges of a disused iron gate, her eyes distant windows full of ghosts. "We feared the worst. But we had no idea that the *worst* was ever so much more horrible than we expected."

She fell silent. Milo's stomach turned, looking at these two people he barely knew, feeling sorry for them. If *he* had gone missing, no doubt Nana would be just as stressed as these two had been, maybe worse, since she'd already buried her daughter. Chester was right; he *couldn't* imagine how horrible it must be for someone to go missing like that. Die, sure, that grief he knew, but missing? The uncertainty of it all? That was an entirely different beast. One with sharp and hungry teeth that ate away at the soul bit by tender bit.

"Did you ever find her?" Milo ventured, dreading the answer but needing to know.

"Oh yes, we found her," Chester said, chuffing out rueful laughter. It was the laugh of a corpse, no life in it at all, and Milo felt the skin on his balls crawl tight at the sound. "Tabby was cleaning Elizabeth's room—dusting, freshening the linens, things we couldn't bear leaving undone lest she return—and I heard her scream. I came running and Tabby was ghostly, pointing a trembling finger at that painting. You see, when we purchased it, the girl in the picture was blonde, with dark brown eyes and a heart-shaped face with pink cheeks, wearing that blue dress and red bow. Captivating eyes that looked so alive they were a bit spooky, if I'm honest. Like they knew something you didn't. Now, though, *now*...the girl in the painting had brown hair, much longer than the previously blonde hair had been, and an oval face. Shaped like mine, see. But the eyes were the worst. Elizabeth had these gorgeous dark blue eyes, the exact shade of dark denim, with an icy blue ring around the pupil. She inherited them from Tabby. We'd found our little girl, Milo old son, and not in any way we'd expected or could comprehend."

Fascinated, utterly chilled, Milo leaned forward. "She was... she *is*...inside the painting?"

Chester sat back in his chair, seemingly spent by the telling of the story, and shrugged. "Your nana seemed to think so. When she came to us, she—"

Tabitha reached over and sharply kicked his ankle.

"Ow, you hag!" Chester exclaimed, leaning over to rub his wounded ankle and slopping scotch on his trousers in the process. "What was that for?"

"We're to honor his mother's wishes," she replied curtly, nodding at Milo. "And you've said too much already, you flappy-lipped drunk."

"Not as though you tried to stop me, did you?" Chester snapped back.

Tabitha sniffed, tutting. "As if I ever could."

"Phroar, you she-devil, I'd like to—"

Beeeeeeeeeep.

They all turned toward the kitchen as the kitchen timer let them know dinner was ready. Tabitha got up, set down her knitting, primly smoothed her skirt and said thickly, "No more of this talk. It's not our place to fill the boy's head with stories of the past. If Astrid thinks he should know, she'll tell him. Milo, let's get up and go to dinner now, dear."

Milo did as he was bade, gathering his school things up into a neat pile as Tabitha left the room to go get everything ready for dinner. Alone with Chester, Milo watched him from the corner of his eye, eyeing the portly man with the sad face and rheumy eyes contemplate the staircase and what lay beyond.

He knows more than his wife will let him tell you, Milo thought. *Maybe he even knows everything.*

"So…" Milo asked, trying to sound more casual than he felt. This next question must be very carefully worded indeed, and he was almost positive this was the right one. "…how *did* you guys end up living in New Orleans?"

"Eh, what?" Chester said, startling out of whatever grim reverie he'd been swimming in. "Hm? Oh. Well. That's…easily answered, I suppose." He scratched his chin thoughtfully. "Your nana—years after the business with the painting, that was—made a very persuasive argument as to how we could change our lives for the better by moving to America. We struggled, you see, to live in that house with all the memories, to live in England at all, and we'd kept in touch enough that she knew our situation. Dutiful in her obligations, is your nana. So we moved, simple as that. Astrid offered us each a job, and the promise that Elizab—the painting was safely ensconced in her home forevermore. That was all we needed, really. A fresh start, and to be close by. In case she…"

He trailed off, his eyes once more drifting back to the stairs.

Dishes clacked together in the kitchen. Tabitha called, "Are you boys about ready to eat?"

"Just about!" Chester called back, shooting a furtive glance toward the kitchen before waving Milo closer. Milo got up and went to him, and Chester pulled him down by the arm of his shirt, liquor fumes wafting off the big man's breath as he whispered. The grip on Milo's shirt was strong, the eyes that looked at him clear, hard, and direct, all their twitching confabulation gone. "It's good you don't like looking at it. Keep it that way. Never, ever look at that painting for long. Especially the eyes. Could be it just works on girls, but taking risks where you needn't take them isn't going to win you any prizes. You hear?"

Milo nodded, his chest tightening under that stare. To him, Chester looked not only firm, but grimly frightened, not of the painting, exactly, but for the boy he held in his grasp.

"Boys?" Tabitha called again.

"Coming!" Chester stood up, lowered his voice. He held Milo by the shoulder in a fatherly way. "Mind what I said. But please don't mention what I said to Tabby."

"I won't." That, the boy knew, wouldn't be prudent at all.

"Good lad." He patted Milo's shoulder absently, his eyes drifting inexorably back to the stairs. They twitched ever so slightly at the corners. "Now let's go see what's for dinner. And Milo?"

Milo looked up at him. "Yes?"

"Don't ask Tabby any more questions about Elizabeth." His eyes softened as he gazed toward the kitchen where his wife clattered around gathering dishes. "She may be a tough old bird, but some things still hurt her, even if they're years behind us. You understand?"

Thinking of his parents, and the ache left behind where their loving presence once stood with him, Milo nodded.

Chester returned the nod, hitching his pants. "Right. To dinner."

Dinner turned out to be slow cooker beef stew with potatoes and carrots, one of Nana's recipes that Milo loved. He supposed she'd chosen it by way of further apology for her absence, and he ate heartily, downing two bowls that left his stomach feeling tight and round as a puppy's. Milo had opened his mouth a time or two to ask the questions burning in his mind—not about Elizabeth, but about his grandmother and what role she may have played— but was silenced by a curt shake of the head from Chester each time. In truth, there was little by way of conversation at all. The two people he shared the table with barely spoke, and Tabitha ate very little, dragging her spoon this way and that through the stew so that it scraped the bowl, but only managing to swallow a few bites. Chester shot Milo a glance as Tabitha cleared the dishes away, holding his finger to his lips when her back was turned.

After dinner, Tabitha set about laying out Milo's clothes for tomorrow on the end of the couch, and Milo trouped upstairs for a shower. He passed by the painting of the girl in the blue dress as he went, and shivered, feeling her gaze on his back as he passed her. Something, *something,* had certainly happened to the people downstairs (and their daughter, certainly) that had to do with this painting, but with the very little information he'd been given, Milo was hard pressed to extrapolate what it was. They certainly seemed to think it was supernatural in nature, but Milo wasn't so sure. Nor was he sure exactly how Nana factored in, only that she'd apparently shown up at some crucial time and was now in possession of the painting that hung in the hall. He mused on this as he showered. Nana collected a great many things, and the important ones—like the books and that painting—were all under glass. Untouchable. Dangerous in the wrong hands, she said, and which he believed wholeheartedly. Hadn't he experienced it for himself, when he read that book that had fallen out of the case and dreamt of the boy with the ruined head? He shuddered despite the pelting hot water. Yes, some things in Nana's house were dangerous indeed.

But some, like the book of poetry owned by Clementine Williams, weren't. They were powerful, certainly, but he had a hard time thinking of Clementine as anything short of beatific in nature. Hadn't she turned him away from his nightmare with the genial ease of her cajoling presence?

And now, his nana was on another business trip, presumably to collect...what? Another book for the shelf? Another painting to put under glass? Would it be another dangerous thing, or something pleasant? And what, exactly, was her business, so shrouded in mystery as it was? A headache began to creep up behind Milo's eye. It was all too much to wrap his head around alone. Milo wiped the steam off the mirror and looked at himself while he dried, and the drippy boy in the mirror looked back.

"Why doesn't she want to tell me what she does?" He asked the mirror-boy. "Why won't anyone give me a straight answer?"

Because what she does is dangerous, the boy replied wordlessly, toweling his hair, *and she doesn't want you to worry. Mama knew it too. You've already lost so much. She doesn't want you to live your life anxious about how much you yet have left to lose.*

But he already did. He'd felt it all night, that tight squeeze of anxiety in his chest, off and on, gripping his lungs like a vice. If Nana thought she was protecting him by keeping him in the dark, she was wrong.

"I'm going to ask her when she gets home," he resolutely told the boy in the mirror, "and this time I won't take no for an answer. This time she won't put me off. I won't cry, I won't beg, but I also won't back down. Then she'll tell me. Right?"

The boy, his hair standing up in wet cowlicks, gave no answer.

Milo looked him in the eyes, squinting. "But before I ask, I need to know they aren't all pulling my leg."

Because yes, that thought had occurred to him too. The story *sounded* real enough, certainly, but with adults there was no telling. They made things up all the time—Santa Claus came to mind, and the Easter Bunny—and lied through their teeth to children. Or they simply made up an answer when they didn't know for sure. His mother had told him swallowing toothpaste was harmful, and he'd spent all of age five wary of any going down his throat, until one tearful dentist visit when he'd cried because he swallowed some, the dentist had told him differently. He believed Nana when she said she would keep her promises, that much went without saying. But maybe—possibly even *likely*—it was just as true that the things in Nana's house, the experiences of the people downstairs, were just more things grownups didn't have a language for, so they made one up. He thought he might be able to put that to the test tonight. He didn't *want* to believe Nana would outright lie to him about who she was and what she did, but if the *Beckenhams* were capable of it...

Well. He would see, wouldn't he?

Once dressed, Milo walked halfway down the stairs to where the wall cut off to a railing, ever so quietly, so as to observe Chester and Tabitha, who were once again in their places in the living room. He crouched low on the fifth stair, peering around the corner, hoping not much of him was visible. He saw Mingus had finally made an appearance and was sitting in the middle of the rug washing his paws, and willed the cat not to sound the alarm if he saw Milo hunched there.

Chester was reading one of the magazines that Nana kept on the coffee table, ruffling the pages as he cleared his throat. He had a fresh drink in one hand and his ankle resting on his knee to support the magazine. Tabitha was back at her knitting, furiously moving the needles to and fro.

"You shouldn't have said so much." Tabitha's back was to Milo, but he saw the minute shake of her head as she spoke in a hiss to her husband. "You've given him more questions than answers, now, and Astrid won't be happy about that."

"Ha," Chester grumbled. "I highly doubt that I gave him any more questions than he already had. He *lives* in this godforsaken mausoleum, for Christ's sake. He either already knows, or he'll figure it out sooner or later. He's too bloody bright to be kept in the dark for long. The child is like a damned lantern, Tabby. And sensitive to boot. He said himself he can feel what the painting gives off, didn't he? Neither you nor I ever felt that. And I'll just bet his nana knows it, too. She thinks she's protecting him." He snorted. "Astrid went on another hunt, didn't she? He'll get it out of her when she gets back, I warrant."

Another hunt. Milo held his breath.

"But did you *have* to tell him about our Elizabeth that way? As though she's…she's some terrible *story* told 'round a campfire instead of our little girl." Tabitha sniffled.

"Oh, confound it, Tabby, I'm sorry," Chester said, stealing a sorrowful glance at his wife. "I didn't mean it like that at all, you know. I loved her. *We* loved her. But she's gone, and Astrid… Astrid made a home for her, somewhere such unpleasantness can never happen again to anyone else. She's safe now, and so is everyone else."

"But Milo…Milo's…she's right across from his *room*, Chez…"

"I know." Chester put down the magazine, set his drink delicately on the table, and scooted closer to his wife, plucking her hands away from her knitting to hold them in both of his. He looked deeply into her eyes, noticing Milo's eye peering around the corner not at all. "But he's been here, full-time, for a year now, and nothing terrible has happened, even as *sensitive* as he seems to be. Do you think Astrid would allow that blasted thing to stay in the house if it was a threat to her *grandson*? After all she's lost already?"

Tabitha sniffled some more, her head moving slowly back and forth. "No," she whispered at last. "No, she wouldn't. She'd... She'd put it somewhere else, away from him. Maybe where she keeps the rest of it. The *really* dangerous stuff."

"That's right." Chester smiled and patted her hand. "Now, no more of this, alright? I admit it was damned stupid of me to talk so bloody much, and I feel like an ass for having said as much as I did. But I had to know if she...if she was..."

"In the house," Tabitha finished. "Yes. Me too. I didn't want to turn a corner, and there she was. It would hurt too much to be surprised that way."

"Yes," Chester agreed, and released his wife's hands as he settled back into his place. "It's best we move on to another subject. He's bound to be nearly done getting dressed by now."

But they didn't move on to another subject. They lapsed into silence, Chester staring at his magazine with faraway eyes and Tabitha sitting still, staring out at the storm. Milo counted down from one hundred before standing and stepping down to the next stair, the one that creaked.

Chester looked up at him, blinking in that twitchy way he had, and smiled. "Milo, old sport! Ready to travel to the land of Bedfordshire?"

"Yes," he laughed, then casually, as if it had just occurred to him, "Nana usually tucks me in and reads me a story. You don't have to read to me, but...Mrs. Beckenham, would you tuck me in? Please?"

Tabitha startled, whirling around, high color in her cheeks evident even in the dim lamplight of the living room. She looked him up and down, took in his cowboy pajamas and well combed, wet hair. She glanced behind him, up the stairs, and swallowed. "Can you not manage on your own?"

"I mean, I *can*..." Milo replied, tucking his hands behind his back in mock embarrassment. "But with the storm... and Nana gone..."

Thunder boomed as if to emphasize his point, making them all jump. The lights flickered momentarily, then became steady again. Rain lashed at the windows, the wind bringing up a scream that sounded like a wailing woman.

"Just tuck the boy in, Tabby," Chester said, then gulped back a yip as another throaty cough of thunder rolled over the roof. "He's a child. A nervous child."

Tabitha opened her mouth to retort, closed it again. Looked at Milo, who gave her his widest eyes, his brow knit together. She sighed, pinching the bridge of her nose. "Alright. Are you sure you won't have a story as well?"

"I'm sure."

"Then up to bed with you." She stood, smoothed her skirt with shaking hands, and traipsed resolutely after Milo up the stairs.

Milo walked up slowly, allowing her to catch up to him. Mingus hauled himself up and darted for the stairs, his body moving like liquid around their feet as he dashed up into Milo's room, eager to be in bed making his razor biscuits against the boy's leg as always.

Milo turned only once, in just enough time to see Tabitha shield her eyes with one hand as she walked past the painting, her face scrunched as if she were in pain, her other hand clutching the tiny silver crucifix she wore around her neck.

TEN

T WO DAYS LATER, Nana came home. It was 8:30 p.m., fifteen minutes before Milo's bedtime, when the front door squalled as it was flung open from outside, allowing the still-pelting rain entrance a few moments before the lady herself stepped over the threshold. She was wearing her rain slicker with the hood pushed back, her loose hair tangled around her in sopping dreadlocks. Her face had a gaunt and haunted look. When lightning flashed, it lit the planes and hollows of her face and made it look like a skull. In her left hand she gripped a cloth grocery tote bag that dripped water onto the welcome mat.

The bang of the door hitting the wall startled everyone, and Milo (who had been watching a short round of cartoons before bed) jumped up immediately when he saw her.

"Nana!" He exclaimed excitedly, running over to her. "You're back!"

"Yes," she replied, not looking at him, her voice a rusty whisper. She pushed the door closed slowly, shutting the gale out inch by inch until it was left outside where it belonged. Then, for several seconds, she just stood there, dripping on the rug, her wind-whipped hair plastered to her face, her gaze fixed on the floor a few feet from her.

Chester and Tabitha exchanged a questioning glance.

Milo's smile faded as he took Nana in, his immediate joy replaced with hesitance as he looked over this bedraggled creature who'd come home to him in place of his jovial and attentive grandmother. "Nana? Are you OK?"

Astrid let out a bark of mirthless laughter. Her eyes drifted down to the bag clutched in her hand, raised it so that she could look at it more closely. It swung, and she tracked it with her eyes before slowly, slowly returning the arm to her side. Then those hollow, empty eyes turned to Milo and hovered there, cold and indifferent. She nodded only once, a slow up and down that seemed to take enormous effort to accomplish. "OK."

"Why don't you come with me, boyo?" Chester said from behind him, making him jump. He looked up at the big man, but Chester's eyes were on Nana. "Why don't we give the ladies some space, what?"

Milo looked first behind Chester—where Tabitha stood, wringing her hands and looking frightened—and then back at Nana, who looked like an animatronic with its wires cut. He finally nodded, and let Chester lead him towards the back of the house to the kitchen.

"You want a little midnight snack?" Chester asked, his hand on Milo's shoulder to steer him.

From behind them, Milo heard Tabitha say, "Why don't you give that to me, dear, there's a love."

Nana murmured something that sounded like it came from a thousand miles away, a whisper in the graveyard.

ELEVEN

T HE BECKENHAMS STAYED on for two more days. Tabitha fed Milo breakfast and made his lunch for school, Chester brought him to the bus stop in the morning and picked him up in the afternoon. At dinner it would be just the three of them, Nana ensconced in her bedroom upstairs, perhaps sleeping, but more likely just staring at the walls. When she did come down, she walked through the house like a zombie, her face ashen and drawn, her hands hanging limply at her sides, her voluminous robe loosely drawn around her thin, frail-looking shoulders. In her nightgown and robe, her feet bare and face slack, she very much looked more her age than Milo had ever seen her.

He tried to carry on as usual at school, but the rat of worry had begun to nibble and fray his tender innards. Cassie especially could tell that something was wrong, but when she asked and Milo changed the subject, she let it drop. He was grateful for that. He wasn't sure he could articulate the shape of his fears if he tried.

The afternoon of the third day, when he got off the bus, Chester's Chevrolet was parked at the corner of State and Clara Street waiting for him. He plodded over to the rumbling Chevy, his mind having sucked in the thunderheads from the night Nana arrived.

"Hot one today, eh, lad?" Chester piped, smiling as Milo got in. Milo didn't respond, and the smile left Chester's face. "What's wrong, my boy? Something happen at school?"

"No," Milo replied glumly, annoyed that his predicament wasn't obvious to Chester after nearly forty-eight hours of unhappy goings-on at the Schulze residence. "I'm just worried about Nana."

The smile reappeared on Chester's face, his muddy eyes twinkling merrily. "Well, worry no more, lad! Your nana is up and about again, good as new. Tabby and I are going home today."

The relief in Chester's voice was almost as great as the wave of relief that washed over Milo. He turned to Chester, grinning, all unhappy thoughts fleeing his mind. "Why didn't you *lead* with that? Hurry up!" He smacked the dashboard with both hands. "Get this barge moving!"

Chester let out one of his great *haw-haw* laughs. "Careful with the merchandise, my fine lad. Away we go, then. Belt in, I'm going to really open her up."

"Ya, mule, ya!" Milo laughed, slapping the dashboard once more, and Chester laughed along with him. Neither of them stopped smiling the whole way home.

Tabitha was coming down the stairs as the two of them came through the front door five minutes later. She pursed her lips tensely, watching Milo as he dropped his backpack and untucked his uniform shirt from his pants. Chester walked around him and disappeared into the back of the house, whistling. Milo stripped off his belt, plopping it on top of his bag, then started for the stairs, but Tabitha put a hand out to stop him.

"Don't get her too excited," she warned, her chilly palm against his chest. "She's still very tired. She insists we can go home tonight, but—" she ran a hand down her face and sighed.

Milo took her in—the brown circles under her eyes, her usually neat hair falling out of its bun in tendrils, the gold cross around her neck tucked into her blouse—and saw her age, all of it, her sadness, her worry. For him, for Nana, or both, he didn't know. He plucked her hand off his chest and held it in both of his. "I won't get too rambunctious. I promise. Can I go see her now?"

Tabitha peered down at him from her adult height, seeming to consider. For a moment it appeared she would say no, that he would be relegated to the downstairs of the house for another day, but then she nodded. Almost imperceptibly, but a nod it was. Milo grinned at her and mounted the stairs.

He could see that Nana's door was cracked open as soon as he reached the landing. The television was on, but the volume low, the irregular blue light of the screen filling the hallway. Laughter rippled from a sitcom laugh track as he reached that partially closed door. Milo wanted more than anything to burst into the room, calling *Nana, I'm home! Here I am! I missed you so much!* But he couldn't do that. He'd promised to be quiet, not to rile her up in any way, so he settled on knocking softly against the door frame.

"Come in," Nana said from inside, but the quality of her voice made him hesitate. She sounded like a person woken from a deep sleep, her throat scratchy, the words a garbled croak. Milo stood frozen outside the door, his hand outstretched to push it open, chewing his lower lip. But a moment later, she spoke again. "Milo, is that you? Please come in. The scary part is over."

Her voice still had that raspy quality, but the words were soothing. *The scary part is over.* He pushed the door open and walked into the room. Nana was propped up in bed wearing her favorite silk nightgown—the one with the cranes on the front and a large tiger emblazoned on the back—half a dozen pillows behind her and under her arms, the covers pulled up to her waist. In front of her was a little serving tray with foldable legs. On this sat a cup of steaming, fragrant tea, a rolled up newspaper, and the television remote. She smiled softly at Milo, and he noticed that her hair was clean now, brushed till it gleamed and braided long and silver, slung over one shoulder. She patted the down comforter next to her. Without any hesitation, he went.

When Nana engulfed him in her embrace and he smelled the scent so particular to her—tea, lemon, cardamom, Dove soap— a sob of pure relief escaped him. Tears fell on her silk gown, but they were happy tears. He'd never in his life been so relieved to know that someone was alright. A kind of illness had washed over her since she returned from her work, but here she was, alive and whole again. She had been right. The scary part *was* over. He clutched at her with both hands, blubbering like an infant, with a total lack of shame.

"Oh, come now," Nana said her creaky, dry voice, "I'm alright, I'm alright, it's alright, my love. Come now, come now."

But she held onto Milo as hard as he hung onto her, and when he looked up at her from where he'd been smothered in her bosom, she was smiling, her eyes also full of tears.

They stayed like that for several minutes, the only sounds the television and their weeping, joyful reunion. At last the tears ran their course, and Milo sat up, swiping at his eyes with the heels of his hands. "You're really better now? The Beckenhams are really going home tonight?"

"Yes, and yes," Nana replied, smiling, her hands folded on her stomach. "I'll admit, things were a bit hairy there for…for a time…but I believe the worst is behind us, and we can go back to our normal, boring routine. More or less."

Milo narrowed his eyes. "More or less?"

Nana looked him over, an expression of great calculation on her face. She reached for her tea, cleared her throat, then took a long sip. She settled it carefully back onto her tray, watching her hands as she did so. Then she picked up the remote and clicked off the TV. Milo thought this was an excellent stalling tactic on her part, but said nothing. He had the feeling that whatever came next would be of great importance, and that it wouldn't do to rush it into existence.

She coughed, cleared her throat again, the raspy rumble inside clearly heard in the quiet of her room. Finally her eyes lit on his face, and stayed there. "More or less. Because there's something I have yet to do, a delicate part of my job. An *important* part of my job. The most key part of it, in fact. It is something you will live with every day if you intend to grow up in this house, and I'm more than a little angry at myself for trying to keep it from you this long. Perhaps it was protective. Perhaps it was simply honoring the dead. Elise...Elise wouldn't have liked me telling you this one bit, with good reason, but I feel it's important all the same. I am sorry to be going against her wishes, though. I feel it's *also* important you know that."

Milo sat silent, but inside he was quivering with anticipation. Here it was, the secret, the elephant in the room, here he would be able to grab its tusks and bring it to heel. The books, the painting, all of it, was finally about to be explained.

Nana bent over, pulled something up from the side of her bed. When her hand came into view, it was grasping the handles of the cloth shopping bag. The one she'd been holding when she came in from the storm, all unseeing eyes and stringy hair plastered to her face. She brought the bag over and set it between them, opening it and reaching inside. Milo's eyes widened in anticipation. Nana pulled something out, something wrapped in tinfoil and stuffed into a gallon Ziploc bag. The thing strained the sides of the bag and kept resisting as Nana tried to pull it out.

Milo reached over to help, but Nana stayed his hands with one of her own. "No. Not with this."

He sat back, slightly put out, and watched her struggle to wrench it free of its plastic prison. After what seemed like forever, one side of the vaguely rectangular, tinfoil-shrouded object slipped free, and Nana pulled it from its bag with a cry of triumph. She placed the rectangle of foil on her tray.

"Now," she said, her hands poised over the object, "when I unwrap this, I want you to tell me what you get from it. Not just what it looks like, mind you, but what it *feels* like. Use all of your senses *except touch*. It is extremely important that you don't touch what I'm about to show you, no matter how great the temptation may be. Understand?"

Utterly enthralled, Milo nodded.

"Good."

Nana began unwrapping the foil around the object. At first Milo saw only a corner, but that was enough to determine that it was a box of some kind. Then Nana pulled away a large swath and he saw—

"A music box!" And a fine example of a music box it was. About six inches long, four wide, four deep, beautifully inlaid with abalone on top, all filigree scrollwork and shining pearlescent leaves, the box itself painted a soft, matte cream shade that looked like fresh vanilla ice cream. Except...

Milo screwed up his face. "Except it's...not, somehow. There's something wrong with it. It's broken, isn't it?"

"Not at all," Nana said, and opened the box. When she did, a little clown popped up from a hole in the center, flanked by four velvet-lined storage containers for jewelry, the little clown beginning to rotate. He was cheerfully painted in primary colors, chubby and jolly-faced in harlequin makeup, clutching three balloons of red, blue, and yellow. As he turned, the familiar song of the circus played—*doot doot doodle-oodle-oot doot doo doo.* Two years ago, Milo and his father had taken apart a music box very similar to this one, and Greg had taken pains to name every part of it for his young, curious son.

This part is called the movement, Greg had told him, holding up the steel cylinder with its wire spokes that plucked at the tiny raised bumps on the barrel. *This is where the sound comes from.*

342

Milo leaned closer to better inspect the clown, then abruptly clapped a hand over his mouth and nose, gagging. "Augh, it *stinks!*"

"Does it?" Nana enquired.

"Yes! Oh God, it's *awful!* You don't smell it?"

"What does it smell like?"

"Like...like...like that dead opossum I found in the shed at Mama and Daddy's house. Worse! Like a hundred dead opossums! And garbage. So much rotten garbage. And...and dirt. But like a graveyard." In truth, Milo had no language to express what he was really smelling: the sour tang of rot in basement earth, the fetid stench of many long-dead things not quite buried. But he was close.

Nana nodded. "And something else, too. Underneath that."

Milo's eyes watered, but he tried to take in another shallow breath, to find what his nana wanted him to find. At first there was only that wet and somehow green stench, but then, amazingly, something else. Something familiar, that brought up memories of birthday parties and family gatherings. His eyes began to water. "B...balloons? Is it balloons?"

Astrid smiled and snapped the box closed, abruptly cutting off the tune mid-*doot*. The smell immediately dissipated, and Milo let go of his nose, breathing in harsh gasps to cleanse his nose and mouth from the lingering aftertaste. He scowled at the box lying mutely malevolent on the tray next to his nana's tea. "You really couldn't smell it?"

"I could," she replied, putting her hand on the abalone inlaid lid, "but it has no more power over me, so the smell wasn't as strong. Now that you've been exposed to this, I'm going to bet you'll have interesting dreams like you did when you read *Poky*, and when I read to you from Clementine Williams' book. But remember, it's only a dream, and it can't hurt you, unless you seek out this box and claim it as your own. Ownership is nine-tenths of the law, after all."

"It's gross," Milo groaned, wiping his eyes of tears not so nearly happy as the others shed in this room today. "I don't know anybody who'd be dumb enough to want something that smelled like *that*."

"'Gross' is one way to put it," Nana said, plucking up the box and beginning to wrap it once more in the foil. Milo felt better watching it disappear from sight. "But no matter. Tomorrow, while you're at school, I'm going to my storage unit across town and putting it with the rest of its vile brethren, to rot in the dark. It'll never be in our home again after today."

"That's what you went out to get?" He pointed at the foil-wrapped box, his face pulled down in a sneer of disgust.

"It is. This, like the books and many other things in my home, is not an average music box. And as with those other things, it is the fact that it *looks* so unobtrusive that makes it dangerous."

"So what's so special about it?"

Nana laid her hand on top of the foil, her eyes distant. "This particular box has something powerful attached to it. The people who owned it thought it was the spirit of a man who did terrible deeds, but he's still alive yet, and so it is something else. Something infinitely worse. A demon."

Milo's eyes went wide. "A...a..."

"Demon. Yes. A very strong, especially vile and unclean spirit, responsible for many deaths and no little chaos." She smiled. "But once it's locked away in my storage unit, it won't be able to do harm to anyone, ever again, as long as I live."

Milo sat, gaping at her, completely shocked to silence. Then he began laughing.

Astrid raised an eyebrow. "And what, young man, is so funny?"

"You're pulling my leg," he replied matter-of-factly. "Demons aren't real. Dad told me that all that weird religious stuff is people trying to lay blame on the supernatural for things that they chose to do on their own. It's all fake."

"Is it?" Nana mused, a smile touching the corners of her mouth. "And I suppose that stink you just experienced was fake too, then, hm? Or Clementine? The boy with the missing eye that so frightened you last year? Perhaps that presence you felt sit right down next to you when you and Cassandra used the witch board was nothing more than superstitious gas as well." She squinted, her smile deepening at his shocked expression. "Did you think I didn't know that she'd brought the thing into my house? Even if I couldn't feel the energies culminating in that room, I saw her come in the house with it when she thought I wasn't looking."

Milo felt his face turn red, the tips of his ears burning. "I was just trying to talk to Mama. I didn't think it would work."

"It *didn't* work," Astrid said, putting a hand on his cheek. "Not the way you thought it did, anyway. What came to you that day was not your mother; never think it. What came to you that day was predatory, a thing that feeds on a mourning child's deepest desires like fine chocolate, and turns those desires against him."

"I just wanted to talk to Mama," he repeated. Milo felt close to tears for the first time in an hour. But then a thought occurred to him, a glimmer of hope. "Have *you* ever talked to Mama? You know, since…"

Astrid shook her head. "No, Milo. Thankfully…mercifully, you understand…your mother has fully crossed over."

"Oh." He considered this. "How do you know?"

"I feel it. The space left behind by a spirit that once was there. As I can feel the presence of one trapped on this plain of existence, desperate to be free to the point of violence against the living. It's why I do what I do."

And now, at last, the question. "What do you do?"

And now, at last, the answer. "Those plagued by trapped spirits and demons contact me for aid. I go to them, when appropriate, and rid them of their problem. Sometimes, these spirits are attached to an object. If that's the case, I remove it from their home and find a place for it where it can no longer do any harm."

"Like the Beckenhams. And Elizabeth."

Now it was Astrid's turn to look shocked. "Yes, like the Beckenhams and their poor, stolen daughter. I would not have that happen to you. I thought for many years that I carried precious cargo, by collecting the things that I do, that my work was of utmost importance above all else. I was wrong, for so many reasons and in so many ways. I failed Elise when she was alive. I simply cannot bear to do so again. *You* are my most precious cargo, which is why I needed to share this with you, despite my Elise's wishes." She squeezed his hand. "And now you know why I tell you not to mess around with the things I keep under glass. You know it all. Can you forgive me, Milo? For keeping this from you, and for putting you in danger?"

She looked so solemn when she said this, her eyes so bright with both hope that he'd accept and fear that he wouldn't, that all of his sadness and anger at her melted away, only to be replaced by a feeling of peace. He took her gnarled old hand in both of his and kissed the knuckles one at a time, before laying his cheek in her palm. "Yes."

That night, after an impromptu ice cream party that went well past his usual bedtime, Milo crept up the stairs to his room (studiously avoiding looking at the painting of Elizabeth) and fell into bed, too emotionally exhausted to even turn out the light. He was asleep in seconds, and when he dreamed, it was of an outdoor birthday party. There were children everywhere, and Milo ran laughing with them, smelling his own sweat, cake, barbecue. He stopped near a tree, his lungs tearing at the air, and leaned against it, watching the other kids run away. A shadow fell over him.

Hey kid, said a voice to his left. *I got something for ya.*

He turned, and behind him was a fat man dressed in a red and yellow clown outfit, a tiny hat stuck to his head. He sweated through his red, white, and blue grease paint, smiling a liar's smile, leaning in to get closer to Milo's face, sizing him up. His teeth, when he smiled, were like razors, yellowed with bits of meat stuck between. A smell was emanating from him—dank, earthy, rotten.

A music box smell, Milo thought, as the man reached out a hand to give him a yellow balloon. He could smell this too, the cheap latex invading his nostrils and mingling with that sour basement smell wafting off the guy in the melting clown face. Milo turned and ran, desperate to catch up to The Other Children. Anything To Not Be Alone With The Clown.

TWELVE

W HAT WITH ONE thing and another, and as all boys must do, Milo grew. His childhood was not an unhappy one, despite the loss of his parents (whom he still dearly missed), and on some level, he was in fact happier than some of his classmates. Nana seemed to know and respect each new need that arose, stepping in when needed, and stepping back where prudent. Milo bloomed under her care, and by the time high school rolled around, had become a handsome and thoughtful young man, blisteringly intelligent and independent.

It wasn't a hard life. Sure, he had lots of chores because Nana was well into her sixties by then and couldn't do as much for herself anymore, but that was a small price to pay to have all the support he could ever ask for, without so much as a question. When he'd picked a private high school to be in his top slot, nervously showing her his short list for schools he wanted to attend, she'd simply put on her reading glasses, nodded, and started making phone calls. He was a member of Jesuit High School the very next day, fully paid. When he wanted to get a summer job to buy himself a car his junior year, she'd encouraged him. When it proved harder than he thought to find a place that would hire him, she'd sent an email to a retired friend in the shipping industry, and suddenly he'd had a secretarial position at a company willing to pay him a whopping fifteen dollars an hour for his services.

And if sometimes Nana went out on an errand for several days at a time, what of that? By sixteen he could do most things on his own, and when she came back hollowed out and glassy-eyed, well, he could take care of her too. It was the least he could do for this mountain of a matriarch who'd tended his every need for so long. He enjoyed giving back. Her one insistence was that he never touch the things she brought home, no matter how harmless they seemed. He'd offered once, when she'd come home with a large and ornate mirror, to bring it to her storage unit for her so she could rest, but she'd refused. Those objects were her burden to bear, and she would carry them until God took her home, so she would. He didn't try to insist, even though he now knew nothing would happen. Since that one weird year of his life after his parents' passing, nothing strange had ever happened to him again as a result of Nana's precious cargo. No dreams, no feelings, nothing. Nana kept all that well away from him, and any memories he had of encounters with ghosts and demons began to be squared away by an ever-increasing rationality of the mind. This, too, is the way of growing to maturity.

Even though he'd changed schools, and made a ton of new friends in the process, Milo never abandoned his friendship with Cassie. They were best friends as children, two souls against the world, and stayed that way. Cassie went to Dominican for eighth grade, a bright student in her own right, and the two whispered to each other late into the night about the trials, heartbreaks, and joys of high school, each curled in their bed with the phone pressed to their ear, cords dangling out from under comforters.

Milo made every effort not to show that he was glad when Nana finally officially retired, meaning that no more objects would be coming in to grow her collection.

"Aren't you worried, though?" He'd asked solemnly, but underneath was a hint of the disbelief he felt. "That some of those…things…may hurt other people without you working to keep them out of circulation? Isn't that your job?"

"I've been doing this over forty years," she'd said simply. "Demon hunting requires a strong back and a stronger spirit. I've got the spirit, but the flesh is brittle and saddle-sore." Seeing his stricken face, she reached over and squeezed his shoulder. "There are always others like me to take up where one of us leaves off. My chapter is finished, that's all."

Cassie graduated a full year ahead of Milo, and went to LSU for premed, but that didn't stop him from nervously asking her to his senior prom. It seemed a cinch after years of living in a reportedly haunted house and being the weird kid with dead parents. She accepted.

When she showed up for their date, Cassie was wearing a sparkly green dress, high black shoes (the kind that clacked on the floor when she walked), her hair in spirals, and her makeup nothing short of perfection. Just seeing her made Milo's mouth dry as a desert and his underarms sweat like deep summer.

Later (after nervously sliding the boutonnière around her wrist and taking what seemed like a thousand pictures with their friends), Milo would take the kiss he'd wanted since he was nine years old deeply, slowly, off Cassie's mouth as they swayed under the revolving shattered light of a disco ball. And when, three months into their relationship, the mutual loss of virginity to one another would bind them even closer, they made a plan. Milo followed her to LSU—he could study business anywhere, he reasoned—and the two became nigh as inseparable as they had been as kids. He moved out of Nana's house with its shadowy, unquiet residents under glass, and into a tatty one-bedroom within walking distance from school, to live with the girl he'd loved all his life. Astrid, for her part, approved. Love bloomed, grew, but didn't fade as first love so often does. He hardly thought of the long years living in Astrid's house anymore, of strange dreams and objects under glass. It was an intense relief to no longer have to rationalize for himself anything in that house, either living or dead. He could see only the face of his love, and he held it in his mind's eye wherever he went, always looking toward the future.

Milo proposed on the night of his college graduation, and Cassie, who had been waiting on this for months, gleefully accepted. They danced around the linoleum of their one-bedroom apartment, drunk on one another, high on the future.

Astrid, overjoyed, gave Milo a check for fifty thousand dollars: enough for a down-payment on a house. Enough to start a family. He hugged her fiercely as his fiancé looked on and wept, promising her over and over that he would take this gift and turn it into a family.

"You'd best do it soon," Astrid said. "I don't want to be so old I can't be trusted to hold my great-grandchildren."

On their wedding day, Milo escorted his nana down the aisle to her seat at the front. Beside her were two empty chairs, both with a single white rose on the seat. When he kissed Cassie after their vows, the whole room went up in applause. Cassie's father and Astrid Schulze hugged one another, tears of joy on their faces.

"I never want this to end," Cassie murmured against his shoulder when they shared their first dance as a couple. Their wedding party looked on with quiet fascination, their faces blurred by the glare of the spotlight above the dancing newlyweds.

Milo kissed his bride's forehead, drawing her closer. "It never will, as long as I'm alive."

In this way, the way of all grandiosely mundane things that happen upon this earth, twenty-two years passed.

THIRTEEN

2016

"D ID YOU SIGN Eddie's papers for school?"
Milo looked up from his phone (and all the damned emails from clients that had appeared in the night somehow—did no one ever *sleep* anymore?) to blink sleepily at his wife. Cassie was standing at the stove, scrambling eggs for their seven-year-old son, Eddie, her pregnant belly protruding from beneath a voluminous night shirt. Her brown legs, bare and lean, looked far more appetizing than anything she could ever cook.

"Sure did. They're in his folder."

"Good." She pulled the pan off the stove and set it aside, wiping her hands on a dishrag and smiling. But there was worry in her eyes, he was sorry to see. "Are you going to see her today?"

"Yes." No need to ask who *her* was. He and Cassie talked about little else besides Astrid these days, preparing themselves for her inevitable exit. The tough old broad had made it in life well into her eighties, but her time on Earth was now beginning to wind down at a rapid pace. Milo had been going to her house—a place she refused to give up despite her advanced age and a wicked case of arthritis—three days a week for five months now. He said it was to help her out, but he supposed what he was really doing was preparing himself for the inevitable. "Are you gonna be OK to go pick Eddie up from school by yourself? I can be home if I need to be."

Cassie smiled wanly, rubbing her belly. "We'll be fine. I think what you're doing is important. Important and right. She took care of you all those years, and now…"

"Now it's my turn," he finished for her. "I know. I feel the same way. But my responsibility to you and our kid—*kids*—is just as important. When Astrid is gone, you guys will still be here, and I want to make sure you get everything you need out of me."

Cassie crossed the room and bent with some effort to plant a kiss on her husband's head. "My hero."

Milo felt a tingle run through him from the spot she'd kissed him, all the way down to his toes.

Over a decade married and she still gives me the shivers. Gotta be something special in that.

He turned, pushing out his chair and pulling Cassie gently into his lap. When she was firmly seated with her arms around his neck and her face close to his, he leaned closer, closer still, and pressed his lips to hers. Her mouth opened immediately, wanting, pulling him deeper, their tongues touching. His hand slid up one of those fantastic legs, to the well-made thigh, under the hem of her T-shirt, farther, farther…

"Ew, gross, you're kissing."

Milo's head snapped around to see Eddie, standing in the kitchen doorway in his pajamas, rubbing sleep from his eyes, his curly brown hair standing up in swoops and swirls from his pillow. In his free hand he clutched his stuffed Kermit the Frog from when he was a baby.

"Morning, bud," Milo said cheerfully, trying gamely not to sound like he had just been thinking lascivious thoughts about his son's mother. "How'd you sleep?"

"OK," Eddie responded, yawning hugely. "I had a weird dream about Nana, though."

"Oh?"

353

"Yeah."

"What about?"

Eddie's lip poked out in thought. "We were riding in this big, grey car, going somewhere special—like, dress-up special—only she wouldn't sit in the front seat with me. You were driving, and you were wearing this weird hat. You couldn't make her get out of the back seat either. She wouldn't listen. Nana just kept saying she was too old for seats now, and had to lie down in the back, where she could stretch out."

"That *is* a weird dream." Milo rasped his palm against the stubble on his cheek. "Did I at least look cool in my hat?"

"No." Eddie gave him a thumbs-down and made his father laugh. His gaze shifted to his mother, still sitting with her arms wrapped lightly around her husband's neck. "Can I have breakfast now, or are you guys not done being gross?"

"Party's over," Cassie murmured, her voice amused as she plucked Milo's hand out from under the hem of her shirt.

FOURTEEN

T HE HOSPICE NURSE, a slim and pretty redhead named Sadie who looked to him like she was little more than a teenager, let Milo into his grandmother's house. She smiled warmly when she saw him on the doorstep, but when he moved to go into the living room, she put a warning hand on his chest (as Tabitha had done all those years ago when Astrid had come home exhausted and half crazed from her hunting expedition), her face turning grave.

"Ms. Astrid isn't doing so well today," she said in a breathy whisper. This close Milo could see all of the freckles running across her nose and cheeks, they and her wide doe eyes conspiring to make her look much younger than she was. "She doesn't like showing it, but I guess you know better than anyone she's doing worse than she lets on."

Milo nodded. "She's a tough old bird. Is she lucid?"

"Well..."Sadie glanced over her shoulder as though her patient might overhear and charge into the room to correct her. She leaned even closer, so close that Milo could smell her shampoo over the antiseptic scent all nurses seemed to wear like perfume. "I wanted to talk to you about that before you went in. When she woke up this morning she seemed agitated. Frightened. She kept asking me if all the things in the glass were still in their cases. I told her they were, of course, and she grabbed my arm. She said, 'You can't be too sure when it comes to those demons.' Mr. Cunningham, that statement gave me a case of the shivers.

I have to say, she is the first of my patients to ever scare me so bad. Her *eyes—*"

"I'm sorry, Sadie," he cut her off, patting her hand, eager to be done with this conversation. "But don't worry. You told me yourself she'd have good days and bad days, with her brain being the way that it is. I'm sure it was only that. What was it you said to me last time?"

Sadie visibly relaxed. "Brain cancer is like that."

"Yes." Milo smiled at her, but under the surface he felt a trill of giddy nerves. "Has she been OK since?"

"Mostly. She's on the oxygen today, and her hands are very shaky, but she's been talking and following conversation just fine."

"Good," he replied, his eyes traveling to the living room, the easy chair in front of the big-screen TV, and the slumped form sitting in it. "Good, good. May I?"

Sadie stepped aside. "Of course. I'll give you some privacy. If you need me I'll be in the back garden."

"Thanks. And Sadie?"

"Yes, Mr. Cunningham?"

"Please don't worry about what she said this morning. If she were in her right mind, she never would have done anything to frighten you. It…it wasn't in her nature."

Sadie brightened. "It's really OK. Happens a lot in this line of work, truly."

Oh my, no, not in her nature to frighten anyone. But it seems it's certainly in your *nature to neatly sidestep the whole truth when it comes to Nana's work.* He watched Sadie leave. *How long until Nana tells her everything? How long until she sees for herself what this old lady slumped in front of* Great British Baking Show *really is?*

Milo turned to the living room, shrugging off his jacket as he stepped toward the small, frail figure nestled in the red armchair by the television. Astrid sat hunched slightly forward, her long white braid now long gone, her hair a short and frazzled white puff around her liver spotted skull. She breathed in raspy wheezes, pulling in air from the oxygen tank sitting at her side, her gnarled and knotted hands lying limply on her blanketed lap. She was so shrunken now, so withered and small, no longer the towering pillar of the family but a broken and shelled out husk. It had been eighteen months since her diagnosis, eighteen months since she had begun to lose herself to the cancer growing, blackly malevolent, inside the pink whorls of her brain. It hadn't been much of a prolonged illness, but it had served to make him strangely grateful that his parents' death hadn't been this drawn out flurry of hospital visits, chemotherapy, and all the waiting for an end that was apt to come at any time. The waiting was the worst part.

How much longer can this possibility go on? Milo thought, not unkindly, setting his jacket on the couch and moving toward the drooling figure. It pained him to see her this way, and more than anything he hoped for an end to her suffering. That it should end this way, after such a tremendous and unique life, was almost unbearable. His eyes fell on the doors to the library, open, to the row of books under glass. *And what will we do when she's gone?*

He dragged an ottoman over and settled himself down at the elbow of his sleeping grandmother, then reached out and gently, oh so gently, squeezed her forearm. He grimaced at how brittle and small that arm felt under his hand.

"Nana," he said quietly, watching her chest rise and fall in short, sharp bursts. "Nana, I'm here."

"Eh?" She grunted. Eyelids now makeupped in only purple veins and red splotches of dried skin fluttered. She coughed, a deep gurgling sound that made Milo wince. Her eyes opened blearily, unfocused, fell on the hand resting on her arm, travelled upwards to the face of her grandson. She smiled. It was a weak and dying thing, but it was warm. "Milo." Her voice was little more than a dry croak. "So good to see you, my beautiful boy. How's Cassandra and...and..."

"Eddie," Milo supplied. "They're doing fine, Nana. How are you feeling?"

"Oh, can't complain," she replied, waving a hand with some effort. "But that never stopped me complaining before, did it?"

She chuckled wetly, then went into a coughing fit, the spasms of her lungs racking her body and tossing her forward. Milo did what Sadie had told him to do in these instances—put a hand out front so Astrid didn't fall forward, rub her back with the other, make soothing sounds until it passed—until she quieted down. When it was over, Astrid fell back into the chair with a soft *whumpf*, gasping for breath.

"You OK?" Milo queried, knowing the answer.

"Fine, my darling, fine," she replied, squeezing his hand. "If I'd known I was still going to be so out of breath, I'd have said no to *this* final indignity." She flicked the oxygen tank, making it *ting*.

"It's to help you."

"It's all to help me. It doesn't mean I like it."

"You shouldn't say things like what you said to Sadie this morning, Nana," he said so suddenly even *he* didn't know he was going to say it, and he blanched. Today wasn't supposed to be about chiding her, it was supposed to be about taking care of her. *Well fucking done, genius. Knocked it out of the park.*

Nana raised an eyebrow, looking at him askance. "You think I said that to scare her? You must not know me at all."

Milo felt his face flush. "I didn't mean—"

358

"Only kidding. You know better than anyone else that the objects in this house hold great power. Deadly power. And that mine used to be the hands that held their flood of terror at bay." She raised her crooked hands to look at them, her mouth working. "Now I can't even hold the spoon to feed myself the oatmeal I have to eat three meals a day. Milo," she leaned in very close to his face, so close he fancied he could smell the rot happening under her skin, "I think they know that."

"Who knows that?" He asked, deeply uncomfortable. He knew that Astrid thought all of this was real, and he was not going to disabuse her of that notion, it was just that...well, he'd been a child, back when all the really scary stuff had happened. A *grieving* child. He didn't blame her for anything she'd said or done, did, in fact, believe she had done everything right. But the truth was that he was older now, a man, and looking at her career through the lens of maturity gave him misgivings about the actual nature of the job. His own experiences, even, once looked at through the carnival glass of childhood, now had a much clearer glass through which to filter. He didn't *want* to believe she was a charlatan, but, well...what other option was there? That there were ghosts living in the books in the library? More likely it was a good way to keep children's hands off valuable antiques.

"You know who," Astrid said simply, looking around at all the things accumulated in her home, her eyes touching them one by one because her hands could not. "I can feel an energy gathering in this place, even as my own clock winds down. They mock me, you know, appearing in my dreams to taunt me. They tell me I'll end up damned like them. My hands used to be the right hands, but alas, not anymore. And when I'm gone, all this," she gestured grandly, "will have to go into a *new* pair of hands, or all my hard work will be for naught. Can you not feel it too, child?"

"I don't feel anything." Milo squirmed, wanting very much to change the subject. "Sadie said you've been doing pretty well this week. She says you've been getting up and down without assistance."

Astrid let out another thick chortle, but this time didn't cough. She sat up a bit straighter, adjusting the blanket on her legs. "Sadie knows same as I do—same as *you* do—that I'm dying no matter *how* many good days I have now and then. One day there's a little less pressure on one area of my brain, and suddenly I can pee without an escort. The next day it shifts and I can't speak a word. How long, do you think, before it presses on the bits that control my heart?"

"Nana—"

"Don't 'Nana' me, young man. I'm not being fatalistic, just *realistic*. I've been here over eighty years without running mad, but human beings aren't edifices. We're just not built to last. But I'll tell you something else. Come closer."

Milo leaned in, and when Astrid met his eyes, hers were clear and sparkling, the eyes of a much younger woman in the face of one that was eighty-six and dying. She lit up with a smile and he smiled back. "What is it, Nana?"

"I'm dying, and that's the truth," she said, "but I think these demons underestimate the fight still left in me. I've got time, Milo. Time to figure out how to keep them at bay when I do at last go to the clearing at the end of the path."

His smile faltered only a little when he replied, "I think you do too, Nana."

She patted his cheeks with her cold, dry hands. "There's a good boy. Now. Would you help get an old lady some tea?"

FIFTEEN

TWO DAYS LATER Sadie called Milo to tell him that Astrid Schulze, with all the wonders that she had performed in this world, had passed from the land of the living as she slept in her bed. He'd woken up, muzzy from sleep still, and answered the insistent ringing from the phone. The news did not come as a particular shock to anyone in the Cunningham household, but Cassie had still pressed against him under the covers and cried, her hands locked around the back of his neck, whispering over and over that she was sorry, so sorry. Milo ran his hand over her back, her swollen belly, her hair, kissing her over and over on each tear-stained cheek, and told her it was alright. At that moment, it seemed like a dream. Even when he went over to Astrid's house, and watched the EMTs wheel her body out into the ambulance on a gurney covered in a sheet, it didn't feel real.

Milo dressed the morning of the combination wake and funeral with uncommon sluggishness, awash in a feeling of unreality. He knotted his tie thinking, *It isn't true. Cannot be true.*

But it was. That sense of unreality followed him all the way up the aisle to Astrid's casket, where he half expected her to be propped up with one elbow on the pink satin pillow, smiling, her eyes sparkling with mischief and saying she'd got him good, hadn't she? But she wasn't. Astrid was lying in a posture of sweet repose, her wrinkled hands clasped lightly at her waist and her eyes closed, with cheeks plumped by saline and skin looking more lively and pink than it had in months. The blue dress he'd chosen for her was knotted primly under the crepe paper skin of her chin, her lips painted a lovely mauve. Her hair was coiffed in a silver cotton ball, curled and set by some careful mortician. Her chest moved not at all, the only thing that suggested she was not merely an exhausted woman deeply sleeping in her church clothes. It was the sight of her stillness that really took it home for him: Nana wasn't sleeping; she was dead.

One more ghost put to rest, Milo thought, and squeezed Cassie and Eddie closer to him.

The funeral was easier than the one for his parents, partially because he was much older now, and partially because he knew many of the people in attendance. But not all. Not all by half. Gaggles of people Milo had never met trailed into the service, not speaking to anyone, but silently wiping tears from their eyes. Many of them were practically ancient, but some were about his age or younger. None came to him to offer their condolences, which was something of relief. He had no desire, on this day of all days, to be told haunting stories of Nana's work. He left them to their grief as they left him to his, and that was alright. Was better than alright; it was *good,* in fact.

I don't need to disabuse anyone of their living visions of who she was today, he thought. *Let them keep their memories the way that I keep mine.*

Once Astrid Schulze was relegated to the family tomb alongside her daughter and son-in-law, the family and friends surviving her drove in a long procession to Milo's house for a post-funeral gathering. None of the silent people who'd crammed into the chapel were present here, and for that he was also grateful. It was hard enough as it was having the ones he knew clogging his kitchen and living room, stuffing their faces with pasta salad and mini muffulettas. From his chair in the kitchen Milo could hear the cacophony of voices as a constant loud susurration, interspersed with the clatter of children's feet as the gaggle of little ones present ran to and fro through the house.

"Why are we doing this?" He asked Cassie as she arranged a charcuterie board, placing Moon Drop grapes and folded meats with great care. The noise and laughter from the living room sounded more like a party than it did a gathering of solemn remembrance. "Just letting people tromp around our house, drinking our booze, eating our food. We did the wake. We did the funeral. I truly don't know how you're still on your feet. I'm so beat I could sleep for fifteen hours."

"Haven't you ever heard of an afterparty?" She retorted, smiling and popping a cube of sharp cheddar into her mouth. "It's tradition. They'll leave soon."

"Yeah, when the liquor is gone," Milo grumbled, rubbing his face with both hands. "I don't even *know* most of these people anymore. Not very well."

"But they knew *her,*" Cassie replied. She leaned onto the counter with both hands, inspecting her handiwork. "It's good for them, especially the older ones, to do something fun after one of them goes. It's hard to lose another person this way, even if it's expected. These things after funerals are kind of like…" she twirled a hand, thinking, "…whistling past the graveyard. It makes them feel better. It might make you feel better too, if you come out and join them. Have a drink. Talk to people."

"I think I'll stay in here for now, thanks."

"My grumpy boy." She picked up the charcuterie board and came to him, bending with some effort to kiss the top of his head, balancing the plate on one hand. Her long black dress swished silkily forward. "You come out when you're ready."

He grabbed her wrist lightly and put his lips against her knuckles. "Thanks for understanding. Don't overwork yourself, OK? If you need my help, just ask."

"Don't worry, I will." She gave him a sly smile that made the hairs on his arms stand up. "I'll save some energy for you, for after Eddie goes to bed."

Milo sighed. "I love the fuck outta you, Cas."

"I love the fuck outta you, too."

She turned and walked out into the fray, and a sound of unified jubilation emitted from the crowd—*heyyyy!*

This city has some weird fucking traditions, he thought, slouching down to rest the back of his head on the chair. Maybe if he caught a little disco nap he'd feel more like joining in. As it was, he wasn't interested in going out and joining the family. Not because he didn't love them—he did, in the distant way you love people you only see on Christmas and Easter for thirty-some odd years—but because, in part, he knew there were two versions of Astrid that were hanging around in his home today. The first version, the blood-relative version, painted her as the kindly grandmother who had taken in her grandson after a tragic accident had claimed both his parents, so she had shouldered the raising of him on her own, despite her advanced age. That one was the truth—the *whole* truth, as far as Milo was concerned. The second version, the one known only by Astrid's adopted family, was stonier and fraught with holes one could break an ankle in, if one wasn't careful. That version painted her as loving grandmother who blah blah blah, but *also* as an entirely different person, one with a secret life, a secret life full of ghosts and demons and God knows what else. It was that version the silent mourners had come to say goodbye to, he knew very well, and it was that version he couldn't allow himself to—

"Milo, my boy, there you are. Been looking everywhere for you, old chap."

Milo startled, turning around to see Chester Beckenham toddling toward him from the living room. Chester, well into his seventies now, nearly entirely bald with his jowls sagging off his smiling cheeks, waggled his glass of punch at him. Milo knew that the old man had gone off drinking ever since his wife had passed six years prior, and marveled at his resolve. And while "hale and healthy" would never be used to describe this bent and elderly gentleman ever again, his brown eyes were clear and full of life. "Hey, Mr. Beckenham. Glad you could make it."

"Chester, please, dear heart," Chester replied, waving the address away as though waving away a particularly rancid passing of gas. "You're far too mature to call anyone Mister but your boss. Especially not me. We've known each other a long time now, eh?"

Milo smiled. "I guess we have. How are you doing?"

"Oh, quite well these days, chappy, can't complain."

"But that won't stop you, right?"

Chester laughed, the sound high and boyish. "You sound like your dearly departed Nana, son. No, it will not."

"Why don't you sit down? I imagine most of the seats out front are taken by now."

"That they are, that they are." Chester limped forward—Milo also knew he'd had a hip replacement last year, but that it still pained him from time to time if he overexerted himself, and the funeral had been a lot of standing—and pulled out the chair opposite Milo, settling his ancient bulk down with a grunt. "I'm sorry about your nana. Astrid was a damn fine woman. Hate to see her go."

"It's not like it wasn't expected," Milo replied, toying with the edge of a party napkin. "She was very sick toward the end, and we had lots of time to prepare."

"Still," Chester mused, "a lady like her only comes around once in a lifetime, if that. Though I will admit, I feel it's a miracle she got as much time as she did, given her vocation. Don't you think so?"

"Yes," Milo admitted grudgingly. He didn't want to talk to Chester, of all people, about this subject. He wanted more than anything for it to die and be left in the ground with Astrid.

"Have you given any thought to what you'll do with her estate?"

The question pulled Milo up short. He *hadn't* thought about it. Truthfully, he'd hoped that her will would leave all of that to people like her, that he'd be washed of it and would be able to move forward with his wife, son, and expected daughter without the burden of Nana's left-behind objects. Her *precious cargo.* "I...haven't, no."

Chester leaned forward, tenting his fingers on the tabletop, his eyes suddenly calculated, his expression shrewd. "As you probably know—or maybe you don't, I've no idea—I am responsible for managing Astrid's estate, but I am also the executor of her will."

Milo raised an eyebrow in surprise. "You are?"

"Yes. She made it so about ten years ago. She said she could tell which way the wind blew when it came to your belief in what she did, and she didn't want any ugliness when she finally passed."

Milo felt the heat of shame creep up his cheeks and to the tips of his ears. So Nana had known all along how he felt about her work. She had known, and said nothing. "Chester, I...I don't know what to..."

Chester held up a hand. "You don't need to justify anything to me, lad. I understand perfectly why you feel the way you do. So did she, and she loved you to the last anyway. She told me it was harder for you to hold onto the beliefs of childhood when you moved into a future full of only the mundane magic of domesticity." He tapped his chin thoughtfully. "I suppose that means she believed you simply outgrew it. Perhaps you did, what?"

"Perhaps I did," Milo replied, a hint of defensiveness in his voice. Of course she would see it that way. Ever the placid acceptance from Astrid, who knew all things came with time, and some things came beyond even that. Astrid with her ghost stories and her *precious cargo* under glass. "So what did the will say? What'll happen to her estate, the house and all the…the…"

"Her collection." Chester nodded. "That's why I came to talk to you, my boy. Astrid left some fairly explicit instructions in her will, that all of her money and her belongings should go directly to you."

"But I don't—"

"And if," Chester continued as if Milo hadn't spoken, "you find you have no use for them, several secondary collectors have been promised to have the keeping of them in your absence. She made only one request before you decide: you must spend one night alone in her house. If, at the end of the night, you find nothing there you wish to have guardianship of, you may relieve yourself of it, and every red cent of her accounts—of which there are several, and all very full—will be transferred over to you. You'll be shed of her business forever, and rich enough to treat your career as a hobby. Quite a fair trade, wouldn't you say?"

Quite a fair trade, indeed. Milo gritted his teeth. He hadn't thought Nana capable of such an underhanded action as this, but he supposed he shouldn't be surprised. She might not have been *upset* with him for growing out of her bullshit, but she certainly had set up one hell of a last push for him believe. One night alone in her house full of creepy, rotting artifacts and all of her money was his. He didn't want to do it—hell, his first thought was to tell Chester to shove it up his narrow keister and spin—but there was his family to consider. Cassie, Eddie, the new one on the way, and enough money on offer that they could have the best of everything for the rest of their lives. *Most grandparents just gift their grandkids money, without all this cloak and dagger shit. Let it never be said Astrid Schulze wasn't extra as fuck, even in death.*

"I'll do it," Milo said.

SIXTEEN

TWO DAYS AFTER Astrid's funeral, Milo slung his red Honda Accord into the driveway of her house just as evening was beginning to fall. In the dying light, he put the balky machine in park with a grinding of gears and waved to Chester, who stood on the porch watching him. Chester waved back, bouncing the keys to the house nervously in his other hand. Milo got out, striding up to the old fellow with brisk steps, trying to avoid getting too wet from the drizzle that had started to fall as soon as he hit the interstate coming from Metairie.

"Don't worry," he'd told Cassie as he kissed her goodbye. "It's only one night in the house I grew up in. It's perfectly safe. We'll be rich by tomorrow."

"I hope you're right," she'd said, kissing the corner of his mouth. "About the safe part, that is. I don't care about the rich part."

Well, maybe *she* didn't care about that part, but *he* did. All Milo saw about this little adventure was a way to put to rest his early life's little spate of weirdness in a way that was lucrative, if time consuming.

Small price to pay, he thought as he reached to shake Chester's hand. *Small price indeed.*

"Good to see you, lad," Chester said distractedly, gazing out at the oncoming gloom. "I'm afraid I can't stay long. Got a meeting with an old business acquaintance for dinner and bridge in about thirty minutes."

"That's fine," Milo said. "Not like I need anyone to hold my hand to get around in here. Can I have the keys, please?"

Chester handed them over reluctantly, biting his lip. "Have you got backup? In case anything goes funny, y'ken."

Milo laughed, but Chester's face remained grave and concerned. *He's taking this so seriously.*

"I'll be fine, I promise," Milo said, squeezing the old man's shoulder. "I've got my phone, and if I get bored, I'll call Cassie for a chat. If she doesn't answer, I'll call you and annoy you during your bridge game. OK?"

"Quite." The word came out clipped. "It's just that…and I know it isn't your way to give credence to this, but…since Astrid passed, things in there have come over a bit queer. It feels less like her home, and more like a…a…cage, I suppose. One where the animals inside have been starving for a long time and are eager to be released so they can gorge themselves. Are you *sure* you want to do this, lad? I wouldn't fault you for saying no at the last moment."

"I'm sure," Milo said, his nose wrinkling in mild contempt for the question. "Why wouldn't I be? It's just a house. One I've lived in, even. One more night won't make a difference either way."

"Better you than me, my boy." Chester glanced down at his car parked in the street, his feet shuffling on the boards of the porch. To Milo he looked like a man ready to dash away at the slightest hint of movement nearby. "Better you than me."

"Thank you for the keys, and thank you for your concern. I promise I'll stay safe." Milo shook out the keys, locating the one that opened the front door. "Now, if it's all the same to you, I'd better get—"

"Oh!" Chester exclaimed, patting his pockets. "I nearly forgot."

He fished around before drawing from his inner jacket pocket a slim, cream-colored envelope, then held it out to Milo.

369

Even in the dim light of dusk Milo could make out his name written in Astrid's neat, spidery handwriting. He took it, and Chester heaved a sigh of relief.

"Would have been damned stupid of me to forget *that*," he said, tapping it. "She left that for you, along with the keys. You're meant to read it as soon as you get into the house."

Milo held up the envelope, inspecting it. "Do you know what it says?"

"I couldn't possibly say, lad," Chester replied (Milo would think later that was a very neat non-answer, very neat indeed) and dug his own keys out from his pocket. "Welp. That's all, then. I'm off to lose my weight in change at bridge. I hope your evening proves less lively than my own." He leaned forward, glancing at the house as though it might be listening in and disapprove. "Remember what I said about having backup. You may need more than one source if things go funny on you. Be watchful. Be wary." He straightened back up and said loudly, "Pleasant evening to you, Milo. Ta-ra!"

And then he turned and trotted down the steps, moving to his car with a gait so rapid it was nigh unbelievable he'd had his hip replaced a year prior, with not even a hint of a limp.

Milo watched him go, bemused. *He sure can move when he wants to. Like someone lit a fire under his ass.*

SEVENTEEN

FIRST ORDER OF business was turning on some lights. Milo wandered through the house, first through the living room—carefully avoiding the easy chair with the oxygen tank still propped next to it—then into the formal den, trailed through the hallway under the stairs, and finally into the kitchen at the back. He was amazed by how little the house had changed since he moved out at eighteen, even though he'd regularly visited until Astrid's death. The amazement came from the knowledge that she never let anything go, that she'd kept up with things in her home in such a way that they rarely needed replacement. Milo supposed that was the kind of effort she'd put into every aspect of her life, from raising her grandson to keeping her glass-covered objects safe: do it right the first time, so you never need to backtrack.

Only she didn't do everything *right,* he thought ruefully, opening the fridge to inspect the contents. *She took a grieving little boy and filled his head with supernatural hooey. She's trying to do it even now, from beyond the grave.*

The cupboards, it seemed, were nearly bare. Half a suspect rotisserie chicken sat in its plastic bubble at the bottom rack in the fridge. In the drawers were one pack of Swiss cheese balefully growing swirls of blue mold, a pack of carrots with only two left in it, and a lone red bell pepper. The freezer held nothing but a tub of Blue Bell Homemade Vanilla ice cream that was, somewhat jarringly, brand new with not even a scoop taken out of it. Similarly, the pantry held little else but the trappings of the weakening palette of advanced age—oatmeal, a flat of Ensure, canned soups heavy on broth.

Milo sighed. "Looks like I'm ordering in."

A small *maow* from his left made him turn. Charlie—so named in memoriam of their first cat, Mingus, who'd passed when Milo was in college—came trotting from around the corner, ginger body rubbing liquidly against the cabinets. He plopped down in front of Milo, showing off his white tummy, and looked up with wide, pleading eyes the color of gold coins.

"Hey, little dude," Milo said, bending to stroke Charlie's soft orange fur. "You out of food?"

Charlie chirped eagerly and trotted away, leading Milo to his dish.

I suppose we'll have the keeping of you as well, he thought, filling the purple bowl that said TIME FOR DINNER at the bottom with kibbles. *Another artifact from Astrid. At least Eddie will be excited.*

He stood up, leaning into his fists to pop his back, staring around him. He felt small, standing here in this kitchen, listening to the grandfather clock tick in the living room, the creaks and groans from above as the house settled its bulk for the night. It wasn't scary at all, this feeling, just…odd. Then it struck him. Had he ever been alone in this house before? Really alone? Milo thought back, to the times in which he'd been left on his own to wander Astrid's home. They'd been few and far between, and only when she'd gone on to collect her *precious cargo*, even though it had been *his* home too for a decade, and someone (usually Tabitha and Chester) had always been appointed to come and look after him in the evenings. Other than a few school afternoons when his caretakers had gotten held up, he'd never really been alone here. Had that happened naturally, or had Nana made certain it was so?

"Questions upon questions," Milo muttered, pulling the envelope Chester had given to him from out of his back pocket. He ran his fingers over the single word printed in Nana's neat, pointed script and underlined with a flourish—*Milo*. That she had cared deeply for his happiness and loved him fiercely there was no doubt, but there was so much that she had said and done that had a ring of such falsehood, he hardly dared open this final letter and examine what it contained. Would it be more lies?

"Or will it finally be the truth?" Milo turned the envelope over and hooked the tip of his pinky into the corner, dragging it along the seam at the top and splitting it open. His fingers shook minutely as he pulled out two pieces of folded paper written front and back in that spidery writing. He allowed the envelope, its job well done, to flutter to the ground, and unfolded the small sheaf of paper in his hands.

At the very top there was the date—February 20, 2014.

"Almost two whole *years* before she died," he murmured. "Christ, but she planned this well."

He squinted at the writing, the swoops and swirls of her letters, and read:

My darling Milo,

(He let out a choked sob, tears already brimming.

"Jesus fuck, Milo, stop being a pussy," he admonished himself, fisting tears from his eyes.)

If you're reading this letter, well, I suppose I've passed to the great beyond. It's been a long time coming, this movement to another type of existence, but it still hurts me to leave you, Cassandra, and sweet little Edward behind. I wish I could see him grow up like I did you, but under better circumstances. Far better circumstances. Since I cannot be there for him, my heart's wish is that you will always be there—to love him, to guide him, to hold him when he's scared, and then one day, to let him go when he needs to go.

I hope I have instilled that instinct in you—to know when it is time to let go.

You know I did the best I could with you, Milo, after Elise and Gregory died. Your mother was my most prized asset, my very first piece of precious cargo, the light of my life after Grandpa Schulze passed when she was only four, and to lose her too was almost too much to bear. They say a parent should never have to bury their child, that it is the deepest pain someone can feel, and they are right. I never got to make things right between your mother and I despite my best efforts and hers, something I will go to my grave feeling sorry for, but there is nothing to be done about that feeling now. It was, even then, the distant past that held us apart, and I never had even the slightest chance of correcting it after your mother went beyond the veil. My one beacon of hope in my dreary life was you. You were so precocious, so good, so absolutely willing to accept me in all my eccentricities as only the very young are capable, that I, in all my immense sorrow, found solace. In you. In us.

Which is why I am sorry to inform you that I lied to you…

"I fucking *knew* it!" Milo shouted at the papers, shaking them violently before crumpling them into a ball and throwing them over-arm across the room where they bounced against the cabinets and landed on the counter. Milo stared at it, lungs heaving air in and out in great gusts, anger swirling red and hot under his skin. He pointed at the crushed mash of vellum with an accusing finger. "Fuck you, you hear me? *Fuck. You.*"

The balled-up paper didn't respond, didn't move an inch. Milo realized he'd been half afraid that something *would* happen, that he had somehow offended Nana's last great confession by balling it up and tossing it aside. That as soon as his angry words were out of his mouth the ball of paper would straighten itself out, perhaps, or that the pages would rise up like the wings of an avenging angel, float into the air and speak in the voice of his dead and buried Nana, chastise him with an otherworldly *language, young man.* He chuffed out a bark of unhappy laughter and shook his head, rubbing his face with both his hands.

"I'm losing my mind," he said from the darkness of his cupped palms, the words garbled by his palms—*um oozim muh mine.* His hands dropped and he looked at the paper ball again. It still hadn't moved. He turned to the cat sitting near his heel, washing its face, and spoke in a rough approximation of Chester's voice. "Losing all my fucking marbles, lad. And you know what we do when we lose our marbles, don't you, Charlie, old boy?"

Charlie gazed up at him, his eyes vacant the way only the eyes of orange cats and some politicians can be.

"That's right!" He pointed at the cat, who looked blankly at the tip of his finger. "We order pizza."

375

EIGHTEEN

A FTER EATING TWO slices of pizza while pacing furiously around the first floor of his dead grandmother's house, Milo wasn't angry anymore. After slice number three, he went back into the kitchen and retrieved the balled-up letter. He smoothed it out using his free hand and the elbow of the one cradling his thick slice of three-meat pie from Reginelli's, careful not to get any grease on the pages. Part of him still *wanted* to be angry—a big part—but the rest of him knew that within these two pages was the way out of that anger. This, too, could be buried, and surely would be. If he allowed it, that was, and he made up his mind to do just that somewhere halfway into slice numero cuatro. What harm, he reasoned, could there possibly be in hearing her out one last time? He would undoubtedly gain a kind of understanding he had spent his whole adult life dreaming of. He may even gain some peace.

He sat on the couch in the living room he'd never been allowed to eat in, chewing thoughtfully and looking at the letter. This could be a blessing in disguise, give him what all his therapists had called *closure*, and allow him to put paid to nightmares he'd carried with him since he was a child.

The boy with his cracked skull, the stinking clown that oozed wrongness, the not-mother from the witch board, and her face, Astrid's face, wild and frightening as she came in from the storm...

He pushed the thought down with a huge bite of pizza, hearing Cassie's voice in his head, *If you choke on that, no one is around to save you.*

He chuckled. No, no one was here. That much was evident from the start. He'd been so afraid to come back here, a fifty-fifty split between traumatic memories and the fear that he *would* see something he couldn't rationalize. The fear that Astrid *hadn't* been lying or a huge charlatan, but acting in earnest against things that weren't, couldn't be, there. It was laughable now, of course. When you're scared of something coming, it always felt too much at once, too big to handle, but then once you were actually *doing* the scary thing, well…

"A body can't keep that level of anxiety up for long," he muttered around his food. Another gem from therapy, but it was accurate. You really couldn't keep that level of excitement forever. People were ever so adaptable that way. Milo drank deeply of the Coke he knew his wife would wrinkle her nose at—*Soda, really? When there are so many other choices?*—and belched expansively. He picked up the letter to read.

Twenty minutes later, he set the pages back down and sat back with a *whumpf*, a dumbfounded look plastered all over his face.

"Bullshit," he said out loud to no one in particular. "Every fucking word. Bullshit. She never let it go, never, even beyond the day she fucking died."

He pushed up from the couch, pizza forgotten, his blood boiling all over again. He paced back and forth, his socked feet whispering over the rug, his fists bunching and unbunching at his side. The grandfather clock let out the first of eight bells and he swung around, startled and angry by its dumb intrusion.

"Shut the fuck up!" He screamed at it, his fists coming up clenched as though ready to fight the sturdy, idiot mechanism that had lived in this house longer than he had, for time out of mind. "*Shut the living fuck up, you dead old bitch!*"

He swung. His fist connected with the wooden side of the clock so hard the entire thing, all one hundred and ten pounds of it, juddered and the glass shook in its frame. Still, it kept on chiming, five, six, seven…He wanted to smash the entire bastard thing, and why not? Didn't this house and everything in it belong to him now, just like the letter said?

The clock let out its final *bong*, the sound reverberating in the room, a vibrating ghost of a chime. Milo glared at it, his face pinched and red, hating it and everything else in this house.

Why are you so furious about this, honey? Cassie asked in his head. *What did she ever do to deserve this much rage? She raised you. She loved you.*

"She used me," he replied, his voice weakening as he spoke aloud the heart of the matter for the first time. "She took the love I had for her, the *trust* I gave to her, and twisted it. She took my desperate need for things to make sense after both my parents died suddenly, and turned it into a ghost story. She made me afraid of things I couldn't even see *for so long,* things that aren't even real. And to top it all off, she did the same thing to *other* people. People who were just as fragile as me. People who were scared and helpless and just itching for their lives to go back to normal, for the nightmare to be over." He thought of Chester and Tabitha, who'd had a daughter named Elizabeth once upon a time. "People who lost people they loved. She lied to them. She lied to all of us. Everything in this house was bought with dirty money. Money she took from people in need."

He glanced at the papers lying on the table and swallowed. "And when she drew me into those lies, she made me her accomplice. And in that…that…letter…" he pointed at it as if Cassie would be able to see it, "she means to try and do it again. Well, I won't do it."

Milo took a deep breath, letting it out slowly. Another.

"I won't," he repeated, but this time his voice was calm and level. His *business voice*, Eddie called it, and that was good, because Milo meant to handle this business once and for all.

Stay in the house for one night, alone, Chester said, and all the money is mine. The assets too. The letter confirms that. One night, one mostly-over-already night, and all the things I don't want will be sold or handed off to people like her. Well, hate to break it to you, Nana, I don't want any of it. Good fucking riddance.

A creak from behind him drew him out of his reverie. He snapped his head around in just enough time to see Charlie, orange tail raised like a flag, push his way into the library and disappear into the darkness beyond. Milo sighed. Nana had never wanted Mingus in there, and he was pretty sure it was also sacrosanct to the new cat as well.

"You dumb little shit," Milo said affectionately, moving to go after him. He didn't particularly care what Nana would have wanted, but the goofy little furball might damage some pricey stuff if left to his own devices for long.

When he flicked the switch just within the library doors, the room was flooded with light and Milo was flooded with memory. It was exactly the way he remembered it, this room, with its deep brown wood floors gleaming, its walls painted the same fading emerald hue it was when he was a child. It was a modest library, to be sure, but had its own grandeur that all houses of books, great and small, possess. There on the wall was another of those paintings of ducks she'd been so fond of, taking wing over a dusk-lit pond and there, below it, the overstuffed reading chair where he'd curled in Nana's lap when she read him stories from her books to help him fall asleep (where, indeed, she'd sat to read him a poem from Clementine Williams' book of poems, but never mind that) and his miniature chair beside it. There was the lamp, tall with a frilly doily shade, standing behind it, the footstool placed so dutifully in front of it. And all around these homey touches, the shelves, stocked full up with other worlds, other voices, other rooms.

Milo surveyed the room with something like wonder, amazed that he should feel such an eerie doubling of past and present, that in this room instead of any other he should feel nine and a half years old again, so small and so fragile. Charlie rubbed at his legs, but he paid the animal no mind even though it was his fault Milo was in here at all. His eyes roamed the room, remembering. They were good memories, the ones from this room, of discovering the pleasures of reading. He'd read nearly every book on these shelves at least once. All of them, that was, except…

His eyes lit on the bookcase stationed at the far wall, the one with the special cabinet inlaid on the middle shelf. The books behind glass.

Milo strode into the room, ignoring every other shelf in favor of that one, the one that had been forbidden to him his entire life. He reached out a hand. Paused.

Yes, the cabinet seemed to call out. *Yes. Come. Touch. Take. We've been waiting.*

He laid his fingers on the glass and immediately pulled them back. A full body shudder ran through him. The glass had an icy, unpleasant feeling, a full ten degrees colder than the rest of the room, and slick as though it were covered in grease. He rubbed his hands against his thigh to rid himself of the sensation and licked his lips with a tongue gone suddenly dry.

"I'm not afraid of you," he whispered. Then, clearing his throat, said louder, "I'm not afraid of you."

The books replied not at all. After all, why would they? They were just books, made of paper, cardboard, leather binding. There was no danger in this room or any other room of the house. There never had been.

So why not take one out and read, Milo, old chap? Chester piped up. *Yellow chicken, are we?*

Milo rubbed his mouth with a shaking hand. Why not indeed? Everything in this house belonged to him now (until tomorrow, that was, when it would all be sold), so there was no reason *not* to take one out and peruse it. It would kill time, if nothing else.

"All your precious cargo belongs to me now, Nana." Milo ran his fingertips over the wood casing of the shelf, marveling at how the little knob fit so well between his index and middle fingers. As if it were meant to be. As if it were made for him.

She wouldn't like you doing that, you know, Cassie spoke up.

"Didn't you read the letter?" He replied, his voice distant to his own ears. "She said herself that all this bullshit belongs to me now. If I want it."

Do you really want it, though, honey? Cassie queried. *Or do you simply want to be defiant?*

"Column A, Column B," he replied, and pulled the knob. The little door came free of the surrounding case with a sigh like pleasure.

Milo stood, simply staring at the books within for several seconds, a giddy feeling of triumph overtaking him. These damned things had haunted him his entire childhood—and beyond, if he was honest—and now no one was here to wag an admonishing finger at him and tell him he may as well be playing with fire. It was utterly thrilling to be free of that anxiety and see them for what they really were: just books, paper gathered together in stories bound with glue, and nothing more. The pleasant smell of old paper and ink wafted out at him, and he smiled. He ran a finger experimentally over the spines, relishing their cool, dry surfaces. He almost expected something to happen (an alarm to blare, perhaps, one final warning *blat* to frighten him away and make him feel nine years old again) but nothing did. He bent and squinted to read the titles of the books, his eyes skating over *The Poky Little Puppy* as quickly as they could. There was the blue bound book of poetry that belonged to Clementine Williams, right where it always had been. He stroked its spine affectionately, moving on. He wanted nothing from that book today. Here was a compendium of the musings of Marcus Aurelius, its spine shiny and almost brand new. Another was a cookbook, *The Joy of Cooking* to be precise, taking up more room than it had any right to. His eyes fell on one slim volume, at the end furthest from him, one with a spine so cracked and battered that the title was unreadable. Milo moved his hand toward it, meaning to pluck it out and see. Hesitated.

It's just a book, he told himself, but his hands were suddenly sweating. *Just a book. Take it out.*

Yes, another voice whispered, a voice like a sighing moan and not his own. *Yes. Take it. Hold it. It's yours. Your birthright. All for you. Always has been. Touch. Take.*

Milo placed his index finger on the top corner of the book and slid it out from the shelf. There was a brief moment where he thought he heard the word *beautiful* sighed almost imperceptibly, but he chalked it up to his imagination working overtime in this house of long-ago horrors. What else, after all, could it be, except the knowledge that what he was doing went against everything he'd been taught by his nana making him jumpy as a long tailed cat in a room full of rocking chairs? He brought the book out and cradled it in both hands, inspecting the cracked and worried front cover.

"*The Metamorphosis*," he read aloud. "By Franz Kafka." He grinned. This had been one of his favorite books in high school, had indeed been one he'd read so many times that his copy was nearly as battered as this one was. "Well, alright, alright, *alright!*"

He opened the inside cover to look at the title page, and found scrawled in red ink beneath the black words of the title:

THIS BOOK BELONGS TO
EDNA CRAVENLY

"Well, Edna," he said, "now your book belongs to Milo Cunningham."

He tucked the book under his arm and traipsed to the living room to retrieve his half-finished Coke and bring it with him back into the library (another rule broken, ye gods, he was racking them up tonight), forgetting entirely that his mission had started as getting Charlie out of a place he didn't belong. At any rate, the cat was gone by the time he clicked the lights off in the living room as well as the library, and settled his bulk into the armchair with the lamp glowing above. A pool of soft yellow light fell around him, warm and comforting. He pulled the soft, fluffy blanket down off the back of the chair and *whooshed* it out over his propped-up feet, tucking it in around him.

This is nice, he thought, relishing the warmth of the blanket and pulling it further up to cover himself up to the chest. *A man could get used to this.*

He opened *The Metamorphosis*, the pages falling apart so easily he didn't even have to hold the book, just lean it against his hand. Whoever Edna Cravenly had been, she'd certainly known how to love a book to death in just the right way. He began reading, almost instantly transported to the world of poor, transformed Gregor Samsa, as the bug with the man's mind trying desperately to communicate to the world what had happened to him. The sap even tried to get out and go to work, unable to accept that his fate had changed, not by his own hands, but by those of unknown (and most likely supernatural) forces. Milo yawned. His eyelids drooped. He read on, his head getting ever heavier. He wondered if he shouldn't just go upstairs to his old room and lie down for a while. The heavy meal had apparently done its work so well that he was ready for sleep at not even nine o'clock.

I think I'll just stay here, he reasoned. *I have to sleep in this house tonight anyway, and it would be too weird to sleep in that room with all those memories. Especially without Nana right down the hall. Besides, I want to get in another chapter.*

And so there he stayed, his limbs turning heavy and his head nodding off and on as he tried (in vain) to power through another chapter of Franz Kafka's most popular work. When the clock in the living room let out a single *bong* to signify the half hour, Milo was already deeply asleep, his feet twitching and his chin on his chest, the book lying open on his lap.

NINETEEN

A SOUND FROM THE living room awoke him. Milo raised his head, his brain muzzy with sleep, and wiped a line of drool from his mouth. He sat, blinking owlishly in the glare from the overhead lamp, listening. Nothing.

Just the cat, he thought, and readjusted himself in the chair. Boy, was his butt numb. His legs, too, had that weird half-dead feeling that he knew from experience would resolve itself with a burning pins and needles sensation. He wiggled his toes experimentally and found that they were also completely numb. He groaned, pushing himself into a sitting position, his back crackling noisily as he sat up, *The Metamorphosis* falling from his lap in a flutter of pages. *Remind me never to sleep in a chair again, even a comfy one. I'm too old for this sh—*

Another sound from the darkened living room. Bigger. A dragging *thump.*

Milo stilled, listening. *Maybe an animal got in the house. One bigger than the cat. More destructive. A raccoon, maybe.*

He thought wistfully of his mobile phone sitting on the couch in the living room, his lifeline to the outside world. If he had it, he could call animal control while his legs woke up. As it was, he was stuck in this room with his ears trained towards the darkness beyond the rim of light in which he sat. Again came the dragging sound, followed by the squeak of the coffee table as something ran into it. A cough, thick-sounding and wet.

Intruder! Someone in the house! His systems sang. A panicked thought flitted over his mind. *I'm going to die in this house just like Nana.*

And on the heels of that, less panic and more sheer gallows humor, *Raccoons don't cough like that.*

Milo felt frozen, unable to rise from the chair and make a decision about what to do, Obviously, to get any kind of help, he'd have to brave going into the living room where the intruder was, and that wasn't going to happen. It would be suicide if the intruder had any kind of a weapon whatsoever. Or God forbid, an accomplice. He thought wistfully of his family, Cassie, Eddie, and the little daughter on the way, and knew that he couldn't put himself in any more danger than he already was. He could wait for the intruder to leave or go into another part of the house, and *then* retrieve his phone and summon help, but from where he was sitting, he couldn't even see into the room where they were. But they could very likely see him, oh yes, because he had what amounted to a goddamn floodlight positioned over his head to light the way. He could lock the doors of the library and stay inside until they left, but that might not be for hours. And if they knew he was in there already (as they surely did), it would simply be a question of busting out the glass panels in the library doors, turning the interior thumb latch on the lock, and coming in to get him. Milo decided that his best course of action was to simply be still, listen, and hope that whoever was in the house hadn't yet noticed his presence. If that held true, he really *could* just wait until they moved into the other part of the house and make a break for it.

Ah, but will that hold water if you still want to claim the money, old boy? Chester spoke up, *Don't recall any caveats for break-ins in the will, do you?*

Milo found he didn't care. With the shuffling, dragging sounds coming from the darkness of the living room, he decided that the money didn't matter. There were other ways to ensure there was enough to go around forever. There was only one Milo. If he were taken from his little tribe, he had no doubt that they would survive, but they'd all be weaker for it. Better to play opossum for a moment while whoever was rifling through the living room absconded with candlesticks and fine china than to be a traumatic event for his wife to discuss in therapy. He tilted his head to the side—slowly, ever so slowly, so as not to attract attention—so that he was facing the living room. To see the intruder might be useful, if, that was, he could get enough light to give a proper description.

The ticking of the grandfather clock went on for many seconds, with no other sounds from the living room. Milo realized he had been holding his breath since the last sound had come, and slowly let it out, not daring to make much sound himself.

Maybe they left. Maybe now is my chance.

He listened for a few more agonizing seconds. Nothing. He sat forwardly slowly, his eyes trained on the living room in case there was anything so much as a rustle of curtains, and then he heard it. Ragged breathing, from near the hallway door, the one under the stairs. It was out of his sight line, but it was clearly the wet, gurgly sort of breathing that came either from the very sick or those with advanced emphysema. He went stock-still again, his ears straining. So whoever it was, they were close to his right, if he chose to walk through the door of the library, about five feet away. Close. Too close for comfort, but not grabbing-distance, and maybe just far enough away for him to make a beeline to the front door and away into the night. He would be on foot, of course, his keys sitting on the dining room table, but if they were breathing like *that*, odds were good that Milo would be able to get away long before whoever it was could give proper chase. And there was something else, niggling at the back of his mind, about the quality of the breathing. It had a high, wheezy quality that denoted itself as feminine to his ears. If it was a woman in the living room, a woman with a gurgling cough who was uncoordinated enough to be bumping into furniture, no less, his odds were even better of getting out of this alive.

If it's a woman, she's probably a vagrant, he thought. *There's a huge homeless population in this neighborhood, and I might have been stupid enough to leave the door unlocked when I grabbed the pizza. If she's drunk or high, that's not so great, but that means she won't have all her wits about her. She'll be at a disadvantage all around, in fact. Plus…plus…*

Plus she sounded *old.* That was it. Her breathing reminded him very much of how Nana had sounded in her last days, her humped old body deteriorating around her, her lungs failing her like everything else. Another cough resounded from the living room, this one going on for several bubbling, wheezy seconds.

OK. An old, sick, homeless, possibly drunk woman wandered her way into the living room. I can handle that. He pushed himself out of the chair.

"Hello?" Milo called out. The breathing stopped. He took a step forward and almost slipped right down on his ass from the Kafka on the floor. Annoyed, he stooped and retrieved the book, holding it loosely in his hand. There was no sound from the living room. "Hello? I know you're in the house, ma'am. I promise not to hurt you. I'm coming out. OK?"

No reply. Whoever was out there was listening, though, of that much he was sure. It took only three steps to put Milo in the doorway of the library, and he stood, feet apart, squinting into the gloom. He turned to his right, and as his eyes adjusted, a shape began to resolve itself. Yes, when she breathed, she sounded like his grandmother, but that was where the comparison ended. Milo gasped. In the half-light cast by the lamp in the library, turned towards the kitchen so that her right side faced him, he saw outlined in blackness a hulking shape, easily six feet tall, as broad as the window that backlit her with silvery moonlight. She was morbidly obese, her slab of a body rising and falling as she breathed in rattling gasps. Her hair was wet, matted to her skull, her lower lip sticking out in a pout from the front of her face. But the strangest part—and indeed the most disturbing—was that she was completely naked as far as he could see. Light touched the side of one leg and one arm, bare white flesh glistening as though she'd come in from a rainstorm. The swell of her breasts was immense, one nipple partially illuminated, over the protrusion of her belly which—thankfully—hung over her pubic mound. She heaved, wheezing, and began to turn her head in a jerky, twitching motion that made Milo feel physically ill, until she was looking at him. Wild eyes gazed out from underneath hair plastered to her face, catching the light and shining back like tiny moons in the gloom.

Milo swallowed. "I don't want to—" his voice caught in his throat, "—I don't want to frighten you, or alarm you, but this is my house. You need to leave. Right now."

She turned the rest of her—more of that jerky, unnatural movement that made his skin crawl—and faced him, her head tilted to one side.

"Mmmmmmmmmmmm…" she moaned, the sound so forlorn Milo almost felt bad for her.

"I know you must be sick, maybe not all there, so I'm not gonna call the cops," he said lamely. "But I do want you to leave. I'm sorry, but you don't belong here."

She only stared at him, body twitching, making that low moaning *mmmmm* sound. Milo wished she would stop.

That sound seemed to drive into his skull like a spike, and it was making him angry that, high as fuck or not, she wouldn't get the hint and beat feet out of this house. She held out her hands in a gesture of supplication, her arms wet and glistening in the lamplight. Milo looked down and away from this pitiful display, and it was then that he noticed that despite having walked bare-ass and dripping all over the living room, she hadn't left so much as a single track. No footprints on the rugs, either. He looked back at the spot in which she stood rooted, and saw that there, too, was no evidence that his soaked guest was anything but totally dry, even as he saw droplets falling from her outstretched fingers.

"What the *fuck?*" Milo exclaimed, his hands coming up to his chest in shock.

Then everything seemed to happen at once. The first thing that happened was that she noticed the Kafka book in his hands. Her eyes went wide, burning, hungry, and her lips peeled open—actually *peeled apart* as though they had been stuck together with glue—with a wet ripping sound, revealing cracked and yellowed teeth. She took a step forward and screamed, "*Mmmmmmmmmine! MINE!*"

Each time her teeth separated, a flood of huge, reddish-brown roaches fell out, their fat bodies falling to the floor and squirming there on their backs, chitinous legs waving in the air much like the ill-fated Gregor Samsa, before flipping themselves right way up and scuttling away. Most made for the safety of the darkness beneath the furniture, but a fair few hurtled towards Milo, who stood with his lips pressed into a tight line until one of them reached his bare foot and began to climb it. He gagged and shook it off. More came now from the mouth of their mistress, some taking to the air with a buzzing hum of insectile wings. Milo cried out in disgust and took two steps back, away from the woman and the roaches, his back hitting the far wall.

She advanced on him, her hands turned into claws, screaming and pouring bugs.

She's full of them, that's why she's so big, came the first insane thoughts. Then, simply, *This is it. I'm never going home again.*

She reached him in four bounding, twitching steps, so much faster than he'd believed her to be able to move, her ragged breath close enough to smell its fetid, rotten odor (maggot-infested seafood and brackish water came to mind), and lunged for Milo. Milo screwed his eyes shut, readying himself for the blow.

But none came. He opened his eyes again, and there she was, screaming and whipping her head back and forth inches from his face, her expression so angry and crazed and ready for his blood, her clawed hands swiping at him over and over in furious gestures of violence...

...and passing straight through him, as if she were no more than air. She howled in misery, raising her fists above her head as she screamed, and the lights began flickering. Lightning forked down from the ceiling fixture and struck her, the smell of ozone filling the room. Still she let out that warbling, phlegmatic cry of unhappiness and cruelty. Milo was by no means an expert on this kind of thing, but he had grown up with someone who was, and he got the idea that what she was doing was drawing power. That once she had enough, she'd be corporeal enough to take the book from his hands. Or the skin from his face, whichever she wanted first. She bent backwards, yelling her head off, as more lightning struck her and roaches tumbled from her mouth in droves. If he was going to make a move, it had to be now.

"Jesus fuck, lady, *here!*" He screamed, throwing the book at her face. It sailed through her head and landed behind her. She whirled and dove after it, mewling her surprise, and Milo saw his opportunity. He turned and, without thinking of anything but *away, away, away,* bounded up the stairs to his childhood bedroom.

He passed the painting in the hallway, and had enough presence of mind to think how stupid this move had been. *Typical horror movie stuff. You always say "I wouldn't do that", but you would. You would. Christ, what an idiot I am. I didn't even bring my shitfucking phone.*

Oh, but there were other phones in the house, weren't there? One in Nana's old bedroom, as a matter of fact, sitting on her bedside table, just as it always had been. It was one of those old rotary jobs, a holdover from when she was young, and it had always fascinated Milo as a child how you had to draw the circles in from the numbers all the way around and let go, watching it spin back to its place before you could dial the next number. It was slow as dogshit and older than God, but it would get the job done to dial 911, alright.

"Where? Where, where, WHERE?" He heard from downstairs, and the crash of something being tipped over.

She hadn't seen him leave, had been too distracted by her precious book, and therefore had no idea where he was for now. That was good. The thought of that monstrosity barreling down on him before he had a chance to even call the cops was terrifying. Especially since now she could apparently move shit around with a fury she hadn't possessed before. There was a shattering crash as something glass broke.

Do you believe now, my darling? Nana said gently.

"Yeah, yeah, I fucking believe. I believe I need some fucking help, is what I believe." He walked softly on the sides of his feet to Nana's bedroom door, careful not to make any noise lest he give away his position. It sounded like Edna (if that was who she was) was still in the living room, banging around. She was slow now, having expended all that energy. Good. He hoped to all that was holy that she spent at least another thirty-five minutes throwing shit around downstairs, enough time for him to get several NOPD officers ready to take her down. But would they do any good? Somehow he didn't think so, although he was loath to admit it. "Just a fucking vagrant. That's all she is. Not Edna. Not a ghost. Just some weird old bum."

He tried Nana's door. It was locked. Milo groaned quietly and put his forehead against the door, thinking. One teenage summer he'd been obsessed with the idea of picking locks. Had even bought a kit and carried it with him everywhere. Still did, as a matter of fact. Nana had laughed about his obsession a bit, and shook her head as she watched him pick every lock in the house. Including, of course, her bedroom door. Milo hope that earnest teenage perseverance would help him now in this hour of need. He fished the little kit of tools out of his pocket and dug around for the right ones. The real question was, did he remember enough about picking locks to get in before the anxious lumbering nightmare harpy downstairs figured out where he was and came up to teach him a thing or two about reading other people's books.

It's not goddamn Edna Cravenly down there. It's some homeless lady—a weird one, yeah, but a living one. He slid the lock picks into the lock and began to root around, his tongue protruding from the side of his mouth. *Gonna get in here, use that dinosaur phone to call the cops, and she'll be gone in less than an hour. She'll spend the night in lockup—won't that be fun in her altogether?— and then they'll let her go to be crazy somewhere else. And I'll get to go home to my family and remember to lock my doors forevermore.*

Even now you deny it? Nana asked, amusement in her voice. *Why do you deny yourself so much understanding?*

"Because it's…not…real." The lock let go with a soft *thunk*, and Milo pushed his way into Nana's room, holding the door as he shut it so as not to make a sound. From below, a thump and squeal of wood on tile told him Edna had moved on to the kitchen. He wondered briefly if Charlie would be OK, and decided he would be. Cats were resilient. And besides, they couldn't read, so he was in no danger of being accused of book thievery.

He scanned the room, a room all too familiar to him for most of his life. The whole room smelled of lemons and lavender, tinged with the medicinal smell of old age. The queen-size bed, with its dusky-rose colored sheets, was dipped in the middle, the mattress having long since conformed to the shape of the person who slept in it. The covers were turned down as if the owner would be back any minute now to slip between the crisp sheets and fall asleep. It occurred to Milo that this was where Astrid had taken her final breath, and he shuddered. Best not to think about that now, under the circumstances. Everywhere in this room were the trappings of a collector. Curios festooned the top of the dresser, tiny porcelain animals swarmed the jewelry caddy, pictures hung on the walls. Some were of him—here, his third-grade headshot, there, a group photo of everyone on the Tigers basketball team in middle school—but even more were older, in black and white. These, Milo supposed, were Astrid's family, and he was sure at one time he'd known who they all were, but not now. The wallpaper was the exact same leaves-and-roses motif as it had been when he was little. Sitting mutely on her bedside table next to the rotary phone was a music box encased in glass. Not the same one she'd brought home that day, with the clown inside, but one similar enough to make his balls crawl.

"Nothing ever changes," he breathed, a trifle amazed. The room was like a time capsule of his grandmother's life. Another screech of fury from downstairs snapped him back to the present. He went around the bed to the far side of the room and sat on the rose-printed duvet. He took the phone out of the cradle and pressed it to his ear.

Nothing.

He toggled the cradle up and down with his fingers, hoping for the dial tone.

Still nothing.

"Fuck," he muttered, and banged it back down harder than he meant to.

The noises from downstairs stopped.

"Oh, fuck," Milo squeaked out, before the sound of heavy, running feet echoed up to him. He looked around wildly, hoping against hope that there would be something in here to help him, save him, from the creature whose footfalls had now reached the stairs. There was nothing he could see. No baseball bat, no axe, and definitely no gun. "How the fuck did you protect yourself from the crazies, Nana?"

You know how. She replied placidly inside his head. *You have always known how.*

"But it's not *true*," he moaned miserably. "You made it all up. To…to scare me? To protect me from reality? I don't know, but you *lied*."

I did not lie about everything. Now the voice was disappointed and sad, like it had been when he didn't learn his lessons well at school or he broke a rule he knew very well how to follow. *Just one thing. For this, you must forgive me.*

Now the footsteps were coming up the stairs, the labored, wheezy breathing loud enough to hear through the door.

Milo sank to the ground, pressed his head against the floorboards, covering his ears. Hot tears ran down his nose and puddled before him on the boards. "I don't know what to do. What do I do?"

I have given you the key to your salvation. Use it.

"It's not going to work." The footsteps were just outside now, the wet squelch of bare toes on hard wood. A cockroach ran under the door ahead of her.

It will if you believe it will. Do you believe me, Milo? Finally believe? Do you believe in me?

Milo let out a choked sob as the door creaked open and Edna stepped into the room, the boards wailing loudly under her bulk. Milo could see her feet from beneath the bed and noted that now the water *was* pooling at her feet, now, when she bounced on the balls of her feet, the wood gave way to accommodate her. Whatever she had been before, whatever aether she had sprung from, Edna was now very real. Very real indeed, and completely able and willing to hurt him when she found him. Maybe kill him. Milo would be one more ghost trapped under the glass of Astrid's house, doomed forever to relive this moment over and over. He thought of Cassie, of how willing she was to put her faith in him, how willing she was to learn and expand her definition of truth, and how donkey-fucking stubborn he had been to be angry at Astrid for doing what she did the way she did it. How wrong he'd been. Edna's bulk settled on the bed, and he could feel her leaning, he could smell her—the clogged, drainpipe odor of the long-drowned—hear her rancid, gurgling breath as she leaned over the side of the bed and her cry of triumph when she saw him, feel the roaches raining down upon him from above. The lights began to flicker as Edna drew more power to herself for her final, killing blow.

And that was all he needed to change his mind.

"Astrid Shulze!" He screamed from his prone place on the floor. "*I call on you in the name of the Father, the Son, and the Holy Spirit! I call on you to protect me now in my hour of need!*" And then, because in some ways he was still very much the child he once was, "*Nana, please help me!*"

"THERE!" Edna's savage cry rang out from above him, her pale and icy fingers closing on the back of his shirt, hauling him up, up, up to face her. Milo was turned like a kitten held by its scruff to face the gargantuan horror of a woman that held him. Up close and fully in the light, her face was even more horrible than he'd thought. The skin was mottled grey-green under the pallor, with purple splotches standing out on the soft parts. Beneath brows completely devoid of hair, her eyes were bloodshot, clouded over, blind, but full of rage nonetheless. Holes dotted her face here and there, and when she lifted the corners of her fish-bitten mouth to grin at him with crooked yellow teeth, one of those holes pulsed, protruded, until a roach popped its head out from underneath, struggling to squeeze the rest of itself out to crawl down and hide in her bosom. Milo screamed and tried to twist away, but Edna held him fast in her grip. She leaned forward and opened her mouth, her black and swollen tongue coming out to lick a long, slow stripe up Milo's face. Roaches crawled out and over his neck, down his shirt, into his hair.

"I believe you! I believe all of it! It's all true!" Milo cried out, sobbing and twisting back and forth, flailing his limbs in an effort to get away. Christ, but she was too strong. Whatever she had planned for him would undoubtedly be slow, horrible, and deeply satisfactory to her soul, such as it was. Milo went limp, resigned to his fate. He had been a fool, to think that he knew better than the woman who had trapped this terrible thing in its glass cage, to think that he was somehow stronger than her for not allowing himself to listen, to deny her trade as charlatanism. He looked up at the ceiling as Edna caressed his chest with one bloated hand. "I'm sorry. Please. I'm so sorry. Please help me, Nana."

A low rumble began in the floorboards, gaining strength until the walls themselves began to shake, the pictures rattling in their frames. Edna startled, dropping Milo and turning around to look behind her as if someone was there.

And, all at once, someone was.

Milo picked himself up from the floor and looked in the direction Edna was facing, her hands clasped to her chest as if in prayer. A bright white light came from the hallway, steadily growing in brilliance until Milo had to shield his eyes from it. Attached to it was a sound like bells, tinkling, delicate ones, but far off as in a distant room. As the sound and the fury filled the room, Edna began to shriek, her skin smoking in noxious waves. She threw herself down on the bed and began to thrash, screaming all the while, her head shaking back and forth in sullen negation of the coming of the light.

"Go back to where you came from, foul thing of darkness," a familiar voice said, "and trouble this child of the light no more."

Edna let out a final shriek—so high-pitched and so long that Milo covered his ears with both hands to block it out—and then her body began to change.

Dimmer, she's getting dimmer.

Dimmer was, in fact, an excellent term to describe what was happening to Edna. First her body became pale, then see-through, then more and more transparent until only her outline remained. Then, even that disappeared, and Edna was no more. With her disappearance, the light itself began to grow dim, no longer such a glare but a soft white, like incandescent bulbs under a lamp shade. Milo put down his hands and opened his eyes. There, standing on the other side of the bed from him, was Nana. Only she wasn't so old and bent as she was when she left the world. Here was a hale and healthy Nana, one with no arthritis, her hair still that shining golden-brown he'd only ever seen in pictures. She was wearing a long-sleeved white dress that flowed around her in waves. If he had to hazard a guess, she looked to be perhaps thirty-five. But still, she *felt* like Nana.

Milo gaped. "Wh...what...how did...how are you...Nana, is that you? Really you?"

She smiled at him. "Articulate as always, my love."

"It *is* you," he breathed, dimly aware that he was kneeling before her, not just out of shock, but out of the sheer awesomeness of her presence. The light shone around her like a halo, her hair blowing as if in a faint breeze. He looked down as his hands, which lay in his lap, at a loss for words. Finally, as they always do, they came in a rush. "I'm so sorry I didn't believe you. Or forgot. Whatever you want to call it, I'm sorry. I spent so long angry at you, thinking you were the problem, that you were the liar, but it was me. I lied to myself. I'm sorry it took all of this," he waved a hand, "to figure that one out. I'm an idiot."

Astrid came around the bed, that halo of light following her. "Rise, my grandson. Come up off your knees."

He did as he was bade, but wouldn't look at her. She put a hand, warm and soft and very much there, on his cheek and made him look at her. Tears overspilled his eyes as he gazed into hers, those deep and limpid pools that held so many wonders. "I wish I could learn more from you. I wish I'd listened. I'm listening now, though. Can you forgive me?"

"My sweet child," she said, cupping his cheeks, "I forgave you long before you forgave yourself." She leaned in and put her arms around him. "I love you, dear heart, so do take care of yourself, and your little family. They are your most precious cargo now. That is something I learned from *you*. Just this time, don't take so gods-damned long to get to the heart of things, yes?"

"I won't," he said, laughing and burying his face into the softness of her shoulder, closing his eyes and holding her, memorizing the feeling of love and acceptance he felt in this embrace, breathing her in as deeply as he could. "I promise to take care of…of everything. Everyone. I love you too. But Nana, what about—"

It was too late. The feeling of weight was gone from his arms, and when he opened his eyes, he saw that she was gone.

Oh well, he thought, *I'll be able to see her again if I ever need to.*

He looked down at the duvet, at the inky black stain that had been left behind by Edna's recent departure, and shivered. He hoped very much to never have to call on Nana again.

TWENTY

Six Months Later

M ILO ROLLED UP the door to the storage unit, grunting with effort. It was a bright, hot summer day, the sky a clear and blameless blue. He had left his little family—Cassie, Eddie, and baby Astrid—home while he went on this most imperative of errands. Eddie had asked to come, bless him, but Milo had refused. His first thought had been of unfriendly entities, but now he added heatstroke to the list of reasons his son was better off waiting in the air-conditioned house uptown. The storage facility custodian stood by and watched him, never even asking if he could help when the roll-up door got stuck about halfway and Milo had to use his shoulder to get it unstuck. Arming sweat off his brow, Milo turned to the custodian and nodded. "This is definitely the only one in her name?"

"Only one I know about," the custodian drawled, chewing on the end of his toothpick. "I ain't got a complete list. That's Tim's job, and he's on vacation."

You seem half on vacation yourself, big man, was right behind his teeth to spit back. But instead, Milo smiled and reached out his hand for a shake. "Then I thank you for your service all these years, keeping this stuff safe and all. It was really important to her."

The custodian shook but looked him up and down as though he'd said something crazy. "Yeah, well, it's paid till the end of the month. You were listed as an emergency contact in case she couldn't be reached. If it's important, you may want to render $124.67

to our little establishment by no later than June 27. Otherwise it's goodbye, so long, farewell to you, my love. We don't hold stuff for free, even for dead old ladies. Got it?"

Milo nodded, not allowing his annoyance to stray onto his face. "Got it. And thank you."

"For what?"

Milo shrugged noncommittally and waved at the open unit that sat in shadow. "This opportunity, I guess."

"Opportunity," the custodian repeated, incredulous. "Yeah. OK, buddy."

He turned on his heel and walked smartly away from Milo, shaking his head. Milo watched him go, amused. That guy would probably be scratching his head about that little conversation for days after this. Might even get a hankering to try and get a peek at what was in Unit 19 on the second floor of the U-Store-It Long Term Storage Facility. Well that was too bad, fella, because this unit was being emptied out ASAP.

"Goodbye, so long, farewell to you, my love," Milo muttered, his hands on his hips. He felt for the switch just inside the door, found it, and flicked it on. Fluorescent light buzzed on, first flickering then holding steady, above four good-sized steel racks with five shelves apiece. The racks were filled with objects—books, children's toys, shoes, Milo even spied way in the back of one an entire Art Deco-style bedside lamp—but that was by no means all of it. Stacked against the walls were paintings, more books, pieces of furniture, pillows, and paper bags bulging with indeterminate contents. Every last one as cursed as the copy of *The Metamorphosis* that had brought Edna Cravenly back from her watery grave. Maybe more so, seeing as this was the place Nana had stored her most dangerous objects. They weren't going out to the trash like the custodian would have surely allowed them to had the rent not gotten paid, but instead being moved to a bigger, climatized unit across town. One where they wouldn't be so cramped, and much closer to Milo's new residence. One that would fit infinitely more.

"We've got a lot of work to do, Nana," he breathed, his hand coming up to tap his shirt pocket and the letter that laid in there, creased and soft from so many foldings and refoldings, its paper now tattered and soft. This was no cursed object, but a holy one, and he kept it with him always.

This is what it said:

My darling Milo,

If you're reading this letter, well, I suppose I've passed to the great beyond. It's been a long time coming, this movement to another type of existence, but it still hurts me to leave you, Cassandra, and sweet little Edward behind. I wish I could see him grow up like I did you, but under better circumstances. Far better circumstances. Since I cannot be there for him, my heart's wish is that you will always be there—to love him, to guide him, to hold him when he's scared, and then one day, to let him go when he needs to go. I hope I have instilled that instinct in you—to know when it is time to let go.

You know I did the best I could with you, Milo, after Elise and Gregory died. Your mother was my most prized asset, my very first piece of precious cargo, the light of my life after Grandpa Schulze passed when she was only four, and to lose her too was almost too much to bear. They say a parent should never have to bury their child, that it is the deepest pain someone can feel, and they are right. I never got to make things right between your mother and I despite my best efforts and hers, something I will go to my grave feeling sorry for, but there is nothing to be done about that feeling now. It was, even then, the distant past that held us apart, and I never had even the slightest chance of correcting it after your mother went beyond the veil. My one beacon of hope in my dreary life was you. You were so precocious, so good, so absolutely willing to accept me in all my eccentricities as only the very young are capable, that I, in all my immense sorrow, found solace. In you. In us.

Which is why I am sorry to inform you that I lied to you. It wasn't a big lie, at first, but it was a necessary one, to keep you safe. Remember when that book fell out in the library, and you read it, how upset it made me? How I told you the story about being chased through my home by Shere Khan? That particular story was fiction, and you knew it, even then, and I'm sorry. It was the first lie I told you (and not even a good one), but I needed to be positive, you see, that you would develop a certain kind of respect for the things in my home. The things behind glass fascinated you, lured you, as they do, and I was afraid in my secret heart that that might mean they would take you away from me the way your dear mother was taken. I was eternally grateful when you, despite your curiosity, obediently kept your hands off of those terrible things, even though then I wouldn't discuss with you why, and kept yourself away from those hungry things without even a question. For they were hungry, Milo. Hungry, but sleeping, dreaming dreams that repeat over and over in all their violent, sickening splendor.

Allow me now to explain some things as I could not before—not even on the day when I finally decided to reveal to you the true nature of my work—about why I hold these things in such high (if horrible) regard. When your grandfather passed away in a terrible factory accident, I was only twenty-two, a mother of one child in a world that was deeply unkind to single widows. Your mother was four years old, still a baby, really, and while she still felt the loss of him that was her father, she didn't feel it as acutely as I did. I was devastated, and not merely because I could no longer stay in the place we once made our home, though that was part of it. Friends and family helped some, but could only do so much to ease the emotional pain and monetary strife of a young woman who, despite the urgings of the world at large, did not wish to remarry. Ever. I loved him too completely to ever move on, and so I stayed, stagnant in my grief for many years. Work was hard to come by. Banking was a nightmare. Our home—the one your grandfather worked so hard to get for us—was taken not two years later, and I fell into a deep depression.

This was all when I lived in Connecticut, mind you, which isn't exactly the roughest of places, but it was still extremely difficult. I was poor, lived with my parents (who were loath to have not just me, but your mother, living under their roof again), and had exactly no prospects with which to lift myself out. I despaired, more often than not, that I couldn't give my daughter, my Elise, the best of everything.

There was a kind woman who lived in our town, not more than a few streets away from my parents, whose name was Lorraine, and it was she and her husband Ed who took pity on me and your mother. Lorraine was also a mother, but a bit older than me, knew the pain of deep loss such as mine, and offered me a job as the personal secretary for their business. Delighted, grateful, and tearful with the milk of human kindness, I accepted. Ed made sure your mother and I had a small apartment nearby—he paid for it himself until I could, sweet man than he was—and I began working for them. And if they were cagey at first with the details of what went on in that business, so what? They put a roof over my head and food in my child's belly, and that was enough for me.

I was a bright girl—I still like to think of myself as a bright girl—so it didn't take long for me to realize exactly what sort of business they were in. They were, to use today's terminology, paranormal investigators, but back then Lorraine was called a medium (a very powerful one, at that) while Ed was known as a demonologist and the only working unordained exorcist. They traveled from town to town, helping people rid themselves of evil spirits, lost souls, and yes, you got it—cursed objects. There was a whole room in their home devoted to the storage of those objects, many of them kept right out in the open, but the most dangerous kept behind glass.

I became obsessed. With them, their work, those objects, but most of all with Lorraine's apparent ability to speak to the dead. I begged many times for her to contact my husband, but she always patted my hand and told me she just didn't feel his energy, that he had surely passed on without lingering. She told me this was a good thing, and that I should be glad. So many lost souls were trapped on earth and lost to the light, she said, that it was a blessing my husband had found his way to it so quickly. This I could not accept, so I watched and learned from them in secret, began accompanying them on investigations under the pretense of taking notes so that they could have clearer records, to which they agreed. I began being gone more than I was home, and your mother basically lived with my parents while I was away. The money still came in, she had the best of everything, just like I wanted, but it wasn't enough. They were not harsh people towards her, my parents, and all of them wanted for nothing, but as she grew to be a teenager, she became bitter towards me. You can only be absent so long before your children no longer feel attached to you, after all, and I had been gone much more than my fair share.

One day I came home to find a note that said simply, 'Do not call me. Do not come find me. You've been gone so long it would be like a call from a stranger, and I am not an object to collect.' I wept over that note, and my own hubris that caused this parting. I'd spent so long with Ed and Lorraine Warren, chasing their ghosts, that I'd become the one haunting the life of my own daughter.

Still, I persevered. Under the tutelage of the Warrens, I'd become a keen medium in my own right, different from Lorraine, but able to sense spirits and cursed objects without her guidance. I could even push back against them, and had a time or two when we'd been in hairy situations that required more than just Lorraine's power to set *it right. When I told her I was shocked that such a thing could be taught, Lorraine had merely shaken her head and said it couldn't be. That my ability had likely been latent, but had been honed to a knife-edge by my many years of practice. She told me thought that, if it was what I wanted, I could go out on my own and begin helping others as she and Ed did, as they were thinking of going into semi-retirement for a time until their daughter went off to college. And, as it turns out, that was exactly what I wanted to do. But not before I had done what I had been training myself to do.*

I went back to the house that I'd lived in with Elise and my husband (Harry, my love), now a long-abandoned, crumbling brick husk of the home it had once been. I went in, sat down in the living room near where his favorite chair had once sat, surrounded myself with candles, and took out a Ouija board. For four days I sat there, calling his name, begging him to answer, and on the fourth day, something did. But it wasn't Harry, no, not he. What I felt was icy cold and black. It pressed itself heavy against my back, and in my ear it whispered, 'You've given so much for this silly little dream of speaking to your husband again. Was it worth it? Was it worth your daughter? Wouldn't it just be better to…give up? Everything, gone in an instant. No more pain. No more light.'

Its voice was like silk, the words like a cool dip in a pond on a hot summer day. Yes, I thought, yes, this was the answer. I would go with this thing to the clearing at the end of the path, and there I would rest. Forever, and always.

The front door banged open, and there was Lorraine, cross raised out in front of her. She shouted, 'Leave, in the name of the Father, the Son, and the Holy Spirit! Begone from this house, foul demon, leave this good woman in peace!'

And just like that, it was gone, the wind of its leaving blowing out every candle I'd had burning. I started to cry, big, ugly tears, and Lorraine came to me. Behind her, in the doorway, was Elise. When I saw her standing there timidly, and the look of immense worry on her face, I cried even harder. She came to me then, and she and Lorraine helped me up and out of the crumbling edifice that was once my home.

Thus began the mending of the relationship between your mother and I. A few years later, she met Gregory. They fell in love and were married. Two years after that, you were born. They were joyous years filled with a type of love that had been sorely missing from my life as I followed Ed and Lorraine, and an easeful sense of belonging that even now makes my eyes sting with happy tears.

But I never stopped my work. Not once. From time to time, I would tell your mother I was going out of town to visit old school chums, or go on a little holiday alone, but what I was really doing was answering the call of some helpless soul or another that had had disastrous circumstances thrust upon them through no apparent fault of their own. Elise never questioned me about these trips. I think she knew, though. I'll never know for sure, but I do believe she knew exactly why I was leaving, and chose not to stop me.

As if she could have, ha.

Sometimes, not always, I would come away from one of these trips with an object. They were (until you, sweet boy) my most precious cargo, my life's work, and it was my duty to protect them even as I protected others from them. I would always wrap such objects in tinfoil and seal them in plastic bags until I could get them home. Then, I would take the most dangerous of them, and place them under glass, just as Ed and Lorraine had taught me (the most active of them were relegated to the storage unit when I found out what havoc they could wreak if they got feisty—lesson learned!).

Which brings me to my point.

When you read that book about the dog—the one that tumbled out all on its own—you dreamed that very night of another little boy, did you not? A lost thing with a bashed-in head and a missing eye, one that wanted very much to reach out and touch you. When I read to you from Clementine's book, I know for certain you dreamed of her, because the next day you were as relaxed and peaceful as a lamb. I thought that, perhaps, the reading of that book couldn't do you any harm—it's more a blessed object than a cursed one—but I know in my deepest heart that the little boy and his wounded head hurt you. I did one more test, just to be sure, when I brought home the music box. How you recoiled from it! How strong was the stench of what it contained to you! And I'll bet any amount of money that that very night, you dreamt of a nasty man dressed as a clown (look him up, he's quite famous). I knew then I'd made a horrible miscalculation. If these things are all true, and I know that they are, they all add up to one thing: as it turns out, you are sensitive like me, possessed of a skill that can't be learned but can be honed. However, unlike me, you didn't need years of teaching to awaken it. It was already awake, and moreover, could wake up the spirits that lie dreaming in these objects under glass.

I became afraid, after that, that if you knew about your gift, you'd end up like me: obsessed, exhausted, alienated from everyone and everything important in your life and thus, ultimately, alone. I couldn't allow you to suffer as I had, in a sad life constantly full of grief, loss, and heartache. So I lied. I told you a story about a tiger and about your dreams being flights of fancy, and I kept my knowledge of what you were close to my vest. But in telling that lie, I spared you. At least for a time. I began to hope that one day, it would be you who would carry the legacy of my collection when I passed away. The sun is setting on my time to walk this earth, and when I'm gone, someone will have to take up the mantle. So allow me to be honest with you to a fault.

My darling, I tell you now, those were not dreams. They were real. The horrible (and beautiful) things that people do to each other live on, attached to objects, homes, people, unable or unwilling to move on. You will see these things, all your life, from the corners of your eyes, feel their tingle on the back of your neck, see them walk in your dreaming mind's eye. And, if you aren't very, very careful, you will see them walking before you, flesh and bone, but crueler, twisted by the cavernous depths of their own unforgotten despair.

But you will not be alone. I have learned many things in my travels during my lone and often lonely (except when you were in it, my love) life. One such thing was how spirits attached themselves to the objects I keep protected under glass. It's difficult to explain, and I shan't tell you lest you curse yourself to try it, but I believe I have accomplished it. As long as this house stands, as long as this letter is in your possession, my darling child, all you need to do is call out my name, and I'll be there at your side. The house is, of course, yours forever, and I trust that you will keep the objects in it safe until your own time comes to pass through the veil. I have used Chester as my mortal conduit to apply my will to this. I believe, in my heart, that if you spend one night here in the house we used to share, that it will all come back to you. That you will remember. And that that remembrance will feel something like relief. If, however you choose not to do this, there are, of course, contingencies—other people like me who will take this burden from you if you wish it. But now that you know the truth, I pray you see that I am not leading you to destruction, but to a greater calling than you've ever known before. I hope you make the right decision. I think you will.

Seek the light, my love. Seek it, and know that I love you.

With all the love that I possess,

Nana

V.
BUT I SEE
THE BRIGHT EYES

And neither the angels in Heaven above
Nor the demons down under the sea
Can ever dissever my soul from the soul
Of the beautiful Annabel Lee

– Edgar Allan Poe, "Annabel Lee"

ONE

BELOVED WIFE

He traced the words over and over again with his fingertip, remembering. He could almost see her there in front of him— her dark eyes under a fringe of wavy brown hair, her skin softly luminescent in the light of their bedroom, pink lips upturned in a dimpled smile that always meant the kind of trouble that made him tingle. How her hands moved when she spoke, never still, pale birds in flight to the cadence of her lilting, deeply pleasing voice. Her laugh, like dark music echoing over the walls of their kitchen as he came up from behind to caress her. Her body, the miracles of love it contained. A thousand memories made over fifteen mostly happy years, reduced to two words etched in marble under the dates, the dash in between them far too short a time.

Beloved wife

"Eddie."

He looked up, his eyes blurry and far away. For a moment, his mind reeled, thinking she was here again, his Anna, her dark hair swirling in the cold cross breeze churning through the tombs. Anna, back from her year-long sleep, come to claim his lips with hers again, to whisper his name into his ear. Come to make it right again with a word, tell him this whole nightmare was over and they could go home, hand in hand, and live again.

He blinked back the tears, and the image dissolved, leaving behind his companion in this journey to the resting place of his— the words stuck like a bitter bolus of regret—beloved wife. "Yes?"

"Can we go? It's getting cold." Samantha tucked a strand of wheat-coloured hair behind her ear as the wind kicked up again before pulling her coat closer around herself protectively.

Eddie glanced back at the entrance to Anna's sepulchre, adjusting the lilies he'd brought, now leaning against white marble wet with condensation from winter humidity, and hauled himself up off his knees. He brushed leaves and pebbles from his trousers, straightened his coat and smiled wanly at Samantha. "Yes."

They wound their way out of the cemetery and back towards the car, Samantha hooking her arm in his so as not to stumble in her boots on the gravel path. He opened the door for her and handed her into the passenger seat, his ears aware she was talking, his mind far away as he climbed into the driver's seat and turned the engine over.

She's not coming back. Not ever. No matter how many times you see her face or hear her voice in your head, Anna is gone. Better to let it go. Forget. Move on. You've got to go forward from here on, because there is no going back.

"…you listening to me?"

"Hm?" Eddie snapped back from his sorrow, glancing over at Samantha, who had her arms folded across her chest.

She sighed. "I guess not."

He reached over and squeezed her thigh, trying for a smile. It felt alien on his face, a rubber mask over a rotten thing. "I'm sorry. I'm listening now. What's up?"

Samantha sucked her teeth and stared at him implacably, her expression difficult to read in hasty glances.

Please don't be angry with me. Not right now.

"I was saying," she said slowly, her voice terse, "that this year my mum and dad are doing Christmas Eve at their house, and we're invited if you want to go. Adam and Rena will be there, and so will Danielle and Mark. They said they'd love to see you again."

The smile on Eddie's face faded. With the anniversary of Anna's death coming up in January, he had completely forgotten other people did normal things like go to Christmas parties that didn't centre around quietly drinking themselves into a stupor alone. A pleasant notion in theory—getting to see friends, toasting the season, eating too many sweets. But the idea of seeing the happy couples eating, drinking, laughing together, of wearing ugly sweaters, shaking hands with relatives as he forced himself to be cheerful, made his stomach lurch. *Their* lives had not been suddenly overturned. *Their* spouses were still here, above the ground, making merry at their sides. And, of course, they would all ask how he was holding up, their faces scrunched in concern, their voices dripping with honeyed, simpering empathy. He was expected to bolster their confidence that they were doing the right thing, to make them feel better about his pain by thanking them for their concern and saying he was fine. Eddie grimaced, momentarily bitter at the thought.

Step right up, folks, and feast your eyes on the wonder of the freak show: The Holiday Widower. Closest you'll get to a living corpse! Pour your sympathy on him and watch him crumple! Remind him how alone he is by snuggling up to your significant other while offering suggestions on how to deal with his grief, though you yourself have no expertise! Careful, he bites!

He took another glance at Samantha. Her face was taut, hopeful. He swallowed, a sudden lump in his throat. "I'll think about it."

She stiffened under his palm.

Fuck.

"Look, Eddie…"

Here it comes.

415

"I'm not trying to make you do anything you don't want to do here. I know it's been hard. For…for me too. But it's *Christmas* and you need to get out of the house. I figured this might be fun, seeing as Mum is inviting some of our friends as well. Get you out of the house, among the living, enjoying a *party* like a normal couple. I mean, we've been dating a while now, and—"

"Four months."

"Excuse me?"

"We've been dating for four months. It's not that long."

She clicked her tongue, crossed her legs so his hand fell off of her thigh. He took it back to himself, gripped the wheel, feeling all at once very tired as Samantha regarded him coolly. "So what are you trying to say?"

Stop talking. Stop. Agree to go to the party and fucking drop it.

"Our friends," she says, as though we've made them together. Anna's friends. "Among the living," she says, as if I'm not constantly aware of—

He bristled slightly, his tone becoming more sarcastic than he'd intended. "I'm saying it's maybe a little too early to be meeting the family."

"You already know my mum and dad. Since uni."

"Yes. I know, but…a big party with all your relatives just isn't where we're at right now, in my opinion. And I'm not so sure I'm ready to face our…any mutual acquaintances just yet. I'm trying to take things one at a time, step lightly, and it's…just not a good time for me," he finished lamely.

"Not where we're at." It wasn't a question. Her voice was flat and low, tinged with disappointment and laced with anger. "Not a good time. For you. Right."

"Samantha…"

"Don't."

Eddie sighed, focused on the road in front of him. *You idiot. You absolute tit. Why are you doing this?*

The answer to that was clear enough, at least. Anna hadn't been dead a year yet, and he still lived with a fealty to her that hadn't been buried alongside her in her family's stone monument. Her death had been sudden, with no preamble of illness to herald what was to come. They had argued one evening—

About doing the dishes, of all fucking things. I'd let them sit for too long and they'd piled up, and she asked me to clean them and put them away. I couldn't be bothered, I'd dismissed her, said I'd get to it eventually, and it started a fight. And Anna—

—and Anna had left to go for a walk, to let off some steam. She had only been crossing the street at the wrong moment, stood on the wrong corner, and the car that had hopped the kerb and ended her life hadn't even been dented in the photographs he'd forced the police to show him. He had walked through life in a fog for six months, propped up by friends and family, his grief a goblin sitting on his chest day and night. He felt guilty for existing, for eating, for breathing when Anna could not. He lived in a hell of wanting her, reaching out for her in the night after dreaming she was near him, and finding her side of the bed empty and cold. He felt like a worthless sham, a mannequin of grief, an empty shell of a man, hollowed out by sorrow and pain. He had had no time to uncouple himself from the idea of being her husband before she was ripped from him forever.

I didn't even get to apologise to her for the goddamn dishes.

Samantha was one of Anna's oldest friends. She had been a regular at their house, she and Anna thick as thieves, and Sam had been a friend to them both in times of turmoil. When he'd had no idea what to get for Anna's birthday the first year of their relationship, Samantha had pointed him in the direction of a beautifully bound copy of her favourite book. When Eddie was nervously fretting over engagement rings, wanting it to be perfect, he had called on Sam's expertise and been soothed by her enthusiasm for his choice in ring. When Anna had had a miscarriage two years later, Samantha had kept them firmly together, comforting each of them, assuaging arguments, wiping tears.

She had stood as maid of honour in their wedding, and fifteen years later, when Anna's groom had found the planning of her funeral too heavy a burden, Samantha had stepped in and helped make the arrangements. They had cried on each other's shoulders more times in the last year than Eddie cared to think about. She had made sure he ate when he was ill inclined to feed himself, had kept him quiet company when he made no attempts to rejoin his friends, had smoothed things over with his boss when he had simply not shown up at work because he couldn't bear to be around people. Samantha had taken all the love and friendship she'd given Anna for all those years and deftly transferred it over to Eddie in his time of need.

He had been grateful to her then, and he still was.

A red light stopped him, and he took the opportunity to look over at Samantha, really look. She was picking at a hangnail, hair draped around her face, a frown creasing her aquiline features. Lines stood out he was sure hadn't been there before, and he supposed those were his fault, as were the tears streaking her ruddy-pink cheeks. Eddie felt a pang of regret for having made her feel inadequate. She wasn't Anna, but nobody was, and living in the shade of a dead woman had to be a feeling that stung. He wasn't sure how to comfort her about this, any of it, because he too lived in that shade.

It's a harder lesson for her, though, because of you. Because—

Because, in a moment of weakness, the tears they'd shared over Anna had turned to kisses, the sorrow to passion, and Eddie had carried Samantha to his bed. No, he could no longer have Anna, but here was someone who had known her, who had loved her too, and who would understand the proximity of Anna's ghost hovering over his life. It was a guilty act of desperation, one he was simultaneously pleased and aggrieved by. Oh, he hated himself for it, but it had been something of a relief to find he still *could* be intimate with someone, however wretched it made him feel.

The first encounter had been rough, hasty, had felt like infidelity of the worst kind, but he'd also needed it in a way he didn't anticipate. Samantha's body was long, lean, boyish, pert breasts small when cupped in his hands, her hair smelling of fruit and sweat. She was so much the diametric opposite of Anna physically that at first it felt awkward to touch her this way. Anna had been full and plush in places Samantha was not, enjoyed a less timid and more liberated type of sex, and his hands had had to find new ways to touch that would please his new partner. All the while, he had felt the ghost of Anna's presence in the room, not judging exactly, but watching this new development unfold. He felt at the time that it had been a shameful blow to her memory, an affair. Afterwards, he had avoided talking about the event with Samantha for a week, then—

Then you felt guilty at having treated her like a fuck-doll, so you caved and called her. Went out for lunch and ended up doing it all again. You could have said no. You could have stopped yourself. But it felt too good to not be alone anymore.

They had fallen into bed together so easily, but their relationship had been stilted and halting, requiring a patience on Sam's part that was almost saint-like. Samantha *had* understood, had applied the patience and care he required, but now it seemed her patience was wearing thin.

It was a stupid, selfish thing to do. You're no more open to her than Anna's tomb is to you. You're sealed, just like that grave. Eddie put his foot down as he turned onto the street where Anna's flat stood. *And about as dead inside.*

They pulled up outside the row of flats.

Say something.

"Sam, I—"

"Are you coming up?"

The question startled him. Had they not just been arguing? Had he imagined the row about the Christmas party? Her face was set, stony, but her eyes were wild in a way that made him feel strangely giddy. There was a desperate edge to her voice, a bid for normality that begged for them to just move on from this unpleasantness, to get to a place where they both felt all right again. The wind buffeted the car, rocking it on its axles.

"Yes," he replied.

TWO

"**D**O YOU REMEMBER where we met?" Anna asked him, pushing her warm body against him in the half light of their evening bedroom.

"Of course I do," Eddie replied, pulling her closer, running his hands down the naked skin of her back. She was so warm, his Anna, so soft. "You slipped and fell on the ice on campus and bruised that pert little bottom."

The bottom of a dark hole. A well of sadness. Why am I

She chuckled and reached down to cup his balls briefly. Eddie shivered and pressed into the touch, breathing in the smell of her freshly washed skin. "You were my saviour that day, you know. I was sure I'd broken my ankle."

Couldn't save her from

"Nah," he said, breathlessly as her hands roamed back up his abdomen in lazy circles. "As I recall, you told me to fuck off when I offered to help you up."

"I did," she sighed, smiling. "But I didn't mean it. In fact, I was embarrassed to be seen so helpless by such a *dashing* man as yourself."

Dashed against the pavement she was struck by the

"Dashing, nothing. I was a gigantic nerd and you know it. I could barely *speak* to a woman, let alone *flirt*. I'd seen you around campus a few times and thought *never in a million years would that girl be interested in me.*"

"I wasn't." She chuckled, laying a kiss on his collarbone.

421

"I know," he grumbled, pinching her nipple lightly. She smacked his hand away, laughing. "So how did we end up here?"

How did I get here, how did I lose you, how did I

Anna shrugged. "I took pity on you, I guess."

"Oh, well, thanks very much!"

"I didn't know you then. My experience had been that when a man offers help, he expects something in return. Usually sex. But you…" She gazed at him, her eyes shining. "You were so clueless it was endearing, and I suppose I thought if anyone could bring you out of that introverted shell of yours, it would be me."

Her eyes are so bright, what is

"I begrudgingly admit you were right, on all counts." He kissed her forehead, cupping her face in his hands. "Plus, you know, I figured the arty girl with the purple hair and the anarchy sign on her backpack would probably fuck me if no one else would."

She laughed loudly, burying her head in his chest. "Cheeky bastard."

Buried in a

She kissed him then, her tongue pushing delicately into his mouth, tasting of red wine they had drunk before bed and an ever-present hint of salt that always reminded him of the breeze coming in off the sea. She had always tasted this way, since the moment they'd first kissed. That kiss had been mere hours after they'd met, and he had thought then, as now, that he would be happy to kiss her forever. Eddie had always found the taste of Anna's mouth sexy, but now, for some reason, an alarm bell sounded in the back of his mind. He pulled back and away from her, scrutinising her face in the dimness.

I wept for so long it felt like I'd never stop, and Samantha had

"What is it?" she asked, her brows coming together over her sparkling eyes, pools of green like deep lake water. She sat up, propping herself on one elbow to look at him better.

The niggling sensation of wrongness, some terrible foreboding eased, but only slightly. "It's…I don't know. I feel strange."

"Well, you're a strange man, Mr. Lee," she replied, snuggling against him again and wrapping her arms around his middle. "That's why I stayed."

Beloved wife

Eddie ran his hands over his wife's body. She was warm, soft, pliant in his arms, so solid and beautiful and *here*. He touched her hair, her face, her back, her arms, marvelling as always at her responsiveness to his every caress. He closed his eyes, leaning into the feel of touching and being touched. He felt very lucky in this moment, despite the feeling of dread still pooling in his stomach.

"Do you love me, Eddie?"

Beloved wife

His eyes snapped open. "What?"

Anna's eyes glistened, tears pooling in the corners. Her voice was thick with sadness as she repeated, "Do you love me?"

Beloved wife

"Anna, of course I do," he replied, the sense of dread in his stomach building, a second alarm bell joining the first. "You know I do. Why are you—"

"I feel so guilty for leaving you behind," she said miserably, tears rolling down her cheeks. "I made a lot of mistakes. I went out that day because we argued, and I was angry. I said a lot of things I didn't mean. But I love you, Eddie."

Now the sirens were going full blast, a chorus before an air raid, the warning of bombs. "Anna, what—"

"I am so sorry, my darling. I love you so much. And I… I miss you."

Beloved wife

The warmth of Anna's body began to drain away, the skin becoming cooler, then cold against his skin. Eddie shivered. He watched as the colour drained from her face, her hair dulling and becoming brittle. His balls retracted as if the skin recoiled from her touch, the rest of his body stiffening and immediately covered in goosebumps. Only the shine of her eyes remained steady, their brightness illuminating her face as it began to sink in.

"Anna," he croaked, his tongue a dry carpet in his mouth, "what is…what's happening?"

To his horror, when Anna spoke, her breath was of earth and rot, the scent of a tomb closed for almost a year now. She dug the bony hooks of her fingers into his chest and leaned in, ever his lover, this rapidly diminishing shell. "If you love me, come to me."

Beloved wife

He was paralysed by fear, his breath coming in harsh gasps, his fingers gripping the covers beneath him.

"A-Anna, st-st-st—" he choked out between gritted teeth. A drop of sweat ran from his forehead into his eye, stinging, blurring the horror in front of him as Anna dwindled. He could see her skull through her skin now, but her eyes were still wet and full of agony, deep, dark pools of the lonely void on the other side.

Her hand came up from beneath the covers, reaching to caress his face. He pulled back in horrified disgust, but her body pinned him down, heavy as a stone despite its rapidly withering appearance, made him unable to escape. He tried to push the hand away and cried out in revulsion as the skin of her wrist flaked under his touch. Her fingertips felt like paper-wrapped icicles as she ran them over his cheek, her face getting closer to his. His eyes bugged out of his skull, his immobile body full of the chill radiating from her corpse as she leaned in, smelling of the grave.

No, no, no, do not do this, no, I can't, Anna, no, please not again

"Come to me, Eddie," she rasped. "If you love me, come to me."

Anna, rotting Anna, with her sunken face and too-bright eyes, his beloved wife, pressed her withered lips to his for a deep soul kiss.

***

Eddie woke with a shout, bathed in the sweat of terror. He scrabbled away from the still body next to him, almost falling out of the bed in his haste to get away, *get away*, from the thing that was Anna and not-Anna, the horror trying to kiss his life to dust. Then the figure beside him sighed and turned over onto its back and moonlight caught blonde hair, turning it silver.

Not Anna. Samantha. He closed his eyes and took a few deep, shuddering breaths, bringing himself back to reality. He was at Samantha's flat uptown, in her queen-sized bed with the blue polka-dot sheets. He'd come up when asked, and they had made love until they were both too exhausted to be angry anymore, then fallen asleep with the sheets still damp. And then—

Then Anna came. He ran shaky hands over his face, staring at Samantha's sleeping form. *Was she in the bed with us?*

The thought sent a shiver down his spine. *No. She wasn't here. Couldn't be. It was just a dream.*

Eddie got up out of bed as carefully as he could so as not to wake Samantha, and padded naked to the bathroom for a piss.

Anna is dead. And you're fucking her best friend.

The light over the sink buzzed into too-bright life, revealing the face of a haggard widower in the mirror. He avoided that man's eyes as he stood at the toilet, choosing to focus instead on the ache in his bladder and the shake in his hands.

Do you love me, Eddie?

He squeezed his eyes shut against sudden tears, shook his dick, and went to wash his hands. Only then did he look himself in the eyes. There were snaps of red in the whites, the blue standing out in all the red. Dark circles underneath. Too long without a shave, far too long without a haircut. The overgrown bush of his curly, dark hair—hair Anna had lovingly mocked but Samantha never commented on—much more streaked with grey than he remembered, sticking up in swirls and pillow-mats. His face sallow and thinner than it had been a year ago, marked with signs of too many drunken nights trying to numb himself from ever-cresting waves of shame and loss. The general effect was of a haunted man, a model of grief, a living ghost.

He ran a hand over his mouth, turned his eyes away from the image as he washed his hands. He cupped some of the cool water in his hands—hands Anna had loved for their strength but which now shook like those of a much older man—over his face and chest, trying to wash away the grotesque miasma of the dream.

Do you love me, Eddie?

"Yes," he whispered back. "But I'm not sure you'd love me. Not anymore."

...eddie...

The breath of a sound, barely audible over the running sink. He whirled around, heart pounding all over again, eyes searching the blackness of the bedroom beyond for the source. Hearing nothing, he turned off the taps, listened again. All was still save for the settling creaks of a sleeping house and Samantha softly snoring in her bed.

Hearing things, he thought wryly as he flipped off the bathroom light and walked morosely back into the bedroom. *Always a good sign.*

The room was still only half lit by moonlight, but Eddie could see Samantha outlined in the bed, on her back, the covers pooling around her legs. Her chest rose up and down in the steady motion of sleep, one breast becoming exposed as her arm came up to tuck under her pillow. She really was lovely, in her way, and he felt sorry for her having to deal with all of this. With him. The thought that she might be doing it because she loved him floated briefly into his mind, but he hastily pushed it away.

Do you love me, Eddie?

He sighed and crossed to the window, intent on pulling the curtains to block the light of the moon from her bed. He gazed outside at the sleeping world, at the other houses on the street where, presumably, other people slept soundly, unvisited by nightmares of desiccated love.

Across the street, within the bright circle of the streetlamp's glow, stood the still figure of a woman. The light didn't seem to touch her but instead flowed through her. He could see the grass of the lawn behind her, the edge of the pavement bisecting her calves. A breeze blew leaves down the street in a swirl, but her long, dark hair didn't move with it. Eddie stopped, his hands on the curtains, his mouth dropping open. The woman wore a blue dress the colour of the summer sky, a dress Eddie knew well. A dress he'd lovingly chosen from a closet full of clothes, because it had been the one Anna had worn the last time they went on a date together for their anniversary.

...eddie...

Not so much a sound as a vibration inside his head. He stood dumbstruck, vaguely aware that he was naked, as the figure turned and began to walk up the street, away from him.

"Wait!" he croaked, but the figure kept moving towards the end of the block. He turned immediately, running from the window, scooping his pyjama pants into his arms as he skidded from the bedroom into the hall. He tugged them on on the way down the stairs, tripping and nearly braining himself on the banister, before he reached the door and was outside.

Panicked, he squinted down the street, seeking the woman in the dark.

Where? Where is—

He spotted her, turning the corner on the left, her dress unmoved by the icy wind knifing through the night. He took after her at a run, his bare feet slapping on the pavement, oblivious to the freezing wind and the gravel biting into the soles of his feet. She disappeared around the side of the first house.

"Anna, wait!" he called, redoubling his efforts and skidding around the corner.

She was gone. Eddie stuttered to a stop, breath pluming out in front of him like clouds from a steam engine, willing himself to find her again, *needing* her to still be there, but to no avail. He let out an anguished sound, tears pooling at the corners of his eyes.

"*Anna!*" he shouted into the dark. "*Anna! Come back!*"

"Eddie?"

He spun around, heart in his throat, expecting her to have heard him and returned. Instead, he saw Samantha standing there, her dressing gown pulled tight around her and her hair getting stuck in her mouth from the wind. She tugged a strand from between her lips as she stared at him, her eyes bleary and confused.

"Eddie, what are you doing out here?" she asked carefully. "It's freezing. Come back home to bed."

Eddie came over to her, his legs leaden and frozen, put his hands on her shoulders. He wanted to shout at her, to scream in her face to leave, get away from him, that her home wasn't his home. That *his* home had walked away and disappeared around the corner moments ago. Samantha recoiled from his touch.

Of course she would, his rational side spoke up. *You look like a madman, out in the cold, screaming at ghosts in the dark.*

"Please come back in," she whispered, and now her voice had a frightened edge to it.

You're scaring her. Stop it. Stop it right now.

"Of course." He tried to smile reassuringly and felt it failing to work on his frozen face.

He was grateful that she made no comment, merely turned and led him back to the house. Every few paces, Eddie glanced over his shoulder towards the empty corner.

THREE

EDDIE TRIED, OVER the next couple of days, to put the incident out of his mind and keep himself busy, but with his office closed for the festive season and seven days of annual leave staring him down, this was mostly a pipe dream. He sat alone in his flat for two days, trying to address Christmas cards, but his attention kept wandering back to the night he'd seen...

Whatever it was I saw. He frowned at the creamy envelope in front of him, the moniker *Dr. and Mr. Vaughn* the furthest he'd managed on the address. Samantha had brought these over yesterday, admonishing him for forgetting this most dutiful of holiday traditions.

He initially objected, wanting only to be left alone in his misery, but Sam gave him a stony look and said flatly, "Anna always sent these out, every year since she was fifteen."

That closed the subject. Eddie took the box of cards and list of addresses from her hands, thanking her. He invited her in, but she declined, saying she was too busy with Christmas preparations to stay lounging in his flat all day.

"My parents asked again if you're coming to the party, though," she ventured delicately, her eyebrows knitted, her voice quiet and unsure. "I still don't know what to tell them."

He sighed. Looked around at the state of his living space and saw only empty whisky bottles and rubbish. His pyjamas—two days old on his unshowered and fairly fragrant body—were grubby and stained. How had he ended up this way?

Exhaustion. Frustration. Guilt. Grief. Take your pick.

"I'm still debating," he replied. "But I think, more than likely, yes."

She smiled, softly. "Really?"

"Really."

You lying sack of shit.

Her brows knitted again. "I'm…I'm really sorry about the other day. I know how hard losing Anna hit you, and I shouldn't push you to—"

Dear god, stop talking about this. Please.

"It's all right." He kissed her forehead, his heart heavy.

When she pulled away, her eyes were wet with unspilled tears. "Will I see you later?"

"Yes."

And with that, she left.

***

Eddie sat where he had been since she'd left, staring at the pile of mutely mocking envelopes and cards, not seeing them.

What am I to write in these? Whose names should I sign? 'Happy Christmas, from Eddie Lee, his recently deceased wife Anna and her best friend Samantha that he's guilt-fucking'? A picture of my empty flat?

He shoved the pile away and got up, walked determinedly to the bathroom. *A shower. I'll be clearer after a shower.*

Eddie stripped and started the water, putting it as hot as he could stand it before stepping in. The immediate relief of feeling water on his skin was amazing, and he scrubbed himself vigorously head to toe, the accumulated hangover of the past two days melting in the heat. *I think I forgot what being clean felt like.*

His thoughts drifted back to Samantha. Her teary eyes, her wounded, giving heart. *I may never be clean again. Not really. And what of the other night? When you saw Anna in the street and you turned on Sam? How did you look then, barely dressed and angry at her for intruding? You probably scared the life out of her.*

He put his head under the spray, rinsing the foam out of his hair. *When you* thought *you saw Anna in the street.* He leaned back and shook his hair vigorously to get it out of his face, blowing water away from his mouth and wiping his eyes. *It couldn't have been real.*

Could it?

He turned off the water, drew back the curtain and reached for his towel, drying himself whilst musing on the subject. Was it so far-fetched, in this world that humans knew so little of, that such things existed? It wasn't as if he were the first to ever contemplate such a thing, or even to see it. There was plenty of evidence out there of people seeing spirits, and surely not all of them were the work of charlatans and the more mentally irregular. But the thought that something like that could happen to *him*, or to *his* Anna seemed...

Distasteful.

He recalled the dream he'd had right before she had appeared, his Anna a rotten thing, a thing from the earth, with her papery skin flaking away from his skull and her too-bright, too-aware eyes. How her mouth hadn't tasted the way he remembered when she gave him her last kiss, but had tasted of death, of the grave in which she'd lain for nearly a year.

Despite the heat collected in his tiny bathroom, he shuddered, a chill running up his spine like Anna's icy fingers had caressed his cheek.

He ran a hand over that same cheek now, feeling more than the rasp of stubble, finding in its place the unkempt, wiry beard of a madman. Eddie went to the sink, ducking under to retrieve his shaving kit from the cabinet below. *You've come this far. Might as well make yourself look like a human being instead of a yeti.*

431

He allowed himself a smile as he dug around, a mote of pride rising from beneath the funk. Here he was, Eddie Lee, carrying on despite his obvious depression, getting himself cleaned up and shaved for the first time in days. It had to be worth something, this small step. All the books he'd read on grief and depression had said so: *one step at a time*. He stood up, set his shaving tools on the sink and lifted a hand to wipe away the fog from the mirror.

That was when he saw the shape.

Even blurred by the fog on the mirror, it was definitely a human shape, the face a pink blob beneath dark hair, directly behind his left shoulder. Eddie froze, his hand midway between himself and the mirror. His breath caught in his chest, his heart pounded, all buoyancy drained in favour of sheer, icy terror.

"A—" His voice stuck in his throat, his mouth suddenly too dry, and even when he cleared it, the word came out in a croak. "Anna?"

Behind him, the shape moved, ever so slightly tilting its head to the side. Then he saw the hand reach up from behind him, the fingers vague and sticklike, seemingly intent on touching his shoulder. He recalled the dream, the feel of those fingers, and a revulsion he never thought possible leapt up in his stomach. He cried out, swiping the fog off the mirror in one go, having to see, having to know if it was her, really her, or some shade here to torment him again.

Lines of water dripped from the cleared part of the glass, and behind him…

Nothing.

Eddie let out a breath he wasn't aware he'd been holding, then gasped in another, and another, desperate to calm the horrible beating of his heart. He leaned against the sink, his hands shaking and his fingers gripping the porcelain so hard his knuckles were white and bloodless.

432

Am I losing my mind?

The thought had occurred to him many times since Anna's passing, but this? This was on a whole other scale.

You're seeing ghosts.

That's inconceivable. Impossible. A daydream.

A nightmare.

He took a few more deep, calming breaths, his heart finally slowing to a normal rhythm. He glanced once more at the bathroom mirror, half expecting to see her there again, no longer blurred, and could not decide whether he was feeling terror, hope, or a sour mixture of the two that she might indeed appear.

I have to get out of here. Sooner the better.

There was a mirror in the hallway, one that faced the big, open lounge where no nasty surprises could lurk.

He gathered his shaving kit and exited the bathroom on legs that shook like a newborn colt's.

FOUR

H ARRODS WAS CROWDED, last-minute shoppers doing their best to scrabble for deals and get in presents that had been dropped on them by expectant children still believing Santa Claus would deliver on all their hopes and dreams. Eddie found the ambient roar strangely comforting, the simplicity of being near a crowd without having to interact with anyone astoundingly pleasurable.

This was a good idea. Samantha said I should get out among the living, and maybe she was right about that. It's not like I could stay home, not after—

He shrugged off the memory of the shape in the mirror with a shiver. *Stop. Right now. Focus.*

He'd left his flat with a single-minded purpose: get out, away from whatever shade was flitting around in that dank and dirty space, as fast as he could. Once ensconced in the Tube, though, he began thinking about Sam, about how kind she had been to bring over the cards and addresses. Always thinking of him. He'd decided then that he was going to get her a Christmas gift, ill-defined relationship or no. She deserved to know that even if he wasn't in the best emotional shape for a deep, heartfelt romance, he appreciated all she had done for him over the last year.

She deserves much more than that, mate, and you know it. She deserves somebody whole, who's capable of giving a damn. Someone who isn't—

'Haunted' was the word that came to mind, and he pushed that away too.

Eddie made his way through the sea of human bodies, his mind turning to the dilemma of what to get her. Jewellery was out of the question—it sent the wrong message. He didn't want to get her hopes up any more than they already were. Books? No. That had been Anna's gift of choice to receive. That would send an entirely different message, which was *also* wrong in its own way. He dug through his internal archives, and to his enormous chagrin, found he couldn't think of a single interest Samantha had. He had taken exactly no time to get to know her in the last four months, it seemed, and his heart sank even further. He couldn't even chalk this one up to sorrow. The truth was, as much as he hated to admit it, knowing more about her personal life and engaging in her interests separated her from being 'Anna's best friend' and put her squarely into the box of 'his romantic partner', the thought of which made him almost ill. It wasn't her; it was one hundred percent him on the pie chart, but it was still the bald truth of it all. He would never, could never commit himself fully to Samantha McLane, and that was that.

You really are a bastard, Eddie Lee.

He ducked out of Harrods and walked on, eyes taking in other stores on the streets. Hallmark. Waterstones. Boutiques with perfumes, shitty bohemian clothes and useless baubles in the windows. He let out an exasperated sigh.

Think harder, you idiot. You know things about Sam. You've known her too fucking long to have retained exactly nothing.

What did she do for a living? He chewed his lip thoughtfully, trying to remember. Something to do with architecture. What?

Drafting. Sam does drafting for a place called Peterson and Vansant. She always calls it P-n-V, which used to make her and Anna laugh like kids.

It was a stupid thing to be proud of, remembering the employment sector of someone you'd known for fifteen years, but he was a little less defeated nonetheless. He at least had a place to start. He wandered a bit, peeking into a few windows. After an hour of searching, going into what felt like a hundred shops, picking things up and putting them down, he decided the trip was going to be less than fruitful and headed home, feeling deflated.

He walked towards the nearest Underground station, miserable at his inability to do even this, the most basic of tasks.

You stupid arsehole. You did this to yourself.

He pulled his collar up against the freezing wind and walked on, turning left at the next crossroads, not bothering to look for cars. It mattered very little if he lived or died, he reasoned. The world would be rid of one more wretch, and even if there wasn't the chance Anna was waiting for him on the other side, at least there would be rest. Darkness. Oblivion.

He glanced up and noticed ahead of him a sign that read *Lance's Woodwork and Hobbies*. He stopped, frowning. Maybe here?

Fuck it. A last hurrah before I go home empty-handed.

He pushed open the door of the shop, a small bell dinging over his head. As soon as the door closed behind him, all outside sound muffled to a degree Eddie wouldn't think possible for crowded daytime London, which was somewhat unsettling. The shop was small, cluttered and smelled of good pine and wood glue. It was extremely warm inside, and Eddie unwound his scarf and unbuttoned his coat, examining the place as he did. Through a slim aisle of boxes and bins of wood pieces, screws and nuts of every shape and size imaginable, he saw a glass counter, at which sat an elderly man, presumably the infamous Lance, hunched over a large book. His head was nearly completely bald, the few stray silver hairs dancing in the shop lighting, his hands gnarled with arthritis and covered in fingerless gloves. The man looked up and promptly shut the book, giving Eddie a smile that was more gums than teeth.

"What can I do for you, young man?" he asked brightly, his voice much louder and deeper than Eddie would have guessed by his appearance.

Eddie walked towards him, having to turn sideways in places to get through despite his slim figure. When he reached the counter, the man looked him over with careful eyes. Eddie noted that one of them was a pearly grey, clouded with blindness. As the man appraised him, Eddie could almost feel that eye looking through him, seeing deeper than he'd like.

"I'm, erm…" He faltered awkwardly, the constant pressure of the man's gaze making him giddy with nerves. "I'm looking for a gift for someone."

"Oh?" Lance asked, his eyes once more roving over Eddie, taking him in. "For whom, may I enquire?"

"A…friend," Eddie replied.

"A lady friend? Or a fella?" The man leaned in, whispering conspiratorially, "No judgement from me, either way. I've been around long enough to have tasted my share of fruits, if you follow."

The man winked with his good eye. For a moment, just the clouded eye was open. Seeing. Knowing. Judging.

Let it go. It's just an eye.

"I follow," Eddie said, smiling nervously despite himself. "But no, it's for my…it's for a woman."

Lance nodded. "A lady friend."

"Yes."

"But not a girlfriend." It wasn't a question. Another flick of the eyes, another appraisal of the wan ghost that had wandered in from the cold.

Eddie ground his teeth. "Not exactly."

Lance nodded again. "Not exactly. And yet, a gift. What type of gift are you looking for?"

"Well, she's an architect. A draughtsperson. She's been in architecture as long as I've known her, went to university for it, actually, and she loves the really old buildings around London, so I was hoping you maybe had something that she would enjoy building?" It all came out in a rush, a hasty ploy to get this conversation over with.

The shopkeeper was having none of that, though, because he sat there, implacable, as if waiting for Eddie to finish. Eddie sighed, waved his hand around vaguely. "I mean, it doesn't have to be huge or complicated or anything, just...fun, you know, to do. Something to pass the time."

"Nothing complicated." Still the feeling of being seen for what he was, the response almost too accurate for the man to not be reading his secret soul with his damned, horrible eye. "Something fun to pass the time."

Eddie resisted the urge to scream, *Do you have anything or not? Fucking tell me so I can get out of this hellhole and away from your fucking, shitting, ugly judgemental eye, you prick!*

But no, he stood there, his tongue stuck dryly to the roof of his mouth, while the man chewed thoughtfully on his gums. After what seemed like an eternity, the shopkeeper slapped the counter with both palms, the force shaking the glass and startling Eddie so badly he nearly screamed.

"I have just the thing!" The old man pointed a misshapen finger at Eddie. "You wait right here, young man, I have just the thing. Won't take a moment."

Eddie watched old man grunt and haul himself off the stool he sat on, and was surprised when Lance unfolded to a towering height before ducking through a doorway in the wall behind him. Eddie himself topped out at six-three and was often the tallest person in the room, but this coot overshadowed him by at least three inches, though age had left him stooped and thin as a whip. Sudden understanding dawned about why the centre aisle was so slender. There was a great deal of rustling from that back room, curses muttered under the old man's breath as he dug through what must be, Eddie supposed, judging by the rest of the shop, and impressive pile of woodworking and sculpting supplies.

Eddie fanned his coat, sweat trickling down his back. *Hurry up, man. I just want to go home.*

The shadow in his bathroom mirror with its reaching hand crept back into his mind.

OK, maybe take your time.

"Ah-ha!" The boom of the shopkeeper's triumphant voice from the back room startled Eddie once more.

If he keeps that up I'm going to kill him with a shovel.

The man returned, stooping under the doorway with a box clenched in one hand. He plopped it on the counter in front of Eddie and smiled. "Well? What do you think?"

Eddie peered at the box. He had thought that in a place like this, anything emerging from the back room would be old and dusty, frayed at the edges like the owner, but the box was shiny and new. A picture on the front showed Westminster Abbey in shining black wood, with the slogan *Build It Yourself!* emblazoned in lurid red letters on the navy blue background. The man rapped the top of the box with one fingertip. "This is damn near-as-damn-it a collector's item by now. Hasn't been in production since, oh, late-sixties, early seventies. It's a woodworking puzzle, you know? Slots that slide together until she's built good and tall."

Eddie touched the top of the box himself, sliding his fingertips over the sleek packaging, gazing at the picture and seeing how it fitted together. It *was* just the thing, he had to admit. He looked up at the man and smiled, genuinely this time. Weird or not, this old man had really pulled him out of a tough spot. "It's perfect."

"Nothing too complicated," the man replied. "Just something fun to pass the time."

Lance grinned his gummy smile and winked again, his cloudy eye ever watchful, making Eddie's stomach do a flip.

Five minutes later, Eddie was back on the street, his purchase slung around his wrist in a plastic bag, the noise and cold of London filling his senses once more. He hurried out of the shop without a backward glance, thankful to be out, away.

FIVE

"I'M REALLY GLAD you decided to come," Samantha whispered, squeezing Eddie's shoulder.

"Me too," he lied, smiling down at her.

The party was in full swing, the house warm and stuffed with people. Children ran here and there, underfoot, in their best Christmas clothes, occasionally screeching at an ear-splitting volume. Sam's parents had been delighted to see him again, and so had a lot of his friends, but Eddie couldn't help but notice a fair few people he'd known most of his life hung back after initial pleasantries had been exchanged. He sipped his whisky, surveying the scene. Don and Mark were chatting together in the kitchen, Mark already red-faced from too much rum punch. Their wives, Karen and Elizabeth, stood conspiratorially off to the side, holding their own conversations, every so often joking about their husbands. Elizabeth turned and briefly caught his eye, the smile fading from her face as she quickly turned away.

This is life now, I guess. People afraid to look at you or talk to you at parties.

Elizabeth whispered something to Karen from behind her cup, and Elizabeth glanced his way. As Samantha kissed him on the cheek and left to mingle, both women turned with raised eyebrows, their gazes following her as she walked. The cups once again came up, their eyes on her back as they conversed. His blood boiled at their obvious judgement, and he felt himself start forward, walking towards them. To confront them, demand answers from them. What did they know? Who were they to judge? Why, if one of their husbands had been laid to pieces on the ground by a car, they'd—

He checked himself, stopping just in time to veer left and into the kitchen past their watchful eyes. *Maybe people are right to be afraid.*

The kitchen was even more hot and crowded than the living room had been, the press of bodies close and uncomfortable. Eddie tugged at the collar of his jumper, willing himself to get through the sea of his peers to the island of the food table set up against the far wall. He finally pushed through the crowd with a fair few 'pardons' and 'excuse me's, and nearly gasped for breath as he emerged. He looked back, saw Karen and Elizabeth watching him from the doorway, but now Mark and Don were with them too, all their eyes silently reproachful.

Eddie turned his back on them, sighing. *Why did I think coming here would be a good idea?*

That had a simple answer: he couldn't think of a reasonable excuse to not come. Samantha had asked him more than once, and he felt a pang of guilt every time he thought about saying no, despite knowing his emergence into this particular group would likely cause him harm.

He perused the offerings on the table, not hungry in the slightest. *These people are no longer my friends.*

He knew that too, as well as he knew that Anna's death was now a permanent milestone in his life. There was *before* and *after*, the two never reconciling into a cohesive whole, ever again. The way that people had reacted upon seeing him come in with Sam had been less than encouraging. They had greeted him, sure, but they had been cold, distant greetings.

That's because they know you're a fuck-up too. They know you haven't let Anna go, but you're fucking Sam all the same. Of course they know. How could they not? Sam has probably told them every detail, has probably cried to at least one of them about what you're doing.

Eddie could feel their accusing eyes as he selected a tiny puff pastry, popping it into his mouth and chewing morosely.

Not only that, they blame you. And they're right to. It was your fault Anna left the house that day—your fault she was standing on that corner. It was you who initiated the contact with Sam, you who used her to try to forget your guilt, your complicity, who buried your grief in her body. And it'll be your fault when that ends in her tears, too. Because it will. Because you're incapable of—

"Edward Lee, do my eyes deceive?" A piping voice rang out close by.

Eddie turned and saw Claire McLane, Samantha's sister, behind him. She was older by only a couple of years, but she and Samantha could have passed for twins. Same hair, same build, the only evidence of difference being her voice, which was deeper and huskier than Sam's. Other than that one difference, though, he had to admit even he had occasionally mistaken the one for the other.

Yes, but you're not fucking her, his mind niggled.

He chewed furiously, trying to swallow the pastry, before answering with a smile, "They do not. How are you, Claire?"

"I'm marvellous, darling," she said, leaning in for a hug. He allowed her to embrace him, briefly circling her waist with the hand not holding his drink. She held him back at arm's length then, concern in her eyes. "But how are you?"

Here we go.

"Oh, you know, holding up," he said lamely, nodding his head.

"Just holding up?" She squeezed his shoulders lightly, her nails digging in.

He shrugged. "It's harder at this time of year."

"Mm," she said, finally pulling away. "Your first Christmas without Anna. It must be terrible living in that old house alone."

"I, erm…I sold it. Months ago."

Claire's eyebrows shot up. "Really? But Anna loved that house so much. It seems such a waste to just—"

"It was too much space for me," Eddie cut her off. "By myself, it was too much to handle. And too…too hard to be there without her."

"Ah," Claire said, nodding sagely. "Too much of her spirit still in the place. Where are you now?"

"Peach Street. Up near Enfield."

Though it doesn't matter where I go, does it? I ran from that house as fast as I could, to get away from her ghost. But it's still following me. Wherever I am, it's always there.

"Enfield," Claire mused. "That's a bit far out, isn't it? From anything fun for you and Sam to do."

And there it is.

"Well, yes, sort of," he said, shrugging again. "But we don't really go out much. It's, ah…it's all a bit touch and go right now."

"That's not what she says. She says the two of you are dating."

Stop asking me questions, you numb cunt! he wanted to scream. *This is none of your business, so keep your horse face out of it!*

Instead he said, "Will you excuse me? I have to go get some air."

A cheap escape route, he knew, but true. The kitchen suddenly felt stifling, the air much too close and thick with the smell of sticky-sweet food and human sweat laced with alcohol. He promptly made for the back door, sparing not a glance for Claire, and pushed through into the freezing night. The air hit him hard in the chest, knifing through his woollen jumper like the blade of a midnight mugger, leaving him momentarily breathless from the shock. He shivered for a few moments, eyes closed, breathing in the comparatively fresher air and allowing himself a moment to calm down.

This was a stupid idea. You knew it was. You should never, ever have come here.

...eddie...

His eyes snapped open, his body going immediately rigid at the sound of her voice. All other sound, all feeling ceased to exist beyond the sudden sight of Anna, his Anna, in this overgrown garden, bare feet standing heedlessly on frozen grass. There she stood beneath a low-hanging tree, the half-light filtering through onto her funeral dress, her eyes reflecting back the brightness of the moon like a cat's eyes caught in the headlamps of a car. He swallowed hard, gazing at her, so close. She took a step forward into the light, and his heart leapt when he saw her hair sway in the breeze and her dress flow around the shape of her legs. She seemed so much more real than she had the first night he'd seen her in the street, so much more—

Solid. His hands twitched with a desire to find out. *My god, this time she's actually here.*

Anna put out her arms. *come to me, eddie.*

Her mouth did not move when she spoke, but instead each word hit him like an ice pick jabbed directly into his brain. His mind reeled at the thought of going nearer to her, the fear that if he did put his arms around her, she'd fade away like smoke, and oh, then he'd be utterly destroyed. This game of knife-edge madness would finally tip him over the side of the ravine, and tomorrow Sam's parents would find him in the garden babbling like an idiot. His mind knew this could be nothing but heart-breaking fantasy, but his heart had other ideas. The strings that tied his soul to Anna's pulled him forward, forward, closer to her waiting embrace. Her eyes glowed that same feral glow even as he got closer, and a soft smile tugged at the corners of her mouth.

And then he was directly in front of her, scant inches from her waiting arms. He lifted his arms to hold her. Hesitated.

Her brow furrowed. *hold me. it's so cold.*

"Anna," he sighed, his hands coming up once more, shaking, not daring. "I…I'm afraid."

oh, eddie. there is nothing to fear. She made the decision for him and stepped into his arms, wrapping her own around his waist in a warm embrace.

Eddie let out a sound of anguished joy, embraced her back. Anna was here, really here, her body warm and soft and solid, in his arms again. He pulled back slightly to look at her face and laughed, actually laughed for the first time in months, cupping her face in his hands and kissing her full on the mouth. She responded, her hands roaming over his back just as they used to whenever they would embrace, the tip of her tongue begging entrance to his mouth. He blissfully obliged and was astounded, delighted, to taste her mouth once again. Tears slipped from the corners of his eyes, left hot trails on his cold face.

All too soon, she pulled back from the kiss to gaze at him with those reflective, unsettling eyes. *do you love me, eddie?*

"My God, Anna, of course! Of course I do," he breathed, leaning in to kiss her once more.

She stopped his mouth with her hand, her brows drawn together, her expression sad. *do you really, truly love me? even now? even still?*

He took her wrist in his hand, pulling her fingertips from his mouth to kiss them. They were warm, her hands smelling faintly of the lotion they'd smoothed on her at his insistence before she'd been buried. "Always. Forever and always."

then come to me, eddie.

"What do you mean?" He chuckled, smiling. "I'm right—"

446

you know where to find me. She unwound herself from his embrace.

He made a sound of dissent, but her hands insisted, and so he finally relented. There would be time now for more embraces, more kisses, because she was here, his Anna. Back from the other side, her love so strong and warm and forever.

Anna pointed to her right, at the fencing, her eyes locked on his, glowing in the moonlight. *come to me, eddie.*

A sudden panic rose in his chest. "What do you mean? I'm right—"

The back door to the house banged open, a loud blast of music and reverie breaking the silence. He turned to see Samantha making her way down the steps and felt a sudden flash of anger at her intrusion. Yet again, she'd come to interrupt him with his wife, and yet again—

The feeling of panic suddenly deepened and he whirled back around.

Where Anna had stood, nothing, save two rapidly re-freezing footprints in the grass. His head swam, his stomach churned. Why had she left again? Why now, when he had been so close to happiness?

"All right then?" Sam said, coming up to his side.

"Ah…" He faltered, looking over to her and not really seeing her. Spots began to cloud his vision.

"Eddie?" she said, her voice now edged with concern. "What's wrong? Has something happened? You look like you've seen a ghost."

"I…I was…I was just…" he stammered, the clouding becoming thicker, blurring and obscuring everything. A ringing sounded in his ears, and the Earth tilted on its axis.

"Eddie!" he heard Sam exclaim as his body hit the icy grass and the world faded to black.

SIX

E DDIE LAY AWAKE in Sam's bed, staring at the ceiling in the dark. She had insisted he come and stay at her house after he'd fainted, and done him the mercy of not trying to touch him once they were in bed. He fidgeted nervously under the covers, uncomfortable. He had told her he was fine, wanting desperately to be alone to figure out what to do, but had to admit that another side of him wanted the exact opposite. The thought of being alone in his flat, that Anna could show up at any time to reel him in again with her warmth and her shining, animal eyes made him at once giddy and repulsed.

At least this time you know she was there. Really there.

Yes, there was that. He shifted again, turning his eyes to the window, the weak moonlight filtering through onto his face. The first time Anna had appeared had been outside this very window, on the street, a shade of herself, and she had walked away from him, avowing his embrace, walking towards—

you know where to find me, eddie.

He sat up in bed, suddenly, remembering. She had walked away, turned the corner, and disappeared. And just tonight, in Sam's parents' garden, Anna had pointed in a direction. In his dreams and now in reality she begged him to come to her. But where?

He threw his legs out of bed and padded out of the room, careful not to wake Sam as he scooped his T-shirt up off the floor and pulled it on. Down the stairs into the kitchen, to dig through a drawer full of junk for a pad of yellow paper and a pencil. These things he brought back upstairs, silently, glancing at Sam's sleeping form as he crossed to the window and stood looking down at the place where Anna had first appeared.

On the pad of paper, he drew a line, in an L-shape, to mark the places she had walked. Across from that, a rectangle to represent Sam's house. More lines to represent the streets between Sam's house and her parents', another rectangle for their house, a bigger square around it for the property. His heart sped up with the sudden knowledge of what he was about to see. He took a deep breath, puffing air out of his cheeks as he drew a hasty circle that was Anna, in the corner of the garden, and a short line for the angle at which she had pointed. This small line he drew across his makeshift map, converging it with the L-shape of Anna's first path. He knew with terrible certainty what lay between the two points, the only place they could possibly intersect.

"The cemetery," he whispered aloud.

come to me, eddie.

He swallowed hard, his heart beating in his throat, his mouth dry as plaster. He looked up and out of the window, half-expecting to see her there again beneath the streetlamp, waiting. But she was not. This was his decision to make, he knew. She could not force his hand. Only ask, beg, and possibly, possibly...

Follow me for the rest of my life. A difficult thought, that. *If I don't go to her, will she haunt me forever? Will I never find peace?*

He took another glance over at Sam, Anna's best friend, a woman he would never love and whom he would inevitably destroy with his inability to move forward and let Anna go. He thought of his friends, and how they were around him now, their watchful, judging eyes, their perception of him forever altered. And his own grief, that nightmare, a black cat that would not stop wailing no matter how many walls he tried to build around it. And Anna, with her feral eyes, and her love for him that brought her back from the grave and into his arms for the briefest of moments.

Do I even want to?

Eddie stared out of the window for a long time, his hands clasped in his lap and his face very still, lost, wakeful, and deeply afraid.

SEVEN

" Y OU HELP WITH that?"

... "Hm?" Eddie sat at Sam's breakfast table, deep in thought, pushing eggs around his plate. The thought of eating made him want to vomit, but she'd offered him breakfast and he couldn't say no without hurting her feelings. Sam had brought him here out of concern, and the last thing he wanted to do was concern her further by rushing away in the morning.

Overnight, sitting at the window, he'd made a decision. He was going to go to the cemetery today, alone, and have a look at Anna's grave. If it was undisturbed, the slab to the tomb firmly closed, he would chalk all of this misery up to his fragile state and consult a physician about therapy. If, by some miraculous turn, he found her sepulchre empty, well...

We'll cross that bridge when we come to it. If we come to it.

"I asked if you'd help me with the tap in the cellar this morning before you leave," Sam replied. "It's been leaking like a sieve, and no matter how many YouTube tutorials I watch on DIY plumbing, I can't seem to get it to stop."

It was just behind his teeth to say, *I have better things to do today, call a fucking plumber*, but he held his tongue. It wouldn't do to be unnecessarily cruel. There was plenty of daylight to do what he had to do, and Sam was in a pleasant mood. No sense ruining it with his bullshit.

"Sure," he said with false levity. "Just show me what's going on."

Sam came over and leaned in, kissing him on the cheek. "My Mr. Fix-It. Thank you."

"My pleasure."

She looked down at him, a reluctant smile touching the corners of her mouth, her hand cupping his chin. "Are you OK? After last night?"

You interrupted me kissing my dead wife in your parents' garden and then I fainted on the grass, and now I'm contemplating breaking into her grave to make sure she's there. I'd say that's a definite 'no' on the 'Is Eddie OK?' scale.

He smiled back at her. "All fine. Just a little under the weather, I think."

"Are *we* OK?"

God, stop asking me questions like this, please. I don't want to hurt you, can't you see that?

"Yes," he lied, kissing her wrist.

***

Eddie grunted, pulling the wrench as hard as he could, trying to tighten the bolt beneath the sink, growing angrier by the second. He'd been at it for hours, and no matter how many trips to the hardware store—three so far—or how many manuals and tutorials he consulted—seven—nothing was stopping the damned thing from leaking a steady stream of chilly water into the basin. The wrench slipped, clattering to the floor and skittering under one of the shelves built into the wall.

"Fuck," he muttered under his breath, wiping sweat from his brow. His back creaked as he stood up, and he leaned backward with his hands pressed in the small of it, hearing joints pop back into place.

Wasting fucking daylight in this spidery bitch of a cellar, he groused silently, looking around at the walls. *What the fuck does she keep all this damn wine for, anyway? I've never even fucking seen her drink.*

Eddie sighed, wiping his hands over his face again before heading up the ladder to the mudroom.

"All OK?" Sam called from the kitchen brightly.

"Yeah," he replied. "Just going to the shed to get a different wrench."

He squinted into the sudden sunlight and was dismayed to see that it had sunk even further than he'd thought. The sky was a much brighter orange than it had been when he'd gone out to the hardware store last. Too soon it would be dark, and he would have to wait another day to bring this plot to its conclusion.

Fuck. Shit. This is taking too fucking long.

He hustled over to the shed, sliding back the bolt and stepping into the cool, pine-fragrant dark. A small mower dominated most of the space, the shelves surrounding full of paint cans and the detritus of the long-standing home owner. Things collected in a shed and were promptly forgotten about, somehow never managing to find their way to the bin. He shuffled around the mower, reaching for the emergency toolbox Sam kept in case the one in the basement 'went missing', she said.

You laughed when she said that. And now look.

His foot caught the end of something heavy and he tripped, just catching himself in time to avoid being brained by the wooden shelf. He looked down at his feet and saw a sledgehammer, presumably left over from when Sam had had the living room redone several years ago, left behind by some construction worker or other who never returned for it. Eddie briefly imagined using it to knock the bastard sink off the wall, wistfully musing on the idea of water spraying out of the pipe in a gush as he smashed the stupid thing to bits.

He toed the sledgehammer aside and snagged the toolbox, heading back in to finish his job.

***

Please, for the love of God, just let me fucking leave.

"You're sure you won't take a shower before you go? You absolutely reek."

He slung his coat around him in the hall. "No, I'm going straight home. I'll get a shower there and then collapse into bed."

Sam tilted her head to the side, a look of slight apprehension on her face. "And you won't take any supper with you? You haven't eaten a thing today. I'd hate for you to come over faint again."

I didn't faint because I was hungry.

"Nah." He smiled, feeling grimy in a way that had nothing to do with hours spent in her cellar sweating. "There's stuff at the flat that I've got to eat before it goes bad. If nothing looks good, I can always order takeaway."

"OK," she replied hesitantly. "But you're sure?"

Yes, I'm fucking sure, Now let me leave.

"Positive." He tried to keep the smile in place as he wound his scarf around his neck. "Right. I'm off."

He started for the door, but Sam caught his hand.

What now, for Christ's sake?

"Thank you so much," she said. "Not just for the sink but for…I don't know. Being here for me, I guess. I miss Anna too, and this Christmas has been…hard. Having you around so much has been more comforting than anything else."

He stilled, looking into her face with surprise. In his misery, it had never occurred to him that Sam had felt anything but miserable around him as well. The thought that he had somehow comforted her with the mere proximity of his hollow bulk made him soften towards her. Maybe he and she were not so different in their motivations after all. He surprised himself by cupping her cheeks in his hands and kissing her softly on the mouth. "It was… It's my pleasure."

"No, it's not," she said quietly. "I know, Eddie. I know that you don't love me. I know you won't, and I can feel you pulling away. But it's still been…been nice to be with you."

Eddie's heart sank, tears welling in his eyes. *Of course she knows. However could she not?*

"I'm sorry, Sam," he whispered, his voice cracking. "I didn't mean to hurt—"

"I know you didn't," she said, chuckling and wiping her eyes. "I knew from the moment it started that it wouldn't last. Couldn't. It was only a question of when. So is it…is it now?"

You idiot. You complete bastard.

Mutely, he nodded.

Sam sighed. "All right, then. Off you go."

"Sam—"

"I said go," she said stonily. Then, more softly, "Please."

Without another word, Eddie went. What more was there to say?

EIGHT

THE CEMETERY WAS mostly deserted by the time Eddie arrived, the sun low and red in the sky. A few elderly people in singles or pairs wandered to and fro, presumably visiting the graves of loved ones despite the bitter cold. A couple of white-haired old ladies huddled in black trench coats and veils of a bygone era shuffled past him with barely a glance, their arms linked and their black-gloved hands clasped tightly together. No one paid much heed to Edward Lee, widower, etched in the sweat and filth of a day's hot work, hair dirty and sticking up in black whorls, striding purposefully towards the back corner of the rows of sepulchres.

All the sepulchres in this area were above the ground—family graves, lineages stretching back over time, monuments built to house the lorded dead. Anna's had been one such family; her tomb was attached to her mother and father, her father's father, and so on, the great stone monolith topped with a marble statue of an angel holding aloft a sword. A large black bird sat watchfully atop the head of the angel, croaking reproachfully at Eddie's intrusion but not flying away as he passed beneath its wary eye. There was a small hallway through the middle, and inside it the stone slab that sealed the final resting place of his beloved wife.

He took a few steps into the rapidly cooling shade, crouched down before her headstone, tracing the words. Her name, her date of birth and death, and those beautiful, fateful words.

Beloved wife

Eddie surveyed the gravesite, looking around for any evidence at all that it had been disturbed. There were no cracks in the marble of the face of the tomb; his fingers found no purchase when they dug into the sealant that kept the stone in place. There were no scuff marks on the walls surrounding, no marks on the ground save for his own footprints.

Nothing. He sighed, pressing his head to the icy marble and closing his eyes. *Not a single sign that she was ever here. Well, what did you expe—*

A sound. Small. Close.

Eddie's eyes snapped open and he lifted his head, ears as alert as those of a cat hunting a mouse in a field. And then it came again, louder, so close he startled, falling onto his backside in surprise.

Scritch, scritch, scritch

Jesus God, is it coming from inside the—

Scriiiiiiiiiitch

Eddie scrambled backwards from the headstone, his eyes wide and mouth open as he fumbled with his limbs until his back hit the far wall and he could escape no more. His breath came like a freight train, breath puffing out in plumes of smoke, his heart a steam engine careering through his chest.

It can't be. Can't be. It has to be rats or something, has to be—

...eddie...

"My god!" he shouted, horrified.

This is what you wanted, this is what you asked for, prayed for, begged for. This is what you—

The scratching again. Louder. More insistent.

...eddie, come to me...

"H—" His voice caught in his throat. "How?"

you know how

"I d-*don't*," he wailed, his teeth beginning to chatter. Whether it was from cold or fear, he couldn't say, but he felt the desire to run from this place, as fast as his legs could carry him. To go back to Sam, tell her he made a mistake, to gather her in his arms and take them both as far away as he could get them, away from this horrible thing. But another, louder part of him was filled with longing and a desire to see, to know, to finally have this burden of grief lifted and have Anna back once more if he could. He crawled over carefully, putting his shaking hand against the cold marble. "Anna, I can't get to you, not when you're behind a—"

do you love me, eddie?

So close. He could practically hear her voice in his ear. Tears streamed down his face in earnest, a sob escaping his throat. "Of course I do. I always have. I always will."

then come to me

The sound of nails dragging across the marble from the other side.

come

A shifting from inside, as if someone were pressing closer to the stone, trying in vain to reach him, the sound of a rustling dress he knew to be cornflower blue.

and we can be together again

A soft thump, as if a head of dark hair rested itself in resignation on the barrier between them.

always

He thrust his fist against the stone in frustration, bruising his frozen knuckles, feeling nothing. "Let me...let me think. Let me figure this out."

His eyes flicked back and forth as he rapidly worked through the problems he faced. Whatever was on the other side of this marble could not possibly be Anna, his rational mind reasoned. It sounded like Anna, might even look like her, but Anna was dead. Dead. And the dead don't return, unchanged, from the grave. He thought back to the garden, to Anna with her too-bright animal eyes, and cringed. If it was not her, what was it? A ghost? A demon? He could leave this place and never, ever find out what horrible thing crouched behind the icy stone that had begun to sweat under his palm. He could choose to let this all go and move on. But, on the other hand…

As I am, I cannot live. And without her, I am not myself.

The scratching resumed from within the grave.

eddie

do you love me, eddie?

"Anna, I—"

do you?

"Yes." It came out in a gasp, barely a word.

***

The drive from the cemetery to Sam's house took half the time it usually took. Eddie ignored all stop signs, streetlights, and speed limits, his eyes wild and haunted as he sped through the dark. He screeched to a halt in front of Sam's place, leaving black tyre-tread marks on the pavement. He hauled himself out, left the engine running as he first carried the gift he'd purchased for Sam to her front door and left it propped up against the wood, then skulked off to the side pathway in the dark. A few moments later, he returned, coat flapping out like dark wings in the breeze, the sledgehammer grasped in his hands. He left as quickly as he had come, only the smell of burning rubber and the distant screech of tyres indicating he had been there at all.

NINE

EDDIE HEAVED THE hammer once more, the sound of the struck marble ringing through the hall of the sepulchre. At first he had been hesitant, frightened that the night watchmen might come upon him and call the police, have him locked away forever before he could free Anna from her prison. But after a few hearty bangs and no one showing up to stop him, Eddie had begun swinging in earnest. His muscles were on fire with the effort, the hammer heavier with each new blow, sweat running down his face and into his eyes so they stung. The face of the marble cracked once, diagonally, all the way across. Eddie's fevered mind rejoiced.

hurry, my love, Anna's voice pleaded from the other side.

"Not long now," he panted back.

He swung again with a great grunt of effort, his back muscles tugging in a painful twinge, his shoulders screaming from the impact as metal hit stone. The crack split further, spiderwebbing outwards, the dent in the centre now shaped like the head of the hammer. Encouraged, he took one final hefty swing, and the front of the tomb cracked, crumbled, large chunks falling away from the opening.

Eddie shouted triumphantly as the pieces fell around his feet, and he threw the hammer aside, ears barely registering the clang and thump of it hitting the ground behind him. He crouched, eagerly hauling the heavy pieces of stone aside, his back yanking so hard he had to clench his teeth around the pain. It didn't matter now, none of it, because he'd done it. He'd reached his goal, he'd opened her prison, and now Anna could be free.

He sat on his heels before the hole he'd made, a lopsided grin on his face, panting and waiting, smelling the earthy, slightly meaty scent of a long-closed grave. Surely now she would come out from hiding, come out and stretch her beautiful body in the moonlight and open her arms to him again, and then they could go back home to his flat.

A need for rest buzzed in the corners of his brain, his eyes heavy as he sat wavering on the ground in exhaustion. Anna would not need sleep when they got home. She'd been asleep for nearly a year now.

She may never need to sleep again.

He chuckled at the thought, his voice ragged and dry. He waited, patiently, for Anna to gather herself. Minutes ticked by, the only sounds around him the breeze and the intermittent lonely croak of the big black bird that still roosted on the statue outside.

Still, she did not emerge.

Eddie frowned. "Anna? Are you in there?"

A rustle from within the grave. He leaned forward further, peering into the dark. His eyes saw nothing at first, just the part of the coffin lid that caught the moonlight. He squinted, his eyes adjusting, and a shape formed, crouched in the back of the inside space against the wall. The shape turned slightly, and the weak moonlight reflected back two silvery spheres. He smiled. So she *was* here after all.

"Come out," he said quietly, scooting forward on his knees, poking his head through the opening. "It's safe. I came, just like you asked. You're free."

The figure didn't move, only stared at him with unblinking eyes.

His smile faded. Why wasn't she coming out? "Anna, please. We have to go."

oh, eddie, i can't

"What?" He scoffed. "Why not?"

461

The figure moved slightly, one bare foot sliding into the moonlight, a sliver of blue dress visible above a dirty ankle. Still the eyes shone brightly, never waning, and a pale hand came out of the darkness towards him, palm upturned.

you love me, eddie? The words were etched in sadness, the pale hand twitching slightly.

"Of course I do," he replied, leaning in to take her hand.

Their fingers met, her hand warm against his, alive, the pulse beneath strong and quick. Joy surged through Eddie's veins, a happiness buoying him he had not felt in a year. Finally, after all this horror, love was coming home. Anna, his Anna, was alive and well, and finally, finally, life could resume its forward motion.

Anna's hand closed around his wrist in an iron grip. Eddie startled, tried compulsively to pull away, but to no avail. She yanked him forward, toppling him into the hole of the grave, his body landing with a crash on top of the coffin below. The wood split and the reek of rot burst forth into his nostrils, a wet and soupy smell that made him retch. Then the thing in the dark was on him, its feet planted neatly on either side of his body, its hands on his chest, dress billowing around it and eyes shining like two bulbs in the dark.

The pressure of its weight pushed him further into the collapsing coffin, a putrid ichor soaking into the back of his shirt as he struggled to get away. Anna, whatever she may now be, was stronger than him, and all his struggles accomplished was to push him farther in, wedging him into the tight space of the open coffin. It leaned in, its face inches from his, a slow grin spreading across its features as Eddie struggled, helpless beneath it, gagging on its fetid breath as he tried to call out for help. The shining silver eyes held his as it leaned in, jaws beginning to spread open, wide, wider than was possible, Anna's features mutating and splitting as it went.

you really do love me

Eddie screamed once, and then there was silence.

TEN

DETECTIVES WATERS AND Gilmour stood at the edge of the open grave, surveying the scene: technicians bustling hither and thither, securing the scene with tape, collecting samples, snapping pictures of evidence marked with little tiles. Above it all, taking note, a large, black bird sat on the head of an angel, its head tilted towards the excitement.

"D'you think they'll find anything?" Gilmour asked, tilting his head to watch one of the officers stoop and peer into the grave with a little flashlight.

Waters rubbed his mouth with his hand, thinking. "Nah. Not much to find, is there? Fuck, it's cold."

Gilmour nodded. "No, not much to find. Still. Morning shift comes in, thinks they've got a grave robbery to report, and then they find...that."

The two detectives glanced behind them. An ambulance stood on the gravel some yards away, a frazzled-looking old man sitting in its doorway wrapped in a blanket, shakily drinking coffee from a foam cup and staring into the middle distance with haunted eyes.

"Yes, well," Waters said, shrugging, "works in a cemetery, doesn't he? Sees dead people all the time. He'll get over it soon enough, I suppose."

"I suppose."

Waters and Gilmour stood silently for a few minutes, watching the technicians busy with their tasks. A light drizzle began.

Waters squinted up at the sky, grimacing as he pulled the hood up on his jacket. "Fucking rain now. Jesus."

Gilmour nodded again but wasn't really listening to Waters' complaining. The truth was, he had been truly disturbed by what they'd found out here this morning.

What kind of ghoul breaks into his own wife's grave, smashes in her coffin, and lies down beside her corpse? What horrible will must he have had, to stay there and freeze to death with his arms wrapped around her in such a way? He shivered, but only partially from the cold.

Not only that, the team was having a hell of a time separating the two of them so they could cart the late Mr. Lee's body away to the morgue for testing. Eventually, he would be interred next to his wife, but there were tests that needed doing, a task against which it seemed, even in death, the Lees stood together in silent protest. Eddie Lee had wrapped his arms and legs around his wife Anna's body, but had also somehow managed to entwine hers around his, and thus together they had frozen in the night. It was a detestable sight, the caved and worm-eaten body glued so perfectly to the freshly blue one, their hands entwined and faces peaceful as though they had just finished making love. There was no sign of violence, but—

It somehow seems violent all the same. That sort of madness never comes without a certain kind of violence.

The technicians were shouting back and forth to one another, the one in the hole of the grave coming out to say something to the other two nearby, who then crouched down to the mouth of the hole. The first technician disappeared and in a moment, a blue foot was thrust from the mouth of the grave. Gilmour startled at the suddenness of it, but quickly relaxed as more body parts started to emerge. The two techs outside helped extract, ever so gently, the bodies of the late Mr. and Mrs. Lee still locked together in their stiff embrace, and load them onto a single stretcher. Seeing them out there in the light, the sadness of the scene struck Gilmour anew.

Something much more than grief and much less than wholesome happened here.

He looked away from them, a lump in his throat, and down into the hallway of the sepulchre. There, mostly obscured by the mid-morning shadows, two figures stood shoulder to shoulder, their eyes reflecting back in the dimness like cats' eyes in an alley. Gilmour blinked in surprise, but all at once they were gone. He stared at the spot a few seconds more, willing them to reappear, but they did not. He shook his head.

Spooked. You're just spooked, is all. Rightly so.

"Detectives," said a voice from behind.

Waters and Gilmour turned to see the face of Officer Eldritch, a young woman of about twenty-five, walking towards them from the barricades, her ponytail swinging behind her as she walked. There were few onlookers—mostly just a scattered group of elderly trying to come in to see relatives resting somewhere behind the tape, waiting patiently as eternal footmen until they could pass—but there had to be a barrier just the same, to preserve the scene.

Such as it is.

"What is it, Eldritch?" Waters asked gruffly. His face was red from the cold and he was getting grumpy with the rain now, Gilmour could see.

"There's a woman here," Eldritch replied. "Samantha McLane. She says she has information regarding the...erm, regarding Mr. Lee."

"What kind of information? Where'd she get it?"

"She didn't say. She says she just knew to come here."

"Well how the devil did she know that? Take down her number. Tell her to go away."

Gilmour glanced up the hill and saw a younger blonde woman, tall, slim, standing on the edge of the tape and shifting from foot to foot, holding a large navy blue box against her chest. She had the resigned look of someone who knew what was behind all the barriers and tape and was not afraid to hear the news. For her, at least, these would be bland headlines indeed. "Let's go and talk to her."

Waters glanced sharply at him. "You go and talk to her. I'm going to look for some chap to get me a coffee."

"All right, I will." Gilmour started up the hill towards Samantha, his eyes trained on her impassive face.

That is a haunted woman if I ever saw one.

Behind him, the black bird took off with a loud croak and flew off into the morning sky.

FIN.

ACKNOWLEDGEMENTS

This book took a really long time to come out, and I want to start by apologizing for that. Depression is a hell of a drug, and it lulls you into thinking you're safe where you are as long as you don't start anything new too quickly. The lapse between books also had a lot to do with COVID, and being stuck inside with no new experiences to stoke the flames and get the mechanism chugging, so to speak. But eventually (as everything does), it came, and this is the result. Three "short" stories, one completely new novella, and one novella previously unreleased on paper. My goodness. My friends, the pride I feel is great, but it's all tinged with a hint of sorrow, because I know one person who is no longer here that would have loved to see this book made flesh. He'd have cheered me on tirelessly, and bought two copies: one to keep, signed and pristine, and another to love to death. That's just who he was.

But I'll get to him. I want to start by thanking the living. Jason, my rock, who encouraged me every step of the way and gave me room to just sit like a lump when that's what I needed to do. You are and always will be my fount of adult wisdom and machine of boundless encouragement, the person who saw fit to love me but leave me wild, and for that I cannot thank you enough. Logan, my responsible monster, who loves me completely, fiercely, unerringly no matter how I feel and puts up with my endless bad jokes, and Dominique, my bestest friend and adventure buddy who for some reason still likes me even when I'm a crabby asshole—the both of you were excellent betas, catching all my continuity mistakes (of which there were many, especially in "Precious Cargo"). Anna Harris, who edited this compilation of misery with a fine-toothed comb and made it shine like a new penny instead of a turd, from the bottom of my heart, thank you. And thank you, as always, to Debbie McGowan over at Beaten Track for sticking with me, and to Deven Balsam for getting me this sweet-ass gig in the first place. You're the real MVPs. And to the Countless Others, who asked me so many uncomfortable questions about when the new book would be ready, which lit a fire under my ass to *do* something, already.

And finally, the person to whom this book is dedicated, Joshua Crimm James (Crimm to his friends). Losing you made the world dimmer, made my life less full, and my heart so much heavier than it used to be, because now I have to carry all of you that's left alive within it. This book was, is, always will be for you. I think that you, my friend, deserve one final story (one for the road, you might say), a little wishful thinking to make things not feel so real. I'll try, in my way, to keep it short. Thank you for every wonderful memory. I hope that wherever you are, you're finally at peace, and that one day when we see each other again, it'll feel like coming home.

"I'll Always Come Back for You"

They met in college, he so much younger than she, but they were instantly as close and inseparable as twins in the womb. They spoke to one another in inside jokes, and laughed at the same time at references only they understood. It was love, but not that kind. They tried dating, but he became afraid of his feelings very quickly, broke up with her over the phone, and disappeared for five months. For her, they were bleak months. She missed her friend, the inside jokes, the laughter. She called and called, sad and angry that he thought this was all they had, that he should disappear so readily from her life. It went to voicemail every time, unanswered.

And then one day, he came back. He knocked on her door— *tap, tap, t-tap, tap*—and she opened it, her relief a palpable wave rolling out of her apartment. She cried then too, rushing into his waiting arms, small fists pounding on his chest, demanding answers.

"Why did you leave me?" she asked, but she didn't mean the relationship. "Why did you disappear?"

"I had to," he sighed, shivering in the cold despite his overcoat, and that was all there was to say on it. He squeezed her gently, breathing in her hair. "But I'll always come back for you."

"Always?"

"Always."

And so that was how it was, the two of them loving each other despite great faults, being there for one another. She escaped an abusive relationship, and he stayed with her while she healed, encircling her in his love. His mother passed away, and he spent every day with her, waiting for the ache to subside. Sometimes, in his grief, he would disappear, but she no longer worried. She knew he was coming back. He always did.

Their lives changed. They grew and got busy—work, partners, children, life—but they never fully separated from one another. She got married, and he came to her wedding without a partner, dressed in a beautiful suit that matched his eyes. He danced with her that night, and told her how proud he was of how far she'd come. She became a writer, something he cheered relentlessly, proud to call her his friend. He said her stories were magic—that they created worlds and brought impossible people to life. He became an EMT, then a bartender, then, then, then…but each new thing was just a facet of him, and she loved each new one that turned up. She reminded him he was more than what he seemed, and he'd squeeze her hand silently, smiling one of his rare smiles. Sometimes it would be months between calls and texts, but that didn't matter. Each time they reconvened, it was like nobody every walked away, because nobody really had. The love was constant, pure, true, the type of love that could break any sleeping spell a witch could ever cast.

Except one.

One day he called her, his voice on the line frazzled and disjointed, afraid.

"What's wrong?" she asked.

"I hate what's been happening," he said miserably. "My brother and his…they…I think they don't like me very much. They keep saying these awful things, and I…I just…"

"Are you safe?"

"What?"

"Are you safe? If you're not safe, you can come here, you know. We'll make room for you, always."

"I…I don't know, I…" He cleared his throat. "Yeah. Yeah, I'm safe. Can we meet up next week, though? On Wednesday? That's my day off."

"Sure! We can go get some pho and talk more."

"That sounds great," he said, with real relief in his voice.

The following Tuesday, she got the call. He was gone. Not just gone for a little while, but gone for good. He'd been killed by the very people he was afraid of, the people he refused to walk away from. She wept bitterly for days, unable to be alone with her thoughts, because of the heavy knowledge of what they'd done to him, her sweet friend who never harmed a soul. She spoke to cops who gave her more details than she strictly needed about his death in exchange for the details of his last conversation. Knowing that hers was, very possibly, his last conversation made her unbelievably sad. Had he really been so isolated at the end? Why hadn't she tried harder to keep in touch? No matter who comforted her, she couldn't feel it, because she didn't want their comfort, she wanted his. She wanted him to show up as he always had, to knock on her door—*tap, tap, t-tap, tap*—and tell her it was all a bad dream, that everything was OK now. But that wouldn't come.

She thought about what he'd said about her stories, how they created worlds and brought impossible people to life. She didn't think it would really do anything, not really, if she wrote a story about him now, but it might get some of the pressure off her chest. The weight of grief was killing her, and any relief was better than none. So she fired up her laptop and she wrote:

He came up the driveway, blond hair shining in the streetlamps, and in his arms were roses.

She frowned at it. Not very good. She backspaced until all that was left was *he* and wrote:

He had promised her he would always come back for her, and death would not stop him keeping that promise. He strode up the walkway to her house, determined to make things right. He lifted one hand, and

She stopped there, closing her eyes, fat tears rolling down her face.

"Please," she whispered to the empty living room, a prayer in one word, "please, I'm begging you. Make it not true. You said you'd always come back. You said—"

A thump from behind startled her. She whirled around, tense, waiting, her heart fluttering like a bird trapped in her chest, listening. Through the frosted glass of the front door, a shadow stood wavering, swaying, tall and lean. The head, she saw, was misshapen, dented in places. It raised one arm, slowly, slowly, as if through very deep water. Then, from the front door, came the very thing she'd prayed for.

Tap, tap, t-tap, tap.

The End.

ALSO BY M.R. HAUCK

Nephthys

Comedenti Dolorum

BEATEN TRACK PUBLISHING

For more titles from Beaten Track Publishing,
please visit our website:

http://www.beatentrackpublishing.com

Thanks for reading!

www.ingramcontent.com/pod-product-compliance
Lightning Source LLC
Chambersburg PA
CBHW010811250626
47169CB00009B/2894